THE LAST FARRINGTON

Benjamin Morris

Illustrations by Sonia Morris

Chapter 1

Warren Farrington sat on his bed, ready to begin reading his eleventh book of the month.
Well, that's eleven including an autobiography by an astronaut and three scientific papers on celestial thesis. So, not really books in the conventional sense.
He'd just had a haircut.
It is vital that Warren, or the Subject, as he is officially referred to, maintains short hair. The risks involved in using scissors or electrical shaving devices are astronomical, so the Director, who oversees everything at Farrington Towers, ordered the engineering department to design a three-tiered metallic dome capable of safely trimming the Subject's hair.
The first tier of the dome, which has gone through several evolutions, is made with a revolutionary impact absorbing layer of cellulose to protect the Subject's scalp. Thanks to a NASA-developed electrostatic generator fitted within the second tier, the Subject's hair gently rises through carefully designed slits. The third tier operates like a seven-blade razor, gently gliding through hair without ever being able to penetrate the protective layer.
As a result, the Subject's hair was cut in clumps. It was untidy and uneven, but the dome ensured that not a single strand of the Subject's hair was beyond two centimetres in length.

The Director considers anything, however implausible, that could jeopardise the Subject's safety. Nothing is left to chance. And it is astonishing how many people have died because of long hair. There was a girl in Sweden whose blonde plaited was caught in the wicker basket of a hot air balloon as it was launching, whilst a diver drowned when her ponytail was gripped by a giant clam. Then there was the case of an Australian surfer who emerged from the waves with long streaks of seaweed entangled in his dreadlocked hair, only to be doused in petrol and burned alive.
Sadly, he was surfing at a location where a film crew were shooting a low-budget horror movie. Moments later, a stuntman wearing a fire-proof outfit underneath his seaweed monster costume emerged from the sea and wondered why the cameras were facing in the opposite direction.

Before reading a word of the book, Warren had to go through a vigorous twenty-four-point safety check, with the assistance of several employees at Farrington Towers. That's nine more than the fifteen checks required before he eats porridge and seven more than the seventeen checks before he brushes his teeth. However, it's one less than the twenty-five checks necessary when he uses the toilet and seven less than what is necessary at bath time.
They are all listed in the Subject's Safety Procedural Manual, which is updated and republished every six months. The manual is carried by all one hundred and seventy employees

at Farrington Towers. Those who come into regular contact with the Subject know the manual inside out.

Precisely twelve minutes before the Subject's scheduled reading time, two members of the housekeeping team entered his bedroom, which is referred to as KR2. KR stands for Key Room, by the way. There are ten key rooms at Farrington Towers, including the Control Room (KR1), the Subject's main bathroom (KR3), the Meeting Room (KR4), the Farrington family library (KR5), the dining room (KR6) and the kitchen (KR7).

There are forty-eight employees in the housekeeping (HK) department, and they work in pairs. They rotate duties to prevent complacency, which is not tolerated by the Director.

For the first time in a week, the two middle-aged ladies in HK22 were working directly with the Subject during their eight-hour shift.

HK22a, who was the treasurer of a church embroidery group in her spare time, carried out the first check outlined in the manual. Having ensured that the cushioned padding on all four walls of KR2 was secure to minimise the risk of head injury, she adjusted the light setting to 'white light.' Of the ten settings available, it was best suited to reading.

She then individually checked that all twelve LEDs were working and tested the two alarm points on the Subject's bed, before closing the electronic window shutters so that no reflective light could pass through.

Meanwhile, the second member of the housekeeping duo, HK22b, who had previously worked at Buckingham Palace, made her way to the Subject's bed. She removed the duvet, protective sheet and pillow, which were swiftly taken away by a separate housekeeping team and replaced by a fresh set that had been meticulously inspected.

HK22b conducted a microscopic analysis of the Subject's non-toxic, organic mattress for bacterial anomalies and dust mites. She read the dust detector display. If it gave a reading over 0.03 dust particles, she was obliged to contact KR1 immediately. Fortunately, that wasn't the case today.

Using an anti-bacterial cloth, she wiped the smooth, rounded cushioned panels around the Subject's specially-adapted bed.

Five minutes before reading time commenced, the two women conducted visual checks to ensure the padded floor of KR2 was free of obstacles and trip hazards. The pair then placed a customised back support on to the Subject's bed, fastening it securely.

At the precise moment of their leaving, four minutes before the arrival of the Subject, the librarian entered to place a book on the bedside table, made from a hardened foam with additional cushioning on the rounded edges. She checked one final time that the book had an approval mark stamped on the inside cover in non-toxic ink.

Only books printed with soft-edge, wax-coated paper could be read by the Subject. This rule was implemented following an incident that occurred whilst Warren was reading a particularly exciting fictional thriller when he was eleven. He was in such a hurry to turn the page that he suffered a one centimetre long paper cut to his forefinger. A

specialist haematologist stayed overnight to monitor his progress, but Warren was mercifully okay.
Three minutes later, two guards serving in the Farrington Protective Force, or FPF for short, entered KR2, alongside the Subject.
Warren was always accompanied by at least two FPF guards. There are forty-four FPF guards employed at Farrington Towers, rotating every day in three eight hour shifts. They all wear black combat uniform and have experience of elite military service.
They are always with the Subject. They are there when he sleeps. They are there when he eats. They are there during academic studies. They sit in the corner of the bathroom when Warren uses the toilet and they never joke about the smell. They are not allowed to make jokes.
In fact, the Director had ruled that the FPF were forbidden from speaking to the Subject unless responding to a direct question.
Warren had reached an age when people seek more privacy. Therefore, his resentment for the guards was growing and he rarely triggered a conversation with them. Consequently, guards he had formed friendships with in his younger years had gradually become more distant.

On this occasion, the Subject was with FPF unit F8, comprised of two friends who had previously served in the British Armed Forces together.
The guards helped the Subject move gently on to his bed. Using an anti-slip sheet, they manoeuvred him delicately

back into the specially moulded seat, built to ensure that the Subject maintained the correct posture whilst reading. The seat includes five belt straps which connect to a central locking system, offering the Subject the same level of security as a fighter pilot whilst he reads on his mite-free mattress in his heavily padded bedroom.

F8a raised the Subject's left leg by six inches and placed a vibrating massage pad underneath it to help prevent deep vein thrombosis. This process was repeated by F8b for the right leg, whilst a wireless heart rate monitor was placed on the Subject's chest. The guards then fitted protective headwear, just in case the Subject should somehow fall from his bed.

With their duties completed, F8 retreated to seats on the opposite side of the room. The FPF must maintain a distance of at least six metres to the Subject, but no more than ten metres, for the duration of sleeping and reading time.

Finally, with the Subject in place, the optician entered. She studied his spectacles, wiped them and checked the lenses. Her final act was to ensure that the distance between the Subject and his reading material was precisely 370mm, to minimise the risk of eye strain.

All of it made sense to Warren, as it was just the way things had always been. Every aspect of his life was regulated in extraordinary detail.

However, he wasn't sure why thirty-two minutes was defined as the limit to his reading time, or why he must observe a minimum break of fourteen minutes between reading sessions, with no more than two sessions in any four-hour period. He assumed that a scientific study carried out at a renowned university must have declared it important.

You may wonder why anyone would worry about eye strain while reading.
Well, the Director had consulted enough medical experts to know that it could potentially pose a threat. Eye strain can cause headaches and double vision and there's even circumstantial evidence to suggest that it has contributed to fatalities.
In 2011, an inquest into the death of nine-year-old Lorenzo Ruiz in the town of Chiclayo, Peru, ruled that he died as a likely consequence of blurred vision after spending six continuous hours reading stories by Enid Blyton.
Lorenzo had been called down for supper by his mother. It was cuy, his favourite meal, so he stopped reading and jumped to his feet.
If you're wondering what cuy is, it's guinea pig. Weird eh? Well, that's Peru for you.
Anyway, after being sat for so long, most of Lorenzo's blood had gathered in the lower part of his body, with less being pumped to his brain. So, when he stood, Lorenzo suffered extreme dizziness. He stumbled forward and inadvertently placed his foot on the end of a skateboard, which caused the other end to rise and whack against his shinbone. This resulted in Lorenzo losing balance and falling out of an open window. Poor Lorenzo landed

directly on top of his father's work equipment on the driveway below.
This would have been fine if his father was a mattress salesman or a maker of trampolines. Sadly, Lorenzo's father performed daredevil acts for a circus and had been practicing a death-defying bed of nails stunt outside his home.
Poor Lorenzo. If he'd followed even a few of the Subject's rules, he'd still be alive.

Having so many rules for reading a book may seem unusual, but the rules are justified. At least in the opinion of the Director, the man responsible for protecting the Subject. He carries out his role with the diligence the boy's extraordinary family history warrants.
That is why the Director insists that everyone at Farrington Towers wears an electronic wristband linked to a satellite navigation system that tracks the whereabouts of all individuals within the grounds. They are fitted to all staff and visitors as they pass through the entrance gate and the Director and his observation team monitor everything from KR1.
As well as being the only person who has never been beyond the perimeter wall of Farrington Towers, Warren is the only person not fitted with a wristband.

Chapter 2

Having gone through the safety checks, Warren was ready to start a new book.
He loved to read and had a remarkable ability for absorbing information. The Subject was especially fascinated by space, mathematics and the natural world, frequently visiting these sections of his family's comprehensive library. He enjoyed fiction too, but the last few novels he'd read had been distinctly lacking in imagination.
There was a reason why. Ever since the paper cut incident, all fictional books had to be independently tested to gauge their excitement level before they could be added to the Farrington library. Only those deemed to have an excitement rating of seven out of ten or less by a panel of twelve readers was approved by the librarian.
That was one of the recommendations of the Bedroom Safety Committee (BSC) which itself is an arm of the Farrington Protective Force (FPF).
Warren rarely ventured into the parts of the library where ancient texts, documents, manuscripts and the personal collections of his long-deceased ancestors gathered dust. He had once visited a small room devoted to his father's love of war movie memorabilia. It was one of Douglas Farrington's two great passions, the other being ornithology, of course. A generation had grown up watching his ground-breaking BBC documentaries on exotic birds.

Douglas had collected Second World War film props, cinematic reels and promotional posters, a dozen of which were framed and displayed in the room.
Based on a recommendation by his only friend, the oldest man at Farrington Towers, Warren had also read a book about the best war movies of all time. However, it was difficult for him to share the writer's enthusiasm for *Apocalypse Now* and *The Bridge on the River Kwai* when Warren had never even watched television, let alone a feature length film.
When it came to fictional books, Warren tended to allow the librarian to select for him, although he had grown increasingly frustrated by her recent choices.
The latest offering was called '*The Boy with the Seventh Sense.*' Warren had only read the first two paragraphs when he launched the book through the air.
F8b, a diminutive man called Stefano Gallo, made the first move. Stefano was born in London, but his father was Italian. Stefano couldn't speak Italian, aside from a couple of swear words his cousin had taught him as a boy, yet he would cheer for Italy during major football championships. Even if they were playing England, where he'd lived all his life.
Stefano made two strides towards the book, removed a transparent bag from his pocket, bent down and placed the book inside it. He then stared at the Subject, and Warren stared right back.
The taller of the guards, F8a, nervously looked up at one of the six security cameras in KR2, as if pleading for

instructions from the Director, who would be watching via the live feed in KR1.

He was always watching.

F8a, Frank Stone, was ten inches taller than his colleague Stefano, who had been the best man at his wedding. His wife had left within a year, but Frank was much happier with just his spaniel, Bandit, for company.

Frank looked tense as he gazed at the camera, but no instructions came over the Internal Communication System (ICS). Finally, Warren broke the silence.

"Can you send Dickie?" His voice frail and hopeful.

"Please."

Warren wasn't talking directly to the guards. He was looking at the camera to the side of his bed, addressing the Director, who would obviously be listening.

He was always listening.

After a couple of seconds, the voice of the Director echoed around KR2 through the ICS.

"Affirmative."

Warren sat in silence, looking away from the guards, who maintained military posture, despite the awkwardness of the situation.

Warren had nicknames for both men. Since he was a five, he'd associated people with an animal. Stefano Gallo was a tapir, as he had a stocky face with a big, curved snout. Frank Stone was a giraffe, as his ears appeared to be set slightly too low and he had a friendly face.

As he crossed over the detection point in the doorway, the ICS announced Dickie's arrival.

'Bernard Page has entered KR2.' The voice was female, robotic and monotone. Warren sometimes imagined how much more exciting the ICS would be if the voice could be altered to adopt the various regional accents that he heard from members of the housekeeping team.
Dickie's favourite grey trousers looked to be a little baggier than usual, Warren noted. Had he reached that strange age where people start to shrink at a more rapid rate?
As you'll have noted from the ICS announcement, Dickie isn't his real name. It's Bernard. But for all of Warren's life and a good many years before that, he'd been called Dickie, as he always wore a bow-tie with a plain white shirt and braces. He was famed for his bow-ties and had over two thousand in his collection. He rotated them every day.
Warren's grandfather Charles Farrington, who had long since passed away, would often seek out a bow-tie whilst on his extensive travels. He'd send them back to his friend at Farrington Towers, where he could be confident that Dickie was taking good care of the home and the Farrington family's many business interests around the world.
This tradition was continued by Warren's father, Douglas, who was often abroad studying or filming rare, interesting and endangered birds.
Over the years, Dickie had accumulated bow-ties from countries as far flung as Vietnam, North Korea, Nicaragua, Togo, New Caledonia, Galapagos Islands, Greenland and the South Pacific islands of Vanuatu. Aside from his first bow-tie from London, the one he most cherished had been hand-made by a beautiful young aboriginal woman from a

small island off Australia's Northern Territory. He never wore it, as he was keeping it safe for Warren.
For Charles and Douglas Farrington, Dickie had been a trusted friend. But they were both dead now and Dickie was looking close to it.

Chapter 3

As Dickie entered the room, he could see that the smaller of the two guards was holding a book.
"Do you mind?" he said, holding out his hand.
Guard F8b responded in an accent that defied his Sicilian heritage. "Rule D77b of the Subject Safety Procedural Manual stipulates that any literature or paraphernalia related to unexpected or unexplained behaviour by the Subject be immediately…"
"I know what the rules are!" interrupted Dickie, calmly. "Just as you know, F8b, that if I, as a member of the Executive Committee of Farrington Enterprises Incorporated, ask you to hand me something, you must oblige. Now, please give me the book. Then kindly leave."
The guard was taller than Dickie and yet he was the smaller of the two guards by a considerable margin. His bulging muscles could crush the old man in a heartbeat. Yet Dickie defiantly held his gaze.
"You're requesting that the Subject be left unguarded?" asked Stefano Gallo, surprised.
"It's within the rules, so long as Warren is accompanied by a member of the Executive Committee," replied Dickie.
"He'll be watching," said Stefano, pointing to a camera.
"I don't doubt it," replied Dickie, as the automated door closed behind the guards.
"F8b has left KR2. F8a has left KR2,' announced the ICS.

"You know, throwing books across your bedroom isn't a particularly endearing trait," said Dickie, talking to but not looking at Warren.
He thumbed through the contents and publisher's details before reading the first paragraph of the first chapter aloud.

"Harley Ryder was an ordinary, unassuming and modest fifteen-year-old boy who wasn't popular at school. But deep inside, he had a secret power. Not just a sixth sense, but a seventh sense, that might be the last hope for a dying planet light years away."

He looked over the top of the book at Warren.
"This could be one of two things," pondered Dickie.
"Either you disapprove of the use of three adjectives in the opening line, or you're dismissing the suggestion that a boy called Harley Ryder could be ordinary and unassuming."
"It rather contradicts the description of a modest character, doesn't it?" replied Warren.
"You think about things too much," said Dickie.
"That's what happens when thinking is all you have time for," replied Warren.
The old man recognised the sadness in his young friend's eyes. He attributed Warren's difficulty in concealing emotion to his aboriginal ancestry, from his mother's side.
"What's really upsetting you?" asked Dickie.
"You wouldn't understand."
"Youth cannot know how age thinks and feels. But old men are guilty if they forget what it was to be young."

"Hemingway?" asked Warren, surprised that he didn't recognise the quote. Dickie was always quoting his favourite books and on the rare occasion that Warren didn't know the author, he'd usually guess at an American.
"J.K Rowling," replied Dickie. "Sadly, her books are no longer authorised by the librarian."
Warren sighed heavily. "I'm fifteen-years-old in a few days, just like Harley Ryder. But I'm not ordinary, am I?"
Dickie didn't answer. He knew it was rhetorical. Warren was starting to ask questions about the world he lived in. While he wasn't allowed to watch television, he knew from the prolific number of books he read that his life was unlike that of anyone else. Also, he'd heard the housekeeping staff say things when they didn't know he was listening.
Warren removed his vibrating leg supports, took off his protective headwear, ripped off his heart monitor and wriggled free of his back support. He stepped off the bed without assistance, in contravention of several rules.
If Dickie cared at all, which he didn't, then he kept it to himself.
Surprisingly, so did the Director, watching from KR1.
"Please can you open the shutters?" said Warren. It came across as more of an order than a request. The Control Room complied and the electric shutters rose.
Warren moved to the window, the only one in his bedroom, and placed the palm of his right hand on the glass.
"Is it ordinary for a boy to have a four-inch thick window that can't be opened because it's made with a palladium-

based metallic glass designed to withstand a Bazooka rocket attack?"
"Well, I believe it's permanently closed to ensure you can't accidentally fall out, more than anything else," replied Dickie.
"Do you know why I read books about space, Dickie?" said Warren, ignoring Dickie's reasoned response. "I like that we barely know anything about it. I read theories on time and space, written by the world's greatest minds. Yet, the reality is, they know nothing. There are ten trillion galaxies out there, going back thirteen billion years. And yet, we don't even know about our own moon. We don't know if it was once part of our planet, or if it wandered through space and was caught in our gravitational field, or if it was a proto planet which collided with Earth. We don't know. When American astronauts brought back lunar rock, they couldn't understand why it was magnetic when the moon has no magnetic field. It was a mystery! And that's just that one little rock in the sky right above us."
Dickie listened. Warren wasn't always in the mood for talking.
"Sometimes, I imagine what it would be like to be up there," he continued. "I think of Gene Shoemaker."
"Who?" asked Dickie.
"He's the only person whose ashes have been scattered on the moon," replied Warren. "It was his dying wish. Can you imagine that, Dickie? He wanted to see the world and he went to the moon. I want to see the world and I've not been beyond the back garden."

"Is life really so bad?" asked Dickie.
"Look out of the window, Dickie. There are two men on their knees, inspecting the surface of my own running track with a magnifying glass so that they might reduce the possibility of me falling over while exercising, even though I run in a protective outfit with foam cushioning. I can see a botanist checking for invading plant species that could potentially trigger an allergic reaction in me. Over there, that's a mycologist, inspecting the grass for signs of poisonous fungi and mushrooms. There's an arborist checking that the trees are in good health and a mathematician ensuring that none of those trees could possibly fall within five metres of my designated walking trails in the unlikely event that they be hit by lightning whilst I'm outside. I can see a seismologist scanning the ground for signs of sudden movement in the Earth's tectonic plates, just to cover the one in a billion scenario of a sinkhole swallowing me up. I can even see a Lockheed Martin F-22 Raptor fighter plane, capable of Mach 2.25, ready to be deployed should any plane threaten the exclusion zone in the skies above the Farrington Estate. Then, surrounding the entire 98-acre gardens, there's a 25-metre high wall, patrolled by men who have served in elite military forces. Beyond it, there's 273,000 acres of fields, woodland and meadows that people can barely step on without being interrogated by the FPF. All of that, just for me. Now, I ask you, is that ordinary?"
"Well, I don't think most kids have an F-22, but the rest of the stuff is pretty run of the mill, I reckon," joked Dickie.

Warren smiled. If it wasn't for Dickie, he would never smile at all.
"Dickie, what did you do when you were my age?"
Dickie was an honest man and a nervous liar. "Me? I'm an old man now. I can barely remember that far back."
"Please," Warren said. "Tell me."
Dickie looked at the young man who stood before him. He was handsome, despite being deprived of most of his auburn hair. He didn't look like a Warren. Then Dickie remembered that he wasn't.
Well, not quite. His aboriginal birth name had been all but forgotten as Warrain had been interpreted as Warren by the world's media when his existence was finally revealed when he was three-years-old.
The boy had the eyes of his mother, a beautiful Aborigine who had stolen the heart of Douglas Farrington. Warren's beguiling brown eyes possessed the same emotional intensity and behind them was a burning passion for adventure that had been instilled in his family for generations.
He was a Farrington, after all.

Dickie sat down on the end of the bed. "We were a close family," he began. "My father was a baker and I must have been your age when I started working for him."
"What about your education?" asked Warren.
"I didn't care much for school when I was fourteen. I wanted to work and help my family make ends meet. My mother would wake me at 5:30 every morning, except on

Sundays and Mondays, and I would deliver bread on my bicycle. People around the village would also place orders for the next day. My aunt let me use her bike until I could afford one of my own. It was green with a little bell and a basket on the front. A girls' bike really, but nobody cared. Everyone had hand-me-downs in those days. It's only nowadays that parents insist on buying everything new. My father would bake all night and by morning there would be a queue of people waiting for the shop to open. Do you know, after a while, I could tell what he was baking just by the smell? Before I could even see the shop, the scent would drift through the streets. I knew if he was baking white loaves or wholemeal, rye or granary, even Sally Lunn buns."

"Did you like working?" asked Warren.

"In the summer, yes. In the winter, it was terrible! I'd get home and my hands would be like claws where they'd frozen around the handlebars. I'd sit in front of the fire for an hour warming them up."

"You could sit by an open fire?" asked Warren, amazed. That was something he'd never be allowed to do.

"With a hot cup of tea too. My father would drop in a teaspoon of sugar, so long as I didn't tell mother! Sometimes I'd sneak into the kitchen and add a second. But mothers know things. Still, she'd give me a hot cross bun after my delivery round, if I'd done a good job. I'd put it in my school bag and save it for lunch."

"Did you have friends?" pressed Warren.

"Lots," said Dickie. "All the boys in the village would meet on the green after school and play football. The green sloped down into a pond on one side and the ball was forever going in it. We'd end up spending half our time trying to fish it out! I was quite a winger in my day, although my boots were too big. I had to share a pair with my brother, who is two years older than me. My parents couldn't afford a pair each and I was saving all my money for a new bike, so we took it in turns to play. I tried playing in my school shoes one time and mother went ballistic! She marched down to the field and dragged me home by my ear. I spent all evening polishing them as she said I couldn't stop until I could see my face in them!"

"Did you like football?" asked Warren.

"Yes, I did."

"Did you like riding a bicycle?"

"Yes," said Dickie. "Even if it was a girls' bike."

"Was it good having a brother?"

"Not always. He gave me a shiner once as he said I stole his delivery round, but I never did. He got ill one day and I took over and the customers seemed to like me. If he were here now, he'd still bring it up! But yes, for the most part, we got on. I wouldn't have traded him for all the money in the world."

"Would you swap your childhood for mine?" asked Warren.

"I'm sorry, Warren." Dickie looked at his friend, sadly. "Sorry for how things are. But we must do everything possible to keep you safe. The final wish of your father was

that you stay here at Farrington Towers, where you can be protected."
Dickie looked down to the ground and shuffled his feet nervously. "You're too important, Warren. You are the last Farrington."

Warrain Farrington
(2003 -)

Chapter 4

You'll have a few questions about what you've read so far, if you possess even the most mildly curious of minds.
Why does Warren require such extraordinary levels of security? How does he afford to pay for it all? Who is the Director? What has happened to Warren's parents? What's so special about the Farrington family?
You'll find out the answers in good time. However, you'll first need to sit through the weekly meeting of the Executive Committee of Farrington Enterprises Incorporated (FEI).
Throughout the week, any employee at Farrington Towers can report any issue to their line manager, who in turn reports to a head of department. Each head of department is a member of the Executive Committee. They are required to attend a meeting every Friday morning to provide a report to the Director.
The Director may also call a meeting in exceptional circumstances. Last year, there were three additional meetings. One related to a proposed Hollywood film about the Farrington family that the Director's legal team ensured never reached development. The second was in response to a flu epidemic amongst the kitchen staff which led to a period of isolation for the Subject. The third followed a psychiatric evaluation of an FPF guard who had seen particularly harrowing things whilst serving with special

forces in Afghanistan. The meeting resulted in his immediate dismissal.

The Executive Committee Meeting Room, KR4, is the only room outside of Zone 6 that the Subject cannot access. Entry can only be gained by the six members of the Executive Committee via a fingerprint recognition system. Inside, the walls are not padded with cushioned panels. In fact, the room is lavishly decorated. There are oriental ceramics that pre-date the Ming dynasty, an early 19th century gilt-bronze and crystal chandelier and a Botticelli painting that once hung in the halls of St Peter's Basilica in The Vatican.

The Executive Committee sat around a beautiful 17th century French dining table originally built for Louis XIV, who can be forgiven for being a lousy King given that he was only five-years-old when his rule began.

In the middle of the table was a gold box of truffles, the Director's favourite. He took great delight in reminding the other Executive Committee members that the truffles were prepared by Belgium's most decorated chocolatier using single bean Ecuadorean dark chocolate. They cost in the region of £200. That's per truffle. There was meant to be one per person, but Dickie would usually decline to eat his and the Director would gladly take it at the end of the meeting, washing it down with a glass of fifty-year-old single malt scotch from The Balvenie.

The Director claimed to be a whiskey expert, although he was anything but. He'd simply read that it was the most highly-sought amongst true connoisseurs.

The Director sat at the head of the table. After pouring whisky into one of six crystal glasses symmetrically placed on a silver tray next to the truffles, he turned to Samuel Tau, Head of Environmental Affairs at Farrington Enterprises Incorporated (FEI).

Samuel Tau was once an interesting man. He had grown up on one of the smaller islands of Papua New Guinea, gaining a reputation as an intrepid young naturalist as he identified new species of flora and fauna. Whilst still a teenager, he led a campaign against island deforestation. Samuel later became a world-renowned expert on macropods, discovering a new sub-species in the Bewani Mountains. You would now think them to have been the actions of a different man. Samuel had practically bitten off the Director's hand when he was offered a post at Farrington Towers. It was, after all, one hundred times his old salary with shares in Farrington Enterprises Incorporated, which even someone growing up in a Pacific island jungle knew to be one of the world's largest corporations.

Samuel could now afford to buy a significant percentage of his homeland's forests and ensure they were protected forever. However, he had no intention of doing anything so noble.

His working life now involved studying environmental reports, mostly concerning toxicology, compiled by his team of twenty-seven staff.

Samuel opened-up his binder. When he first arrived, the binder was hand-made, with a photograph of the distinctive

Victoria crown pigeon glued to the cover. He had taken the photo himself.
"It reminds me of home," he would say, in his gentle islander's accent.
A decade on, he owned a leather binder from *Aspinal's* of London and was more interested in the FEI share price than the wildlife of his homeland. He'd happily see every tree in Papua New Guinea torn down for another good day on the stock exchange.
Samuel was always the first to eat his truffle during Executive Committee meetings. As he licked his lips, catching the last chocolate flake with the end of his tongue, Samuel glanced down at the binder before addressing the Director.
"There are no areas of serious concern from a safety perspective following analysis of my team's weekly reports. However, I should declare that we recorded the dark clouded yellow butterfly in the south west region of the inner grounds."
The inner grounds meant the 98 acres within the perimeter wall that enclosed the Towers and the gardens.
"My natural inclination is to ask how a butterfly was able to gain entry?" asked the Director. "Did it slip through the rooftop lasers?"
He was referring to the thousands of lasers placed eight millimetres apart and positioned two metres below the top of the twenty-five-metre high perimeter wall, spanning the length and breadth of the inner grounds. The lasers contain a deadly amount of photon energy, generating previously

unknown levels of gamma radiation. Anything unfortunate enough to fly or fall into the lasers is toasted in a fraction of a second. Its crispy carcass falls into protective netting a further ten metres closer to the ground.
It is one person's full-time job just to collate data and dispose of flying insects and birds obliterated by the lasers. The Royal Society for the Protection of Birds (RSPB) is among the organisations lobbying the government for their removal, blaming the lasers for the virtual extinction of one migrating species. However, the RSPB had not been able to conduct an official investigation, as its regular pleas for access had been refused.
"Nothing escapes our lasers," replied Samuel to the Director's concern. "Over the last seven days, the retractable gates at the main entrance have been opened on seventeen occasions. Fourteen of those relate to shift changes. Two were for distinguished guests, namely his Holiness the Sultan and the Secretary of State for the Environment."
"Vile man," interrupted the Director. "I'm still angry by the price of his silence."
"The final time the gates were opened was for the deployment of FPF guards on to the outer estate, which no doubt Mr Johnson will expand on in his report on security matters. On three of these occasions, animal species were recorded by our motion detection sensors entering the inner grounds. The first two invaders were a hoverfly and a bluebottle, respectively. As known species, both were swiftly caught and terminated. In the third instance, a

butterfly entered the gardens. However, it was not immediately terminated as the specimen was not on our list of recorded species. Consequently, the Subject's scheduled walk around the gardens was abandoned."
"Is this species native to the UK?" asked the Director.
"The dark clouded yellow butterfly breeds in southern Europe and northern Africa and is merely a summer migrant here. It's relatively common in southern England, where it's drawn to the wild clovers. However, it's comparatively rare this far north and we were surprised to find one at this late stage of summer."
"Africa?" questioned the Director. "Was the butterfly analysed for disease?"
"Naturally," replied Samuel. "And no threat was detected. In terms of safety, the primary risk is that this species of butterfly could collide with the Subject during his daily exercises. After consulting with a Lepidopterist, we learned that the dark clouded yellow is an active and naturally inquisitive butterfly. However, if the Subject follows protocol and wears eye protection outside, I cannot foresee a circumstance in which the extremely unlikely probability of a dark clouded yellow butterfly again successfully entering the grounds could cause harm to the Subject."
"This is a Farrington we're talking about; anything could happen!" remarked the Director.
Samuel politely nodded.
"I would like you to review our procedures for gate openings at the main entrance and the quarantine zone," said the Director. "Three invasions in one week is

unacceptable. To have none at the trade entrance in Zone 6, which is far busier, proves that there's room for improvement. We need to tighten defences. What if a wasp, or heaven forbid a bee, should gain entry? Do I need to remind you what happened to Douglas Farrington?"

"Understood, sir," said Samuel.

The Director took a sip of whiskey and turned his leather chair to face Mitchell Johnson, Head of Security.

Mitchell is a former Green Beret, a member of the US Army Special Forces. He received the Medal of Honour for rescuing three civilian hostages during the War in Afghanistan. After a hero's return, he worked with the Central Intelligence Agency (CIA), leading the counter-terrorism department for seven years. He was almost certainly involved in Operation Neptune Spear – the mission that ended with the death of Osama Bin Laden. However, you can't help but sense that he might be exaggerating his involvement by the bullish way he claims to be "sworn to secrecy."

"Drones!" boomed Mitchell, placing the palm of his right hand firmly down on the table for dramatic effect. "We had a drone problem!"

This was his typical method of communication: Say one word, let it sink in for a couple of seconds, expand with slightly more information, then provide a detailed analysis. When Mitchell first arrived in 2013, the Director had found this method irritating, particularly when coupled with Mitchell's strong Texan accent. But he had come to appreciate that the American's repetitive method was

effective when used to give explicit instructions to his team of fifty, made up primarily of FPF guards.
"Do we know where the drone came from?" asked the Director.
"Documentary makers," replied Mitchell. "Tried to film us without authorisation. The drone was operated from a van parked on a rural lane 8.2 miles east of the perimeter wall, just beyond the boundaries of the Farrington Estate. Our satellites picked up a U.F.O within our airspace at 1:59pm on Wednesday afternoon. The pilot was possibly attempting to exploit any potential weakness in our security procedures during a shift change. We monitored the U.F.O as it moved through our airspace at an average speed of 7mph. However, we were initially unable to positively identify it as a drone."
"Why?" asked the Director. "Was it a new model?"
"Paint!" said Mitchell. "The drone was painted to look like the sky. They painted a square slab of foam and attached it to the underside of the drone in the hope we wouldn't be able to see it from our ground surveillance cameras. They cut a hole in the foam just big enough for the drone's camera to record an overhead perspective."
"What happened to the drone?" asked the Director.
"Boom!" replied Mitchell. "We blew that bird out of the sky!"
He was a true American.
"We sent one of our own light-artillery drones to intercept the U.F.O once it came within three miles of the perimeter wall. The invading drone was shot down. The wreckage was

retrieved, investigated and declared safe. We removed the surveillance footage, which wasn't anything to be concerned about, and identified the invading drone as a specialist model which retails for around fifty thousand US. It is owned by an independent production company called Mystery Media Limited."

"I know of Mystery Media," said the Director. "They produce television documentaries about unexplained or unsolved mysteries. They've contacted us on several occasions."

"That's correct, sir," said Mitchell. "We were quickly able to ascertain that only one of the company's employees, Barry Fenwick, is authorised to operate a drone. Using our satellites, we located a white Ford Transit registered to Fenwick. He was apprehended by the FPF eleven minutes after the drone was shot down. When our boys arrived, he was still stood there with his remote control, wondering what the hell had happened. During interrogation, Fenwick informed us that he used the drone as a last resort, as every attempt made by Mystery Media to gain access to the Farrington Estate had been ignored."

"Well, what do they expect?" said the Director, shrugging his shoulders. "So, how did this incident conclude?"

"Fenwick was warned that any further excursions into Farrington airspace would result in criminal charges," said Mitchell.

"You took the decision not to press charges without consulting me?" asked the Director.

"I did, sir," replied Mitchell, almost apologetically. Not that he'd ever apologise. His father had told him as a child that saying sorry was a sign of weakness and Mitchell had never forgotten that. "I decided that the destruction of the most expensive drone on the market for a small film company that is yet to turn a profit in its five-year lifespan, was probably sufficient punishment," he said.
"Did you return the drone?" asked the Director.
"All 78 pieces of it!" beamed the American.

Chapter 5

Next to Mitchell Johnson sat one of the very few people in the world that the former CIA man found intimidating. She is 5'1", weighs 104 pounds and speaks with a frail delicence that demands the absolute silence of everybody in the room. Her name is Anna Kraus, Head of Lifestyle and Education. Important men had been known to sweat in Anna's presence for fear of interrupting her by pouring a glass of water or even removing their suit jacket. Of the four heads of department, it was Anna who the Director most respected.

Ultimately, the other three were motivated by money. Anna was different. She believed that nobody else could do the job of looking after the world's most vulnerable boy as well as she could.

She was probably right.

Anna had enjoyed a remarkable career, firstly at Deutsch Bank in her homeland, where she combined a ruthless command of business to negotiate the acquisition of several financial institutions. Often, men enticed by her beauty were too egotistical to realise that they were the ones being preyed upon until it was too late for their business.

Anna was then head-hunted by the Chinese. She was instrumental in persuading leading banks to float on the Shanghai Stock Exchange. With China attracting more investment, Anna's expertise came to the attention of the monarchy of Saudi Arabia. She was recruited to manage the finances of the Crown Prince, but was soon in charge of all business affairs of The House of Saud. When she foiled an attempt to poison the King, Anna was given an infinite budget to dictate all aspects of the family's welfare too. But she could not turn down the greatest challenge of them all: ensuring the safety of the last Farrington.

Anna is ultimately responsible for much of Warren's daily routine. His education, physical well-being and diet is all organised by Anna and her carefully selected team of seventy-six employees. Many of these work in housekeeping, with an additional nine focusing on Warren's diet and nutrition, whilst fourteen are teachers.

Anna decides when the Subject wakes up, when he eats breakfast, when he brushes his teeth, when he participates in physical exercises, when he studies, when he reads, when he practises a musical instrument and when he goes to bed. Every moment of every day is executed with an exhaustive attention to detail.

Anna is also known for being fiercely patriotic and rarely passes up an opportunity to promote German culture and cuisine. At a Christmas party that she hosted, Anna served sekt, a fruity variety of sparkling wine popular in Germany. The choice of food wasn't quite so well received. Few people went back for a second serving of wiener schnitzel and spätzle. However, when a pizza delivery van arrived late in the evening with an order for everyone else at the party, Anna took it in good humour.

Anna did not believe in the 'curse' of the Farringtons. She was too clinical in her approach to life to believe that a person was not the master of their own destiny.
The idea that an evil force could somehow be integrated into a jade dragon ornament, which could subsequently inflict a hereditary curse on the man who took it from a sacred temple, was ludicrous to Anna.
"What is it about this jade dragon that gives it the ability to grasp the legal difference between ownership and possession?" she once asked the Director, who was unwavering in his belief in the curse.
Anna hoped she was right, given that the jade dragon was on display at Farrington Towers. It was still attached, as it had been for over one hundred and twenty-five years, to the end of a walking cane that once belonged to Richard Farrington.
Now encased in glass, the cane had been displayed above the main entrance of Farrington Towers for as long as she'd worked there.
Curse or not, Anna had been given the responsibility of ensuring that the Subject reached his sixteenth birthday alive. That was all she'd agreed to.
She could see Warren was becoming increasingly frustrated with his constant surveillance and manicured lifestyle. He was also asking questions about his family's history.
Anna didn't like the way Warren was being treated and had reservations about the excessive levels of protection. The Director was aware of her intention to leave when the Subject turned sixteen and inherited full control of the

estate and business empire. But for now, it was Anna's job to ensure his safety and she carried out the role to perfection.
"There are two matters that I must bring to your attention," she said, softly. You could hear a pin drop. "The first is an educational matter. As you know, the Subject is making remarkable progress through the curriculum, as you would expect with the calibre of his tuition. He demonstrates a natural aptitude for mathematics and science. Professor Tengku has noted the Subject's fascination for geology and archaeology and has stated that the Subject is already a match for any student he encountered during his fourteen years as a lecturer at Oxford."
"I'm delighted that the Subject continues to progress at such a rapid rate," said the Director.
"As we've discussed previously, chemistry classes can be difficult to conduct, due to the syllabus," continued Anna. "We've always found a way to carry out practical experiments involving chemicals for the academic benefit of the Subject, by implementing safety precautions, such as bomb-proof glass."
"It's important that the Subject's academic progress is not hindered by the restrictions imposed upon him," said the Director.
"I appreciate that support and previously we've always found a way to work through stumbling blocks," Anna continued. "However, I am having difficulty finding a way to conduct a hydrogen pop test. It's a basic experiment that demonstrates the reaction of a magnesium strip with

hydrochloric acid. For the Subject, it's a simple task. However, creating the 'pop' requires an open flame, typically produced by a Bunsen burner."

"I see," pondered the Director. "An open flame presents thirty-seven safety concerns and needless to say, a Bunsen burner is out of the question."

The Director thought for a moment. "Does this experiment have to be carried out directly by the Subject?"

"It's a requirement of the examination board," answered Anna. "However, there are no restrictions on the length of the lighting apparatus. In theory, we could create an extended grip to hold the magnesium strip that would allow the Subject to remain safely behind protective material far away from the open flame. He could hear the 'pop' through headphones."

"That sounds plausible," nodded the Director. "Consult with the fire safety officer on this matter and discuss the construction of this lighting apparatus with the appliances engineer. We'll also need to conduct sound tests with the audiologist to ensure no damage is caused to the Subject's hearing."

Anna nodded. "It's imperative that this is achieved, as it's the last of his Key Stage 4 components, which are frankly well below his ability levels."

"That's all well and good, but I must demand a full risk assessment and six successful simulations before I give approval for the Subject to conduct this experiment. Is that clear?" asked the Director, sternly.

"He's an extraordinarily bright boy…" protested Anna.

"I know, he's a Farrington. Fate is the problem, not a lack of intelligence," replied the Director.
Anna let the comment slide.
"There are additional minor points for concern. They are listed in my weekly report," she continued, tapping the file in front of her. "For the record, we have a new oatmeal supplier. We were concerned by the methods of our previous provider. The farm was using herbicides to combat broadleaf weeds spreading through the crop in its US state of origin."
"It's pronounced Oreg*on*," chipped in Mitchell Johnson, smugly.
"No, I mean origin, as in the state where we source the oatmeal. It's actually South Dakota," replied Anna, throwing a scornful gaze Mitchell's way. He reminded himself that he should never interrupt Anna Kraus, let alone assume she'd made a mistake.
"Anyway," continued Anna. "I have approved the oatmeal produced by a Scottish farm that has adopted a cleaner de-husking process that goes a little against the grain, if you'll excuse the pun." Anna couldn't help but look across at Mitchell, knowing he'd be baffled by the remark.
"Also, the kitchen team have been instructed to attend a safety refresher course after an incident with vegetables on Sunday. Carrots were sliced horizontally rather than being mashed into puree. Consequently, eight slices ranging from 2.2cm to 3.7cm in diameter were placed in the Subject's food bowl. Fortunately, the serving staff immediately recognised this as a potential choking hazard."

"Was the chef responsible disciplined?" asked the Director.
"Such a fundamental error could have had catastrophic consequences. Once we identified the chef at the root of the problem, he was dismissed," said Anna.
"If you'll excuse the pun," the Director remarked.
Anna smiled.
Once again, it went over the head of Mitchell Johnson.

Chapter 6

Hisoka Saito had been sitting patiently. He knew he would, as always, be the last of the four heads of department to speak. The Director rubbed his hands together in anticipation of the latest report from his Head of Finance. "Hisoka," he said, excited. "What news?"
Hisoka Saito had striking hair - white at the front and sides and black on top, giving him the appearance of a badger in a Savile Row suit. Indeed, badger was the animal that Warren associated with him.
Hisoka lived, breathed and slept money. He had a wife and three children, but was guilty of allowing the controlled, safety-driven paranoia of Farrington Towers to influence his personal life. He took the regimental world of work back home and didn't allow his children to play outside, join sports teams or play computer games. When his sons secretly visited Alton Towers together, Hisoka was apoplectic with rage. When he discovered his wife knew of the trip, he took it as a personal betrayal by his family. They duly returned to their native Japan. They're now living on the beautiful inland island of Shodoshima, where Hisoka's sons enjoy scuba diving and rock climbing. His wife runs the island's largest plantation of olive trees and finds her tennis instructor a more than adequate substitute for her bean-counting husband.
Hisoka ignored his marital problems by immersing himself in work. He was seen by others on the Executive

Committee as being little more than a puppet for the Director. But Hisoka was astute and thorough when it came to investments and acquisitions.
Whilst it was the Director who decided which commodities and industries to invest in, Hisoka ensured that everything appeared legal on the surface.
Over the course of his tenure, Farrington Enterprises Incorporated had become global leaders in lead smelting, lead acid batteries for the automotive industry, plastics manufacturing, and tanneries producing leather from animal hides.
The amount of money Hisoka and his equally corrupt team paid to officials and politicians to keep the company's more polluting enterprises out of the headlines was staggering. The bribes were worth every penny, as such investments reaped considerable profits.
Hisoka shuffled the papers in front of him, but he didn't require them. He knew the figures by heart. "Our advisers in South America were accurate with their predictions," he began. "The Bolivian government has vowed to invest billions of dollars on infrastructure projects. We anticipated this as we lobbied hard for the government to open-up areas of protected rainforest for development. Consequently, our partner businesses in the country are well positioned to benefit and the value of our Bolivian subsidiaries will increase substantially."
"That's wonderful!" said the Director. "Have you completed your research into new opportunities in Central America too?"

"Nearly there," replied Hisoka. "Certainly, there is potential for further cultivation of the Nicotiana Tabacum plant in subtropical America, for use in the tobacco industry. There's been a huge increase in the amount of young people smoking in Africa and it would be prudent to exploit that. I only have one piece of bad news. Our attempts to lobby governments into ending the international ban on whaling have not yet been successful. For now, we'll have to make do with the two Japanese ships operating for what we call research purposes. Elsewhere, our decision to remove support for fair trade cooperatives is paying dividend. With lower wages, our clothing and footwear manufacturing firms in Cambodia and Laos are returning larger profits. We also continue to make steps towards the expansion of oil drilling in the Arctic Circle and have made a significant political payment to an influential figure. We are hopeful that it will help us secure future opportunities, particularly in Russia. In terms of our African investments, one minor cause for concern is cocoa. Not only has the price dipped due to a predicted surplus in crops, but we have discovered that some of our Ghanaian farmers have been smuggling cocoa over the border into the Ivory Coast for personal profit."

The Director shook his head. "Why bite the hand that feeds them?"

"My sentiment precisely," replied Hisoka. "We sent in an operational team to bring the situation back under control and have arrested several protagonists. Prosecutors in Ghana are preparing charges. A human rights organisation has accused us of exploiting the farmers, claiming that we are paying them less than similar workers in the Ivory Coast. Amnesty International says that we are forcing farmers to make the trip across the border for higher wages."

"Bloody Amnesty International!" said the Director, exasperated.

"I know," sighed Hisoka sympathetically. "They won't let this matter lie, even though our legal team has provided evidence that we are paying our workers three Ghanaian cedi per hour. That's 7% above the current average pay in Ghana."

"What's that in US dollars?" asked the Director.

"It is very close to one dollar," responded Hisoka, smoothing out a crease in the sleeve of his shirt caused by his diamond cufflink, without a hint of guilt.

"There's some positive news on this front. Our research has predicted another surplus of cocoa for the coming year, so we will soon close two of our more troublesome farms in Ghana, saving us the salary of more than three hundred people. This will allow us to shift resources, perhaps increasing our shark finning operations in the Far East, where the price of fin soup has risen sharply. This is due to tighter regulation when it comes to the conservation of certain species. It's an increasingly lucrative opportunity. We must, however, continue to be wary of environmental campaigners. Earlier this month, a film crew aboard a vessel operated by the Sea Shepherd Conservation Society secretly recorded a boat belonging to one of our subsidiaries

catching an Oceanic Whitetip Shark, an endangered species, and removing its fins."
"Why was I not made aware of this?" said the Director.
"The footage only emerged two days ago," replied Hisoka. "We made sure it was impossible to link the activity to Farrington Enterprises Incorporated. I have warned those responsible to be more diligent."
"You mean to ensure they don't kill endangered sharks?" interrupted Anna.
"No," smiled Hisoka. "To ensure that they all not being filmed!"
"Good work, Hisoka" said the Director. 'So, how does the annual balance sheet look?"
"Net assets of Farrington Enterprises Incorporated currently stand at $49.7billion. Whilst we are still awaiting financial reports from our crude oil production in Saudi Arabia before signing off our quarterly statement, I anticipate a healthy return for our shareholders. For those around the table, based on provisional figures, I predict a bonus payment of approximately $2.6million for the four minor shareholders on the Executive Committee and $26million for the two of you who are lucky enough to have a one percent share."
"Did you hear that Dickie?" said the Director, beaming from ear-to-ear. "Not a bad day's work, eh? Don't go spending it all on bow-ties!" he laughed, to the visible delight of Hisoka.

Dickie had heard just fine, but he was not smiling. He was busy scribbling a note about Ghanaian cocoa farms in his notebook.
He couldn't fathom how the Director had wrangled enough power to be able to transform a once great, noble company into a corporation that butchered the majestic Oceanic Whitetip for the benefit of wealthy Chinese diners. He regretted not doing more to stop him years ago, when he might have had the strength and influence.
What made it worse was that it was Dickie who had hired him, after the death of Douglas Farrington.
He had needed a man of ambition. Michael Manalton was not his first choice, not by a long chalk, although he had talent and a proven track record of identifying opportunities in emerging global markets. However, upon visiting Farrington Towers for his interview, he formed an immediate bond with Warren, who was only three years old at the time. The two of them played an imaginary game of dinosaurs. Michael pretended to be a big sauropod, stomping around, whilst Warren laughed as he flew across the room like a pterodactyl.
So, Dickie had offered him a golden opportunity to become Director of Farrington Enterprises Incorporated. That was on the proviso that he agreed to maintain the company's commitment to promoting sustainability, sharing wealth and fighting inequality around the world.
Michael Manalton had done that for a brief time, but he never displayed any affection towards Warren again. Within a year, he insisted on being referred to as the Director and

issued an order to all employees that Warren was to be called 'the Subject'.
Only Dickie had refused to abide by it.

"I think you're forgetting something," said Dickie to the other five in the Meeting Room.
"What's that?" asked the Director.
"It's Warren's birthday next week."
"Nobody has forgotten, Dickie. Everyone will gather outside to sing 'Happy Birthday' and one of the world's finest chefs is preparing a space-themed cake. I've also arranged for a special gift."
"Is it something he can play with?" asked Dickie, knowing very well that Warren was not allowed toys.
"No, but it's something the Subject will appreciate," replied the Director. "It's a sample of moon rock, taken during the Apollo 17 mission. It's costing us in the region of $5million."
Dickie couldn't hide his surprise. "Moon rock? That's not something you can simply pick up off the shelf."
"Tell me about it!" said the Director. "Let's just say a former world leader isn't finding corporate consultancy as lucrative as his lavish lifestyle demands. He is grateful for the additional income."
"I see," said Dickie. "Whilst I can't say I approve of this former leader's decision, I'm sure that Warren would enjoy the chance to study moon rock. He has a fascination for all things celestial."

"Oh, he won't be allowed to touch it," smiled the Director. "But he can observe it at a safe distance."
Dickie sighed. Perhaps Warren can stick it on the fridge, he thought. He didn't say it aloud as he didn't want to have to explain the magnetised moon rock mystery to Mitchell Johnson. So, Dickie changed tact. "I was wondering if perhaps Warren might be allowed a candle on his cake this year?" he said, without any sense of expectancy.
"Absolutely not!" responded the Director. "Why would the Subject want a candle?"
"Perhaps he'd like to wish for something. Like a means of escape. A jet pack, maybe?" said Dickie, sarcastically.
"If he does, then it's your doing," replied the Director, angrily. "Conversations like the one you shared with the Subject yesterday…"
"His name is Warren," interrupted Dickie.
"Conversations of that nature put ideas in his head," continued the Director, without correcting himself. "We have safely contained and managed the Subject by controlling the necessary reality of his existence. Quite frankly, your nostalgic reminiscing of football matches and bread deliveries jeopardise our ability to continue doing so."
"He is nearly fifteen-years-old," argued Dickie, against his better judgment. "He knows that his is not an ordinary life. When exactly do you propose that we start providing him with some answers about who he really is?"
"I will know when the time is right," replied the Director, defensively.

"When?" asked Dickie. "When he's sixteen and you stop benefitting financially from keeping him locked up like an animal?"

He held the Director's gaze. But whilst he maintained an air of defiance, Dickie regretted that he'd allowed his emotions to get the better of him.

"Let me remind you, Mr Page, that you make just as much money from Farrington Enterprises Incorporated as I do," said the Director.

This time, Dickie held his tongue.

"This meeting is over," said the Director.

He stood, ate Dickie's truffle and left the room.

Chapter 7

Warren's fifteenth birthday was largely a day on which everyone other than Warren had a good time.
However, it was to end with a revelation.
During lunch, most of the employees gathered on the south lawn of Farrington Towers, sampling appetisers prepared by one of only four chefs in the country with three Michelin stars to his name. Treats included caviar and smoked salmon, warm deviled egg with Provolone cheese and ratatouille crostini.
The nibbles were complemented by Dom Perignon Champagne. Most present would testify that it doesn't quite taste the same from a foam cup. But the guests were aware that glass was strictly forbidden, as the Subject was expected to be making an appearance. Giving people glass wasn't worth the risk. What if someone were to suffer a previously undiagnosed allergic reaction to caviar and in a state of panic inadvertently launch their glass in the Subject's direction?
What if a disagreement was to break out over the last cup of Champagne and in the ensuing fracas, a glass was thrown and severed the Subject's carotid artery? These were all scenarios considered in the thirty-page pre-event risk assessment.
Warren's party differed from most in that nobody could really be classed as a friend or relative of the birthday boy.

That's because his family are all dead and he has no friends, except for an 80-year-old with a fondness for bow-ties. Instead, Warren's birthday had evolved into an occasion where the staff at Farrington Towers could enjoy themselves. To a degree, anyway; it wasn't exactly an unreserved free-for-all. With safety at an absolute paramount, everyone was restricted to one cup of Champagne and guests needed to conform to the same meticulous security checks as the staff. Even the Stradivarius violin being played by one of the musicians in the visiting woodwind ensemble had to pass through the scanners.

During the hour-long celebration, only a skeleton crew remained on duty, as most took advantage of the rare opportunity to relax with colleagues. To ensure this would not place Farrington Towers in a vulnerable position, should anyone try to exploit the reduced staffing levels by launching an offensive attack, the Director never organised the party on the Subject's actual birthday. It was always one or two days either side, with employees given little notification.

Incidentally, there's no suggestion that anyone has ever considered attacking Farrington Towers. If anyone wants Warren dead, they'd yet to declare such an intention. The far greater concern was that he would die in an incomprehensible accident.

Warren was not permitted to mingle with the staff. There were far too many people and most had consumed a small amount of alcohol. However, he was briefly allowed on to the lawn, accompanied by six FPF guards and the Director. The Chief Observer (CO) had temporarily taken the Director's seat in KR1. The CO, Julius Reed, was skilled in surveillance, but did not have the Director's authoritarian presence. He was usually in charge of KR1 during the night shift, when there was little to do other than watch the Subject sleep and monitor his heart rate. To relieve the boredom, Julius and the three-man observation team would bet on trivial matters. Would the Subject break wind during his sleep? Which one of the two FPF guards supervising him would be the first to pick his nose? That sort of thing. It helped pass the time.

Every time Warren ventured outside, he was required to wear a protective outfit made of tightly woven layers of Kevlar, much like a bullet-proof vest but for the whole body, with an added layer of foam cushioning. It was designed to ensure that Warren could survive a bullet from a 9mm handgun at point blank range.

Such a scenario was all but impossible, given the intense security at the entrance, with all manner of X-ray surveillance and detection devices deployed by the FPF to keep the Subject safe.

Still, because of the family's history, it was deemed necessary for Warren to wear the outfit while outside.

The sponge layer caused him to walk in long, clumsy strides, and because the outfit was coated in a white fabric, he looked like a mummy from classic horror movies.

Dickie was among those mingling on the lawn, wincing with embarrassment as Warren swung his arms and legs forward in huge strides because of the restrictions of his ludicrous outfit. He moved like Tik-Tok in *Return to Oz* as he walked towards a podium, where the Director was waiting to address the crowd. FPF guards created a human wall to ensure that employees were no closer than twenty metres to the Subject.

"Good afternoon, ladies and gentlemen. I hope you are all enjoying your Champagne," said the Director through a microphone.

"You bet! It's free!" shouted a younger member of the perimeter security team who was relatively new and hadn't yet been worn down by the monotonous routine of the job. The remark garnered polite laughter.

The Director smiled as he continued his address. "In what is a special treat for you, the hard-working employees of Farrington Towers, I've laid on black gold caviar. It's produced from the eggs of the rare Iranian beluga fish, an albino sturgeon found only in the southern Caspian Sea. Trust me when I say it was difficult and very expensive to acquire!"

Dickie noticed a gardener lean towards a woman who worked in housekeeping. He whispered: "I'd have preferred a Christmas bonus, wouldn't you?"

"Damn right I would, Craig!" came the quiet reply.

"But we're not just here to enjoy this wonderful, expensive caviar," continued the Director. "We're here to celebrate

the fifteenth birthday of the Subject. To mark the occasion, we have prepared this!"
As he spoke, a huge cake, shaped like a space shuttle, was wheeled across the lawn.
"I hope you appreciate the effort," said the Director, facing Warren. "We liaised with the European Space Agency on its design. It's a scaled reproduction of a conceptual shuttle."
The Director turned to face the crowd. "Don't worry, everyone will receive a slice, just as soon as it has been cut by our world-renowned chef. Everyone that is, except for the Subject, who I'm sorry to announce won't be able to enjoy any of his own birthday cake," he said, in mock sadness.
"The cake was produced by an independent catering company and unfortunately we cannot verify the source of the strawberry jam. But don't let that get you down," he added, facing Warren but still speaking into the microphone. "We have received dozens of birthday cards since your actual birthday two days ago. Seeing as you are not permitted to open post and they haven't been wax coated, I can't pass them to you. However, I will read out a selection."
One of the FPF guards passed the Director a small pile of envelopes. Warren stared at him, hoping that his natural disliking of the man wasn't too obvious to those present. Of all Warren's animal affiliations, the Director was perhaps the most convincing. The falcon. His sharp, angular features, the curved nose and inward lower lip gave you the impression that underneath his suit was a pair of wings. He

even turned his head in short, stuttered movements, like a hawk surveying the horizon for prey.
The Director cleared his throat as he opened the top card. "*Dear subscriber, wishing you fond regards on your birthday. With best wishes, The Smithsonian.* I think that has something to do with science!"
Warren had been in correspondence with *The Smithsonian* after the magazine published his ground-breaking findings on the Navier-Stokes equations, one of the greatest conundrums in the field of mathematics. They had no idea the author was only fourteen at the time.
The Director took the next card from the pile, faking giddy excitement.
"*Dear Valued Reader, we hope your birthday is out of this world. We have teamed up with the National Space Centre to offer you 20% off entry price, for up to four people, valid within thirty days of your birthday, not to be used in conjunction with any other offer.* And that's from Astronomy Now magazine."
As the Director looked at a third card, he was aware of a commotion to his left. The matter was swiftly dealt with by the FPF and he continued, barely breaking stride.
"Here's another lovely card. *Dear Master Farrington, Many happy returns on your birthday. We look forward to continuing our commercial partnership for another successful year. From your friends at JPMorgan & Chase, New York City.* How lovely of the bank to send its regards," said the Director, as he handed envelopes back to the guard.
"I won't read all of them, as most are affiliated to our business contacts throughout the world. There's a lovely

note from one of our logging firms in Nicaragua and the entire workforce of our industrial fluids team in Bangladesh has signed their name in a card, so hopefully you can find some time to read them all later, once they've been wax coated. Now, I would like for us to sing 'Happy Birthday' to the Subject. Naturally, the audiologist has tested and measured vocal readings for everyone gathered here today. So, could all of those wearing red stickers please refrain from participating and momentarily enter the sound-proof booth at the back of the garden. If all of you with a green sticker could join me in singing at the prescribed decibel level, as rehearsed."

The Director led a muted, monotone chorus of the celebratory anthem.

Happy birthday to you,
Happy birthday to you,
Happy birthday dear the Subject,
Happy birthday to you.

The Director left the podium and Warren was escorted back to the secure environment of KR2, whilst those on the lawn chatted. A few sought out the caviar. After all, where else would gardeners and cleaners have the chance to enjoy canapes that cost more than their weekly wage?

Dickie however, approached the Director, a man he normally tried to avoid.

"That was a fine cake," said Dickie. "I'm sure Warren appreciated the effort."

"I hope so. This is his special day, after all."
"Yes, I'm sure he's overwhelmed," said Dickie, a touch sarcastically.
"I'd like to apologise," continued the old man. "For telling Warren those stories about my childhood. Also, for what I said in the meeting about you keeping him locked up. That was unfair."
"Dickie, I know that your relationship with the Subject is different to mine," said the Director, adopting a reflective tone. "I know you have more of an emotional connection with the Farrington family, having served them for three generations. It is natural that feelings will occasionally rise to the surface."
"Thank you for being so understanding," said Dickie.
"We'll speak no more of it," said the Director. "I do hope that in future you'll keep such emotions in check. Unless that is, you believe the Subject should be free to chance his luck in the real world?"
"No, of course not," replied Dickie.
"Good, then we'll continue as we are."
"I have one further request," said Dickie. "Would you mind if I spoke alone with Warren once more this evening?"
"What about?" asked the Director, suspiciously.
"I fear Warren may dwell on what I told him. I feel I should reiterate the dangers of the world, to help him understand that the environment created here is best for him. I have a gift that I think will help. It's just a book, but a special one. It belonged to Warren's great-grandfather."

"If it's not been verified by the librarian, then I would need to know what it's about," said the Director. Dickie's apologetic stance had meant he felt obliged to listen, but in truth the Director didn't like the sound of this unorthodox gift.
"It's just a travel guide," said Dickie. "*The Road to Oxiana*, by Robert Byron. It's a first edition, published in 1937. It's considered to be one of the great travel journals. Warren's great-grandfather, Ernest, took a copy with him on his own travels to the Middle East in the 1960s and added notes throughout his journey."
"I see," said the Director, rubbing his chin. "You know how strongly I feel about keeping the Farrington family's history concealed from the Subject. You once spoke to the Subject about his mother's upbringing in Australia and revealed some of the customs of her indigenous people. I know I expressed reservations at the time, although I appreciate it had a positive effect on the Subject. He enjoyed researching tribes of the Northern Territory. But where the Farrington family line is concerned - the curse, the deaths, the business empire - that must remain secret. For the good of the Subject, of course."
"It is not my intention to reveal any such information," said Dickie. "I have read both the book and the notes written by Ernest Farrington and I assure you that nothing of consequence is revealed. With Warren's interest in foreign lands and customs, he would find it fascinating."
"Can I see this book?" asked the Director.

Dickie reached into his left inside pocket and pulled out a plain, dark-brown leather-bound book and passed it to the Director. "It's not been given a wax coating yet," said Dickie as the Director inspected it. "I'll be sure to do that before presenting it to Warren."

"Indeed," replied the Director, flicking through the journal, noticing that several pages were loose where the stitching had eroded.

"I am concerned Dickie, that reading such exploits might encourage the Subject to contemplate similarly grand fantasies of adventure."

"I'm not sure I follow," said Dickie.

"Well, could reading this book inspire the Subject to yearn for a life beyond the perimeter wall?" asked the Director.

Dickie smiled. "I should think that after reading about the three days of vomiting, diarrhoea and fever his great-grandfather endured after eating dumplings in Afghanistan, it might actually have the opposite effect on Warren!"

"Very well, Dickie. I'll allow it. But you must present it to the librarian of course, so she can make the necessary safety additions and issue authorisation."

"Of course, and I am grateful," said Dickie. "I shall visit Warren soon. If I stay outside, I simply wouldn't be able to resist eating more of that caviar."

"Really Dickie? I didn't think you cared for delicacies?" replied the Director. After all, this was a man who chose not to eat his Belgian truffle solely out of stubbornness.

"I don't, normally," said Dickie, noting the scepticism of the Director. "But who knows when I'll next come across an albino sturgeon?"
In truth, he'd never eaten caviar in his life and wasn't interested in starting now.
"However, I can't drink my Champagne if I'm to speak to Warren. Would you care for it?" asked Dickie, handing the Director his foam cup.
"Thank you, but I should head back to KR1 if you're planning to converse directly with the Subject. I would like to hear the conversation."
"Go on, take it," said Dickie, passing the Director the cup. "Can't you relax for one day? This business with Warren is my mess, so let me put it right. Besides, the Chief Observer will be watching and Julius is extremely vigilant, as you know. You stay here and talk to some of the staff. Have you met Craig over there, on the gardening team? He was just telling me how much he appreciated the caviar."

Chapter 8

The time allotted to the birthday celebrations meant that there was a rare break in the Subject's schedule. Dickie intended to use this time to his advantage.

"You looked magnificent on the lawn," said Dickie, grinning at Warren as he paced across KR2. "Simply splendid!"

Warren smiled, although he couldn't move much as he was in a harness, strapped to the bedframe. With only three minutes until reading time commenced, the optician was quietly securing his glasses.

"You try walking in that suit! It's impossible! Since they added the sponge, I can't even bend my knees."

Dickie laughed as the ICS announced that the optician had left the room.

"The Director felt that you needed an additional layer of protection as so many people were outside. Your outfit was amended quickly and therefore lacks a little refinement, shall we say. Unlike my bow-tie," Dickie added, drawing attention to its design.

"Where's that one from?" asked Warren.

"Lower Silesia in Germany. It was made during the Second World War. Do you like it?"

"Not my favourite, if I'm honest," replied Warren. "It's not as colourful as some. Anyway, never mind your bow-tie. What happened on the lawn?"

"What?" shrugged Dickie.

"Soon after I arrived at the podium, one of the chefs appeared, carrying a knife."
"Really?" said Dickie, astonished. "What happened?"
"He was disarmed by the FPF, thrown to the floor and escorted away. Anna Kraus was there too. She said to him, '*Vincent, are you trying to get yourself killed?*'"
"That must be Vincent Lindberg, from Stockholm," said Dickie. "He's one of our finest chefs. Was he trying to confront you?"
"No," replied Warren. "I don't believe he realised that I was on the lawn. I think he was heading over to cut the cake."
"That would make sense," pondered Dickie.
"What did she mean?" asked Warren.
"What did who mean?"
"Anna! What did she mean when she asked Vincent Lindberg if he was trying to get himself killed?"
Dickie turned to face the two guards in the corner, keeping a watchful eye on the Subject. He knew he was about to discuss something that the Director wouldn't want him talking about.
"You're aware of the metallic wristbands that everyone other than you must wear from the moment they enter Farrington Towers?"
"Of course," replied Warren.
"Do you know why they're worn?"
"For security reasons," Warren replied. "They have location sensors so that everyone can be monitored from KR1 at all times."

"That's right," said Dickie. "They are used to ensure all employees remain in their permitted zone. A chef or a teacher could not gain entry to your private quarters, for example. The automated doors simply wouldn't open."
"I know that," said Warren. "But that doesn't explain what Anna said to the chef."
"The wristbands have another function," said Dickie, staring out of the window. "They have an inner chamber, filled with a deadly neurotoxin extracted from the golden poison frog of Colombia. The frogs are kept in a laboratory in Zone 6. This poison can be injected directly into a person's bloodstream through eight needles concealed within the wristband. This weaponry can be activated instantaneously under the Director's order."
"Under what circumstances would he give such an order?" asked Warren.
"If it is perceived there is a threat to you, Warren. If your safety is compromised, the Director will not hesitate in administering the poison. The toxin attacks the nerves, causing almost immediate paralysis. Death comes within ten seconds. It's more of a deterrent than anything. None of the guards would risk attacking you, as they know it would prove fatal to them."
Warren could not believe what he was hearing. "Has the poison ever been deployed?"
"No," said Dickie, looking at Warren directly. He was telling the truth. Warren was certain. He considered himself an expert in reading body language.

"But why? None of this makes sense. Why is this allowed to happen? What makes me so important?"
"I'm sorry, I really am," said Dickie, turning away. "You know I can't tell you what you wish to know. Not now. Maybe that will change, when you're older."
"In that case, I don't care for being young."
"It is better to be a young June bug than an old bird of paradise," said Dickie. "Do you know who said that?"
Warren laughed. "You've recited Mark Twain many times! Still, it doesn't make me feel any better."
Dickie retrieved a brown leather-bound book from his inside right pocket. "Then maybe this will," he said. "A present."
"A book? Great, I've only got three on the go already!" said Warren, sarcastically.
Knowing he was facing away from the cameras, Dickie winked at Warren. "Trust me. You'll like it. Anyway, I need to go or Anna will complain that I've put you behind schedule."
The ICS announced Dickie's departure.
Warren picked up the book, which Dickie had left on top of a copy of *Paradise Lost* by John Milton. Warren was reading classic poetry for English Literature studies. But he was intrigued by this mysterious book.
He opened it and read a handwritten note on the inside cover. And for the first time in his life, Warren felt dangerously excited.

Dear Warren,
My life may depend on you continuing to read as if this were a normal book.

Warren's heart was racing.

Take a few deep breaths, bring your heart rate back down and do not look at any of the cameras. It is imperative that the Director does not discover what you are reading. Give no cause for suspicion.
The Director believes I have given you a book entitled 'The Road to Oxiana'. It was once owned by your great-grandfather, Ernest Farrington. It was written by Robert Byron and is based on his ten-month trip through the Middle East in 1933-34. Byron travelled by ship from Venice to Cyprus before visiting Palestine, Syria, Iraq, Persia and Afghanistan. Your great-grandfather visited many of the same places in 1962 and made additional notes to update his first edition copy of Byron's book, which he travelled with.
I am telling you this as the Director may ask you about it and you'll need to convince him that I've given you nothing more than a travel guide. Should you need an anecdote to fend off the Director's questions, both Byron and your great-grandfather were fascinated by the Mosque of Sheikh Lotfullah in Iran.
But this is not a travel journal. It is a hand-written account of the tragic events that have affected the Farrington family. You will read how, with each untimely death, fears of a family curse grow. Eventually your father, with only the best intentions, laid the foundations for the protected world you now inhabit.

Be prepared, for there is tragedy with each passing page. However, I know you will take inspiration from the lives, however brief, led by generations of Farrington men and women.

I also want to tell you that I'm sorry, Warren. I could not prevent your father from building the restrictive world you occupy. Neither could I stop the Director from making you a prisoner in your own home after your father's death. I have failed too in preventing him from destroying all that was good about your family's vast and once noble business empire.

I believe you will one day change this, Warren. Your grandfather, Charles, was the greatest man I had ever known. That was until I met your father. You have the same spirit, Warren. You are a Farrington.

I give you my word that I will be ready to help you, when you truly need it.

Your friend,

Bernard 'Dickie' Page.

Chapter 9

After reading Dickie's note twice, Warren turned the page. There, written in ink, were the words: *The Book of the Farrington Family.*
In smaller writing underneath was the signature of Egbert Farrington. Warren began reading the words of his great great-great-grandfather. His life would never be the same again.

Wednesday 3rd August 1904
Long have I dismissed the notion of a family curse, despite the rumours that are circulated amongst the populace. However, recent events have caused me to consider even the most irrational theories.
Three years ago, when we lost uncle Stanley, the famous mountaineer, the circumstances were strange and yet ludicrously plausible. It was simply highly unfortunate that a Himalayan golden eagle would swoop down, grab Stanley in its huge talons and drop him 1,000ft on to the rocks below. From the account provided by his guide, the mighty bird of prey may have been attracted to Stanley's coat, made from the fur of the tahr, an Asian wild goat commonly preyed upon by the eagle.
But the misfortune that recently befell my only sibling, Howard, at Black Rock Desert in Nevada, has shaken me to the core.
Could the curse of the Farringtons be true?
When friends begged Howard not to risk his life in the pursuit of the land speed record, my fearless brother laughed off their concerns.
Howard smashed the record, becoming the first man to surpass 100mph. Suddenly, the Farrington Flyer suffered a puncture. It was

sent somersaulting through the air. Amongst the debris, we found Howard's limp body, a broken neck causing his mercilessly instantaneous death.

Whilst such pursuits regularly end in tragedy, the crash was not caused by automotive failure or driver error. Instead, the puncture was caused by arrows fired from the bow of native Indians of the Paiute civilisation, an indigenous people who have inhabited Black Rock for generations. Howard was unaware that he was driving over a sacred Indian burial ground. He'd employed the services of a local guide to consult on precisely such matters and paid the ultimate price for inaccurate information.

In search of answers to our family's unwanted record for tragedy, I studied the archives of national museums and unearthed the story of John Farrington (1790-1809). I believe his story represents the source of the so-called 'curse of the Farringtons'.

John, who had been born into poverty, was a master's servant on his first sea voyage at the age of fourteen. By his nineteenth birthday, he was an able seaman with the East India Company. Little record of his service exists. However, the following extract was written on Sunday 15th October 1809 by Malcolm Middleton, who worked for the East India Company on trade ships to India and the Far East.

'In the summer of the Year of our Lord 1809, we dropped anchor near the Chinese port of Canton. It had been six weeks since men swearing allegiance to the notorious pirate, Ching Shih, attacked the Marquis of Ely, a trade ship of the East India Company, and took nine British sailors hostage.

The Captain condemned the actions as an attack on the King himself and sought the assistance of Emperor Jiaqing of China to find the pirate and rescue his captured men. The Emperor's Imperial Guards sent word that the sailors were being held captive at a Taoist temple on an island off Macau.

I was one of a group of five men who volunteered for a daring rescue mission.

We steered a launch to the island under the cover of darkness. It was a relief to reach the beach without detection. We battled our way through thick bushes towards a light emanating from the temple. When we peered inside, we saw seven British merchant sailors tied up, gagged and lying face down on the floor, with only one man protecting them. This man, wearing Chinese robes, was armed with a gilt-bronze sword. He walked amongst the captives, kicking them violently.

One of our number looked out to sea and there, silhouetted by the moonlight, stood a diminutive figure at the bow of a Chinese junk ship fast approaching the island. It was flying the flag of Ching Shih's Red Fleet.

We could not delay.

The Captain had been impressed by able seaman John Farrington, a man I had not previously encountered. During a rough trip around the Cape of Good Hope, he had demonstrated astonishing strength and his determination inspired his fellow crewmen. The Captain advised that Farrington be promoted to the role of Master's Mate for his next expedition.

This man, John Farrington, must have been part conjurer, for he could render people unconscious by using a cloth soaked in a strange, sweet-smelling liquid. He would hold it tight to their face and they would sink to the floor in seconds. It had worked sufficiently on two drunken Chinese pirates guarding the temple entrance. Farrington again

administered this potent chemical on the robed assailant, whilst the rest of us set about freeing the sailors.
It was to our surprise that these fine men of the merchant navy, far from wallowing in grief after their harrowing period of captivity, immediately informed us of two startling revelations. Firstly, the robed man now slumped on the floor with his head resting on the vestry, was in fact one of the nine missing sailors. He had turned traitor, passing on sensitive information about British ships transporting silver to Chinese ports. He demonstrated his loyalty to the pirate Ching Shih by slaying the only officer amongst the captured men.
In return, he was rewarded with some of Madame Ching's plundered loot.
The second revelation was that Ching Shih had concealed her substantial bounty, the result of six months of piracy, in a chamber within the temple. We found gold, pearls, rubies, diamonds, emeralds and a great deal of silver originally stolen from British ships. A hoard like it we'd never seen.
It was then that the murderous traitor woke from his slumber.
He went for his sword, but we'd deprived him of it. Instead, he removed a heavy item from his pocket and charged at John Farrington with the intention of sending him straight to his grave. A scuffle ensued during which Farrington, an athletic young man, overpowered his attacker and pulled the weapon from his grasp. It was a beautiful jade ornament, carved into the shape of a dragon and decorated with Chinese symbols.
The traitor cried out in anguish.
"No! The dragon must not leave the temple! It is cursed!"

Farrington paid no heed to such claims and placed the jade dragon in his pocket, as the traitor was tied up by the men he'd tortured. These loyal men of the merchant navy demonstrated remarkable constraint.
Farrington suggested we create a static line of men across the stony beach to transfer the hoard quietly on to our boat. It was a simple but ingenious idea that kept our presence hidden from Ching Shih, who had anchored on the opposite side of the island.
We stepped aboard the 24-four-foot launch, which was just big enough to accommodate us all, before rowing for an hour to reach a light frigate that would transport us to port. We heard the tortured screams of a man enduring a cruel, painful death in the temple. Despite his actions, the traitor's dreadful wailing brought us no pleasure.
Eleven men boarded the light frigate along with the bounty. John Farrington passed me the jade dragon and asked if I would personally ensure that it was given to his young wife back in England.
We set sail, heading north easterly to the port of Hong Kong, where we could join an armed fleet of Royal Navy ships that could easily fend off piracy.
Only Farrington was aboard the launch as it continued in a westerly direction, pursued by a frantic Madame Ching, chasing her plundered treasure. It is said that she spent a day chasing down the launch, crewed with relentless determination by a lone seaman with the stamina of ten men.
When she finally caught him and realised she had been tricked, Ching Shih launched a blistering attack to restore her dented pride.
If the stories are true, Farrington stood proudly at the bow as the far larger and faster ship began its assault. And there, John Farrington remained, motionless, with a startled, statuesque expression.

He did not move, not even an inch, as he was pierced through the heart by a spear which formed part of a carved statue of the Chinese sea goddess, Mazu. The statue had been fitted to the bowsprit of Ching Shih's ship to protect its crew from evil spirits.
Farrington floundered briefly, like a fish on a hook, dangling above the water whilst his launch was effortlessly crushed by the keel of the red fleet's flagship vessel. He died right there at the end of the bowsprit.
The pirates couldn't fathom what had caused his strange state of paralysis. However, clenched in Farrington's hand was a half-eaten xiaolongbao, a steamed dumpling popular in southern China.
We were devastated when word reached us of young Farrington's demise. His chance of escaping the pirates was slim, but the manner of his death was a shock. Had he truly been speared by a sea goddess?
I made a solemn vow to honour the agreement I had made with my fearless colleague. I would hand his family the jade dragon.
The East India Company agreed that in return for his brave actions, it would ensure that Farrington's widow and two young children were looked after. "John Farrington's noble sacrifice will not be forgotten by his family for a thousand years," said the Captain in a solemn toast.
M.E Middleton

Warren took his eyes away from the page for a moment. There was a lot to take in, but he remembered Dickie's note at the start of the book.
'You must not arouse suspicion.'
Warren took a break, as procedure required, before continuing.
He wasn't upset by the unfortunate manner of the deaths. He had read books like *Moby Dick* and *Mutiny on the Bounty*.

The thought of one of his ancestors being a seafaring man fuelled Warren's desire for adventure.
He could barely contain his excitement as he continued to read Egbert Farrington's words.

Since Howard's death, I have been immersed in researching my family's past. Thanks to the British Library, I have been able to locate records of births, deaths, Christenings, marriages and even the financial affairs of my relatives.
The documents and newspaper articles I have unearthed provide fascinating information.
John Farrington's wife, Kathleen, was indeed rewarded by the East India Company as the widow of a naval hero, who had not only saved the lives of several men, but recouped priceless treasures for the Empire. Kathleen invested wisely in financial institutions, including the East India Company itself. During the industrial revolution of the 19th century, the family established engineering and textile manufacturing operations. Kathleen's son, Edward, founded Farrington Enterprises Incorporated to create a hub for their growing worldwide interests.
The company expanded into agricultural commodities, from cocoa beans to rice, providing jobs and opportunities for communities on every continent. In a legacy that survives to this day, the Farrington family made spreading wealth its key focus, helping people prosper all over the world.
Money has also provided those blessed with the Farrington name with opportunities to pursue personal glory. And yet happiness has been fleeting, for tragedy is never far away. For all their brilliance, Farringtons have died in the most unlikely ways.

John Farrington's brother, Gordon (1788 - 1815) fought with distinction alongside the Duke of Wellington during the Waterloo campaign. As a Commander in the King's Dragoons, he fought with the skill of a dozen men and defeated the French cavalry regiment. With the battle won, Gordon scaled a fence to chase a cowardly deserter who he had spotted fleeing battle. He found him hiding behind a cattle trough. During his disciplinary hearing, the coward himself told how Farrington had died. He had taken off his dark red jacket, stained with the blood of a hundred men, soaked it in the trough and then shaken it. Sadly, this attracted the attention of an aggressive bull, who charged at Gordon, piercing him through the heart.
John's widow, Kathleen Farrington, died in 1840, shortly after she delivered documents to the Prime Minister as she lobbied for a parliamentary review of women's rights. She was killed when the Prime Minister closed the door to Number 10 Downing Street as Kathleen left, spooking a parliamentary carriage waiting outside. She was trampled to death.
Information on death certificates of other family members hint at a consistent theme of unfortunate fatalities. The esteemed adventurer Edward Farrington (1807 – 1850) was impaled by a narwhal whilst mapping Antarctica coastlines, whilst John's sister Gertrude (1793 – 1826), died when a weathervane was blown from the roof of her cottage. The arrow pointing north pierced her skull.
Edward had one son, the engineer Nicholas Farrington (1843 – 73). He was killed whilst demonstrating a prototype steam roller's effectiveness on a new tarred road surface. On what was the hottest day of the year, Nicholas' feet stuck to the tar whilst he showcased the capabilities of his pioneering new roller. Sadly, his young apprentice collapsed with heat exhaustion while at the wheel. Nicholas tried to

untie his laces and escape from the tar, but he was unable to bend down, owing to a leg injury sustained years earlier during an explosion in a Welsh coal mine. Sadly, Nicholas was squashed in front of screaming onlookers.

Nicholas had two sons. Stanley was to die on Everest, of course, whilst Richard Farrington (1863 – 1892) was my father. I would only see him fleetingly, as he was often in South Africa. I knew that he worked in diamonds, smoked cigars and enjoyed Punch magazine.

Here is an account of his death, written by Grant Burrell, Head of Operations at Kimberley Mining Company, a subsidiary of Farrington Enterprises Incorporated.

Thursday 4th August 1892

By now, word will have reached you of the tragic death of your husband and my employer, Richard Farrington.

Allowing for a period of mourning, I felt compelled to write to describe the circumstances of his death, with the hope that they may bring some comfort. Since the discovery of the Star of South Africa diamond in Kimberley, Farrington Enterprises Incorporated has increased its mining operations, bringing prosperity to the local people with fair pay, health care and educational provision for the workers' children.

Richard developed an uncanny ability to locate kimberlite, the rock that contains diamonds. He joked that his ability derived from the powers of a jade dragon that has long been in his family's possession and is now mounted on the end of his walking cane.

This incredible knowledge nearly saved his life and were it not for an incalculable twist of fate, Richard would have emerged from the Kimberley Mine Disaster as a hero.

Richard requested that the mine shaft be extended to reach depths previously unexplored. Within days of this extension being completed, news of an astonishing diamond discovery reached the surface.
Upon stepping off the shaft to see the diamond as it was being extracted, Richard noticed that the water level was rising fast and the pump operator was nowhere to be found. Realising the danger, he ordered the miners to leave their tools and head to the mine shaft. His quick-thinking saved the lives of one hundred and fourteen working men with families.
Having saved as many as possible, Richard was left in a raging torrent of rapidly rising water, engulfing the mine. He used the sloping roof of the pit to feel his way out, clambering through a tunnel above him.
He made it to the surface alive, still clutching his cane.
There was a moment of celebration, but the joyous scene was interrupted by a sudden hydrothermal explosion. A hitherto unseen geyser – a huge pressurised mass of boiling hot water and steam - shot up through the Earth directly below Richard. He was sent fifty feet into the air, landing face first on the ground. Whether he would have survived the fall and the burns to his body is not clear.
However, he was killed by the jade dragon on his walking cane, which fell from the sky seconds later, striking his head.
How could fate deal such a poor hand to a man who had forsaken his own safety to save the lives of his workers?
We have named the hydrothermal hotspot 'Diamond Geyser' and hope that it may be forever associated with a fine gentleman.
G.F Burrell

Gordon Farrington
(1788 - 1815)

Commander in the King's Dragoons. Speared through the heart by a bull whilst reprimanding a cowardly deserter at Waterloo.

Gertrude Farrington
(1793 - 1826)

Pioneering trade negotiator with East India Company. Died when a weathervane fell from a roof and pierced her skull.

John Farrington
(1789 - 1809)

Sailor. Died whilst pursued by feared pirate Ching Shih. Speared by a statue of sea Goddess Mazu attached to a ship's bowsprit.

Kathleen Farrington
(1791 - 1840)

(Nee Henderson) Widow of John. A pivotal figure in the campaign for women's rights. Died when trampled by startled horses.

Edward Farrington
(1807 - 1850)

Son of John & Kathleen. Explorer. Killed in north Canada by a narwhal tusk while protecting animals from poaching.

Nicholas Farrington
(1843 - 1873)

Son of Edward & Margaret. Renowned engineer and creator of tarred surfaces. Killed by steam roller during a demonstration.

Richard Farrington
(1863 - 1892)

Son of Nicholas & Sylvia. Saved the life of 114 men during mining disaster. Killed by geyser and head wound caused by his cane.

Stanley Farrington
(1868 - 1901)

Son of Nicholas & Sylvia. Famed mountaineer killed by Himalayan golden eagle whilst attempting to reach summit of Everest.

Howard Farrington
(1884 - 1904)

Son of Richard & Eleanor. Land Speed Record Holder. Killed in the Farrington Flyer when arrows fired by natives caused crash.

Son of Richard & Eleanor. Naval Captain. Died when his vessel sunk while laying Atlantic cables that were struck by the Titanic.

Daughter of Egbert & Pamela. World famous archaeologist. Died when T-Rex exhibit collapsed at Natural History Museum.

Son of Egbert & Pamela. Spitfire Ace. Shot down. Died when German plane ran out of fuel and crashed into his ambulance.

Son of George & Edith. Environmentalist. Died when parachuting into a woodchipper in the Brazilian rainforest.

Daughter of Ernest & Penny. Americas Cup Winning Captain. Died after being knocked into the sea by an inflatable orca.

Son of Ernest & Penny. Nobel Prize winning Scientist. Died inhaling CFCs when trapped by collapsing Antarctic hut.

Son of Charles & Wendy. Ornithologist. Killed when an estate agency 'Sold' board speared him and agitated a swarm of bees.

Daughter of Charles & Wendy. World Motocross Champion. Decapitated during race by a tree felled by Canadian beaver.

Wife of Douglas. Aborigine. Born in Australia's Northern Territory. Killed by a black widow in a didgeridoo and a blow from a boomerang.

Chapter 10

The Director was not happy as he entered the Control Room.
He did not appreciate having to fend off the trivial problems of Craig Mantle, who only needed one cup of Champagne to give him the courage to complain about Christmas bonuses.
Had Dickie tricked him in some way? If he hadn't, then he had hugely misjudged the gardener's passion for caviar.
He looked up at the display of camera screens in KR1. There were three separate units, with each one providing a live feed from sixteen cameras in four rows of four monitors.
On the central unit, all four screens on the second row (camera feeds 21 - 24) beamed images direct from KR2.
The Director double-clicked on monitor twenty-four, providing a feed from the camera placed at the end of the Subject's bed. As he did so, the image enlarged across all sixteen screens on the central unit. But it did not provide the view he wanted, so he resorted to an overview of the bedroom.
Still, the Director wasn't satisfied. He was trying to see the name of the book Warren was reading.
He turned to the Chief Observer. "Is the Subject reading the book given to him by Dickie Page?"
"Yes, sir," replied Julius.
"How long has he been reading for?" asked the Director.

"He read for thirty minutes, thirty-seven seconds, during which time he turned the page six times before taking a break," replied the CO. "He then resumed his position and has since been reading for sixteen minutes, turning the page an additional five times."
"The Subject only turned six pages in a full session?" asked the Director.
"He appeared to read the first page twice, sir," replied Julius.
"You didn't find that unusual?"
"Of course, but it has happened before with books that have a complicated introduction."
"Were you monitoring his heart rate?" asked the Director.
"Yes," answered Julius. "It raised briefly by six beats, then returned to normal."
The Director frowned. "Did Dickie make any reference to the book's title when he gave it to the Subject?"
"No sir, he did not."
The Director switched on the ICS.
"Good evening. Are you enjoying your book?"
Warren looked towards the camera at the end of his bed.
"It's interesting. Thank you for asking," he responded.
"May I ask what you're reading?"
"*The Road to Oxiana*, by Robert Byron," replied Warren. "It's about one man's travels in the Middle East."
"The Middle East? That's not a part of the world that has interested you of late?" pressed the Director, adopting an inquisitive tone.

"What is interesting is that my great-grandfather, Ernest Farrington, has added notes about his own experiences of a similar journey he made. Once I've finished reading this, I'd like to learn more about the Mosque of Sheikh Lotfullah, which he considered spectacular."
"That's fascinating," said the Director, not meaning it. "I shall leave you to enjoy your great-grandfather's adventure. You still have some reading time remaining."
"It's okay," replied Warren, putting the book down. "That's enough for tonight anyway. I'm going to read a little poetry for the last few minutes."
The Director smiled.
Everything seemed to be in order.

Chapter 11

It was 6:15am, thirty minutes after Warren had risen been woken and helped from his bed.
He had fulfilled a morning wash and dressing procedure that would sound exhausting to anyone else, but was merely routine for him. Perhaps the most trying part of the morning was brushing his teeth at 6:03am.
By the time that Warren had reached the bathroom, the floor had been sterilised, with a housekeeping unit ensuring that there were no traces of water, although anti-slip flooring, cushioned furnishings and padded walls guaranteed that the Subject couldn't be injured.
The dental hygienist had placed an approval sticker on a new tube of specially made toothpaste, confirming it had been tested for antibacterial chemicals such as triclosan and other surfactants on the 'red list'. An extensive filtering system to ensure minimal levels of contaminants, including fluoride and chlorine, kept the water purified.
Warren was then placed in a cushioned chair, secured with strapping, much like those found at any dental surgery. He was gently lowered backwards and a bespoke gum protector was placed inside his mouth. Six different electric brushes were utilised at a variety of ultrasonic levels. The sulcabrush was used along the gum lines, whilst brushes with softer bristles reached into gaps between the molars.
Two FPF guards watched, as always, from the corner of the bathroom as the hygienist removed the gum protector for a

final microscopic inspection and to record any bacterial anomalies.
Nothing in Warren's body language suggested he was unsettled. However, inside his head was a swirling mass of questions. Was there a curse hanging over his family dating back to the actions of a seaman two-hundred years ago? Why did the Director want to keep his family's past a secret? And how on Earth did Edward Farrington come to be speared through the heart by a narwhal?
He looked forward to the single reading session before breakfast and morning exercises, prior to academic lessons.

Once back in KR2, Warren picked up his book, having undergone the regular procedures before reading time. He noticed that the librarian took a second glance at the leather-bound book in the small pile of books by his bed. The librarian thought the binding of the book she'd authorised at Dickie's urgent request had been a darker shade of brown. But she decided against checking for the approval stamp, as she feared it would make her appear complacent in the eyes of the Director, who would be watching.
Once she had departed, Warren took the book resting underneath *Paradise Lost* and turned the page. He noted a change in handwriting, which did not bode well for Egbert Farrington.
He briefly skipped ahead a few pages, to see who had penned the next entry. It was Ernest Farrington. How appropriate. If the Director asked any more questions, part

of Warren's response might contain an element of truth, given that he was now reading the words of his great-grandfather!
Warren flicked back to read Ernest's entry from the beginning.

Friday 10th October 1947
My world has been turned upside down by the discovery of this book, hidden in a rarely visited section of the Farrington library.
I was saddened to find that it contained numerous tragic accounts of my family's past, recorded by my grandfather, Egbert.
Regrettably, I must add more tales of woe.
I spent the years of the Second World War in the Scottish Highlands, only recently returning to Farrington Towers, bought by my grandfather in 1908. Whilst other men fought for their country, I was absorbed in my studies. I was desperate to join the war effort and indeed attempted to enlist on several occasions, hoping my height would convince recruitment officers that I was as old as I claimed to be. But I was unsuccessful.
I was fourteen when the Germans surrendered.
Perhaps my desire to enlist would have been dampened had I known of the unusual deaths of many a Farrington before me.
I cannot give credence to the notion of a family curse. However, I acknowledge that the stories that follow have fuelled the belief amongst some that the Farrington family is inflicted by a curse. This has become a national topic of conversation, thanks to speculative articles by Fleet Street hacks.
My grandfather died in 1912, eight years after he wrote in this book. As the family business developed a communications network, Egbert

used his vast nautical expertise to lead an operation laying deep sea cables on the bed of the Atlantic. His vessel was towing cables that could withstand the high pressure of the deep sea. However, fate cruelly intervened after six months of faultless operation.

As a 100-mile stretch of cable was slowly being ploughed into the seabed two miles below the surface, the line was struck by a huge force, violently pulling on the cable and capsizing my grandfather's vessel. Unbeknown to Egbert and his crew, the cable had been struck by the RMS Titanic as it sank to the bottom of the ocean, having capsized in the fog some fifteen miles away. With all rescue efforts concentrated on the much-heralded liner, no ship responded to my grandfather's mayday call.

Egbert left behind a wife, Pamela, and two children, Stephanie and George. Pamela perished during the Great War. She'd volunteered to assist in coastal patrols and in 1918 was a passenger in a sidecar being ridden by another volunteer. The sidecar came loose from the motorcycle and hurtled off a cliff in to the sea below. Pamela remarkably survived the fall, but the sidecar was swept out by the current, where it was mistaken for a sea mine by HMS Dreadnought and destroyed by a torpedo.

Aunt Stephanie became a leading palaeontologist and was the first to produce indisputable scientific evidence linking dinosaurs to birds. Whilst unearthing fossils in Montana in 1938, Stephanie discovered a near complete Tyrannosaurus Rex fossil. After she had painstakingly reconstructed the dinosaur at the Natural History Museum, part of the steel structure she had requested for the exhibit collapsed.

The neck of the dinosaur lurched forward and Stephanie was effectively 'eaten' by the T-Rex, with its teeth causing a fatal haemorrhage.

My father, George Farrington, was one of the great pilots of the Second World War. Flying his Spitfire, George accounted for sixteen Luftwaffe fighter planes, making him the leading ace of the Battle of Britain in 1940. When three Iron Cross pilots of the Luftwaffe launched a surprise attack on a coastal base, George took to the skies before an order could even be issued. He single-handedly engaged in a fierce battle with a trio of Hitler's finest fliers. He sent two of them crashing into the Channel.

However, the third German fighter struck George's tail from the blind side. George deliberately stalled his engine, sending his Spitfire into a tail-first descent towards the beach. To the astonishment of onlookers, as the third Messerschmitt Bf 109 flew directly above him, George fired his machine guns, killing the German pilot. The Spitfire hurtled into the Channel, but George dragged himself out and scrambled to shore, despite a broken leg.

Tragically, the Messerschmitt, which had been aimlessly circulating with the pilot slumped dead at the controls, ran out of fuel twenty minutes later. It crashed directly into the ambulance transporting George to the hospital five miles away, killing him instantly.

Before I left for Scotland, and my father proudly left to serve with the RAF, he told me about this book. "No matter what you read, do not allow it to dictate your life, or you'll have no life at all. There is no curse. It is just a pretty stone," he said, pointing to the jade dragon on the end of Richard Farrington's old cane, hanging above the fireplace. I may only be sixteen years of age, but I understand what he meant. Maybe I too will be lost in tragic circumstances. Perhaps I will be the last Farrington. Nonetheless, I am determined to live a full life.

We are not made for an ordinary existence.

Ernest Farrington.

Warren looked at the clock. He'd been reading for nine minutes. He turned the page to see that the next section was written by Charles Farrington, his grandfather.
Warren could not resist the urge to continue, even though he suspected that the most shocking revelations were yet to come.
He had to face them. He was ready to face them.

Chapter 12

Dickie sat down for dinner at the opposite end of the table to Warren. They hadn't seen each other all day. Not that there was anything unusual about that.

"How has your day been?" asked Dickie.

"Maths was interesting. Differential calculus. You know, Newton's second law of motion; simple stuff."

Warren knew that Dickie struggled with mathematics and couldn't engage in a meaningful discussion. So, he changed the subject. "The porridge tasted unusual at breakfast."

"Oh. That'll be the oats," replied Dickie.

"The oats?"

"During the Executive Committee meeting, Anna mentioned that she's changed your oatmeal supplier."

"Why?" asked Warren.

"Something to do with herbicides, apparently," said Dickie. "The old oatmeal came from South Dakota, or was it Oregon? Anyway, it was somewhere in America. Now they bring it in from Scotland."

"I prefer the old oatmeal," said Warren. "It's sweeter."

"That's probably because it's American," said Dickie. "They put sugar in everything. That's why they're all fat."

"That's a misconception," replied Warren. "The South Pacific islands have the highest proportion of obese people because their diet is based on fried fish. In American Samoa, three quarters of the population are clinically obese, compared to approximately a third in the United States."

"They didn't carry out that poll at *Disneyworld*, let me tell you!" remarked Dickie. "It's 90% there!"
Warren resisted the temptation to challenge Dickie's baseless statistic. "Can you ask the chefs to add more sugar to the oatmeal or whatever's required to make it more American?"
"I doubt they'll be allowed. It's all to do with calories. This is Anna's area of expertise, really. You know how meticulous she is. The decision won't have been taken lightly."
"Can we ask her then?" said Warren.
"Now?"
"Yes, if there's even a remote possibility of bringing back my American oatmeal!"
"KR1, is Anna Kraus available to join us for dinner?" said Dickie, speaking into the air.
They waited in silence for a few moments.
"Affirmative. Miss Kraus will be joining you soon." It was the voice of the Director over the ICS.
Dickie and Warren continued eating. Beef, roast potatoes, carrots and parsnips are all on the list of choking hazards, so Warren's meal was blended and served more as a roast soup, placed in an anti-contamination pouch and consumed through a straw. Even still, a doctor trained in the Heimlich manoeuvre was sat nearby, alongside two FPF guards.
"Have you had the chance to read the travel book I gave you?" asked Dickie, nonchalantly.

"Yes, it was fascinating," replied Warren. "The journey must have been quite emotionally draining. There's a lot to take in."
The old man understood its meaning.
"Indeed," he replied. "How far have you read?"
"All of it," said Warren, without emotion. "All of it that was there, anyway. Some pages are missing. I suppose that's understandable, given how old the book is. Perhaps they'll turn up one day. Somewhere unexpected, perhaps?"
"I'm sure of it," said Dickie.
He was impressed. This fifteen-year-old boy had discovered the unbelievable truth about his family. Yet he was still in control of his emotions. Dickie was careful not to go too far with coded speech, as the Director was listening in. So, he changed topic.
"And what are your reading next?"
"I have requested *The Aeneid*, as I'm finding advanced Latin relatively challenging," said Warren. "I'll be requesting some information about agricultural farming as well, as this oatmeal discussion has made me realise how little I know about arable crops and harvesting methods. I've also asked my physics professor to source Professor Stephen Hawking's theories on space and time warps. I couldn't substantiate the calculations when I read them a few years ago, but he thinks I'm ready now."
"Quantum theory and that kind of thing?" asked Dickie.
"You don't have to pretend you're interested," smiled Warren. He knew that while Dickie was interested in space

exploration, he was nonplussed about theoretical aspects of the universe.

"Whilst we're talking about quantum worlds, I'm sure I saw you wearing that bow-tie two days ago. You never wear the same one, Dickie. Is everything okay? Have we entered a parallel dimension in which you've finally run out of fresh bow-ties?"

"You're quite right, it is the same one!" said Dickie, looking down at it, as if he was surprised. "I'm fond of this one. It comes from..."

"Lower Silesia!" interrupted Warren.

"That's right!" said Dickie. "Do you know, the first time I wore this was to see a war movie at the theatre back in 1963?"

"How would I possibly know that?" replied Warren. Out of politeness, he chose not to mention that Dickie couldn't have worn it in 1963, as he didn't own a bow-tie until he met Warren's grandfather, Charles, some years later. He'd recited the story of their first encounter many times.

The conversation was interrupted by the ICS.

"Anna Kraus has entered KR7."

Anna was wearing standard issue flat-bottomed shoes, her feet barely making a dent in the padded floor. She walked up to the circular table. A seat, securely built into the floor, automatically moved backwards, initiating a beeping sound and a robotic 'Danger: chair reversing' warning. Once Anna was securely sat down, the chair edged slowly towards the table with another warning.

The chair was the same as Warren's in that it was padded, reinforced and secured to the floor to prevent it collapsing or toppling over. However, Anna wasn't required to wear the protective strapping or body armour that Warren wore during meal times.
"In need of some intelligent company, are you Warren?" she said, softly, before winking at Dickie.
They were separated by transparent sections of a plastic material, which divided the table like a pie sliced into quarters. This was to prevent non-diced food from entering the Subject's eating area. Sound devices were installed to allow for conversation between those dining.
"Actually, we invited you to join us as we have a crisis on our hands." Dickie looked momentarily serious, before a smile broke out across his face. "Warren would like to know if he can have sugar on his porridge?"
Anna laughed. So much of her daily routine at Farrington Towers was studious, formal and regimented. This was the first time she had laughed all day. "I'm afraid sugar is out of the question," she politely replied.
"How about honey then?" pushed Dickie. He knew that there was no chance of Anna ever agreeing to honey on oatmeal, but he also knew that these rare, informal conversations were good for Warren's sanity. His too, for that matter.
Anna's tone remained diplomatic. "Raw honey is difficult. We couldn't allow bees on the premises for safety reasons and there is a risk, albeit infinitely small, that honey from outside sources could cause botulism."

"So, must I live with this tasteless Scottish wallpaper paste instead?" asked Warren. "Surely, you could allow me just one spoonful of sugar to help it go down?"
Anna was bemused by the scenario. A fifteen-year-old heir to the world's largest business empire and an eighty-year-old bow-tie collector made unlikely comrades.
"The nutritionist recommends that you consume no more than fifty calories in added sugar per day, which equates to three teaspoons. A can of fizzy drink alone may have three times that amount and a chocolate bar contains one hundred calories, so you can understand the limitations."
"But I never have any fizzy drink!" reasoned Warren. "And I'm only given a liquefied form of chocolate on special occasions."
Dickie, meanwhile, had momentarily lost concentration and started humming '*A Spoonful of Sugar*' from the film, *Mary Poppins*.
"That's true," replied Anna. But you do consume pureed fruit and fruit juice, which may have health benefits but does contain sugar. You also have occasional baked treats, such as cookies and birthday cake."
"Don't mention birthday cake!" Dickie interjected. "Warren wasn't allowed a slice of that spaceship, remember?"
"Space shuttle," corrected Warren.
"Right you are!" conceded Dickie.
"So, there's no leeway when it comes to my porridge?"
"I'll speak to the chefs," sighed Anna. "You are currently consuming slightly less than fifty calories of added sugar per day, so perhaps we can alter the recipe. I can't promise that

we'll add sugar, but we can conduct trials with ginger, lemon, cinnamon, vanilla and other ingredients to create something more appetising. It may take a few days though, to pass compliance tests."

"Thank you, Anna, I appreciate it."

"Do you know this boy has never eaten a hot dog?" interrupted Dickie, abruptly, like it was impossible to believe that someone could reach the age or fifteen without visiting a summer fete or roadside layby and paying over the odds for hot food.

Anna frowned. "Now you're just causing trouble, Dickie! You know that sausages are high on the list of choking hazards. Hot dogs are off the menu just so long as Warren is here, I'm in charge of his diet and that camera is looking down on us all!" she said, pointing to the corner of KR7.

Unexpectedly, one of the two FPF guards observing the Subject received a transmission in his earpiece. He rose from his seat and approached the table.

"The Director requests the presence of you all in KR1 immediately."

"Including Warren?" asked Dickie, surprised. "He's never been to the Control Room!"

"My orders are to summon the Subject and members of the Executive Committee as a matter of urgency," said F16a, with F16b dutifully stood alongside him.

"Well then, we'd best get on with it," said Dickie.

Chapter 13

Warren might have expressed amazement at the technological wonders of the Control Room, were it not for something unexpected dominating the central block of monitors.

On screen was someone dressed in a bird costume. The kind of heavy costume worn by mascots of sporting teams, which concealed an individual's identity.

Warren took a few steps towards the screen and was surprised when the bird addressed him directly.

"Master Farrington, there you are!" said the bird in a bubbly, camp male voice. "Oh, my days! Who's your hairdresser, Edward Scissorhands?"

"Excuse me?" asked Warren.

"Don't worry. You wouldn't understand the reference if what I've heard about you not watching any TV is true. I just wondered how they cut it, that's all," continued the bird. "I know they're right sticklers for safety there at FT. I bet bath time's a right old drama for you! Having to get your willy out in front of them guards and having them sit there to make sure you don't fart in the tub. Must be right embarrassing!"

"Who are you?" asked Warren, sternly.

"Oh, my God! Haven't they told you anything?" said the bird. "That Director bloke, he's a sneaky rascal! You wouldn't believe the threats I had to make before he'd let

me meet you, Warren. To answer your question, I'm what people would call the baddie."
"You mean, you're a criminal?" asked Warren.
"Well, yes, I suppose! But I have a flair for the dramatic, Warren! There is an element of criminal activity in what I've done on this specific occasion, yes. But without wanting to sound egotistical, I like to think I'm more of a malevolent, vengeful mastermind."
"Why are you dressed as a giant sparrow?"
"I thought you'd never ask! It's not actually a sparrow costume, although I know why you'd think that, what with the grey and brown plumage. It's supposed to be a hawfinch. If you look closely, there's a red tint to the head. It was specially made."
"Well, I shouldn't think there's much demand for hawfinch costumes at fancy dress shops," said Warren.
The hawfinch swayed backwards, laughing. "That's true, Warren, very true! Oh, you are funny!"
His voice was becoming even more ludicrous.
"Still, it was important for you to wear that costume, wasn't it?" pressed Warren.
"It was, Warren. Do you know why?"
"I can take a guess. I'm assuming the costume was created as a mascot for the estate agents, Hawfinch & MacLean."
"Good, Warren!" said the hawfinch. "And what do you know about that company?"
"Hawfinch & MacLean was found guilty of corporate manslaughter following the death of my father," said Warren.

The hawfinch flapped its wings, excitedly. "I knew you wouldn't let me down, Warren. That's the thing with your family; you're all so bloody clever!"
Warren's knowledge about Douglas Farrington's death took the Director by surprise. How did he know about it?
"You look ridiculous," said Warren, attempting to turn the tables on the mysterious man who was yet to declare his intentions.
"I know," replied the hawfinch, mournfully. "I don't know why they had the costume made, to be honest. It doesn't make sense to have a mascot named after only half the company. So, anyway, Warren, tell me; am I Hawfinch or MacLean?"
"I don't think you're either partner."
"What makes you say that?" asked the hawfinch.
"Well, both directors would surely be in their fifties now," answered Warren. "I suspect you're younger than that, judging by the exuberance in your voice and the youthful way you're flapping those wings."
"Brilliant, Warren!" said the hawfinch. "Top marks!"
"And of course, that's not your natural voice, is it?" continued Warren. "And the most logical reason for adopting such an eccentric persona is that you have a distinctive accent. Which might well be the case for a relative of Cameron MacLean, who I believe was from Glasgow?"
The birdman paused, scratched the head of his costume and in a Scottish accent in stark contrast to his adopted voice, said: "I'm impressed. Genuinely, I am. It is a pleasure and a

privilege to meet you, Warren. My name is Fergus MacLean, Cameron son. I'm twenty-years-old and, ironically, I quite like birds."

"I do too," said Warren.

"I'm aware of your interest, Warren. That's somewhat ironic too, given that the RSPB is lobbying the Government for the removal of the laser beams above Farrington Towers which kill hundreds of birds every year."

"I didn't know that," uttered Warren, ashamed. The daily extermination of bird carcasses was unbeknown to him.

"Do you know something, Warren?" asked Fergus. "In another world, I believe you and I could have been friends."

"Why not in this world?"

"Because of the torment and suffering your family has inflicted upon mine," replied Fergus.

Warren was confused. "Your suffering? It was my father who was killed!"

"So, you know what happened that day, Warren? The day your father died?"

"I was told about it a long time ago," he replied, aware that Dickie and the Director were stood behind him. In truth, Warren had only read the harrowing account of Douglas' death that very morning.

His attempted cover-up didn't fool the Director. Such a conversation wasn't possible without his knowledge. Someone had been feeding the Subject information.

"Please, enlighten me!" said Fergus.

Warren felt a lump in his throat. "My father was killed when he was speared by a Hawfinch & MacLean 'For Sale' board and subsequently attacked by a swarm of bees."
"That's right," said Fergus. "But they weren't 'For Sale' boards, Warren. They were 'Sold' boards."
"A trivial point, don't you think?" asked Warren.
"Perhaps," replied Fergus.
"Well do tell if I've missed something?"
"There's a lot more to be honest, but that's for another time," said Fergus. "It's a long story and it's hot in this ridiculous costume. Dusty too. It's been in the attic for a fair while. So, I'll get to my point, Warren. Have you ever seen this girl?"
Fergus held a photo close to the screen. "Can you see it? It's very awkward to show you without getting these big furry hands in the way."
"No, I haven't seen her before," replied Warren, honestly.
"I didn't think you would have," said Fergus. "I kidnapped her today while she was at school. Well, I didn't, but I had my men do it. My men? That sounds ridiculous! I mean men who I'm paying extortionate amounts of money to commit abhorrent crimes. I'll tell you though, the kidnapping wasn't easy. She's a real fighter. She took down two of my men, which is impressive for a fifteen-year-old. One of them had a computer monitor smashed over his head and another guy needed a compass surgically removed from his eye. I did tell them not to underestimate her; I knew she'd be feisty. But these ex-special forces soldiers

think they're so great, don't they? They couldn't comprehend that a wee lass could pose a threat."
"Why did you kidnap her?" asked Warren.
"Well, the primary reason was to bribe you, Warren. Try to entice you from your weird little world there at Farrington Towers."
"Why?"
"Why? Because I feel we owe it to generations of our ancestors who have shared such tragic misfortune."
"What shared misfortune?"
"Like I said, I don't have time to explain as I'm sweating buckets under this costume," replied Fergus. "Do some research into our families Warren; you'll see what I'm talking about."
"Why kidnap this girl?" grinned Warren. "Did you think I would take leave of my senses and rush out to rescue her, just because she also appears to have aboriginal ancestry?"
"Dear boy. Did you not see the family resemblance?"
The sentence hit Warren like a steam train.
"Come on Warren, take a wild guess!" teased Fergus.
"She can't be..." uttered Warren.
"Can't be what?" asked Fergus, enjoying the game.
"I have a sister?"
"Clever boy!" smiled Fergus. "A twin sister, in fact."
"You're lying!"
"Why, because you thought you were the last one? The last Farrington? I assure you, it is true. You ask your friend there, the old man who dresses like it's the 19th century."
Warren turned around. "Dickie?"

Dickie put his head to the floor and didn't say a word.
"What exactly do you want from me?" said Warren, turning back to the screen with a look of defiance.
"Isn't it obvious, Warren? I want you to rescue your sister," replied Fergus.
"And if I refuse?"
"I won't lie, I'll be disappointed," said Fergus. "And your poor twin will be in a perilous situation. I was thinking of getting four elephants and tying each of them to one of her limbs. It would be great to see what happens when you put a mouse in the middle of all that. I've always wondered if elephants really are frightened by mice. I'm not sure. I've got a feeling it would be a massive anti-climax. What do you think?"
"I don't think you have four elephants."
"You've got me on that one! But I'll come up with something suitably revolting. That's a promise."
"You're deranged," said Warren.
"Oh, no doubt!" smirked Fergus. "But this is a sick planet, overflowing with sick individuals. I think you'll find there would be overwhelming public interest in seeing the world's safest boy – that's you Warren - take on a dangerous, life-threatening mission."
"Why would it be life-threatening?" asked Warren.
"Because I'll be trying to kill you, Warren," said Fergus, matter-of-factly. "You can be certain of that. So, what do you say? Are you ready to be a hero?"
"Where is she?"

"I've sent everything you need to know to the Director there," replied Fergus. "Location, time limits, rules, everything. Does that mean you're coming then?"
"You'd better believe it," said Warren.
"Oh, that's great," exclaimed Fergus, flapping his wings with joy "Really great. Nice chatting to you, Warren. See you soon."

Chapter 14

Three hours had passed since a man dressed in a bird costume had introduced Warren to the concept of sibling dismemberment by startled elephants.
Warren had immediately turned to the Director, asking if he could take a handful of FPF guards to pursue the captor of his twin sister and lead a rescue mission.
The Director refused.
Not only that, he coldly dismissed Warren's request for the information Fergus MacLean claimed to have sent.
With tears streaming down his face, displaying a petulant anger that not even Dickie had witnessed before, he screamed, cried and begged. Then he became aggressive. Incensed by the hopelessness of his situation, he began throwing himself into the walls and windows of KR2. The FPF guards found the situation difficult to control, as there were strict limitations regarding contact with the Subject. Eventually, Warren collapsed, partly from exhaustion and partly from the realisation that any attempt to inflict pain upon himself was futile in his cushioned room. He was placed into a padded suit and secured to the wall of KR8 with huge Velcro strips.
KR8 was designed for such a scenario. Some of the staff called it the stroppy room.
With the Subject under control and supervision enhanced with additional guards and medical staff, the Director set about locating the book that Dickie had given Warren.

Early the next morning, he sat with an arrogant expression at the head of the table in KR4, pouring himself a glass of scotch as other members of the Executive Committee waited for him to convene the unscheduled meeting.
For the first time that any of them could recall, Samuel Tau had not eaten his truffle within seconds of sitting down. He'd stood with other members of the Executive Committee during the extraordinary call from Fergus MacLean. Like everyone, he was astonished by the composure the Subject had demonstrated. What had happened since had shaken Samuel.
He'd seen the Subject escorted from KR1 in tears and heard him screaming until he choked. Consequently, Samuel didn't have the appetite for lavish treats.
However, the Director sat calmly, unruffled, eating his truffle as though nothing of consequence had occurred. The fingers of one hand were tapping the desk and the other hand rested on a book. It was a well-aged, dark brown hardback called '*The Road to Oxiana.*'
"This book was supposed to have been given to the Subject two days ago," said the Director, as the other five listened. "It was a gift from Dickie," he added, refusing to look at the old man. He spoke as if Dickie wasn't even in the room. "Dickie told me it was all about rail travel in the Middle East. But he deceived me. Instead, he presented the Subject with a different book altogether, one unauthorised by the librarian. This book, here," he said, removing a second book from under the table.

He placed the similarly-sized journal in front of him. It looked to have more wear and tear and the leather was of a lighter tone.
"The book he really gave the Subject has been written by generations of Farringtons. It's a book I didn't know existed. It reveals how they made their fortune and the extraordinary ways in which they have died."
"Warren deserves to know the truth," said Dickie, still looking down.
Unflustered, the Director continued. "Dickie was aware of the book's contents and of the impact it would surely have on the Subject's naïve, impressionable mind. Overnight, we reviewed surveillance footage and there's no doubt that the Subject read the book in its entirety, reading poetry in-between so as not to arouse suspicion. Having read Dickie's note to the Subject on the inside sleeve, I know why. Now, I appreciate that Dickie could not have foreseen last night's astonishing turn of events with Fergus MacLean. However, by reading stories of his intrepid ancestors, the Subject will naturally want to demonstrate the same heroic characteristics."
The Director faced Dickie for the first time. "The impact of your actions could be devastating. Perhaps even more importantly, you have broken the sacred bond of trust within this committee."
"My bond of trust with Warren is what's important to me," snapped Dickie.
This caused the Director to grunt. "Do you think the Subject will trust you now? The loyal servant and friend

who never told him about his twin sister? Because this MacLean chap was right, wasn't he? You knew she was out there somewhere and yet you never uttered a word about it to the Subject."

Dickie's bottom lip quivered. He was right.

The Director smirked wickedly, relishing the moment.

In a show of solidarity that surprised other members of the Executive Committee, Anna Kraus placed her hand over Dickie's. "I'm sure you had your reasons. You have nothing to be ashamed of."

"Or perhaps you have?" interrupted the Director. "Several pages have been removed from the Farrington book. I believe these pages contain the part of the story written by the Subject's father, Douglas. You wouldn't know where these might be would you, Dickie?"

The old man didn't respond.

It was Anna who broke the silence. "Rather than playing the blame game, shouldn't we be working together to resolve this matter? Perhaps we should start with the information Fergus MacLean sent?"

"That will remain confidential," said the Director.

"On what grounds?" fired back Dickie.

"You've read the Subject's Safety Procedural Manual," replied the Director, sharply. "I can withhold any information if there are reasonable grounds to suspect that disclosure may place the Subject in jeopardy, directly or indirectly. Considering what has happened, I'd say I have reasonable grounds to assume that you would leak the information to the Subject. This could in turn lead to him

attempting to escape from Farrington Towers and drastically increase the threat to his life. Wouldn't you agree?"
"The boy is changing," replied Dickie, staring at the Director. "You can't maintain this charade forever."
"You would do well to remember that I have the power to propose a motion that could see you voted off the board of the Executive Committee," smirked the Director. "If you would like to continue serving the Subject, you might consider co-operating."
It was a threat he had issued before to prevent Dickie from challenging business decisions.
"Okay," said the Director, appeased by Dickie's silence. "Let's move on. Details of the missing Farrington girl will remain confidential. However, it is necessary to build a profile of Fergus MacLean, considering the threat he poses to the Subject. Do we know anything about him?"
"Issues!" boomed Mitchell Johnson. "This guy has issues, I'll tell you that. Lousy childhood by any standards and it all started with the death of Douglas Farrington. For the benefit of those unaware of the contents of this Farrington book, I'll read an entry actually written by Dickie on 7th July 2007."
Mitchell Johnson began.

'It is with great dismay that I report the death of my friend, Douglas Farrington, who I have proudly served for many years.
He was revered as the world's leading ornithologist. His remarkable documentaries brought to the world's attention species including the

hornbill, kakapo, Christmas frigate bird and the Eskimo curlew. He also successfully established conservation areas on every continent. Following the death of his wife, Kala, Douglas became increasingly concerned with safety, withdrawing entirely from public life as an obsessional fear of the Farrington curse took hold.

When his sister, Tara, was killed in 2002 whilst leading the Canadian round of the World Motocross Championship, Douglas questioned whether there could indeed be a curse on his family. Could it be solely down to misfortune that Tara should be crushed by a tree mid-race, after it had been felled by a beaver?

This only three years after their aunt Phoebe (1958 - 1999), the famed captain of the Americas Cup winning sailing team, perished in a freak accident at the port of Cowes, where she was preparing for a round-the world challenge. Having navigated tropical storms in the most inhospitable seas, it seemed preposterous that she should be knocked off a harbour wall by an inflatable orca that had blown away from a tourist gift shop.

Charles Farrington, Phoebe's older brother and father to Douglas and Tara, died during an Antarctic expedition in 1987. As the oldest sibling, it was Douglas who inherited the estate and assets of Farrington Enterprises Incorporated.

However, I managed the corporation while he continued his education and later pursued his own interests, usually concerning bird conservation.

Douglas was on a trip to Australia when news of Tara's death reached him. Whilst filming a documentary on an outlying island of the Northern Territory, Douglas had fallen in love with a beautiful, intelligent young aboriginal woman who was the very definition of her name, Kala, meaning fire.

However, as the sole remaining Farrington, Douglas felt obliged to take a more active role in the family business. He asked for Kala's hand in marriage before returning to England.
Kala, aged only nineteen and eight years his junior, agreed on the condition that they have a traditional Aboriginal wedding ceremony. It was only fair, as she was prepared to give up a happy life in Australia to travel to the other side of the world with her new husband. All she knew about England was it always rained.
When Kala tragically died only months later, Douglas expanded on the safety measures first introduced by his father. He set about offering around the clock protection for his infant son, Warrain. He stated that any threat, however implausible, must be considered to enhance the child's long-term survival prospects.
Douglas felt that his own untimely death was inevitable. Sadly, three years after his entry into this journal, he was proved right.
He endured a death that only led to more media speculation of a family curse.
Much like his father before him, Douglas was beginning to regret the self-imposed prison he had built for himself and Warrain. He was questioning the purpose of an isolated existence and felt it was having a detrimental impact on the development of his three-year-old son.
The first step towards change was to journey beyond the perimeter wall for the first time since Kala had fallen to her death in 2003.
Douglas was deeply affected by the plight of refugees in Sudan, a country he had visited whilst filming the secretary bird for a BBC documentary. So,
in-keeping with his family's reputation for helping those less fortunate, he bought an entire estate of new homes to provide free accommodation for thirty-six families from the war-torn nation.

When the media expressed an interest in the story, Douglas was convinced by the publicity-seeking estate agents for the development, Hawfinch & MacLean, to step back into the public eye and attend a ribbon-cutting event at the marketing suite.
Douglas only agreed as he liked the fact that Ted Hawfinch, one of the partners, was named after a bird.
Ted's business partner, Cameron MacLean, had ordered thirty-six company-branded 'Sold' boards for the media photo call. He nailed the boards to the wooden ground stakes in his back garden where his wife, Morag, kept an apiary. That same day, by coincidence, she had opened the beehives to extract honey. The Queen bee escaped and unknown to her, found a new home within the corrugated plastic sheeting of one of the 'Sold' boards.
Cameron loaded the thirty-six boards on to the back of a company pick-up truck and made his way to the marketing suite.
As he neared the new development, he noticed a swarm of bees filling his rear-view mirror. Within seconds, the swarm engulfed his truck. Unable to see where he was going, Cameron crashed into a low wall at speed, sending the 'Sold' signs flying.
By miraculous misfortune, Douglas was impaled in the stomach by the pointed wooden stake of one of the signs, just as he was about to cut the ribbon to declare the estate open. The scene was captured by several photographers and television broadcasters.
He might have survived, had that board not been the very one carrying the Queen bee. Douglas was attacked by the swarm.
The autopsy estimated between 1,250 and 1,500 stings on his body.
I lost someone who I considered a close friend. I may not have served Douglas for as long as I served his father, Charles. But I had great admiration for him and believe Douglas was on the verge of altering his

outlook on life, which might have led to a relaxation of the stringent rules governing Warrain's upbringing.
Now, sadly, I am obliged to carry out the wishes outlined in his last will. I am to appoint an Executive Committee, comprising myself and four individuals to head departments responsible for various aspects of Warrain's health and wellbeing. These include security, lifestyle and the environment, whilst a finance expert will look after the company's worldwide business interests.
The Executive Committee is to be headed by a Director, who will have the responsibility of overseeing every aspect of this work.
I will do my best to ensure that we appoint the finest candidate for this role, but I harbour grave concerns for the boy. I fear that the committee will only impose more regulations for Warrain to live and abide by.
I vow to do my best to guide this adventurous spirit, the last of the Farrington men, in the hope that he will one day emulate the feats of those before him.
Bernard 'Dickie' Page.

There was silence across KR4.
"My God," said Samuel Tau. "Every time I hear about it, I cannot believe how unlucky Douglas Farrington was. There are dark forces working against this family."
Anna rolled her eyes. "Why would this incident with the bees trigger an act of revenge by Fergus MacLean?" she asked. "Douglas was clearly the victim."
"Litigation!" replied Mitchell. "This incident led to a whole world of pain. Cameron MacLean was charged with causing death by dangerous driving. Whilst awaiting trial, he broke into the home of his estranged wife and killed himself. His

widow, Morag, took over Cameron's role in the business and started an intimate relationship with Ted Hawfinch. They planned to re-name the estate agency Hawfinch & Hawfinch after they married. But then corporate manslaughter charges were brought against the company, as it turned out the pick-up truck's MOT had expired. As it was owned by the business, they were culpable. Anyway, to cut a long story short, the business went bust, Cameron was dead and his wife gave up their only son for adoption. I guess Fergus MacLean, who was only eight-years-old at the time, was left feeling pretty pissed about the whole damn deal."

"Still, it seems strange to blame the Farringtons for what happened subsequently," remarked Samuel.

"Agreed," said Mitchell. "Unless there's something else we don't know about."

"So, what do we do now?" asked Anna. "Could we locate the missing sister, even without Warren's knowledge?"

"That won't be happening," interjected The Director. "There will be no rescue mission and the Subject is going nowhere."

"Surely you're not going to keep him stuck to the wall of the stroppy room for the rest of his life?" said Anna.

"No, of course not," replied The Director. "He'll calm down, eventually."

"You can't be serious?" said Anna, turning to Dickie as she looked for support around the table. "Are you going to allow this to happen?"

Dickie sighed heavily and kept his head down. "I'm sorry, Anna, but the Director's right. It would be ridiculous to allow Warren to pursue a suicidal fantasy, purely to prove himself worthy of the Farrington name."
"Well you've changed your tune!" she said, her voice rising above its normal whisper. "I don't believe I'm hearing this. You would betray your friendship? Why, just so you can keep your millions in the bank?"
Dickie looked frail and unprepared for a confrontation.
"I would take a vote on this, Anna," smirked the Director. "But clearly the rest of us agree. There will be no rescue mission."
"Hisoka?" said Anna, in desperation.
"If the Subject were to be killed before his sixteenth birthday, we would lose everything, Anna," pleaded Hisoka. "All of us would lose the assets and shares that we've accumulated over the…"
"I don't give a damn about my shares!" shouted Anna, rising from her seat. None of them had ever seen her so emotional.
"One more year, Anna," said the Director, trying to retain calm. "The will stipulates that if we ensure the Subject reaches adulthood, we will all be entitled to maintain our individual stake in Farrington Enterprises Incorporated. We've sacrificed a great deal for that boy. We've given up normal lives and we deserve to be rewarded."
Anna shook her head. "And what of the girl? What does she deserve?"

"We are not a hostage rescue task force," replied the Director. "Yes, it's unfortunate. But the will of Douglas Farrington clearly states that this committee was created to protect one person and one person only. There is no mention of a second child. In terms of our commitment, nothing changes."
Anna rose from her seat. "Excuse me, gentlemen. I need some air."
When she reached the door, she turned to face Dickie. "You are his only friend in the world. The first time he truly needs you..."
Her voice started to crack.
Disgusted, Anna turned and left KR4.

Chapter 15

Warren sat in the bath tub with two FPF guards in attendance, which as Fergus MacLean suggested would be a humiliating experience for most people. But for Warren, it was part of life's routine.
The water temperature was 98.6 degrees, two above body temperature, with no bubbles. The water was tested for potential chemical interference and fluoride levels before Warren was hoisted into an anti-slick seat firmly secured to the tub, so that his head could not go beneath the surface of the water.
The soap was made with naturally-sourced, vegetable-based ingredients including coconut and jojoba oils. The formula had been altered countless times over the years. A hygienist gently dabbed it on to the Subject's skin with a sponge. He didn't always require soap, but it was necessary today as Warren had sweated profusely whilst stuck to the wall of KR8.
Dickie entered the bathroom. He stood next to the two guards, but they didn't greet him, as their attention was solely on the Subject.
"You asked to see me?" said Dickie, apprehensively.
"Do you know why I'm only permitted to spend eight minutes in the bath?" asked Warren. There was a softness to his voice, with a hint of rebellion.
"Is it something to do with wrinkles?" guessed Dickie.

"That's right!" said Warren. "But I've researched the matter and I don't understand why an eight-minute limit is imposed. There are so many variables involved that it's impossible to know exactly how long it will take before wrinkles appear on a person's hands and feet. It could be five minutes, it could be an hour."
"Really?" said Dickie, unsure of what Warren was implying.
"The strange thing is, there's nothing wrong with having wrinkles. It's a natural adaptation of our body that allows us to grip in wet and dry conditions. The wrinkles act like grooves on a tyre, so they channel water away from our fingers. Now, if that's a fact, I would be safer staying in the bath tub for longer. My wrinkled hands could grip the side of the tub and there would be less need for the anti-slip surface."
Dickie didn't know how to respond.
Warren raised an eyebrow. "My point Dickie, is that not all of the rules here make sense. In fact, I will go further and say that some are fabricated to suit other people."
"Would you like me to request a review of your bath time limitations?" asked Dickie.
"No! I would like you to help me save my twin sister," said Warren, his voice gradually rising.
"I would like you to convince *him* that we should do something," he added, nodding his head towards a camera as though it represented the Director himself.
"I'm sorry, Warren, I really am," replied Dickie. "But such a mission would be suicide."
"What happened to you?"

"I only want what is best for you, Warren."
"Is this best for me? Sat here with a hygienist dabbing me with a sponge and two guards hoisting me in and out as if my legs were glued together?" said Warren, sadly. He looked away from his old friend. "You talk of your childhood memories, yet you deprive me of any of my own. Leave. I want you to leave."
"You're wrong if you think I don't care about you," said Dickie.
"All you care about is my family's money," said Warren, who was trying not to sound upset. "That's all you ever cared about."
"That's not true!" replied Dickie, hurt by the words. "I've served your family…"
"My family?" shouted Warren. "My family are all dead, Dickie. Where is your loyalty to me?"
Even the hygienist backed away owing to the sudden outburst, although she was still wary of exceeding the eight minutes and disrupting Anna Kraus' carefully planned daily schedule.
"Maybe it's time to call it a day, Dickie," said Warren. "I think you're becoming confused and forgetful. Do you even know you've worn that same bow-tie three times in the last week?"
Dickie looked down, as if he doubted Warren's claim.
The Director's voice came over the ICS. "Guards, remove Bernard Page from KR3. Duty Doctor, please attend KR3 immediately." The heated conversation had increased the

Subject's heartbeat and the Director felt it necessary to request a check-up.
"I used to know where every one of my bow-ties came from and even who made it," Dickie said, as the guards approached him. "This one was given to me by a Prisoner of War, but for the life of me, I can't remember his name," he said, as the guards gently took his arm.
Then, with a wry smile, the old man held Warren's gaze for just a moment. "Could have been any Tom, Dick or Harry."
"Bernard Page has left KR3," came the robotised announcement.
A tear rolled down Warren's cheek as he sat in the bath tub. He thought about Dickie's words. Something about them sounded familiar.
And then it clicked.

Chapter 16

Two days after Warren had spoken so bitterly to Dickie in the bathroom, the pair shared a brief but more civilised conversation over breakfast.
It was Warren who broke the silence. "I have requested access to the library during my free session at 4pm."
Dickie looked up, surprised.
"I was thinking of viewing my father's cinematic collection," added Warren.
Dickie smiled in a way he hadn't smiled in a long time.
"I'm pleased to hear it," he said, relieved. "Your father was very fond of those old war movies and built up a remarkable amount of memorabilia. The detail in some of those old posters is fascinating."
"It's a shame I've not had the opportunity to ever watch any of the films they're promoting," replied Warren. "That's impossible with the regulations here."
"It's a pity," said Dickie. "I find a good movie can offer an escape from reality."

With that, Dickie rose and returned to his quarters.
He shined his shoes, ironed his trousers and a clean white shirt and placed on the first bow-tie that Charles Farrington ever bought for him. It was from *Harrods* and depicted little London buses.
He'd not worn it in forty years.

Nobody paid Dickie much attention as he walked outside the Towers and across the south lawns later that day. The FPF guards had always begrudgingly paid him respect, owing to his close relationship with the Subject. But word had spread about the Subject's remarks in KR3. They all knew the special bond had been broken and suddenly Dickie was vulnerable.

Some expressed the opinion that his days at Farrington Towers were numbered.

Dickie sauntered up to Major Jack Reynolds. The two spoke regularly, as Jack had little to do other than polish the F-22 Raptor fighter jet and carry out maintenance work.

"One hell of a day for flying?" said Dickie, looking up at the blue sky.

"Tell that to the birds being zapped by those laser beams!" replied Jack.

Major Reynolds had been one of the most decorated pilots in the Royal Australian Air Force (RAAF). After retiring from active service, he spent several more years touring air shows as part of the Roulettes, the RAAF's aeronautical display team.

"So, did you read about Josef Frantisek?" asked Dickie.

"I did," replied Jack. "That guy had problems mate! Undoubtedly one hell of a pilot, but there are rules of engagement and it doesn't sound like he had much time for them. The guy was a rogue. You ask me, I don't think he deserves a place."

Dickie loved military history and often shared stories of the great wartime pilots with Jack. They had created their own

Hall of Fame in the cockpit of the F-22. Already, it featured eight acclaimed pilots including the 'Red Baron' Manfred von Richthofen and Russian Ivan Kozhedub. George Farrington was on it too.
Every few months, they each suggested a different candidate for inclusion on the Hall of Fame, but only one was selected.
"Fair enough," responded Dickie, although he was disappointed. Frantisek's desire to fight his own private battle against the Nazis during the Second World War had made him a hero in Dickie's eyes.
"What about my suggestion, the frog?" asked Major Reynolds.
"Adolphe Pegaud?" said Dickie, ignoring Jack's derogatory term for the Frenchman. "I wasn't entirely convinced, seeing as he only achieved five victories. And he was shot down by a rookie. But as he was the first ever pilot to be declared an Ace and the first to parachute out of a plane, I'd say he's earned a place."
"I'm glad to hear it," grinned Jack. "I've got his picture here with me. It's a bit grainy because I printed it off the internet, but it'll do. I'll add it next time I test the controls."
"I was wondering, if it's not too much trouble, can I put this one up?" asked Dickie.
Jack smiled, but he was apprehensive. "It is too much trouble and you know it!" he replied, as kindly as he could. "I can't just pop open the cockpit of the world's most dangerous military aircraft and let you hop on in!"

Dickie knew how rigid the safety protocol was around the plane. To open the canopy required the entry of a five-digit code, known only by Major Reynolds, followed by a different five-digit code, only known by members of the Executive Committee.
"I know that," said Dickie. "I know about the codes."
"Right," said Jack. "So, if I go mad, or one of you guys goes mad, or that hot German chick goes mad, and decides to take it out on a reclusive billionaire teenager, you can't dive in an F-22 and fire sidewinders all over the place!"
"I'm not going mad," said Dickie. He lowered his head and drooped his shoulders. "I'm dying, Jack."
Jack sighed. "I'm sorry. I didn't know."
"Nobody does," said Dickie. "I've not told anyone. But I've not got long left."
"Strewth mate. I don't know what to say," said Jack.
"You don't have to say anything. But seeing as I might not get to do this again, I was hoping you would let me sit in an F-22 and stick the frog and the rogue up on the Hall of Fame?"
"Frantisek's not going up! No way! I don't care if you are dying, buddy, that bloke wasn't right in the head!" laughed Jack. He was the sort of Australian who could make a joke of anything and get away with it.
"You'll let me put the Frenchman up though?" pleaded Dickie.
"Johnson's going to have my balls for breakfast for this, you know that?" frowned Jack.

"I'll smooth it over with him," said Dickie. "I'll be in and out in ten seconds."
Jack looked around. "Oh, Christ. Hurry up, before I regain my senses!"
"You're a good man!"
"Tell that to my ex-wives!" quipped Jack.
Dickie climbed the steps and punched in his five-digit code. Major Jack Reynolds did the same whilst looking around, still muttering concerns about the whole crazy idea.
The canopy opened and Dickie dragged his frail body over the side and settled into the cockpit, amazed at the array of controls around him.
"How do you fly this thing?" he joked.
"Oh, we definitely don't have time for that!" smiled Jack. "Besides, you've forgotten to turn the lasers off above us!"
Jack passed Dickie a picture of the French First World War pilot. "Here, stick this on the dash quickly and jump on out of there!"
As Dickie went to reach for it, he pressed a button to close the canopy. Jack tried to prevent it from shutting, but to no avail.
"Dickie? Dickie, don't joke around! What are you doing?" said Jack, worried.
When the old man didn't acknowledge him, Jack's fears increased and he beat his fist furiously on the canopy. The noise barely registered through the thick, polycarbonate structure.
"I'm sorry Jack, but I'm going rogue!" said Dickie to himself.

He pulled a picture of Josef Frantisek from his shirt pocket and placed it on the Hall of Fame. His watched beeped. 16:05 exactly. Right on schedule.
Dickie had studied the pilot's manual meticulously, so he knew how to launch the F-22's jet fuel starter system. He fired it up. It sounded like being inside a vacuum cleaner. He saw Jack jump down from the wing and run towards FPF guards, who were converging on the jet from all corners of the grounds.
Dickie smiled. "For Queen and country!" he said, as he fired a short-range AIM-9 Sidewinder missile towards the perimeter wall of Farrington Towers.
From Dickie's perspective, it seemed to travel in slow motion. It was as though the missile was riding on an invisible horse as it skirted the lawn for about three hundred metres before smashing into the bricks, sending an anti-artillery weapons post along the wall crashing to the ground. Once the dust settled, Dickie could see that a section of the wall had been reduced to rubble. Thanks to the positioning of the jet, facing away from the Towers, the missile had also taken out part of the main entrance gate. Dickie couldn't help but smile. Is this how Josef Frantisek felt when he shot down those German bombers?
And then it came. The poison.
Dickie thought it might happen. It hadn't been inevitable. After all, it meant authorising the execution of a member of the Executive Committee. It turned out the Director was every bit as ruthless as he suspected.

Dickie felt no pain. Whilst eight needles had pieced his wrist, the effect of the world's most deadly natural poison felt oddly soothing. Better this than alone in a hospital bed, he thought.

With the last of his strength, Dickie maintained a grip on the controls.

His vision was failing, but he could see straight ahead, beyond the flattened wall and into the employee car park. And what should he see but the Director's gleaming Ferrari F50, bought from the vast profits of the many immoral business ventures he'd financed since the death of Douglas Farrington.

Dickie smiled.

"For Warrain and Nerida," he uttered with his final breath as he fired a second Sidewinder.

The Director looked out of the window to see his beautiful supercar flying 100ft into the air.

Then the situation got a whole lot worse.

As the V12 engine landed in the centre of the perimeter footpath on the south lawns, where hours earlier the Subject had been walking, the Director received a call from guard F8b.

"Code red. I repeat, code red! The Subject…he's gone."

Chapter 17

After three years in the Royal Parachute Regiment, Stefano Gallo had served with the Special Air Service (SAS), an elite unit of the British Armed Forces.
He'd faced perilous situations whilst in Syria, tracking down members of the terrorist group Islamic State of Iraq and the Levant (ISIL).
So, he could certainly face being grilled by the Director, who was furiously pacing across KR1, firing out questions.
Compared to his fellow guard and close friend Frank Stone, Stefano had got off lightly. Frank had several years of experience with the Intelligence, Surveillance and Reconnaissance Brigade of Special Forces, so it didn't reflect well on him that he'd lost sight of a fifteen-year-old boy in a library.
"Let's try again, shall we?" said the Director, failing in his efforts to stay calm. "Take me through exactly what happened, step by step."
Stefano took a deep breath.
"I entered KR5 with F8a and the Subject at precisely 16:00, as scheduled. The Subject outlined his intention to head to a room containing his father's collection of film memorabilia. This had been listed in the Subject's daily schedule. I was walking in front of the Subject with F8a to the rear. We reached the reference section fifty seconds later and turned left from the central aisle to face north. At the end of that aisle, we met the librarian. She unlocked the door, three of

us entered the film room and the librarian returned to her office. On each wall are four separate units for books or cinematic reels, filed alphabetically. We knew that the units were secure as we tested them during reconnaissance this morning. We had sealed off access to the unit containing photographic film, which is coated with a gelatin emulsion. The central display cabinet contains items of movie memorabilia, including a red bandana worn by Christopher Walken in *The Deer Hunter* and the US Army uniform worn by John Wayne in *The Longest Day*. This cabinet had already been protected with cushioned panels. On the south facing wall, there are twelve cinematic posters on display. We placed a restriction zone around them, so that should any come loose, the Subject would not be harmed. As there are no windows in the room, we maintained surveillance from the entrance. Then, we heard a loud noise behind us."

"And what did you do?" asked the Director.

"I opened the door and went outside," admitted Stefano. "I looked towards the south facing window at the opposite end of the aisle. I could see that part of the perimeter wall had been destroyed. I walked to the window to monitor the situation and evaluate. I was aware that if the F-22 was to alter its position so that its weaponry was aimed at the Towers, we would need to initiate emergency procedures."

"And you, F8a? Where were you?" asked the Director.

"I continued surveillance of the Subject in the movie room," replied Frank Stone. "The Subject had been unmoved by the commotion outside. Well, I say unmoved. He smiled."

"He smiled?" queried the Director. "Didn't that strike you as strange?"
"Not at the time. But on reflection, it was an unusual reaction," replied Frank.
"And what happened next?"
"I heard another explosion. I partially opened the door and called out to F8b, asking what was happening. He advised that we should leave immediately and head for the bunker. Then I turned around and the Subject was gone. I had taken my eyes off him for approximately ten seconds."
"He snuck past you, undetected?" suggested the Director.
"No sir, I do not believe he did," interrupted Mitchell Johnson, who had been reviewing camera footage.
"The Subject disappeared from a blind spot," said Mitchell. "Sadly, we have no eyes in the movie room. However, we have cameras along the aisles of KR5. I've studied the recordings and the Subject does not come back out of that room."
"Well, he hasn't vanished into thin air!" raged The Director. "Could there be a rotating wall?"
"Already considered that," replied Mitchell. "I've checked the structural plans and that's not possible."
"Then it makes no sense!" said the Director, incensed. "He can't have vanished!"
He paced up and down the room, before stopping. A creepy smile swept over his face.
"What is it?" asked Mitchell.
"Guards, was there anything in that room that the Subject seemed particularly interested in?"

"He seemed intrigued by the posters, sir," replied Frank Stone.
The Director smirked.
"What?" asked Mitchell.
"In all the years you've known Dickie, did you ever see him wear the same bow-tie twice?"
"Can't say I did," pondered Mitchell. "It's his thing, isn't it? Wearing a different one every day?"
"It was," said the Director. "But he wore the same one on three different occasions recently. The Subject picked him up on it. Dickie said it was made in Lower Silesia in Germany, then a few days later said he'd worn it to watch a war movie in 1963. Then, he mentioned it a couple of days ago in the bathroom."
"How do you remember that?" asked Mitchell.
"That's my job," replied the Director, before turning to the Chief Observer. "Bring up that conversation in KR3, could you?"
While Julius went through the recordings, the Director buzzed through to the librarian, Wendy Henderson. She was devastated as she felt partly to blame for the Subject's disappearance.
"Librarian, what do you know about Lower Silesia?"
"Well, it doesn't exist today," Wendy replied, nervously. She was petrified of the Director. "It's part of Poland now. But during the Second World War there were several concentration camps in the region. Perhaps the most famous was the Gross-Rosen camp."
"Is there a film about Gross-Rosen?" asked the Director.

"Oh, I'm not sure," replied Wendy. "Films aren't really my area."
The Chief Observer shouted across KR1. "There's nothing here. All Dickie said was that the bow-tie could have been made by any Tom, Dick or Harry."
"Oh, that'll be the tunnels then!" chirped Wendy, who overheard Julius' remark.
"What?" said the Director.
"Haven't you ever seen *The Great Escape*?" she said. "That was the first time that my Kenneth took me to the pictures, you know? Must have been 1963! The escape tunnels built by the prisoners were called Tom, Dick and Harry."
"Is there anything about *The Great Escape* in that room?" pleaded the Director, with great urgency.
"Yes!" Wendy replied. "There's a poster on the wall. It's in front of me now. Starring Steve McQueen, James Garner and Richard Attenborough. Blimey, I forgot Attenborough was in it!"
"Librarian, now listen carefully," said the Director. "Is there anything unusual about the poster? Does it come away from the wall?"
The Director waited impatiently.
"Hold on," said Wendy. "Well, it doesn't want to budge."
Another pause.
"Oh, hang on, that's…there's a button! On Steve McQueen's chest. There's a small button!"
"A button?" repeated the Director.
"Yes, it's made of silver," replied Wendy. "It's engraved with the Farrington family crest."

Chapter 18

Warren had been crawling for twenty-eight minutes, give or take fourteen seconds.
When you don't have any friends, aren't allowed to watch television and don't have access to the internet, you have a lot of time to perform mundane tasks. One of Warren's mundane tasks was to count.
Consequently, Warren had become accurate at counting minutes. It was rare for him to be even half a second too slow or too fast over a single minute.
He once measured his walking pace at 2.1mph without the protective suit on and estimated his crawling speed to be between 40-45% of his regular walking speed. Warren conservatively estimated that he was crawling at around 0.85mph, although he suspected it was closer to 0.9mph.
It was a tight squeeze and Warren needed to be on his knees. But he was nimble.
Farrington Towers is placed centrally within the ninety-eight-acre gardens, with approximately four hundred and forty-five metres to the entrance gate from the front door.
Warren assumed that his grandfather would have ensured the tunnel ended at a location well beyond the perimeter wall. So, he figured that he'd need to crawl for at least one mile, no matter what direction he was heading in.
That's what he hoped, anyway.

When he spotted the poster for *The Great Escape*, he knew it somehow offered salvation. He'd never seen the film. However, he'd read a book entitled *'The 50 Greatest War Movies'* just a few months previously, so knew about *The Great Escape.*

He read that it was one of the highest grossing films of 1963 and featured Allied prisoners of war escaping a concentration camp in Lower Silesia, through three secret tunnels named Tom, Dick and Harry.

Warren spotted a button concealed within the blue shirt of one of three men depicted running on the poster. Then, seconds later, he saw that the FPF guards were distracted by an explosion. Warren suspected that his only friend, a man he'd wrongly doubted, was offering him the opportunity to escape.

So, he pressed the button.

The ground had opened-up beneath him and Warren had disappeared before he had time to react. His heart froze as he fell in total darkness. Then suddenly, there was light and Warren could see he was plummeting towards an underground lake.

He tried to turn in the air to land feet first, but failed and hit the water sideways with a heavy thud. His feet almost touched the bottom and Warren looked up through crystal-clear water as he rose gently to the surface.

He made the conscious decision not to panic, which is quite something, considering he'd never been taught to swim. There were too many safety permutations.

Warren recognised that the water was low in salinity, with little salt content. He had read about places like the Dead Sea and Great Salt Lake where you could just lie back and drift to safety by using the water's natural buoyancy. But he couldn't do that here, which posed a problem.
He reached the surface. Whilst trying to keep his head above water, he saw that the nearest rocks were seven metres away. But it was a sheer face and did not offer safety. To his right, fourteen metres away, were rocks he could clamber up. Beyond them, he spotted a tunnel.
'Remain calm,' Warren told himself.
He remembered instruction he'd been given on treading water in a practical skills class. A specialist instructor remarked that it was the first time he'd ever taught someone without the involvement of water.
Warren recalled the simulations, moving his legs in a continuous circular motion that allowed him to keep his head above water. But when he attempted to move his arms horizontally too, he found that it upset his rhythm and he slipped under the surface immediately, swallowing a mouthful of water.
He stopped flapping and made a concerted effort to regain his composure, treading water by maintaining circular kicks for a moment longer. But he wasn't moving.
He dipped his head below the surface and, allowing for enlarged size perception, estimated that the lake was six metres deep. There were rocks below him too.
There was no time to have any regret at having pushed the button, as he knew his life was in danger.

Warren took a deep breath and exhaling slightly, allowed himself to sink gently to the bottom. He picked up two large rocks from the bed of the lake and held one under each arm to weigh him down and help gain balance. He normally wouldn't have been able to pick them both up, but having studied mineralogy, Warren knew that water supported at least a third of the weight of a submerged rock. He was in luck, as the sandstone rocks he had found weighed forty percent less under water.

One step at a time, he began walking towards the sloping rocks in the distance. He moved slowly, squeezing the rocks tightly against his body, edging closer as the seconds ticked by.

Having been under water for a minute, Warren had only managed to walk eight metres and was starting to struggle. He once sat in bed and held his breath for two minutes and eleven seconds before the Director noticed his fluctuating heart rate and called for immediate medical assistance.

But this felt harder. Was it the pressure of the water, or had he let out too much air while dropping to the bottom of the lake?

Warren tried to walk faster and felt the urge to hold his nose as desperation crept in. His knees buckled as he dropped the rocks, before the water stopped supporting their weight. As he did so, he spluttered, blowing hard through his hand and opening his mouth, swallowing water. He tilted his head up, desperately trying to reach the ever-nearing surface. It was so close.

He couldn't fail now.

With one final effort, Warren lurched forward, pushing him briefly above the surface. He slid under again, but clambered for his life up the slippery slope, finally reaching dry rocks where he keeled over, choking up water.
After a minute spent regaining his breath, Warren realised how cold he was. The water was freezing.
He stripped down to his pants, leaving his clothes on the rocks. He knew he would dry faster without them.
Warren was certain that the Director would soon discover what had happened. He half expected to see an FPF guard dropping into the lake behind him. There was no time to waste and the best way to generate body heat was to keep moving. So, Warren staggered to the tunnel, still gagging from having swallowed water. Chiselled into the rock beside the entrance were the initials C.F and the year 1980.
"This had better work, Grandfather!" he said as he climbed in to the tunnel.

After crawling for one hour and sixteen minutes, Warren finally saw light breaking through.
Despite the claustrophobic environment, he hadn't been fearful. All he felt was excitement. He was both hunter and the hunted. Warren assumed that the Director would not allow him to escape. Yet at the same time, he was focusing on the search for Fergus MacLean and his kidnapped sister. Not that he had the faintest idea of where to start looking.
Following the light, he clambered up between the roots of a huge cedar tree. Warren was climbing within what appeared to be its hollow interior.

Sticky, amber-coloured resin from the sapwood dripped down the inside of the tree, where roots overlapped to create a natural ladder. He climbed higher towards the light and reached out of a hollow, grabbing a branch.
He peered out and could see that his hand was on top of an envelope, with his name written on it. It was wrapped around the branch with string.
Warren put the envelope in his mouth, biting down so he could use his hands to pull himself out of the hollow, before swinging down and dropping to the ground.
He was barely a mile beyond the perimeter wall and guards would be scouring the estate looking for him. He didn't have time to hang around. However, he had to read the letter.

Dear Warren,
If you are reading this, then by miraculous good fortune you unravelled my clues and have escaped.
If that is the case then, at best, I am firmly off the Director's Christmas card list. At worst, I've become the first pensioner from Inverness to be killed by frog poison while at the controls of an American fighter jet. If this is so, please do not regret our recent conversation. I know that our bond of friendship was true, as now do you.
Head north, north westerly for 11.4 miles, passing the east bank of the lake. At the most northern tip, you'll see a dilapidated storage shed in woodland 100m beyond an old boathouse. Hidden there, you'll find food, water and information concerning your sister's whereabouts.

Also, you'll find the four missing pages from the Farrington book. I had to tear them out as they included details of the tunnels and I was fearful that the Director would read it before you did.
You have nothing to fear. Remember, you are a Farrington.
Your friend,
Dickie.
PS – "A boy's story is the best that is ever told." Charles Dickens.

Chapter 19

Warren was happy to follow Dickie's instructions. However, his immediate concern was footwear. He'd not been wearing any shoes on his visit to the library, as he didn't wear shoes inside Farrington Towers.
He was fortunate that he had emerged from a grand cedar tree, a non-native species that are a common feature of stately homes but quite out of place in dense woodland. Warren spotted a fallen cedar branch and tore off a piece of bark. He peeled away a handful of the long, course fibrous strands from the inner bark and twisted them round to make a strong, rope-like fabric.
He then broke off two smaller pieces of bark with curved sides, before scouring the woodland for soft leaves.
There were plenty of trees around, but most were horse chestnut. He'd hoped to find a sycamore, as he had read its leaves were large and soft. He settled on a maple tree and gathered as many leaves as he could.
Warren returned to the cedar tree to extract sap with the envelope from Dickie's letter. He smeared it over the leaves to stick them together before distributed the leaves across the two chunks of bark and tying them around his feet with the natural rope.
Warren stood up and took a few strides, like he would have done if he'd been trying on a new pair of shoes at a shop. He was surprised that his footwear was relatively comfortable.

He set about finding his location. Estimating the time at 17:38, he found a thin stick and stood it on its end, marking its shadow on a rock with a white stone.
Then he waited a few minutes and repeated the process. Warren was about to set off in the direction between the two marks when he sensed a presence behind him.
"I'd ask what you're doing, but I'm not sure I want to know."
Warren turned around to see a boy not much older than him standing on a rock ten metres away. He was dressed entirely inappropriately for the surroundings. His jeans flapped over white trainers and he wore a bright red shirt with a logo emblazoned across the front. He was skinny, which made him look taller than he was, with a floppy blonde fringe that drooped over his eyes. But Warren was more concerned with the small blade he was holding in his right hand.
"Hello. What is your name?" asked Warren, softly. He didn't want to provoke the stranger.
"Listen here, you just appeared out of nowhere, wearing nothing but a pair of dirty kecks, so I'll ask the questions, all right?" replied the boy. "What are you doing out here with no clobber on?"
His accent was unusual. Northern, certainly, thought Warren. He tended to affricate the stressed 't' with an 's' suggesting the 'slit t' accentuation of Irish English or Scouse. He'd heard it once before, from one of the ladies in housekeeping.
"Are you from Liverpool?" asked Warren.

"Are you from another frigging planet?" came the response. "What the hell do you think this is?" he said, grabbing the emblem on his shirt.
"A cormorant?" guessed Warren.
"Liverpool!" said the boy. "Anfield? The Kop? You'll Never Walk Alone? The Miracle of Istanbul?"
"I did read something about the miracle of Istanbul!" said Warren, recalling familiarity with the expression. "Isn't it connected to the painted icons of the Hagia Sophia Basilica?"
The boy hopped down off the rock and strutted towards Warren. He was trying to look menacing but didn't pull it off with his slight stature.
"You're either a United fan taking the piss, or a total dickhead who's never heard of Liverpool Football Club. Either way, you'd best start making some sense, lad."
Warren took a deep breath and decided to tell the truth.
"My name is Warren. I took my clothes off, or my clobber if you prefer, after falling into an underground lake. I wanted to prevent hyperthermia whilst I crawled through a tunnel in darkness. I need to reach a location beyond a lake to the north before nightfall. It's eleven miles away and I must keep moving, so I don't want any confrontation if I can possibly avoid it."
"Confrontation? Big words, lad," replied the stranger. "Why would I want a confrontation with you?"
"Well, you are holding a knife," reasoned Warren.

"Course I'm holding a frigging knife!" said the boy. "I've not seen anyone all day and then you come bouncing out of a tree with just your skidders on and grab a frigging stick!"
"I was using it to calculate which way is north," said Warren.
"You what?"
"If you mark two points of a stick's shadow a few minutes apart they…"
Warren stopped as he could see the boy looked confused.
"Look, my sincere apologies, but I don't have time to explain. I must keep moving."
"That must hurt, lad?" said the boy, looking down at Warren.
"My knees?" replied Warren, noticing that they were a swollen mix of reds and purples. "Yes, they're very sore."
"I wasn't talking about your knees. I meant walking around with a plum up your arse."
"You mean plum in your mouth?" corrected Warren. "The simulative phrase for the upper classes? Yes, I suppose you're right. Now, can I please go?"
"Go where?" asked the boy.
"North!" said Warren, increasingly frustrated.
"Which way's that then?" asked the boy.
"That way!" pointed Warren.
"Great!" said the boy. "I'm going with you!"
He slid the knife in his pocket, strutted over to Warren and held out a hand.
"Gary."
"Warren," he replied, shaking the hand, reluctantly.

"I know. You said that already," said Gary. "You're not one of those leukaemia kids, are you? I mean, don't want to come across being all insensitive, like."
"Leukaemia?" asked Warren. "What makes you say that?"
"You're practically bald!"
"No," replied Warren. "My hair is cut every few days."
"Cut?" sneered Gary. "Butchered, more like! I mean, no offence, but that's a shocking Barnet mate."
"I've never really thought about it," replied Warren. "I need short hair so it doesn't get tangled up with seaweed or hot air balloons."

Chapter 20

The two teenagers had walked for two hours, during which time Gary had hardly stopped talking.
Warren would have been happier on his own, as Gary's red shirt stood out like a flashing beacon. But asking him to remove or cover it would only lead to more questions.
On a positive note, Warren was pleased that his unwanted companion was at least fast and nimble over the wild, rugged landscape.
Gary had told Warren a great deal about his life. At the age of fifteen, he'd been spotted by scouts for Liverpool Football Club whilst having a kick-about down the park. He was invited along for a trial and Gary had "absolutely smashed it." The Liverpool manager was watching and offered him a fifty grand a week contract on the spot. Gary's debut coincided with his sixteenth birthday. They were 1-0 down against United with ten minutes to go. Gary then "walloped one clean on the volley," which hit the underside of the crossbar and bounced in. The Kop had gone berserk. Then, in the last minute of the match, someone tried to break his legs, so the referee gave a penalty and the United captain walked for an early bath. Liverpool came away with a 2-1 win.
The following day, there was a picture of Gary on the back page of the *Echo* with the headline, *'The Kop's New Hero.'* Gary framed it and hung it in the snooker room of his new mansion.

Warren was fascinated by Gary's exciting life, but it was not without problems. Gary ripped up his contract with Liverpool as his step-mum had signed it. He went back to the gaffer and demanded one hundred grand a week. Liverpool agreed as Real Madrid were already sniffing about.

"So, what about you. What do you do?" asked Gary, finally.

"Well, I read a lot," replied Warren, starting to come to terms with his companion's accent.

"Did you read the Zlatan Ibrahimovic autobiography?" asked Gary.

"I don't think so," replied Warren. He had read many autobiographies by scientists, explorers, conservationists, astronauts and political figures over the years. But Zlatan Ibrahimovic wasn't a name familiar to him.

"You should," said Gary. "I know he played for United, but his book is spot on. Tells it like it is."

Warren decided to change the subject. "I like music too."

"Oh yeah, who do you like?"

"It depends on my mood. Sometimes Bach, sometimes Grieg. Occasionally, I need the darkness of Shostakovich."

"Can't say I've heard of them," said Gary. "Though to be honest, I've never heard of half the people in the charts."

Warren continued to make his way along the east bank of the lake. There wasn't a footpath, but the grazed land made for easy hiking. He'd been careful to steer clear of long grass to make it harder for any pursuing FPF guards to track him. However, Gary had snapped a few twigs in the woods out of boredom and Warren was certain that a good tracker would spot this. He'd once read about tactics used by the Shadow Wolves, a team of expert trackers working for the American Government to prevent drug smuggling. So, Warren tried to avoid leaving obvious signs.

Only on one occasion had Warren heard the gentle humming sound of an FPF drone. He'd immediately clambered behind rocks.

"What are you doing?" asked Gary.

"Hiding. There's a surveillance drone coming. I can hear it. Quick, up here!"

Gary leapt over the rocks and clambered down a hole, squeezing in next to Warren.

"A drone?" said Gary. "What for?"

"I have no idea," lied Warren. He listened as the humming noise grew louder, before disappearing into the distance. Warren's actions had presented him with a problem; how would he explain this to his companion?

"I knew it!" said Gary.

"Knew what?"

"They're after me," said Gary, nodding as though it was obvious.

"They are?" asked Warren, as they climbed out from the rocks.

"Course they are! Makes sense, don't it? A footballer idolised by millions goes missing, there's going to be a massive manhunt. They've probably got the Army out looking for me too. And the navy."

"Because you're a football player?"

"That's one thing, yeah," shrugged Gary. "But I'm famous for music too. More people know me as a guitarist."
"Really? You play guitar?" asked Warren, excited.
"Aye, the electric guitar," replied Gary, looking up to the skies as if he was recalling a treasured memory. "I'll tell you mate, when you're up on stage in front of thousands of screaming fans, no other feeling like it in the world."
"You're in a band?"
"Biggest band in the world. Well, one of them," said Gary. "Sold out Wembley. Funny thing is, the next day, I played there in the FA Cup and bagged the winner."
"You must be an extraordinarily talented individual," enthused Warren.
"Yeah," said Gary. "But I had to give up the band. Lasses started turning up at the training ground every day, screaming for me. We love you Gary! Will you go out with us Gary? Will you sign my tits Gary?"
"Tits? As in birds?" asked Warren, hoping that Gary might also have an interest in ornithology.
"Sure, loads of birds," replied Gary. "Any bird you want. Anyway, gaffer said I had to choose between footy and the band."
"And you chose football?"
"The band gave me memories I'll never forget. Biggest debut album ever; headlining Glastonbury and all that. But it was non-stop. Sometimes, I'd be playing those five strings so hard, my fingers would bleed. I was that good."
"Five strings?" asked Warren. "Don't you mean six?"
"Five strings, mate. I play the electric guitar, remember?"

"Guitars tend to have six strings," said Warren, confused. "I've studied music intensely. Banjos have five strings and you have some five string bass guitars, although they typically have four. It's unusual to hear of a rock guitar with five strings."
"That's why I was so different," said Gary. "I had to have guitars specially made by some Japanese warrior. Only makes guitars for the best in the world, like *Kill Bill*, but with guitars instead of swords. They cost a million dollars a pop and he never lowers his price. But he made mine for free as he wanted me playing his brand. For the publicity, you know?"
"So, this Japanese guitar maker, does he omit the Low E?" asked Warren.
"Eh?"
"On a six-string guitar, the top string is the Low E," said Warren.
"Mate, honestly, don't talk to me about chords! I never needed to know them. I learnt to play through sound, like Hendrix."
"Oh," said Warren.
"Anyway, I gave it all up," said Gary. "That were last year. You gave me a guitar now, I couldn't play a note. Whereas I could kick a ball from here to that boathouse."
"Boathouse?"
"Yeah. Over there, at the edge of the lake."

Chapter 21

Warren found the shed in woodland just north of the boathouse, as Dickie had claimed.
There was no bolt or lock and the dilapidated door had come off its lower hinges, so one of the corners was resting against the ground.
Warren entered the shed and noticed that, whilst spacious, there was practically nothing inside. Just some empty bottles and an old table. No food and certainly no map.
Warren got on his hands and knees and studied the floor. He'd forgotten how sore his knees were until he began crawling on the floorboards.
"You're not all there, are you?" said Gary, watching his companion inspect the rotting wood.
"I'm looking for a trapdoor or loose flooring," said Warren. "Maybe you could help, rather than just standing there?"
"I would, but I'm coming back from a nasty knee injury. Got taken out in the Champions League against Bayern, didn't I?"
"Then have a look at the table," said Warren. "Are there any markings on the wood? Anything that looks like a code?"
Gary took a quick glance. "Aye! Someone's drawn a cock."
"Perfect! That could mean all sorts of things. The cockerel is used in astro-mythology as the animal symbol of the Orion constellation. Dickie knows I love space, so perhaps…"

"No lad," interrupted Gary. "I mean cock as in penis. They've drawn a cock and balls. They've even added some squiggly lines to make them look hairy."
"Oh," said Warren, disappointed.
"I'll check if these bottles are empty," said Gary.
He was just about to pick one up, when Warren called out.
"Wait! Don't touch them!"
The bottles were in two rows. On the first row, two were stood upright and one was on its side. Below them, two bottles were on their side, flanked on both sides by a standing bottle.
"It's Morse code," said Warren.
"You what? From the Viking days?"
"No, you're thinking of Norse," replied Warren. "This is from Dickie. It means 'Up.'
Warren looked up and noticed that the centre of the shed had been boarded. It had been too subtle to spot at first glance. He stood on the table, reached up and pushed against the five wooden panels bridging the centre of the shed roof. None of them budged, so he went outside and around to the rear of the shed.
"Could you raise me up?" he asked.
Gary looked baffled.
"I mean give me a lift, so I can reach that triangular panel up there?"
"Are you kidding?" replied Gary. "No way! I don't want to feel your balls on the back of my head!"
"Do you want a drink or not?" asked Warren, impatiently.

Gary sighed, then crouched down, put his head between Warren's legs and stood up, with Warren using the rear of the shed to keep his balance.
Warren reached up and found that the triangular panel moved sideways. He moved it across and even though the sun was almost set and darkness was creeping in, he could make out a small backpack at the other end of the shed. He slid in and wriggled down. It was a tight fit. Warren felt a zip and opened the top compartment. He felt a torch inside and turned it on. He then opened the main compartment and found food and water.
"Anything?" shouted up Gary.
"Supplies."
"Wouldn't happen to be any Coca-Cola?"
With that, Gary heard something roll along the boards, and a bottle of water dropped to the floor. "Save some if you can," said Warren.
"No worries," replied Gary. "Need a lift down?"
"I will do. Just give me five minutes," said Warren, as he pulled a plastic folder from the bag. It contained a note from Dickie, a hand-drawn map, money, a set of keys and an envelope. Warren opened the envelope and found the four missing pages from the Farrington family book.
"I'm taking me trainers off," said Gary. "My feet are killing me!" He sat down on a rock and drank his water.
There was something strange about this lad, he thought. Why would someone be leaving Morse code messages for him? Gary was tempted to leg it and leave Warren in the

shed. But something stopped him. Maybe he should stick with him, just for a while.
After all, what did he have to lose?

Chapter 22

Stefano Gallo, F8b, was well camouflaged amid the bulrushes, one hundred metres from the shed.
He hadn't stopped moving since the Director had ordered him back to KR5 to press a button hidden within a poster for *The Great Escape*.
His colleague, Frank Stone, had watched him instantaneously fall through a mechanised trapdoor. It had opened in a circular motion and two seconds later had completely closed with barely a sound. Even on close inspection, Frank and the Director, standing alongside him, could barely see its outer edges.
Stefano had fallen into a small lake. He feared it would be shallow, so was relieved when he barely touched the bottom. He had no problem swimming to the rocks, despite wearing military-issue boots and a rucksack.
Having left the water, Stefano surveyed the surroundings, before opening his waterproof pack and retrieving a two-way military radio transceiver.
"This is F8b reporting, over."
"10-4, F8b," said the Director, who was still in the library. "Do you receive me, over?"
"10-2, over," replied Stefano, informing the Director that the reception was good.
"Can you report your position? Over," said the Director.
"Affirmative," replied Stefano. "I fell for approximately one hundred and forty feet into a small lake with a depth of

twenty feet. I'm now on dry rocks. I have located clothing belonging to the Subject. They are wet and piled on rocks. I have no visual on the Subject, but I can see the entrance of a narrow, man-made tunnel. Over."

"Is there any sign of the Subject in the tunnel? Over," asked the Director.

"Negative," replied Stefano, shining a torch into the darkness. He opened one of the many pockets of his combat trousers and removed a navigational compass. "The tunnel heads north. Should I continue in pursuit? Over."

"Affirmative," said the Director. "Your orders are to follow the Subject without apprehending him. Stay hidden from his view. I want to see how he copes. Do you copy? Over."

"Roger that, sir. Over and out," said Stefano, as he clambered into the tunnel and started crawling.

Once he'd climbed out of the hollow tree almost two exhausting hours later, Stefano radioed his position and was met by Frank Stone, with a clean uniform. Stefano rejected it and insisted they immediately continue the pursuit on foot. He felt humiliated at losing sight of the Subject in the first place.

Every man in the Farrington Protective Force was summoned to aid in the search.

Most were directed to the eastern and southern ends of the vast estate, as it was the logical direction for the Subject to head in. Just beyond the eastern border was a village with a bus stop, with links to a rail station. So, it was probable he would head there.

Whilst waiting for his colleague to arrive, Stefano spotted a stick on a rock, alongside two small white marks. He suspected that the Subject had been using the stick to find his bearings. Stefano learned a similar trick when he was a scout.
Something told him that the Subject would head north, into the wilderness. It wasn't logical, but the Subject was clever. Surely, he'd know that the search effort would be focused closer to the towns with public transportation links?
So, based on his instinct, Stefano and Frank trekked north. Frank's experience in reconnaissance had proven beneficial. After a while, he'd been able to track not one but two sets of footprints. One belonged to a pair of trainers, almost certainly size nine, which presented a mystery. The tread pattern suggested they were not multi-terrain shoes, while it was evident from the stride pattern that they were not being used for running. They were a casual trainer unsuitable for the conditions.
Crucially, there had been a hint of another set of prints. It was not the print of a boot or shoe, but in Frank's expert opinion a foot wrapped in bark.
Finally, they had a breakthrough. Stefano was peering through military-standard night vision scopes at a pair of trainers, placed on a rock outside a shed in woodland near the lake.
Stefano put the scopes down, as visibility was still better with the naked eye. The sun had set, but his vision had adjusted to the fading light.

He radioed KR1, where the Director was coordinating the search operation. Stefano provided his location and a description of a boy, perhaps sixteen or seventeen years of age. The Director was hopeful. This boy may have seen the Subject and the FPF might soon be on his tail.
Frank Stone moved slowly through the trees. Gary, who was drinking from a bottle, didn't think anything of the hump in the undergrowth five yards away.
"Don't move!"
Gary jumped up in shock, spilling water over his Liverpool shirt. He turned around to see a man dressed in black, camouflaged with grass and twigs. He was pointing a gun at him.
"Don't shoot me!" said Gary, panicking. "Please don't shoot. I'll go back. I don't want to die!"
"We are not going to shoot you. You are not in any danger," said the figure, calmly but with authority, as he stepped slowly through the undergrowth towards Gary. "Just don't move and answer my questions with a simple 'yes' or 'no', do you understand?"
"Aye," whimpered Gary. One of his legs was shaking.
"Are you alone?"
"Aye," replied Gary.
"If you could stick to 'yes' or 'no' this will be much easier," said F8a. "There's nobody else inside the shed?"
Gary shook his head, absolutely petrified.
"Is the shed safe to enter?"
Gary nodded.

"Are you absolutely certain there's nobody else here?" asked F8a.
"Aye!"
"My name is Frank. I'm with the Farrington Protective Force. Do you know who we are?"
"Course I do!" replied Gary. Everyone knew about Farrington Towers. The weird deaths, the reclusive heir who'd never been seen and his elite guards dressed in black. It was always talked about on TV.
"What's your name?"
"Gary," he replied, still shaking. "Gary Morton."
"I'm going to lower my gun, Gary. I need you to stay where you are as I want to ask you a few questions. There's no point running, as we will catch you. Do you understand?"
"Aye," nodded Gary.
Stefano appeared to Gary's right, as if sprouting straight from the Earth, and approached the shed. He lifted the edge of the door resting on the ground and pulled it open. He scanned the room but it was empty, aside from a table and a few empty bottles.
"Clear!" he shouted, before carrying out a perimeter sweep.
"Keep your hands in the air for me," said Frank, as he approached Gary.
Frank went through the left pocket of Gary's jeans, pulling out a Liverpool FC wallet which carried £1.73 in change, a Liverpool FC Supporter's Club ID card for Gary Morton, a membership card for The Wirral branch of the Young Farmers' Association, two football trading cards both

depicting Liverpool players, and a business card for Yvonne West, a Care Support Manager at Birkenhead YMCA.
Frank then went through Gary's right pocket and pulled out a small knife. It had a wooden handle with a slit running through the middle so that the three-inch blade could slide inside. The handle was inscribed with the message 'You'll Never Walk Alone.'
"What's this for?" asked Frank, pulling out the blade, which was blunt.
"It's for fishing," said Gary, angry that they'd taken it. "It's from my dad, so give it back!"
"What are you doing out here in the middle of nowhere?" asked F8a, putting the knife in his own pocket.
"Just training," said Gary.
"You're a long way from home," said Frank, tossing the wallet to Stefano, who was setting up a laptop computer. "Have you seen anybody today?"
"Yeah, you two!" replied Gary, regaining his natural cockiness.
"We're looking for a young man who is missing and we're very concerned for his welfare," said Frank, keeping calm. "He's about your age, 1.72 metres tall, 67 kilograms, light brown skin with short hair."
Gary nodded. "Only seen one lad all day, but it sounds like the same kid. Didn't have short hair though. He had weird clumps of hair, like he'd cut it himself. Looked proper crap it did. And he had next to nothing on. Just his kecks!"
Frank looked up. "When was this?"
"Don't know. Four hours ago?" guessed Gary.

"Where?"
"Miles back. He was sat on a rock, holding a stick up to the sun like a frigging nut job."
"Did you speak to him?" asked Frank.
"You joking? I'm out in the countryside and I see a lad wearing just his kecks. Course I didn't talk to him! I damn near soiled myself. I hid until he'd gone."
"Which way did he go?" asked Frank.
"He went one way, I went the other. Like anyone would!"
Frank eyed him with suspicion. "We've been tracking your prints for miles and I can tell from the stride pattern that you've not run, even for five seconds. So, what are you doing out here, Gary?"
"I told you, I'm training. I've got a Champions League qualifier coming up. I play for Liverpool mate, so you'd best let me go or you'll be hearing from my judge."
"You play for Liverpool?" asked Frank, grinning. "So, you thought you'd test your fitness skills in the wilderness, did you? Without any medical supplies, food or even a phone?"
"It's called extreme physical training, mate!" sneered Gary.
"Hold on, did you come through the youth system at Anfield?" asked Frank.
"Aye," replied Gary. "Chief scout spotted me when I was just a lad, scoring a hat-trick for the local men's team. Signed me on the spot."
"The chief scout? Is it still Ted Chadwick, that bloody old timer?" asked Frank, looking genuinely interested.
"Yeah, he's still going!" smiled Gary. "Good old Ted!"

"That's funny," said Frank. "Ted Chadwick is the name of my milkman. So why don't you stop talking bullshit, sunshine, and start making some sense?"
"Maybe I can help you out?" interrupted Stefano, who had been tapping away on the laptop. "This is Gary Morton, aged 16, currently unemployed without any fixed abode. Reported missing by his youth counsellor at the YMCA two days ago. Records suggest he previously lived with his stepmother, Irene, in a village a few miles west of Birkenhead. His father, Neville, a farmer by occupation, is serving four years at Her Majesty's pleasure for assaulting a labourer called Dean Mack."
"My dad did nought wrong!" shouted Gary, angrily. "You'd have hit the bastard too if it were you!"
"Not quite a Liverpool player then?" Frank mocked.
"Seemingly not," replied Stefano. "His membership to Liverpool FC Supporter's Club expired two years ago, along with his father's. However, it looks like our boy did score a consolation goal for his school's B team in a 6-1 defeat five months ago, earning a brief mention in the school's newsletter. That was before he was permanently excluded."
"Oh yeah?" smirked Frank.
"According to local newspaper reports, Gary orchestrated a bomb hoax to escape a science exam. He went to the effort of making it look like a real bomb, using two bottles of Tizer and some electrical wiring. Funnily enough, the science exam wasn't scheduled until the following day."
"Tizer?" queried Frank. "I didn't know it was still around."

"Stupid bloody reporter got it wrong," sneered Gary. "It was cherryade."
Frank sniggered, before he turned to face the boy.
"Champions League footballer eh?"
"Shut your face!" Gary bit back.
"This is interesting though," said Stefano. "Gary is Vice President of The Wirral Young Farmers' Association. He came third in a ploughing match at the Southport Town and Country Fair."
"Bit of a farm boy at heart, are we?" teased Frank.
Gary said nothing.
"Let's call this in," said Frank. "Get a mobile unit out here to take Mr Morton to the Towers for further questioning. He knows more than he's letting on. Then we can concentrate on picking up the second set of footprints."
"You won't be calling anything in," came a voice from behind them.

Chapter 23

Frank Stone turned to see the Subject leaning over a rock, with Stefano's gun pointing directly at him. F8b had left it unattended while setting up his laptop.
Warren pointed the gun at the guard who looked like a tapir.
"You're not going to shoot," said Stefano, inching slowly towards the Subject. "There must be fifty guards scouring the countryside. You pull the trigger and they'll be another unit here within minutes. It's over. Give me the gun. Let's go back to the Towers."
Warren fired a shot straight over Stefano's shoulder, narrowly missing him.
"Now they all know where we are," grinned Warren, nonplussed. "You!" he said, addressing F8a, the one who looked like a giraffe. "You were a Brigadier, were you not?"
"That's correct," replied Frank, surprised by the boy's knowledge.
"To have reached a senior rank within the British Armed Forces, you'll have experience in quickly assessing an enemy in a combat situation. Do you question my will to use this weapon if necessary?"
"No," replied Frank. "I do not."
Stefano remained still, with the sound of the gunshot still ringing in his ears.

"Good," said Warren. "There's a rowing boat by the boathouse. Turn around and walk to it. Otherwise, my next shot will be on target."
Warren and Gary walked behind the two guards. Gary was smirking as he held his gun, retrieved from Frank Stone.
As they walked, they heard F8b's radio transceiver. A request from KR1 for an update went unanswered.
Warren was conscious that a second request would be transmitted soon. If that also went without reply, the Director would surely send more guards to the last known location of unit F8.
"Take off your clothes and boots," ordered Warren, as they reached the edge of the lake. "Gary, keep the gun trained on them."
Warren went through their backpacks and took out the radio transceiver and a survival kit.
"Do you have flares?" asked Warren.
"We're not allowed pyrotechnics," replied Frank.
"Nylon?" asked Warren.
"Only paracord," replied Frank.
"It's been a long time since you were in the parachute regiment," said Warren.
"It makes quite a handy snare wire," replied Frank.
Warren took out the cord and ordered F8a to tie one end to the front of the rowing boat. Next, he ordered Frank to remove a silver ring on his finger.
Warren knew it was important.

The two FPF guards were then told to climb aboard the boat, before Warren tossed Frank Stone one of the two transceivers.
"Channel Six," he said.
With the teenagers still pointing their rifles at them, the guards pushed the boat away from the bank and rowed towards a floating wooden platform in the middle of the lake, built as a roosting spot for grebes by Douglas Farrington some twenty years earlier.
It took a few minutes for F8 to reach the platform. When they did, Warren spoke into his transceiver.
"Climb on to the nesting site."
When the guards appeared reluctant to do so, he took Frank's ring out of his pocket.
"You've got five seconds or I throw the ring in the lake."
Frank looked across at the Subject and sighed. The boat rocked wildly as he followed Stefano on to the platform.
Gary used the cord to pull the boat away from the stranded guards.
"I'd think twice about jumping in," said Warren on the transceiver. "This lake was created by glacial movement in the last ice age. Its current temperature is about 2.5 degrees, which means you could swim for about a minute before your muscles seize and you succumb to exhaustion and hyperthermia. Personally, I'd wait for a rescue team."
"Is that true?" whispered Gary, stood by his side.
"I've embellished a little."
The two boys watched as the boat bobbed back towards the bank, far out of reach of the two humiliated FPF guards.

"Now, toss your radio into the water."
As it splashed on the surface and disappeared, Warren placed Frank's ring on a rock by the side of the lake. He let the guard see him do it.
"What do we do now?" asked Gary.
"We're going to put on the clothes that our kind, seafaring friends have left us."
"Then what?" asked Gary.
"A dear friend has provided me with a plan," replied Warren, taking off his makeshift shoes and slipping on combat trousers, jacket and boots. The boots were too big, but he tightened the laces and they were comfortable enough.
"Back at the hut, the guard mentioned that you're a member of a young farmers' association. Is that true?"
"Aye," said Gary. "That bit was true. The rest of what I said was mostly bollocks though."
"Bollocks?" asked Warren.
"Aye," said Gary. "Total Bullshit."
"Bullshit?"
"Bloody hell mate, you really do have a plum up your arse!" said Gary. "It was all lies. All the footy nonsense and stuff about the band. All crap."
Warren frowned, but he felt sympathy for his companion and was starting to like having him around.
"Back at the shed, when the guards asked if you were alone, why did you lie?"
"Don't know," said Gary. "I'm just so used to it, it seemed normal. I won the World Championships for lying, you

know? The trophy was huge. Ten-foot high, made of solid gold. Shaped like a giant bull taking a crap."
For the first time in his life, Warren laughed with someone his own age.
"Why do you ask about the farming thing?" said Gary.
"I was hoping you might have experience of driving a tractor with front loading machinery?"
"Course I have," replied Gary. "We always had tractors on the farm. Why?"
"Because I have the keys to a tractor and I don't know how to drive it."
"What do you need a tractor for?" asked Gary.
"Well, my plan is to escape the Farrington estate so that I can rescue my twin sister, who I never knew existed until three days ago, from a deranged lunatic trying to seek revenge on my family for reasons I don't yet understand."
Gary raised his eyebrows. "What do I get out of it?"
Warren took off his backpack. It was the bag Dickie had left for him in the shed. Inside was a food container with energy bars, a bag of dried fruit, a sealed packet of crackers, a lump of cheddar cheese and a small tin of tuna. There were six bottles of water, although Gary had gulped one down already.
In a separate compartment, he had found items of greater interest, including an envelope containing five wads of £20 notes wrapped in a red paper band, marking each one as £1,000.
Warren removed some food and a wad of cash.

"You can either take five crackers with half my cheese, or take one wedge of this currency, which can be traded nationally for goods and services?" he said.
Gary looked gob-smacked. "Are you for real?"
Warren shrugged "Okay, six crackers."
"It's a tough one," said Gary, sensing an opportunity. "I'll tell you what. Make it two wedges of your currency and you've got yourself a deal!"
"Done!"

Chapter 24

The Director paced around KR1.
Unusually, the monitors were not displaying footage from the cameras inside Farrington Towers. Instead, they were providing a live feed from drones around the estate.
It had been a busy yet unproductive night for the FPF. Twenty units, encompassing forty guards, ended the active search for the Subject at midnight. They were instead placed near exit points along the heavily wooded northern border, with strict instructions to covertly pursue and monitor the Subject's movements.
No-one understood the reasons behind the Director's order, but knew better than to question it.
However, the FPF had failed to uncover any significant leads as to the Subject's whereabouts following his encounter with F8. The drones also returned to Farrington Towers without making visual contact.
Mitchell Johnson had been coordinating the FPF throughout the night and was still working at 6am when the active search restarted.
Two hours later, the Director arrived.
"Mitchell," he said, forsaking pleasantries. "What's the latest?"
"Challenging," replied the Head of Security. "The Subject is smart and he's throwing us curve balls."

"What do you mean curve balls?" asked Anna Kraus, who was also present in the Control Room. She secretly hoped Warren would succeed in his escape bid.
"He's inventive," conceded Mitchell. "He's thinking of creative ways to aid his escape. Last night, the Subject eluded two of our most experienced guards, taking their clothing and leading them at gunpoint to a rowing boat, where he left them stranded in the middle of a freezing lake. During a debrief, the guards in unit F8 revealed that the Subject has an accomplice, 16-year-old Gary Morton from Birkenhead."
"F8?" queried the Director. "The unit who were monitoring the Subject when he escaped?"
"That's affirmative," replied Mitchell, acknowledging the Director's misgivings about the ability of two men who he regarded as the best in the FPF.
"Have we tried contacting Warren through the radio he took?" asked the Director.
"Affirmative," replied Mitchell. "When an expected update from F8 never came, we diverted guards located nearby to their last known location. It took over an hour minutes to locate the two missing guards. In the meantime, we received a radio transmission from the Subject. It turned out to be an inventive ploy to deceive us."
Mitchell opened his laptop and clicked on a sound application. A crackling noise came from a recording. He increased the volume.
"This is a recording of the transmission from the Subject," said Mitchell, pressing the 'play' button.

"Hello. This is Warren calling Farrington Towers. Do you copy? Over."
"This is Mitchell Johnson, Head of Security. We copy. Where are you? Over."
"At the north end of a lake, near a boathouse. I don't have long, there's someone here with me. He has taken a gun from an FPF guard and fired a shot. Nobody is injured but he's now leading me away in an easterly direction."

In the background of the recording, another voice is heard. It's the sound of a young man with a distinctive scouse accent.

"Hey, what are you doing with the radio? Give it here!"

A struggle breaks out and there are muffled noises before the transmission ended. Mitchell Johnson closed his laptop.

"Smart!" said Mitchell. "If that came from a green beret, I'd be impressed."
"What do you mean?" asked the Director.
"At the time, we had every reason to think the Subject's concern was genuine. But following the debrief with F8, it became apparent that the recording contains a false message and that the confrontation between the Subject and Gary Morton was staged," said Mitchell.
"So, let me guess," interjected the Director, with his head in his hand. "After hearing this communication from the

Subject, we sent every available man east in immediate pursuit?"
"It was the appropriate course of action, given the information we had at our disposal," said Mitchell, embarrassed. "It was only when we were able to retrieve F8 from the lake that we discovered that the two accounts did not corroborate."
"Okay. What progress has been made this morning?" asked the Director, hoping for some positive news.
"Very little," replied Mitchell, wearily. "At least in terms of discovering the Subject's location. Given that they are now wearing camouflaged FPF clothing, the two targets are most likely moving through the forest near the northern boundary. They're probably looking for an escape route but the border is surrounded by thick hedging. Their chances of slipping through without us spotting them are extremely slim."
"What of this Morton fellow?" asked the Director.
"We have a team assigned to finding out everything about him," replied Mitchell. "We have spoken to the boy's stepmother, Irene Morton. She reported that her stepson has been staying at a YMCA in Birkenhead for three months. We contacted the centre and found out that Morton did not return to his room three nights ago. With no money, food or clothing, they feared the worst. His youth counsellor considers Morton to be vulnerable because of his strained relationship with his father, Neville Morton, who is in jail for the assault of Dean Mack, a labourer on the family farm. Gary falsely claimed that Mack

was in a relationship with his stepmother, which led to his father assaulting the labourer. At his father's trial, it was revealed that Gary Morton suffers from Compulsive Lying Disorder. This consequently caused a rift with his father, who was jailed for actions directly caused by his son's fabricated stories."

"Strange boy. Should we consider him a threat to the Subject?" asked the Director.

"It appears that Morton is ill-equipped for survival," replied Mitchell. "It's difficult to know how the two have become companions. We also don't know what he's doing this far from home. We're searching for any local link but their meeting was most likely a chance encounter. Irene Morton insists that, while Gary is often in trouble due to his incessant lying, he has never been violent."

"What else did we learn from our two former special forces soldiers who were outmanoeuvred by a teenage boy in his pants?" asked the Director sarcastically, shaking his head at the ridiculousness of the situation.

"Supplies!" replied the American. "We believe that the Subject has supplies. Morton was seen to consume a bottle of water in its entirety. As he had no bag on his person, we believe it unlikely he would spend two days wandering the wilderness before having a drink. Therefore, it's probable that the water was supplied by the Subject. A bag may have been left for him in the shed where they encountered F8."

"Who would have left a bag for him?" asked Anna.

"The same man who orchestrated his escape yesterday, of course," replied the Director.

"Dickie?" asked Anna.
"That's right," said Mitchell, picking up the baton. "But we don't know what instructions he may have given the Subject to aid his escape, or his efforts to reach his sister. We don't know if Dickie had any knowledge of the girl's whereabouts. Could he have accessed the material sent to you by Fergus MacLean?"
"There is a public footpath running across the northern section of the estate," said the Director, ignoring Mitchell's question. "I know as I fought the council tooth and nail to get it removed, unsuccessfully, I might add. Have we asked walkers if they have seen anything?"
"Of course," replied Mitchell. "The FPF spoke to a middle-aged couple out hiking at 7:18am and a man out walking two dogs, both Labrador retrievers, at 7:53am. But nothing of interest has come up. There is a derelict farm 2.3 miles from the boys' last known location, which we've searched thoroughly. The only drone sighting of anyone other than the walkers was of a man at the wheel of a John Deere tractor at 7:06am."
"A tractor?" asked The Director. "Where was that?"
"It can't be the Subject, sir," replied Mitchell, pre-empting the next question. "This was approximately four miles south of the Towers and six miles west. That's over fifteen miles from where the Subject was seen last. There's little agricultural activity now as we've closed most of the farms on the estate. But some of the land in the south west zone is still used for sheep grazing and arable farming, until the last of the old tenancy agreements end."

"You didn't think it wise to investigate this sighting further?" asked the Director.
"No sir. The tractor was briefly monitored by our drones but, given the evidence, it seemed logical to focus our efforts in the north. Why would the Subject trek eleven miles through the forest with bark and leaves strapped around his feet, only to then head in the opposite direction?"
"Johnson, what are the chances of the Subject escaping unseen to the north?" asked the Director.
"Impossible," he replied. "We've covered every conceivable exit."
"That's my point," said the Director. "You've got nobody in the south. What if he picked up a tractor at that derelict farm in the middle of the night and headed in the opposite direction?"
Mitchell Johnson didn't appreciate being spoken to like he was an idiot, but he kept calm.
"Sir, that derelict farm is barely a mile from the northern border. In the dead of night, trained reconnaissance soldiers are not going to miss the sound of a John Deere tractor firing up!"
"That's true," conceded the Director. But something about it still niggled.
He turned to the Chief Observer, who'd worked through the night. "Bring up the drone footage of that tractor."
The recording appeared on screen within a few seconds. It showed a brand new green tractor slowly transporting a single bale of hay on top of a front loader, raised in the air.

Julius, the Chief Observer, zoomed in for a closer look at the driver.
"The picture doesn't give us the best angle, but that's definitely not the Subject," noted Mitchell, a touch relieved. "It doesn't match the picture we have of Gary Morton, either. We know that Morton is wearing combat clothing. This man is wearing a straw hat and a tweed jacket that's torn on the left shoulder."
The Director agreed. The driver looked more like Worzel Gummidge than a special forces soldier. However, he noticed something else.
"The sound! Why can I hear the drone buzzing, but not the tractor?"
"That is strange," stated the Chief Observer, unhelpfully.
"Find out who farms that land and call them," said the Director. "Just check that it is their tractor."
"Sir, this footage was taken one hour ago," whispered Mitchell. "The tractor was travelling at eight miles an hour. If it continued at that speed, it will be beyond the southern boundary at any moment. We can't get a drone or an FPF unit there quickly enough to continue the pursuit."
"Then let's hope the Subject isn't on it!" replied the Director.
"Sir," said the CO, with a phone cusped to his ear. "The farmer doesn't drive a John Deere. He says that if anyone local had forked out for a new tractor, he'd know about it."
"Get on to every John Deere dealership, authorised or not, within a hundred miles," shouted the Director with a sudden urgency. "Now!"

"We're on it!" said Julius, directing his team of three observers in KR1, just as a transmission came in from the FPF.
"Sir, we've got a message from F6a in the northern sector," said Mitchell. "They've found a scarecrow that may be of interest."
"Why would I be interested in a bloody scarecrow?" replied the Director, losing patience.
"Well, it's wearing Stefano Gallo's uniform," replied Mitchell.

Trevor King was one of the three observers who had been making telephone calls.
He found the morning's developments enthralling and, like Anna, secretly hoped that the Subject might make it. So, he couldn't help but grin as he turned and addressed the Director.
"Sir, I've got an independent dealership on the line. They sold a John Deere a few days ago. It stuck in their mind for two reasons. Firstly, the buyer paid up front in cash and was…"
"Yes!" screamed the Director. "Was what?"
"He was wearing a bow-tie."
The Director looked bewildered as it dawned on him that, for the first time in his life, he'd been out-smarted.
"There's another thing," added Trevor. "The tractor, sir. It's electric. First one they've ever sold. That's why the soldiers didn't hear it."

The Director looked up at the big screen and turned to his bewildered Head of Security. "Morton lived on a farm, didn't he? No doubt he learned how to drive a tractor."
"Are you saying that's Morton, dressed as a scarecrow?" replied Mitchell.
The Director nodded.
"But where's the Subject?"
"My guess is, he's under that hay bale on the front loader," replied the Director.
"I'm sorry sir," interrupted the Chief Observer. "We've just checked our radar scanners. The tractor is just about to pass beyond the estate boundary."
The Director gave a wry smile. "Then the boy is on his own. For now."

Chapter 25

Warren peeked through the hay bale to survey his surroundings.
The tractor's front loader didn't offer the most comfortable ride, but he'd managed to work himself enough space to survey the estate map that Dickie had left for him.
Back in the derelict barn near the northern border, where Dickie had left a battery-powered tractor, Warren had dipped two sticks in paint pots. One cedar red, as it was used to paint fences, and the other blue lagoon, left over from when the tenant farmer painted the farmhouse kitchen many years ago.
Using the map to navigate, Warren would hold up the sticks through the hay bale to give directions to Gary, who was driving. Red cedar meant head left. Blue lagoon meant head right.
Gary was having the time of his life. Whenever Warren gave instructions, he would shout 'Aye-aye captain!"
Warren didn't know why his companion adopted the voice of a pirate.
He was surprised that they had eluded the FPF and assumed that the staged argument transmission had worked. But only now, when he was within quarter of a mile of the boundary, did Warren finally believe he was going to make it.

"What do I do now?" shouted Gary as they approached a large, wild hedgerow running across the field as far as the eye could see.
"Put your foot on the accelerator," shouted Warren, poking his head out from the side of the bale. "We're going straight through it!"
"Aye-aye!" replied Gary, whooping jubilantly, whilst Warren gazed ahead at the looming hedge.
"Let's do this!" Warren uttered, aware that he was far more precariously positioned than his companion.
As the tractor crashed into the hedgerow, its front wheels rose violently in the air. It rocked wildly from side to side upon landing, until somehow all four wheels were firmly back on the ground. The hay bale was tossed aside and Warren emerged from his tucked position inside the bucket.
"Warren! You're alive!" shouted Gary.
Warren didn't know what to say. He just smiled. It had been the single most exhilarating moment of his life.

Chapter 26

Warren and Gary made an odd couple.
One a pale-skinned Liverpool-supporting teenager with floppy blonde hair, legally declared a compulsive liar, who was already failing school when he was excluded for fabricating a bomb shortly before running away from a troubled home life with pennies to his name.
The other, a highly-academic, half-aboriginal violin-playing teenager and heir to the accumulated wealth of the world's richest family, who had run away from an enormous mansion with wads of bank notes in a backpack.
But both were starting to find themselves grateful for the company.
If Warren had been bothered by Gary's presence initially, he now appreciated his experience of operating a tractor.

Nine hours had passed since the John Deere barged its way through a hedge on the southern border. The two companions continued south through the sheep farms and peaceful rural lanes of Wales, as Dickie had instructed. They were one hundred miles beyond the south-eastern tip of the Farrington Estate when the tractor's battery died. This came as no surprise to Warren, as the dashboard instruments provided him with an accurate power reading. However, he'd been hoping for a few extra miles as Gary insisted that batteries usually lasted "way longer" than what the display stated.

The two comrades walked across hills, trampled over heathland and trekked through woodland for three hours before taking a break by a river. Warren took out crackers and cheese, a bottle of water and two energy bars, one of which he threw to Gary.
"I can't get this morning out my head!" smiled Gary, chomping on the bar. "When we drove through that hedge, I thought the whole bloody tractor was going over! I don't know how you never fell out that bucket! Fair play to you!"
Warren didn't know how to respond to that.
"So, you're a runaway, just like me?" he asked, casually.
"Don't make out me and you are the same, mate," replied Gary. "I'm nothing like you. Nobody powdering my arse after I take a dump."
The barbed response took Warren by surprise. "You think I've had it easy?"
"You going to pretend you haven't?" replied Gary. "I've seen the TV shows about you. Know all about your global empire. Let me tell you, life's a bit harder in the real world."
"My life's not great, believe me," said Warren.
"Oh aye?" said Gary, sarcastically. "Had it tough, have you?"
"Well, I've never been to school, as I have one-to-one tuition for every subject, and I have to abide by a meticulous diet with a carefully managed sugar intake to maintain peak health."
"Crap, I take it all back then!" said Gary, mockingly.
"I can't enter certain sections of my family library without advance notification," added Warren.

Gary pretended to play the violin. "That's the world's smallest harp, playing just for you!"
Warren was already aware of Gary's limited knowledge of instruments, so didn't question the accuracy of the mocking statement.
"Well, whilst we're on the subject of violins, I have to play with cloth covering the strings and a face guard to protect me, in case a string snaps."
"Oh Christ, my heart!" said Gary, clutching his chest dramatically. "It's bleeding! Really, it is. Look! There's blood spurting out everywhere!" he added, simulating a violent heart explosion.
"I've never been invited to a birthday party," continued Warren, reflectively. "I've never kicked a football. Never caught a fish. Never carved my name on a tree. Never kissed a girl. Never had a friend. My dad is dead and my mother died before she could even hold me in her arms. And to top it all, nobody ever told me that I had a twin sister."
Gary had no smart remark this time. He sat down and stared ahead, throwing a stone aimlessly into a pool below a small waterfall.
"When you put it like that, it does sound a bit shit," he said. "To be honest, you should have said that stuff about your mum and dad first, instead of the crap about the violin."
Warren smiled.
"What's all this never had a friend stuff though?" said Gary. "What about us?"

"Well, we're not really friends, are we?" replied Warren. "More like companions."
"Oh, cheers mate!" said Gary, sarcastically.
Warren passed him a fresh bottle of water before he also threw a stone in the pool.
"So, why are you out here?" asked Warren.
"Don't know. Just needed to get away," replied Gary.
"From what?"
"Home. Life. Everything really," said Gary. He tossed another stone aimlessly.
"I always wanted to be like my dad. He'd wake me every morning by coming in my room, singing Elvis songs. After moaning for a minute, I'd drag myself out of bed and help him on the farm. Sowing seeds, ploughing the fields, rolling the hay, anything that needed doing. It was our farm, so we had to work hard to make a living. He could fix anything, my old man. One of them who could just do stuff, you know? He was never clever or nothing. Don't know names of capital cities and flags and crap like that. But when it comes to nuts and bolts, he's a genius. If there were something wrong with the tractor, he'd sort it. One time, he came home with one of those sit-on lawnmowers and we fixed it up and entered a proper race. One twelve hours long. Goes on all through the night. I'm telling you, our mower went like a bloody rocket. Forty miles an hour down the straight. We tuned it up together, me and dad. People say I'm just like him. Well, they used to say that."
Gary picked up another stone and threw it the water.

"Teachers at my old school thought I were stupid. I get shit grades for not knowing algebra or who won out of Napoleon and Hitler. But I can tune a bloody engine. No exam for that though, eh? Anyway, we took part in this race. Must have been fifty mowers from all over Merseyside, Cheshire, Lancashire, Yorkshire. But we were winning it. We ended up 39th as we got a puncture half way through and had to push it back to the pits. But we were winning. Nobody ever believes me when I tell them, as I lie about everything else. But that one's true. We were bloody winning."

That day were great. But most days, it was crap living on the farm. I wanted to be out with mates, playing footy, meeting up with the lasses in town. But instead, I was stuck on a farm. Felt like I was missing out. So, I started lying. I told my mates that I had a go-kart track where all the Formula One drivers went. Said we'd found a diamond mine at the bottom of a well. Thought I had to impress people, so I kept lying. I lied about snogging a teacher and that got me into more trouble than I'd had been in if I had proper done it. I lied about having trials for Liverpool. In the end, nobody believed anything I said. Then one day, I left school early. Said I had a funeral to go to, but I didn't. Went home, walked through the front door and my step-mum, she was…"

Warren could see Gary was crying.

"She was with Dean," said Gary, almost spitting out the words.

"What do you mean with him?" asked Warren.

"With him, with him, you know!" said Gary, impatiently. "On top of him! My dad gave him a job when no-one else would have given the prick a chance. Even converted the barn for him to live in. And that's the thanks he gets. Anyway, I ran out the house to find dad. Started shouting me mouth off and dad charges back home. And he's angry. I cannot even describe it. He starts hitting Dean and it were brutal. He was hitting him, again and again, like he was a rag doll or something. I was terrified, as I thought he were going to kill him. Then Irene comes running out the house, screaming, "Nev! Stop! What are you doing?"

"My dad turns around and she's stood there with her clothes on. She's wearing an apron, with one hand tucked inside an oven glove and a potato peeler in the other. Says she's been preparing dinner all afternoon and she don't know what the bloody hell he's going on about. Anyway, the police turn up and the shit hits the fan. They took dad away and Dean got carted off to hospital. A few weeks later, Irene stands up in court. She denies having an affair and blames me for everything. Some judge reads out reports from my teachers and so-called friends. They make it look like I lie all the time. Said I had Compulsive Lying Disorder."

"What happened to your dad?" asked Warren, delicately.

"Got four years," sobbed Gary. "Last thing he said to me was that I'd ruined his life. Said he never wanted to see me again. Anyway, I didn't want to go back to the farm, not with my step-mum and that prick laughing behind my back. So, I left. Stayed at the YMCA in Birkenhead for a while.

Then reached a point where I'd had enough. I'd had enough of everything."

"Where did you go?" asked Warren.

"Nowhere," said Gary. "I knew people would think that I'd top myself, but I weren't thinking that. Don't know what I was thinking. Jumped on a train and when I got caught without a ticket I was chucked off and just started walking. Didn't think about food or where I'd sleep. Just kept thinking of my dad. How I could prove to him I was telling the truth. After walking for bloody ages, I stopped for a lie down on the moss. You know that light green moss which is all soft and when you push it down it rises back up, like a trampoline? I just sat and listened to the river. Then I heard something else. It was a red squirrel. I swear I'd never seen one before. He'd scuttle down the tree, grab a pine cone, have a little look at me and then scuttle back up. He kept doing it, over and again. The more I watched him, the more I thought that this little squirrel had it all figured out. Nobody taking the piss because his phone doesn't have internet or because he's the only boy in the class not invited to Amelia Green's party. Nobody telling him to get a job, go to college, or apologise to his bitch of a step-mum. Just a simple life. Eat nuts, make a nest, live in a tree."

"They're called dreys," said Warren.

"You what?"

"Squirrel nests are called dreys."

"Dreys then, for Christ's sake," said Gary. "What does that even matter?"

"Just making a correction. So, then what happened?"

"Not a lot," said Gary, grinning. "I got bored and tried to hit the little furry prick with a rock. But I missed. Then I heard a branch snap and saw your pampered backside poking out of a tree."
Warren smiled. "What happened to your real mum?"
"She died when I was three," replied Gary.
"My mum's dead too. How did your mum die?"
"She got cancer," replied Gary. "Yours?"
"Black widow in a didgeridoo."
"Bullshit!" said Gary.
Warren handed him four folded pieces of paper.
"What's this?"
"These are the pages missing from a book all about my family. This section was written by my father, three years before he was killed by a swarm of bees."
"Shit yeah, I've heard about that one. Maybe your life is worse than mine!" said Gary, before reading the words of Douglas Farrington.

Chapter 27

Saturday 21st November 2004

When I was ten years old, my father, Charles Farrington, sat with me and my sister Tara and read extracts of this book. He thought it would help explain why our lives had altered so drastically.

We enjoyed an adventurous and carefree childhood, but that all changed when our father discovered this book in the family archives.

I knew that my grandfather, Ernest, was a great environmentalist. My father proudly told me that, for Ernest, generating profits was secondary to helping those less fortunate. It was an ethos that my father also lived by.

It wasn't until that day in 1984 that my father told us about the manner of Ernest's untimely demise almost twenty years earlier. He met a horrific end, landing in a wood chipper as he parachuted into the Brazilian rainforest while attempting to shut down an illegal logging operation.

My father, a world-renowned scientist and explorer, initially considered his father's death to be a cruel twist of fate. However, upon unearthing this book and reading how generations of Farringtons had died, his opinion changed. He found old news articles about the family curse, which had been all but forgotten in a fast-changing world.

Almost overnight, my fun-filled childhood was over.

My father insisted that me and my sister were home schooled. We were forbidden from playing sports and could not venture outside alone. My circle of friends quickly diminished.

Paralysed by fear, my father made sweeping changes to Farrington Towers. He built a huge perimeter wall around the gardens. He

invoked strict security, with people only allowed in and out through one entrance at certain times of the day. He constructed a secret underground tunnel, accessed via a trapdoor within the library, as an escape route during an attack.
But such a sheltered life was ill-fitting for a Farrington. Naturally, I rebelled. I was young, fearless and intolerant of the notion of a curse. I possessed the same desire for adventure that inspired generations of Farrington men and women to reach great heights.
So, I walked away from my father's rules when I was twelve.
I was living with a relative when news of my father's death reached me. Dickie Page would later inform me that my departure, coupled with the increasingly rebellious behaviour of my younger sibling, had led my father to question the purpose of his life. The darkness of an isolated existence wasn't worth the sacrifice.
Gradually, he altered his perspective. He even allowed Tara to pursue hobbies, including skiing, horse riding and motocross.
Then, in 1987, my father planned his first scientific expedition in years. He privately funded a research trip to Antarctica, leading a team of scientists conducting experiments into the ozone layer. It was to become one of the most important scientific missions of the 20th century. This trip was fuelled by a renewed desire to live life in the true Farrington spirit. I only wish my father had written to me and expressed this change of outlook, for I shall always regret that we never reconciled.

Whilst his team's huge research base was being dismantled after months of research, my father's team temporarily stayed inside a hut built by the Soviets several years earlier.

One night, a shift in the glacial plateau caused the hut to collapse. A shelf of toiletries fell on top of my father's sleeping bag, followed by the side panel of the hut. By miraculous misfortune, a bottle of deodorant landed next to my father's mouth and the collapsed panel compressed the bottle, spraying chlorofluorocarbon propellants and other volatile substances down his throat passage. This caused inflammation and triggered a fatal heart attack.

It was only months later, when my father's expedition published findings that proved the devastating impact that CFC's were having on the ozone layer, that the undeniable irony of Charles' death reignited speculation of a Farrington curse.

For a week, it was all the tabloids could write about.

Even still, this did not dampen my enthusiasm for adventure, or that of my sister. I continued to travel the world to study, film and protect rare birds. Tara indulged in motorsport, becoming a feminist icon for excelling in a male-dominated environment. That was until 2002, when she was crushed by a tree felled by a Canadian beaver during a motocross race.

News of my sister's death reached me whilst I was in Australia. Even on the other side of the world, another Farrington being killed in unusual circumstances dominated the papers.

As the last surviving member of the family, I had to return to England to take a more active role as the head of Farrington Enterprises Incorporated. However, it was not what my heart desired. In Australia, I'd met Kala, an aborigine of the Tiwi tribe, living on islands off the Northern Territory. I was conducting a study into the population of the red goshawk, a rare Australian bird of prey, when I was struck on the head and knocked unconscious. Kala had believed me to be hunting this sacred bird and had taken me down with a boomerang from eighty yards.

I do not know why I fell immediately in love with Kala. Perhaps it was her big, sorrowful brown eyes, or her stunning smile, or the yellow and white streaks painted around her face and shoulders. Perhaps it was the effect of the medicinal concoction she insisted I drink! Whatever it was, I believed I would be spending the rest of my life with her.

My family's wealth and influence seemed secondary compared to the jubilant existence I briefly shared with Kala, the chief's beautiful daughter.

Kalti, a wise chief and fine hunter, initiated the smoke ceremony as we were married under the bright red sun.

Life was perfect, but fate had other plans.

Still mourning the loss of my sister, I left Melville Island and returned to Farrington Towers with Kala, who was now pregnant. While I was consumed with the task of taking control of my family's vast business affairs, I spent less time with my wife and she found life at the Towers oppressive. It was only when her most beloved belongings arrived from Australia, some months later, that her smile re-appeared.

Among these possessions was a boomerang that she'd carved from the roots of the mulga tree, and a didgeridoo, made from eucalyptus from Arnhem land. Despite the joy they brought, these wonderful relics were to claim her life.

During the transportation of the didgeridoo, a deadly black widow spider made its nest within the mouthpiece. The loud resonance of Kala's playing must have startled the spider into biting her lip. In great pain and desperate to attract attention, Kala threw her boomerang towards me as I was jogging in the grounds. I heard its blissful, whirling sound splitting the air overhead, before watching it return

through an open window, hitting a paralysed Kala on the head and sending her hurtling to the lawn far below.
Mercifully, doctors saved the life of our two unborn children, delivering them as Kala died in my arms.
There could be no doubt as to the validity of the Farrington curse. Kala was raised in one of the world's most dangerous environments. During her youth, she had lived among poisonous snakes and man-eating crocodiles. Yet months after arriving at the Towers, she was another tragic story in the never-ending sorrow my family seems destined to endure.
It was then that I began to understand my father's stance on safety. Although I was reluctant to deny my own children a life of freedom and adventure, it was imperative that I do everything possible to keep them safe.
I increased the protective measures introduced by my father, raising the height of the perimeter wall and introducing security scanners to ensure no-one could gain unlawful access. I replaced the windows with bulletproof glass, obtained flight restrictions in the skies above the estate and introduced a quarantine zone, which all visitors were required to pass through.
No stone was left unturned in my quest for safety.
Should the curse strike me down, my will outlines how a newly-created Executive Committee will ensure my son's protection, while also maintaining the family's business interests.
I have assigned to Dickie the role of nurturing my only son and heir to the Farrington fortune, Warrain (Belonging to the Sea).
I made the difficult decision to separate the twins to enhance their chances of survival. No-one at Farrington Towers knows of the existence of Nerida, aside from Dickie and the family doctor.

Both men are sworn to secrecy.
Dickie felt that Nerida should live with Kala's family and honour the traditions of her mother. But such a life is fraught with danger. So, Nerida was secretly moved to a safe house far away, under the supervision of Dickie's brother. She will remain unaware of her identity, unless Warrain dies and Nerida becomes the sole remaining heir.
Perhaps a change of name may free my daughter from the curse that has come to define the Farrington name.
Should my children ever read these words, I hope they will find forgiveness in their heart. My son, my daughter – I fear I may come to regret some of my actions. I am gripped by the fear that defined a dark period of my father's life. But every decision was born out of love and a desire to protect you.
Perhaps one day, you will understand. Perhaps one day, you will find each other. Perhaps, one day, you will break this dreadful curse.
Douglas Farrington.

Chapter 28

"Wow," said Gary, putting the pages down. "Your actual name is War Rain?"
"Seriously?"
"What?"
"After all that, the thing that shocks you most is my name?" asked Warren. "And it's not War Rain, it's Warrain. It means Belonging to the Sea."
"Your dad died soon after he wrote this then?" asked Gary.
"Yes. Two years later."
"Where did you get this then?" said Gary, holding up the four double-sided pages.
"A few days ago, Dickie gave me a book all about my family history, but pages were missing. He tore them out because they contained details about the underground tunnels. So, he left these pages for me in the shed, after he'd helped me escape."
"Escape from Farrington Towers?"
"Yes."
"You know that sounds ridiculous?" said Gary. "Makes you sound like you were a prisoner in your own home."
"I was."
"Why didn't this Dickie bloke help you out before then?"
"I've been thinking about that. I think it was because of a promise he made to my father."
"Why now then?"

"My sister was kidnapped," replied Warren, after a moment's thought. "A twin sister I never knew existed. The Director stopped me from launching a rescue mission. I guess Dickie decided to finally intervene."
"So, that's where we're going next then? To find her?" asked Gary.
"That's the plan. Make camp here tonight and depart at daybreak."
"Is she fit?" asked Gary.
"Who?"
"Your sister!"
"Seriously? "Do you expect me to dignify that with a response?"
"Oh yeah, right!" said Gary. "You've never seen her, have you? You wouldn't know what she looks like, I suppose."
There was an uncomfortable silence until Gary opened his big mouth again. "So, what's the deal with all these weird deaths then?"
"Oh, for crying out loud!" exclaimed Warren.
"What? Don't mean to sound harsh, but it's proper mental."
"I'd rather not talk about it. Anyway, you said that you'd seen documentaries about us," said Warren. "Presumably you know about the curse?"
"Aye. But I never believed any of that curse crap."
Warren was surprised. "Why not?"
"Don't take this the wrong way mate, but that motocross lass died as she was riding in a place where beavers sometimes knock down trees. Your grandad died as he

chose to sleep in some crap hut built by the Russians and everyone knows they can't build for shite. Your mum, yeah, she was unlucky. But if I ever got anything sent to me from Australia, I'd check it inside out, as everything in that country is like, insanely poisonous. That black widow didn't know anything about a curse. Sorry if I'm being out of order. That's just my God's honest take on it."
"Oddly, I find that quite reassuring," replied Warren.
"How can any of that be reassuring?"
"Well, if it were a curse, it would mean anything could kill me at any time," reasoned Warren. "Your theory puts me in control of my own destiny. That I can live with."
"Aye, that's what I meant!"

Chapter 29

For most of the pupils at Beacons Grange, singing in the chapel was a chore to be endured rather than enjoyed. But for Nadia Fisher, it was a cherished weekly highlight. A moment of euphoria to break up the demanding pursuit of academic excellence that defined most of her school life.
As well as the Sunday morning service, pupils were obliged to attend a Tuesday evening service of prayer, sermons and hymns. Nadia possessed a voice or rare beauty and was the lead singer in an elite choir that represented the school at competitions and public events.
Nadia was standing alongside other senior pupils, three pews back from the Senior Chaplain, who was stood behind a Victorian lectern. She looked around at yawning faces as Father Harold Bradshaw delivered his sermon.
Did Judas Iscariot deserve to be vilified and be forever synonymous with betrayal?
Father Bradshaw suggested that, considering his actions led to Christ offering salvation to all humanity, perhaps we ought to review our opinion of Judas? Nadia wasn't swayed. Judas was a Judas. Although in truth, she didn't care much either way. She just wanted to sing another hymn.
Finally, the sermon was over.
The organist struck the first key, signalling the moment for Nadia to lead the choir in hymn. She looked down at the initials scratched across the back of the pew in front of her. It was a traditional rite of passage for pupils to carve their

initials into the chapel pews after completing their A' levels or International Baccalaureate. Occasionally, a pupil was caught and served with an immediate suspension. There was a plastic container tucked inside the vestry that included several compasses, made for mathematics but occasionally utilised for petty vandalism.

After scratching their names into the wood, many had gone on to successful careers as scientists, doctors, lawyers, politicians and artists.

It's unlikely that any of them were as revered during their time at Beacons Grange as Nadia Fisher. Captain of the school hockey team, regional chess champion, captain of a Model United Nations debating team that was undefeated in eight months, junior pilot with eleven hours logged with the Combined Cadet Force, an accomplished pianist and flutist, convincing winner of the under 16 girls' national tennis championship and a Wimbledon junior championship runner-up, winner of seven of the school's sixteen individual prizes for academic excellence (Biology, Chemistry, Mathematics, English Literature, Latin, Japanese and Music) and school record holder for every individual girls' track athletics discipline from 400m to 5000m, as well as the long jump and high jump.

The only blemish in Nadia's copybook was Art, where her work was not shortlisted for the school prize by a tutor known to prefer conceptual design over artistic flair. Nadia had thrown her canvas painting in a skip. However, somebody must've liked it, as an hour later, it had disappeared.

Nadia felt no nerves as she alone sang the opening verse of *Make Me a Channel of Your Peace*, her favourite hymn. The rest of the choir remained silent as Nadia's voice soared through the chapel. Even the Chaplain closed his eyes, a pleasurable smirk sweeping across his face.

Ralph, the resident caretaker at Beacons Grange, was trimming the hedges outside. During the summer months, he always worked close to chapel on Tuesday evenings, as it enabled him to hear the voice of Nadia Fisher.

He had once rescued a piece of her artwork, which had been tossed out soon after he'd overheard the Head of Art suggesting that Nadia broaden her artistic horizons beyond aboriginal influences. Ralph didn't agree with this assessment.

The painting comprised hundreds, maybe thousands, of brightly coloured dots all colluding to form a pink crocodile. Ralph had placed it on his bedroom wall, although nobody knew he'd done so.

He'd never shared a proper conversation with Nadia. Not on a one-to-one basis. However, he loved to hear her sing and the sight of her incredible smile would make his day. Ralph had never seen another smile like it. That was until he caught a glimpse of two boys while pruning an increasingly invasive purple splendor rhododendron bush.

Both boys were wearing school uniform, but Ralph was certain they were not pupils of Beacons Grange. One was pale-skinned and glanced around uneasily, in the manner of a working-class lad looking for an excuse to start a fight with a public schoolboy. The other, who was wearing a school cap, had aboriginal ancestry. Ralph had no doubt about it.

"Can I help you boys?" asked the elderly caretaker.

"Just keep walking," Warren whispered to Gary. This was just what he didn't need. Minutes earlier, they'd stolen two uniforms hanging up in the changing room of the school swimming pool, leaving Warren's combat uniform and Gary's scarecrow jacket and hat in a locker. Warren had hoped to move around the school unchallenged, with the intention of questioning pupils about what had happened to his sister. But his attempts to ignore the caretaker were unsuccessful.

The old man stepped closer, holding his garden shears.

"I said, can I help you boys?"

"You may be able to," replied Warren, pretending he was pleased to be asked. "We're still trying to familiarise ourselves with the grounds. It's easy to lose your bearings here, isn't it?"

"New then, are we?" questioned Ralph.

"Is it that obvious?" replied Warren, ignoring the gardener's slightly confrontational tone and trying to keep the conversation light-hearted. "I only transferred to BG yesterday," said Warren. He'd heard a girl refer to the abbreviated name at the pool.

"That right?" said Ralph, unconvinced.

"It's my father's work you see. He works in renewable energies and he's involved in a study on tidal power in the Channel. He reckons it'll be a two-year project, so I'm here in the meantime."

"Are you new here too?" asked Ralph, turning to Gary.
"Aye," said Gary, nervously. "Well, sort of!"
"Barry is on a cultural exchange initiative," interrupted Warren. "It's part of the school's Care in the Community scheme. We bring in less privileged pupils from inner-city schools. Not only does it benefit their education, but it also enhances our own understanding of people from all walks of life. Like Barry."
Gary scowled at Warren, who was aware that he might have overplayed the part of a snobby public schoolboy.
"I see," replied Ralph. "So, where are you boys heading now?"
"Mathematics," replied Warren. "I don't suppose you can point us in the right direction?"
"I doubt you have mathematics now," said Ralph, grinning.
"Don't tell me I've got my weekly timetables mixed up?" smiled Warren.
"Well, none of the pupils tend to have lessons at ten past six in the evening," said Ralph, throwing his shears on top of a wheelbarrow full of brambles. "That's why most of the boarding pupils you see around campus are out of uniform."
Ralph stood with his arms folded, as if waiting for a more believable explanation.
Warren laughed. "I don't know what's the matter with us! I guess we're still in shock after what happened to that poor girl."
"What happened?"

"You know," said Warren, leaning in towards the caretaker. "The girl who was kidnapped."
"Oh, I see!" said Ralph, feigning surprise. "You know about that?"
"Everyone knows!" frowned Warren, believing he was successfully digging himself out of a hole. "I heard that one of the kidnappers had a computer smashed over his head and that she rammed a compass in his eye before she was taken!"
"Astonishing, isn't it?" replied Ralph, bewildered. "What a fighter!"
"Does anyone have any idea where she might be now?" asked Warren, trying to be subtle.
Ralph looked the boy up and down. "There's a small cottage beyond the north end of the Quadrant. It has camellias climbing all over the front."
"Okay," replied Warren, thrown by the change of subject.
"Go around the back of the cottage and let yourselves in," said Ralph. "I'll be there in a few minutes."
"Why would we do that?"
"It's either that or I call security? I just heard on my radio that a teacher is busy searching the swimming pool for two missing uniforms. I've got a feeling you know something about that, don't you? Sorry, what was your name again?" said Ralph, turning abruptly to the taller of the two boys.
"Gary!"
Warren closed his eyes and shook his head.
"I mean Barry!"
Ralph laughed.

"Go the cottage and don't even think about running off. I'm sure you haven't come all this way for nothing."

Ralph removed his gloves and placed them next to the shears on top of the brambles. He pushed the wheelbarrow up the impeccably trimmed pathway and left it below the nativity scene window. Then, he stepped inside the chapel, ready to spark a conversation with the most important person in his life.

For the very first time.

Chapter 30

A short time later, Ralph re-appeared and pushed the wheelbarrow back towards his cottage. He left it on the front lawn and walked around to the back garden, which was wild and unkempt. Weeds sprouted from the pathway and lavender drooped over both sides. It was quite unlike the grounds of the school, which were manicured to an award-winning standard.

Ralph whistled as he approached the back door, pushing away the camellias that partially concealed the handle. The door was tight, but he leant against it with his shoulder, pushed hard and it opened with a squeak. He stamped his feet on the stone slab floor to clear some of the freshly mown grass from his boots.

Warren and Gary were stood waiting in the small, cold room which contained several other pairs of boots. Some were covered in clumps of dried mud, making them almost sculptural.

"Come on through," said Ralph. "Don't worry about your combat boots as I don't have carpet."

Once in the living room, Ralph noticed that the fire was almost out, so he threw on two logs.

"That should keep it going for a while."

The room was small, with bookshelves covering three of the four walls. There was a two-seater sofa covered in wood splinters, as it was usually occupied by logs.

"Take a seat," said Ralph, gesturing towards the sofa.

"Sorry," he added, as Warren and Gary looked unsure about sitting on it. "As you can tell, it's not often that I receive guests."
Gary smiled out of politeness and sat on the edge of the sofa, but Warren remained standing as he'd seen a painting on the wall. It depicted a Spitfire and three German fighter planes. It was titled 'The Greatest of the Few.'
"Is this you?"
"Well, sadly that confirms what I feared," replied Ralph.
"And what's that?" asked Warren, baffled.
"That I'm not as old as I look!" said Ralph. "I was just a young boy during the Battle of Britain. I was of the generation that was regularly reminded how fortunate we were to have missed the war. I never understood that view, since most of those who served could hardly stop talking about it for the rest of their lives!"
"Why do you have this picture hanging up?" asked Warren.
"Does it matter?"
"Not really. It's just that you don't have any others. No photos either. Makes me wonder what's so special about this Spitfire?"
Ralph picked up a bottle of single malt scotch and poured some into a chipped tea cup before sitting down on a chair. It was in equally bad shape as the sofa, although it was covered with a tartan rug which kept it moderately clean.
"Well, it's not my only picture," said Ralph. "I have a painting by a pupil hanging in my bedroom. You'd like it. It's inspired by aboriginal art from the Northern Territory."
"Scotland?" chipped in Gary.

"No, a little further to the east," replied Ralph, without belittling his guest. "Australia, in fact."
"Who are you?" asked Warren. There was more to this old man than he had initially thought, of that he was certain.
"Just the caretaker. But seeing as you're so interested, that there is George Farrington. He was the bravest of all Allied fighter pilots during the war. If there was any justice, every child would learn about him at school. But instead they learn about our revolting Royals. When I was growing up, Farrington was my idol."
"Why?" asked Warren.
"He gave the country hope," said Ralph. "Every boy wanted to grow up and be a legendary pilot like Farrington. He died when a Messerschmitt ran out of fuel, with its pilot dead at the controls. The plane crashed into the ambulance transporting Farrington to hospital. A death quite undeserving of such a great man. But you already knew all that, didn't you?"
"Excuse me?" said Warren, startled.
Ralph stared at Warren, before a loud clunking noise from the lion's head door knocker broke the silence.
"Ah, that'll be your sister," said Ralph, rising from his chair.
"My sister?"
Ralph Smiled. "Yes, Warrain, your sister."
"I prefer Warren, actually," he replied, before realising he'd never told the old man his name.
Ralph turned to Warren before he reached the front door.
"I was hoping to break the news to you gently, but I suspect we don't have much time."

Ralph greeted Nadia with a warm smile and a handshake. "Hello, my dear. It's a pleasure to meet you."
"It's a pleasure to meet you too, Mr Page," smiled Nadia, firmly shaking the old man's hand. "Although I feel like I know you already. I see you around the grounds practically every day."
"I know what you mean!" replied the caretaker. "Come on through to the living room. And please, call me Ralph."
Nadia hoped this errand she'd been asked to carry out by the caretaker didn't take up too much time. She was happy to help, as the old man was very well respected. During open days, everyone remarked on the perfection of the lawns and flower beds. However, she'd booked a lesson with the school's professional tennis coach and didn't want to be late.
"I don't mean to sound rude, but will this take long?" she asked. "I was hoping to hit the court to practice my backhand."
"Ah yes, I've heard about your tennis prowess," replied Ralph, ignoring the question. "Is it right you'll be playing at Wimbledon next year?"
"We'll see," replied Nadia, modestly. "I have several pre-qualifying stages to win if that's to happen."
Nadia followed Ralph into the lounge and was surprised to see two boys of about her own age sitting on the sofa.
"My sincerest apologies, Nadia," said Ralph. "I have brought you here on a false pretense."
"What's going on?" she asked, nervously.

"I'm not entirely sure myself. I suspect the best thing would be for you to take a seat while I tell you what I know. Hopefully, our guests here will be able to fill in any gaps. However, before I begin, you should know that this boy here is your brother, Warren. Twin brother, in fact."
Nadia was speechless.
"I'm sorry for the clumsiness of your reunion," added Ralph.
Nadia looked at Warren but said nothing. There was no hug shared between the two. No smiles or tears. Just shock.
"I know this is like, really bad timing," interrupted Gary. "But is there a tuck shop where I could grab a Coke? I'm parched. Besides, I should probably leave you lot to it for a bit."
Ralph tutted.
"The canteen is closed. There's a vending machine in the corridor outside the main hall. Walk straight across the quadrant, turn right and go through the door next to the Shakespeare statue."
"Got it!" said Gary, stepping towards the door.
"Shakespeare? Is that the guy on the horse?"
"No. It's the chap with the quill."
"Is that the thing that's a bit like a duck?"
"You're thinking of a quail. A quill is like a long pen with feathers," clarified Ralph.
"Oh right! Cheers!" said Gary, as he left via the back door.
"Please tell me he's not related to me too?" said Nadia.
Ralph smiled, before walking over to the coffee table and picking up a brown envelope.

"This arrived by special delivery today. It's the final will of my younger brother, Bernard. I called him Bernie, but you knew him as Dickie," he said, smiling at Warren.
"I did," said Warren, sadly.
"Do you know how my brother died?"
"I had hoped there was a chance he might still be alive," replied Warren. "He helped me escape Farrington Towers. He left clues to a secret tunnel and then diverted the guards by firing a rocket from an F-22 Raptor."
Ralph smiled. "That old cliché!"
"I don't know what happened to him after that," added Warren. "He must have been killed by…"
"The Director?" interrupted Ralph.
"Possibly. Did Dickie ever tell you about the toxic wristbands?"
"Hmmm," mumbled Ralph. "Not pleasant."
"I'm sorry," said Warren, as though Dickie's death had been his fault.
"Please, don't be," replied Ralph, sitting down and reflecting for a moment. "We were always close as children, even though he took my job delivering for the family bakery. I was ill one day – just one day – and I never got my job back. By all accounts, the customers liked him more than me, so my parents let him carry on. He was more of a people person, you might say. I took up gardening instead and after winning a Silver Gilt at the Chelsea Flower Show, my landscaping services were in demand. I built quite a successful business and was looking forward to early

retirement. But that all changed when Bernie called me fifteen years ago."

Ralph leant towards Nadia and Warren.

"Whilst on business in London, Bernie saved the life of Charles Farrington, your grandfather. He was about to be hit by a double-decker bus when Bernie leapt from the pavement and pushed him out of the way. To show his gratitude, Charles bought Bernie a bow-tie from Harrods, with red buses on it, giving birth to his nickname. It was the start of a life-long friendship. My brother helped your grandfather develop his family's business links all over the world. The relationship continued with your father, Douglas."

"Farrington?" interrupted Nadia. "As in…"

"Yes, Nadia," frowned Dickie. "*The* Farringtons."

Nadia sat back wide-eyed as Ralph continued.

"For a long time, Bernie's focus was the financial interests of Farrington Enterprises Incorporated. However, your father became increasingly obsessed with safety. When your mother died when you two were born, it convinced your father that the Farrington curse was real."

"My mother died during childbirth?" asked Nadia.

"She died from a fall whilst heavily pregnant. The doctor delivered you both at the very spot where she died. You were given Aboriginal names in her memory. Warrain and Nerida."

Ralph smiled at Nadia. "Your name means flower."

"Your father was inconsolable and devoted his life to ensuring that the curse would not claim his two children.

He used his wealth to ensure that every aspect of his son's life was controlled by meticulous levels of safety. My brother was asked to step back from managing the family's business affairs and instead provide companionship and guidance to you, Warrain."
"Please, just Warren."
"My apologies. Privately, my brother never accepted that your father's approach to your upbringing was best for you."
"And what about me?" asked Nadia.
"You were sent away with few people know of your existence. Douglas hoped that by changing your name, you might avoid the tragic and untimely death that has befallen so many of your relatives. You took the name Nadia Fisher, after your foster parents, who had no knowledge of your parentage. Unknowingly, you have been financially supported by a sponsor since the day you were born."
"A sponsor? Who?"
"Me," said Ralph.
"You? Do you really expect me to believe this? You're the caretaker!"
"When you were growing up, I lived in a house opposite you in Primrose Court," said Ralph. "When you attended playschool at St David's, I was the warden. I grew a beard and spoke with my natural Scottish accent. When you progressed to primary school, I was the librarian. I pretended to be a retired French professor and regularly wore a beret."

"You're Claude the librarian?" said Nadia, taking a closer look. "You had a puppet?"
"Oui, Jean-Pierre," replied Ralph, in a French accent. "I used him to teach children how to count in French."
Nadia laughed as she recalled the memory, but there were tears in her eyes.
"You had an intense passion for learning," smiled Ralph. "Numerous books on dinosaurs and fossils. I sponsored your academic scholarship at Beacons Grange and altered my appearance once again to become a scruffy caretaker renowned for his rhododendron hybrids. When your foster parents were struggling to fund your coaching and international tennis excursions, they threw some bits and pieces in a box and headed off to a car boot sale, wonderful people that they are. There, they sold a Venetian landscape painting for £400,000, with a mysterious buyer suggesting it could be an original by the Italian master, Canaletto. He offered them the chance to take his price or take the painting to a dealer instead, where it could be worth nothing at all or millions. They took the money. I threw the picture in the bin when I returned home, as I can assure you it wasn't the work of an Italian master. I far prefer the picture hanging in my bedroom. It's a pink aboriginal crocodile."
Nadia smiled. "My parents told me about the Canaletto! That money changed our lives."
"You deserved every penny."
Nadia sniffed and regained her composure. "I knew I was adopted, of course. My parents told me on the first

occasion I raised the matter. But I never imagined that I'd been given up because of a stupid curse."

"Douglas, your father…"

"He's not my father," interrupted Nadia. "My father is Gerald Fisher."

"My apologies, Nadia. Douglas Farrington feared that a disaster – natural or otherwise - might strike Farrington Towers and eliminate him and both his children. That would be the end of the family line. So, he sent you away to live a normal life. He needed someone to look out for you and wanted someone like Bernie. That is why I got the call. I devoted fifteen years of my life to a child barely aware of my existence. My brother and I agreed to maintain minimal contact to offer no clue that it was me who was secretly looking over the second twin."

"You didn't know he had died?" asked Warren.

"Not until this morning, when this arrived," said Ralph, tapping the brown envelope containing the will. "I suspect you are not aware of this Warren, but Bernie established a substantial business empire of his own. Since the death of your father, Farrington Enterprises Incorporated has changed beyond recognition. Your family's reputation for supporting environmentally-friendly businesses and fair trade co-operatives has been destroyed. Under the Director's leadership, the company now invests in weapons, oil, toxic chemicals, blood diamonds, tobacco production and even shark fin soup. Just a few days ago, he shut down a cocoa plant in Ghana when workers rebelled as they earned less than a dollar an hour."

"I had no idea," said Warren.
"You weren't supposed to. My brother couldn't prevent it from happening. So, instead, he used the considerable revenue from his shares in FEI and founded his own company. He named the business after a style of bow-tie. He quietly re-opened many of the enterprises initially established by the Farringtons, but shut down by the Director. He formed fair trade collaborations in third world countries, providing decent working conditions and higher incomes. Among the not-for-profit interests in his name are a textiles company in Afghanistan, a firm specialising in jute products in Bangladesh and a commercial shipping repair business in Angola. In Burma, he transformed agricultural land once devoted to growing poppies for the opium trade into areas for growing new varieties of rice. He's also created eleven wildlife reserves, protecting rare and endangered species."
"My God! What will happen to them now?" asked Warren.
"Bernie left all his material assets and full ownership of Batwing Limited to just one individual."
"You?" asked Warren.
"No," replied Ralph. "You!" he said, turning to Nadia.
"Me?" asked Nadia. "But that's absurd!"
"My brother was an extraordinarily intelligent man. He did not make absurd decisions. If he left his empire to you, it's because he believed you capable of continuing his work. Work that was started by your ancestors, don't forget."
"But he didn't even know me!" said Nadia.

"He didn't need to," replied Ralph, taking a sip of whisky. "You are a Farrington. That is all he needed to know."
"Then why not leave it to Warren?"
"Warren's death would see the Batwing Limited passed back to the Director," answered Ralph.
"If Dickie cared for us so much, why didn't he tell me that I have a sister?" asked Warren.
"He was sworn not too," replied Ralph. "Your father ordered that Nadia's existence was only to be revealed in the event of your own death, Warren. Either that or following the first birthday of your first child."
"Why is that relevant?"
"I'm not certain, but I believe that your father hoped that, one day, the two of you would reunite. However, his immediate priority was ensuring the survival of the Farrington line. If one of you were to have children, then the need for you to be separated was no longer so important, as there was another heir."
"How did he expect me to have children when I wasn't even allowed beyond the perimeter wall?"
"Which leads me to the question I've been itching to ask since you popped up wearing a stolen uniform," replied Ralph. "Why are you here?"
"I came to rescue my sister!"

Nerida Farrington
(2003 -)

Chapter 31

Nadia and Ralph looked confused and Warren understood the need to explain.
"A man calling himself Fergus MacLean contacted Farrington Towers, claiming to have kidnapped my twin sister. He dared me to try and save her from an elaborate execution."
"Elaborate execution?" questioned Nadia.
"Yes. Something involving elephants. It wasn't pleasant. I wanted to launch a rescue mission but the Director wouldn't allow it."
"He refused to help you?" asked Ralph.
"That's correct. But Dickie left me a note, advising me to begin my search at Beacons Grange, where I would find help. So, here I am."
"Fascinating," said Ralph. "This Fergus MacLean chap. Is he related to…"
"He's the son of Cameron MacLean," anticipated Warren.
"You know what happened to your father, then?" asked Ralph.
"Dickie gave me the book. On my birthday."
Ralph pondered for a moment.
"So, MacLean didn't tell you himself where Nadia was being held captive?"
"He said he'd given the Director that information."
"Was the Director there when he said that?" asked Ralph, rubbing his chin.

"Yes. He was standing behind me throughout my conversation with Fergus MacLean."
Ralph paced around the room. "Yet no such kidnap occurred and Nadia remains safe and well."
"There's another thing," said Warren. "MacLean showed me a picture of the kidnapped girl. She was an aborigine, but it definitely wasn't Nadia."
Ralph considered this information and sat down.
"From what I can fathom, there are two possibilities. The first is that Fergus MacLean violently kidnapped the wrong girl and this incident has miraculously escaped national media attention. Or…"
"Or what?" asked Warren.
"It was an elaborate hoax."
"With what purpose?"
"What if Fergus MacLean had discovered the existence of a second Farrington?" suggested Ralph. "I recently read an obituary for Doctor Graham Draper in *The Times*. He was the man who delivered you both. He was murdered at his clinic. What if MacLean tracked him down and forced him to confirm the existence of a second Farrington before committing murder?"
"Okay. But why stage a kidnapping?" asked Warren.
"Let's say MacLean wants you or Nadia, or both of you, dead. It's impossible to get into Farrington Towers, so instead he finds a way to entice you out. With you on the outside, he could…"
"Follow you?" interrupted Nadia.

"Right," said Ralph. "He never kidnapped Nadia because he didn't know where she was. So, he follows you when you escape, and you lead him straight here."
"Thanks!" said Nadia, sarcastically.
'You're forgetting something," said Warren. "He sent the Director information on Nadia's whereabouts. He didn't need to follow me."
"That's only what he claimed he'd done," frowned Ralph. "What if…"
"The Director's in on it!" interrupted Nadia for a second time.
"Exactly!" said Ralph. "What's your opinion of the Director?"
"He's unusual. Enigmatic. But I've always thought there's a dark side to him."
"My brother thought so too. Regretted employing him. He was just a financial whizz in the City at the time. His real name's Michael Manalton."
"Unusual surname," remarked Warren.
Ralph paced around the room.
"Assuming MacLean is seeking revenge on the Farrington family, the big question is, what's the Director's motivation?"
They were startled by the clunking noise from the lion's head door knocker. It was Gary. He rocked into the living room with a smile beaming across his face.
"You wouldn't believe what just happened. I put a quid in, right, and the circle bit in the vending machine didn't go all the way round, so this Mars bar was hanging out, literally

right on the edge. I nudged the machine but it still wouldn't drop. I thought, Gary, don't get angry, get smart! So, I stuck my hand right up inside the machine, but I still couldn't reach. Talk about bad luck!"

"But, you're eating a Mars bar?" said Nadia, baffled.

"Aye," said Gary. "I had to smash the glass in the end. Only way I could get it."

"Oh dear!" sighed Ralph. "It's imperative that we don't draw attention to ourselves, so if you could refrain from such actions in future, we'd all be grateful. We have to assume Fergus MacLean and possibly the FPF is out there somewhere."

"Who? What? Have I missed something?"

"I'll explain later," said Warren, before turning to Ralph. "Where should we go?"

"I've got an idea about that. It's a long way from here, but if Bernie's right, you'll be safe there for a while."

"We can go to my parents' house," said Nadia.

"I'm sorry," said Ralph. "We can't do that. If Fergus MacLean has any idea of the direction Warren was heading, he'll come across Beacons Grange, as this is hardly the most built up part of the country. And if you search the school online, your picture is everywhere. The fact that the star pupil is of aboriginal descent will not go unnoticed."

"Meaning?" asked Nadia.

"Meaning that he may consider the possibility of you going home. That might place you and your foster parents in danger."

"Then I must warn them!"

"I understand that. But we can't call them from here. We don't know who might be listening in. I will find your parents and tell them everything, okay? We'll leave here first thing in the morning."
"Do you have a car?" asked Nadia.
"Yes, but not here," replied Ralph. "It's in storage at Farrington Towers of all places. Our best bet might be to catch the morning bus that passes by the school. Then we could board a train in town. The only thing around here that moves are old lawnmowers."
"Lawnmowers?" said Gary. "What type of lawnmowers?"

Chapter 32

Fergus MacLean was eight-years-old when his father woke him and told him that he loved him.
This was not normal parenting behaviour for Cameron MacLean. He was not an affectionate father.
Just the night before, Fergus had heard him banging on the front door, having not seen his father for several days.
"Morag, let me in! Let me in, you bitch!" he yelled.
Fergus slipped out of bed, poked his head through the curtains and opened his window. He could see his father below, with the porch light shining on his face. Cameron looked up and smiled as blood trickled down his chin and into his mouth.
"Son! My boy! Let your old man in!" he slurred, trying to maintain his balance by leaning against his estranged wife's car.
"What are you doing dad? Why are you bleeding?" asked Fergus, trying to keep his voice down so that his mum didn't hear.
"They got me son! Took all my money. Our money, son!" he shouted angrily, slamming his clenched fist down on the roof of the hatchback.
"They took everything, my boy. I've got nothing left. Nothing!" he cried as he collapsed to the floor.
Morag appeared behind Fergus, closed the window and roughly grabbed her son's wrist before dragging him back

to his bed. "Don't you dare open that window again, do you understand?" she yelled.
"I'd be better off without the pair of them!" she muttered to herself after slamming his bedroom door shut and storming back downstairs.
Fergus lay still. He didn't understand what was happening. He knew somebody had died because of his dad's work. Somebody famous. Now dad wasn't allowed back. He'd been drinking a lot and mum didn't want him around. She had a black eye. It was an accident, she said. But still, she didn't want him in the house.
Yet somehow, the very next night after his appearance on the driveway, Cameron MacLean was sat on the edge of his son's bed. Fergus rubbed his eyes, blinked a couple of times and smiled. He gave his dad a hug.
Cameron looked smart and there was no blood on his face. Fergus wondered if everything would be better now. Maybe mum had let dad come home.
Then Fergus drifted back to sleep.
Cameron had lovingly kissed his sleeping son's forehead. Then, he'd walked downstairs, sat in his old chair in the dining room and took the pills from his pocket.
He left a book on the table nearby, scribbling two words on the cover.
'For Fergus.'

Fergus didn't read the book for a while, as it didn't have any pictures in it. But eventually, he read it with a relative. A man he'd never met until his dad's funeral.

And from that day onwards, his life had a purpose: to bring down the Farrington family.

It was more a journal than a book. It contained hand-written accounts from dozens of MacLean men, passed down through generations.

Fergus discovered how, in the early 19th century, John Farrington had stolen treasure that belonged to one of his own ancestors, leading to two hundred years of misery for the MacLeans.

All the while, the Farringtons paraded their fame and fortune to the world.

The story began with Lachlan MacLean in 1809.

Lachlan was a colourful character; a gambling man who left Scotland when he was caught with an ace up his sleeve. He stowed away aboard a merchant vessel and eventually found himself in China, where he employed his old tricks with renewed success. When word spread of Lachlan's skilful manipulation of a card deck, he found himself barred from gambling establishments. He took a job with the East India Company to bring in some money, working as a boatswain on ships operating along the south China coast.

Lachlan's luck changed one night when he was one of nine British men taken captive by Ching Shih. Rather than adopting the naïve stance of the other crewmen and refuse to help the feared pirate, Lachlan smartly chose to become an informer. He provided insider information on British merchant ships carrying silver.

His intelligence reaped great rewards for Ching Shih. Lachlan became a trusted ally of the pirate and was assigned the job of guarding the remaining captured British sailors. For carrying out this duty with unswerving loyalty, Ching Shih presented Lachlan with a jade dragon ornament, dating back a thousand years to the Jin dynasty.

Then, one night, Lachlan was robbed by a cowardly sailor, John Farrington. As well stealing all of Ching Shih's hard-won treasures and handing it to the British, Farrington selfishly took the dragon for himself, despite Lachlan claiming that the jade was cursed.

Lachlan was then tied up by sailors he could have killed at any time during their captivity, but had chosen not to out of the goodness of his heart. When he was found by Ching Shih, Lachlan was treated as a traitor and butchered.

But he was still able to enact revenge, even from beyond the grave. He managed to sneak a small Chinese dumpling, or *xiaolongbao,* into Farrington's pocket.

Lachlan hoped that, upon his escape, Farrington would find it and eat it. For the dumpling had been coated with a traditional Chinese concoction called gu, a potent blend of toxins taken from five poisonous creatures: the viper, centipede, scorpion, toad and spider. The poison caused paralysis across the entire body, then a slow, painful death.

If you thought that this action made them even, then you'd be wrong. Justice had not been served. For Farrington's widow had been lavished with financial rewards by the East India Company and shared her undeserved wealth with her late husband's siblings.

This was how John Farrington triggered a story of vengeance that would define the MacLean family for generations.
In 1815, Lachlan's son Calum claimed the life of Gordon Farrington during the Battle of Waterloo, forcing a bayonet into his torso, blaming a rampaging bull for the attack.
He later became an ironmonger, claiming the life of Gertrude Farrington by scaling a roof and dropping a weathervane on her head.
After re-training as a coachman, Calum brilliantly orchestrated the demise of meddlesome women's rights campaigner Kathleen, running her down with horses outside Downing Street. Tragically, an umbrella, a decorative accessory of the wealthy widow, became lodged in the carriage wheels. They buckled and hurled the poor coachman head first into a wall.
Calum's son, Irvine, ingeniously killed Edward Farrington with a giant icicle in Canada, blaming it on a narwhal.
Irvine was to become one of the hundred and forty-two men to perish at Risca coal mine in 1860. He triggered an explosion whilst attempting to kill the precocious teenager Nicholas Farrington, who was working in the mine to gain an experience of hard work. More lives had been needlessly lost, because of a Farrington.
In 1892, Richard Farrington died during a mining disaster. But it was no accident. In fact, it was almost a perfect execution by Gregor MacLean.

Gregor had demonstrated talent in the field of engineering, but sacrificed a blossoming career to devote his life to the same noble mission that had obsessed his father, Irvine. Whilst only fifteen, Gregor finally claimed the life of Nicholas Farrington, whilst serving as the engineer's apprentice. He applied a strong glue to the sole of his master's shoes before he was due to publicly demonstrate a new tarred road surface. He then proceeded to run him over with a steam roller, avoiding prosecution by claiming to have collapsed at the wheel with heat exhaustion!
Gregor then secured a job at Richard Farrington's South African mine. There, he deliberately triggered a flood which ultimately led to Richard's demise. However, an investigation found that the pump operator was to blame. Gregor was arrested and tragically died of starvation in prison seven years later.
His son, Iain MacLean, was determined to complete his father's work. He landed a fabulous hat-trick of Farrington scalps.
Hearing of Stanley Farrington's attempt to become the first man to scale Mount Everest, Iain falsely claimed to be an expert on Himalayan trails and joined the support team. He masterfully manipulated Stanley's route to the summit before severing his rope, sending the mountaineer plummeting to his death. He blamed a golden eagle after cutting shreds into Farrington's fur coat.
Three years later, Iain sabotaged Howard Farrington's land speed record attempt at Black Rock Desert. Disguised as a local guide, Iain told the Paiute indigenous people of

Nevada that the car would be driving over an Indian burial ground. The natives exacted revenge by launching arrows at the Farrington Flyer, one of which punctured a tyre and caused the fatal accident.

Iain's final act was to bring down Egbert Farrington's vessel, which was laying deep sea cables across the Atlantic. Having acquired a boat of his own, Iain headed for the freezing north seas and sought out an iceberg. He drilled a hole into a huge block of drifting ice and towed it slowly south, intending to use the thick fog to place it directly in the path of Farrington's vessel.

However, in the misty darkness, Iain targeted the wrong ship, placing the iceberg in the path of a commercial liner, the Titanic. Iain was killed by falling ice in the initial impact with the liner, which caused his own vessel to capsize.

Iain was not to know that his masterful plan would inadvertently succeed, as the Titanic would subsequently bring about Egbert's demise.

Iain had not travelled alone. His young son, Angus, was with him on the journey and managed to beat away a few passengers to clamber aboard a lifeboat from the Titanic. This meant news of Iain's sterling efforts would reach home.

His heroic hat-trick had long been part of MacLean family folklore.

Angus MacLean set about surpassing even his father's achievements. While only a teenager, he tracked down Egbert's widow, Pamela Farrington. He volunteered to join her on a coastal patrol along the cliffs, driving a motorcycle while she was confined to a sidecar. He loosened the connecting bolt and cheered as the sidecar became detached and flew off the side of the cliff. Angus was shocked to see her survive the fall into the sea. However, he later described the sight of the Navy slamming a torpedo into Farrington's cockpit as it bobbled on the surface as the most exhilarating and gratifying moment of his life.

Angus used the same trusty spanner to take out Stephanie Farrington, breaking into the Natural History Museum and sabotaging her T-Rex exhibit. The fact that Stephanie was effectively 'eaten' by the dinosaur was a bonus.

George Farrington was a more difficult target, as this personal duel would have to be conducted amid a world war. Angus joined the British Free Corps, which was established by a fascist group to give people the chance to fight for Hitler. Angus didn't consider himself a true Nazi sympathiser, although at the time he was happy to join the side that was winning. Upon hearing that George had joined the Royal Air Force, Angus devoted a year of his life to flying and became a distinguished pilot in the Luftwaffe, earning the Iron Cross.

In 1940, he led an attack on a Bomber Command airfield in the south of England, where George was stationed. Angus got the better of his opponent in a thrilling aerial duel and sent Farrington's Spitfire hurtling into the Channel. However, a lucky shot from Farrington's plane somehow entered the cabin of Angus' Messerschmitt, mortally wounding him. Despite the pain, he continued to circulate

for twenty minutes before crashing his plane into the ambulance transporting his enemy to hospital.
The mission of destroying the Farringtons fell to Gavin MacLean. Having read a report in *The Times* about Ernest Farrington's publicity-seeking attempt to tackle illegal logging operations in the Amazon, Gavin infiltrated Ernest's team of conservationists. Having gained the trust of his adversary, he provided Ernest with a location for a parachute landing site in an area of rainforest earmarked for destruction. Gavin marked it with a flashing beacon, which he placed on top of a bed of twigs and leaves concealing an industrial wood chipper. Gavin's plan was a masterclass in meticulous, military-level preparation, so he decided to watch the drama unfold.
Tragically, Ernest Farrington's dismembered left arm was spat out of the chipper and a serrated bone sliced into Gavin's leg. The wound caused a severe gangrenous infection and he died in a Brazilian hospital weeks later. The actions of a Farrington had claimed the life of another great MacLean.
Hamish MacLean took a different approach. He did not want to just kill the Farringtons; he wanted to humiliate them and prove that the MacLeans were equally as pioneering and adventurous.
A brilliant scientist, Hamish went to the Antarctic to carry out studies into the ozone layer. He was aware that Charles Farrington was already there, leading his own expedition. Farrington was not willing to share his findings and selfishly insisted that Hamish conduct his own research. So, Hamish

devised a plan to look through Farrington's papers. But while Hamish was in the process of reading his narcissistic rival's notes, Farrington woke from his sleep. Hamish took the first item he could find, an aerosol can, and sprayed it into Farrington's mouth until his foe was no longer breathing.

Fortunately, the high winds meant that others in the hut didn't hear a thing. So, Hamish proceeded to detonate explosives in the ice around the Soviet hut and claimed that a shift in the glacial plateau was responsible for its subsequent collapse. A masterstroke from a brilliant mind!

But Hamish could not believe his eyes when he read the research notes he had taken. Farrington claimed that CFC gases were causing a hole in the ozone layer. Hamish dismissed the idea as preposterous and concluded that his rival had fabricated his research in anticipation of it being stolen.

Hamish called his bluff and publicly rubbished all claims made by Farrington's team.

Whilst Charles Farrington's findings were universally hailed, Hamish was ridiculed by his peers. His research funding was withdrawn and he fell into a great depression, not helped by the disappearance of his young son, Hamilton, on a camping expedition.

Hamish suffered a fatal heart attack upon hearing that his arch rival was posthumously being awarded a Nobel prize.

Gambler and loyal servant to Ching Shih, the Chinese pirate. Murdered by Shing Shih due to actions of John Farrington.

Son of Lachlan. Ironmonger and Coachman. Speared by Kathleen Farrington's umbrella while steering horse & carriage.

Son of Calum. Explorer. Died in a mining disaster in 1860 caused by the presence of Nicholas Farrington.

Son of Irvine. Mining pump operator. Died in prison seven years after being blamed for death of Richard Farrington.

Son of Gregor. Sailor. Killed by falling ice created by collision with the Titanic whilst searching for Egbert Farrington's vessel.

Son of Gregor. Luftwaffe flying Ace. Struck by a lucky shot from George Farrington's Spitfire. Died during crash landing.

Son of Angus. Logger. Died of gangrene in Brazil after shard from Ernest Farrington's leg was thrown from woodchipper.

Son of Gavin. Scientist. Died of a heart attack caused by Nobel prize being awarded to Charles Farrington.

Son of Hamish. Took his own life due to pressure of criminal charges brought about by death of Douglas Farrington.

Chapter 33

Cameron MacLean had seen his father become a wretch of a man. A once acclaimed scientist now a laughing stock in his field.

Having been orphaned at the age of fourteen and passed between foster homes, Cameron was consumed by hatred for the Farringtons.

First, he targeted Phoebe Farrington, the over-hyped sailor adored by the public just for winning one yacht race. As she made her way from her sail boat to the harbour, Cameron initiated his audacious plan. He tied a remote-controlled plane to an inflatable orca, which he acquired from a shop in town where he'd taken a part-time job. Cameron flew it directly into Farrington with such force that she fell from the harbour wall and hit her head on the jetty below, before being swept away by the waves.

Passers-by tried to save her and someone even attempted to seize the offending orca. But it was instantly blown - or flown - out to sea, until crashing out of range.

Then there was Tara Farrington, Charles' daughter. Tara was so arrogant in the way she exploited her family's ill-gotten wealth to finance her pathetic tomboy lifestyle, revelling in her role as a so-called 'feminist icon'.

During the Canadian round of the World Motocross Championship, Cameron chopped down a tree and shoved it on to a quiet part of the circuit, just as Tara was approaching. His timing was impeccable. As the track ran

alongside a river, beavers were wrongly blamed as gullible journalists droned on about the Farrington curse.
After laying low for a year, Cameron decided to finish the job. He learned that Douglas had returned to England from Australia, where he had married an Aboriginal woman who had fallen pregnant. Cameron knew he had to act fast, before a whole new brood of Farringtons were born.
He secured a job in the sorting room of the local Post Office and waited for an opportunity. The arrival of a didgeridoo in the parcels room presented him with an enthralling idea.
Cameron tracked down a reptile and arachnid expert called Jonty, who was selling black widow spiders. This strange, pale-faced chap sold many deadly animals, including rattlesnakes and scorpions. The black widow cost £20 and Jonty didn't even ask Cameron for the fake Dangerous Wild Animals (DWA) licence he'd spent hours forging.
Cameron could barely believe his luck when Kala Farrington proceeded to not only be bitten by the spider, but also be walloped on the head with a boomerang she had herself thrown, before falling out of her window. It looked so much like another tragic Farrington death that it wasn't even investigated. No-one suspected the cunning genius in the mail room.
His life's work was almost complete. The only Farrington remaining was the heartbroken Douglas. With Kala's death bringing about changes in postal security checks, Cameron adopted a new approach, plotting his execution with the same meticulous detail.

It was no accident that a Queen bee escaped and found a new home within one of the 'Sold' boards of his newly-founded estate agency. Cameron had shown an interest in his wife's apiary project and developed his own bee-keeping skills. He extracted the Queen and concealed her within a hidden compartment of a corrugated 'Sold' board.
Ensuring that the swarm had latched on to the Queen's pheromones, Cameron angled the 'Sold' board in the back of his pick-up truck. Unlike the other thirty-five boards, this one was not tied down. So, when he arrived slightly late for a photo call at a new housing development, he knew precisely where Douglas Farrington would be standing. After all, he'd personally put the blue ribbon in place. He simply had to drive his van into a marked spot on a low wall outside the Marketing Suite, and he'd send the board flying in the air, like a javelin.
It worked perfectly.
Cameron was overcome with a sense of euphoria as he saw Douglas floundering on the floor with a stake in his guts, covered in a swarm of bees.
Finally, after two hundred years, his ancestors could rest in peace.
He was charged with causing death by dangerous driving, but he could live with that. But he couldn't live with the revelation that there was another Farrington. A boy had been delivered as Kala lay dying on the steps of Farrington Towers.
It was not over.

The boy's birth, three years previously, had been kept secret. But with Douglas' death, he was the last of the Farrington lineage, so his existence was revealed and reported around the world.
Every media outlet wanted a photo of the boy, Warren Farrington, and huge prices were offered to anyone who could capture the first image of the world's richest and most reclusive child.
But security around the estate had reached obsessive levels. There was nothing Cameron could do.
He was mortified by his failure to complete his mission. He turned to the bottle whilst counting down the days to a trial that would inevitably lead to a prison sentence. He'd killed Douglas Farrington for Christ's sake, the world's most famous ornithologist. The British public were demanding justice.
He could only see one option. On the night before his court appearance, Cameron returned to his marital home. Morag had changed the locks of course, which wasn't a surprise after his behaviour the night before. But Morag wasn't aware that Cameron always left a back window off the latch. Cameron snuck in, crept upstairs and kissed his son as he slept. Poor little Fergus. He'd barely given the boy the time of day, so committed had he been to his noble cause in recent years. Yet, that night, he felt like he could sit and watch his son sleep for hours. Fergus briefly stirred, but after a hug, he turned on to his side and was soon dreaming again.
It was time.

Cameron updated the family journal with his own story and scribbled 'For Fergus' on to a scrap of paper.
Fergus was the last hope for the MacLean family. Unless...
No, it was impossible. Hamilton couldn't still be alive.
Then, Cameron swallowed the pills.

Chapter 34

As the Director entered the Meeting Room, he was delighted to see that six truffles had been neatly presented on the table.
It had irritated him that in executing that old fool Dickie Page, he might have inadvertently sacrificed his second truffle. But thanks to the confusion engulfing the household following the Subject's disappearance, the truffle order had not yet been altered.
The Director, who'd decided to hold a meeting of the Executive Committee every day until the Subject returned, rose from his seat and paced around the room with arrogant confidence.
"Gentleman," he said. "This is a good news day!"
"Forgive the interruption," said Samuel Tau. "But shouldn't we wait for Anna?"
"I'm afraid Anna Kraus will not be joining us," said the Director, smirking individually at Samuel, Mitchell Johnson and Hisoka Saito.
"Why is that?" asked Samuel.
"She has been dismissed with immediate effect. I have already identified a suitable replacement."
The announcement took all three men by surprise, not least Mitchell Johnson. Although she was constantly belittling him, he was fond of Anna. Even after several years of failed advances, he still had the deluded belief that she would one day cave in to his requests for a date.

"May I ask why?" said Mitchell, cautiously. "I mean, women of Anna's business capabilities are few and far between."
"Anna's relationship with the Subject has become increasingly informal over recent months," replied the Director. "You've all seen it. The seeds of friendship had been sown. So, reluctantly, I terminated her employment as I believe that she would not have supported the action I am considering taking."
"What action?" asked Mitchell.
"Before I come to that, you should know that all our futures hang in the balance. As we speak, the Subject could be at the Principal Probate Registry Office reading his father's will. In doing so, he'll discover that he can now assume full control of his family's assets. That means he could strip us of our individual shares in Farrington Enterprises Incorporated."
"I don't understand," said Mitchell. "I thought the Subject only inherited control on his sixteenth birthday?"
"Hisoka," said the Director. "Would you explain to Mitchell?"
"Of course. I have acquired the original will of Douglas Farrington," began the Japanese, opening a binder. The top sheet was stamped with the Farrington seal.
"Douglas regularly revised his will, although the principal components remained unaltered. Namely, Warrain Farrington is the sole heir to the family's assets, including the business and estate. Also, he should remain in the care of Bernard Page, who would have a position in a five-strong Executive Committee under the leadership of an appointed

Director. The sole heir has the opportunity to dismiss the Committee and the Director upon his sixteenth birthday."

"We know this," replied Mitchell, impatiently. "What's changed? Last I checked, the boy had only just turned fifteen!"

"Douglas Farrington added conditions that have become of relevance in light of recent events," replied Hisoka, as he flipped to the last page of the will and read aloud. "Should Warrain wilfully pass beyond the boundaries of the Farrington Estate before his sixteenth birthday, this will alter the terms outlined in my last will. My son will possess the authority to dismiss, with immediate effect, the Director and members of the Executive Committee, who must relinquish all assets of Farrington Enterprises Incorporated."

"Why would Douglas apply such a condition?" asked Samuel.

"I should think the key reason was probably to prevent the Subject from being manipulated," replied the Director, calmly.

"So, we're finished?" sighed Hisoka.

"Not necessarily," replied the Director. "There is one last option. We could deploy the Ashta squadron."

There was silence around the room.

"I'm sorry?" said Samuel. "What's the Ashta squadron?"

Mitchell Johnson took a deep breath. "It's a secret assassination team within the Farrington Protective Force. It's a squadron of six highly-skilled motorcyclists, trained to track down and destroy a target."

"What does Ashta even mean?' asked Hisoka.
"Ashta is a village in India where a pack of six man-eating wolves killed dozens of people," answered the Director. "They spread so much fear that people didn't believe they were wolves at all, but demons. Nowadays, people remember them as the wolves of Ashta."
"We have an assassination team?" asked Samuel, incredulous. "But why?"
"I don't know," replied Mitchell, honestly. "It's never been deployed."
"Until now!" said the Director in celebratory fashion. "The Ashta will find the Subject, of that I have no doubt."
"And then what?" asked Samuel.
"Well, the wolves of Ashta didn't leave much trace of their victims," replied the Director. "Just pools of blood."
Samuel Tau laughed. "I'm sorry, is this some kind of joke?"
"Oh, there's no joke," replied the Director. "The only joke is that we are on the verge of losing everything we have worked for. But not if we terminate the Subject before anyone outside these walls discovers he has escaped."
"You can't be serious?" frowned Samuel.
"I'm absolutely serious. Eliminate the Subject and with a little restructuring, we will assume full control of the business, gentlemen. No 0.1% shareholdings any longer. We'll be the owners of the world's largest and most powerful global corporation. Of course, we'll have to kill the sister too."
"The second Farrington child? Why?" asked Samuel, sensing that the situation was getting out of hand.

"Because in the event of the Subject's death, she will inherit the fortune of the family she didn't even know she had. Ridiculous as that sounds! Isn't that right, Hisoka?"
The Head of Finance scanned over the will.
"That is unfortunately the case," confirmed Hisoka. "In the event of the Subject's death, notification must be sent immediately to a solicitor, who is named in Douglas' will. Only upon the written confirmation from this solicitor that the Farrington lineage has ended will full control of Farrington Enterprises Incorporated pass on to the Director and the Executive Committee."
"Fascinating, isn't it?" interrupted the Director. "Douglas was so determined to keep the identity of his daughter a secret that she wasn't even named in his will. But this solicitor must know where she is. And this is, I hope, where you give me good news, Johnson?"
Mitchell Johnson sighed.
It had been some twelve hours since the Director asked him, as a matter of extreme urgency, to uncover as much information as he could about a legal firm, Baker Brothers Solicitors, registered in Scotland. Only now did Mitchell understand the significance of the small amount of information he could unearth in such a short space of time.
"There's not much to report," replied Mitchell. "Baker Brothers has only ever had one employee. And it's only ever had one client."
The Director leant forward in great anticipation. "One employee? Please, tell me who?"
"Ralph Page."

"Page?" replied the Director. "As in…"
"As in the older brother of Bernard Page," anticipated the Head of Security.
"Fascinating!" said the Director. "So, what do we know about Dickie's big brother?"
"We know from phone and postal records that Ralph had infrequent contact with his brother," replied Mitchell, without his usual energy. "To our knowledge, they'd not met in person for a long time. For the last four years, Ralph has been working as a caretaker at Beacons Grange, a mixed independent boarding school in the heart of the Brecon Beacons. It was founded in the 18th century and is renowned for its Georgian uniform and brass band."
"Would you happen to know if a fifteen-year-old girl of aboriginal descent is amongst its current crop of pupils?" asked the Director, excitedly.
"There is one girl who initially appeared to match the profile," said Mitchell. "She crops up regularly in searches on the school. Nadia Fisher, a promising junior tennis player. She also recently led the school choir in an international singing competition in Russia. She was photographed in *The Moscow Times* as she delivered her victory speech in Russian, much to the delight of dignitaries, including the Russian Minister of Culture."
"That must be her!" said the Director. "Academic excellence, unique talent; the classic hallmarks of a Farrington."
"I initially suspected that too," replied Mitchell. "However, that's incorrect. Whilst the photo Fergus MacLean held up

for us was not of excellent quality, the photo in the Russian press and articles about Nadia Fisher's tennis career clearly depict a different girl entirely."

"Ah," said the Director. "Don't worry about that! I'm afraid I've been just a tiny bit naughty!"

He pulled a face that the Executive Committee members hadn't seen before. The look of someone who'd been caught stealing cookies from the jar and thought a cheeky smirk might help them get away with it. "I have a confession. The picture MacLean showed us wasn't the missing Farrington girl at all."

"Then who was it?" asked Samuel.

"Who knows? I found it on Google."

"*You* found it?" asked Mitchell. "Am I missing something?"

"I think this would be an ideal time to introduce the newest member of the Executive Committee," smiled the Director.

In walked a man who was not recognisable to Samuel, Mitchell or Hisoka. They'd seen him before, but he'd been dressed as a hawfinch.

"Gentlemen, meet Fergus MacLean," announced the Director, before the two embraced like old friends.

"The birdman?" asked Mitchell.

"The one and only!" replied the Director. "Fergus and I concocted the kidnapping story. We anticipated that it would trigger an escape bid from the Subject. Naturally, I'd heard of the secret tunnels, but radar surveys of the grounds offered no indication as to where they were. They were too deep! I suspected that Dickie knew though and he would find a way of letting the Subject know. As luck would have it, the old man delivered! My intention was to pursue the Subject so that he could lead us straight to Subject B, his twin sister. But I confess, I underestimated the boy. He is smart, at least compared to that dim-witted Italian and the long-necked buffoon who you still believe to be your finest guards."

The Director looked at his Head of Security, who offered no defence for the F8 team of Gallo and Stone.

"Still, although we lost sight of the Subject, we've been fortunate in unearthing this vital piece of information from Douglas Farrington's will," continued the Director. "I have no doubt that Nadia Fisher is indeed the missing Farrington and that the Subject is with her at Beacons Grange School as we speak. Now, all we need to do is finish the job."

The Director perched himself on the corner of the Louis XIV table.

"So, there we are gentleman. We come to a pivotal moment. Our livelihoods are on the line. We must seize what's rightfully ours! Make no mistake, it's the decisions made here in this room that has turned Farrington Enterprises Incorporated from saintly do-gooders into the most powerful corporation in the world. The Subject wasn't involved. So, are you with me?"

"With you for what?" shrugged Mitchell. "Are you asking us to kill two fifteen-year-olds?"

"Who would know?" gestured the Director, leaning against a Botticelli statue. "Who would find out? We send in the Ashta team, they do the job quickly and quietly. Then we inform the world that the last Farrington has died."

Fergus MacLean
(1998 -)

"And what do we say happened to him?" asked Mitchell.
"It doesn't matter!" replied the Director. "That's the wonderful thing about it! We could say a bag of seed fell on his head and he was pecked to death by pigeons and people would believe it. He's a Farrington! That's what they do. They die in stupid ways! The alternative is we just walk away. With nothing."
The Director turned to his Head of Finance.
"Hisoka? You with me?"
Hisoka thought about the financial implications of his divorce settlement and reluctantly nodded.
"Samuel?" said the Director, turning to the Head of Environmental Affairs.
The big islander was surprised to see that he'd been subconsciously doodling on the cover of his leather-bound binder throughout this most astonishing of meetings.
He looked down and wondered what he'd done with his original binder with the picture of the Victoria crown pigeon.
For the first time in years, Samuel missed the simplicity of life in Papua New Guinea.
"I would rather walk away with honour than be a part of what you're proposing," he stated, boldly but emotionally.
"I resign. With immediate effect."
Samuel Tau was approaching the door when he was stopped in his tracks.
"KR1."
It was the voice of the Director.

"You are to initiate the poison sequence of Samuel Tau's wristband in twenty seconds."
"Sir, what are you doing?" asked Mitchell, rising from his seat. "You can't do that!"
"Can't I?" replied the Director, sternly. "Fifteen seconds, Samuel."
"I am not a murderer," he said, staring at the Director.
"Are you crazy?" panicked Mitchell. "Call it off!" he shouted to the Director, who didn't flinch. "KR1, call it off now!"
"Overruled!" shouted the Director, angrily. "Last chance, Samuel."
"Go to hell," whispered back the islander.
Then came a sudden pain from the needles being thrust into his wrist. The poison felt light and gentle, almost hypnotic. His binder fell to the floor and he couldn't move his arms or hands. His legs felt like they weren't even there. Like they were made of jelly. He'd felt that sensation once before, during an initiation ritual when he was eleven-years-old. He'd drank juice from the kava plant and found that he didn't have the strength in his legs to walk afterwards.
He remembered that feeling as he collapsed to his knees in KR4.
Samuel could see someone in front of him, crying and shouting incoherently. Someone was holding his face. He recognised the man from somewhere. But he was fuzzy and Samuel couldn't understand what he was saying.
And why was he crying?

Samuel's head slumped sideways, towards his binder. He could make out his last doodle. It was becoming clearer. It was a spotted cuscus. When he was little, he'd found one in the woods and taken the animal home, feeding it lettuce until it was strong enough to be returned to the wild. Samuel Tau pictured that cuscus, with its soft fur and grateful eyes, munching on lettuce, as the last ember of life left him.

"Prepare the Ashta," said the Director, briefly placing his hand on the shoulder of Mitchell Johnson, who was on his knees, in tears. He cradled Samuel's lifeless head in his arms. The Director took a second truffle from the table and placed it in his mouth.

"Delicious!"

Chapter 35

Gary worked through the night in Ralph's workshop, which was a mechanic's dream.
Boxes were piled upon boxes of wheels, pulleys, transmissions, chains, axles, spindles, sprockets, drive belts, blades and old engine parts. Gary could hardly contain his excitement.
He'd fixed one ride-on lawnmower within a couple of hours, although it didn't need a great deal of work. Just a few modifications to make it run faster, mainly removing the blades and the lower deck to raise the ride height.
A second lawnmower hadn't been working since the previous summer, while a third was in bad shape. It was just a shell with two flat wheels and the engine sat on a worktop covered in cobwebs.
But Gary reckoned he had enough parts to fix up all three. He wasn't sure what kind of an escape plan they were hatching in the lounge, but he wasn't worried about it. His last tractor adventure with Warren had been awesome and Gary was hoping for something similar.
Warren popped into the workshop to inspect the results of Gary's incessant tinkering.
"How's it progressing?"
"Aye, pretty good, I reckon," replied Gary, lifting the front end of a mower and resting it on its rear, with a blue milk crate holding up the front. "That one's done and it'll go like

shit off a shovel," he said, pointing to a mower in the corner.

It was an expression Warren had never heard before. "Like what?"

"Shit off a shovel!" repeated Gary, amazed that Warren had never heard of it.

"It means dead fast! I'm working on the second one now. Biggest job is swapping the pulleys round, putting the bigger one round the motor and the smaller end round the transmission."

"That'll make it faster?"

"Oh yeah! I'll have to cut away some of the metal frame to make way for the bigger pulley. That brings a couple of problems."

"What problems?"

"The brakes," replied Gary. "They won't work that well. Scratch that, they won't work at all! You won't want to take a tight bend on this thing once I'm done with it. Also, these'll go like a rocket on the flat and downhill, but lose a bit of power uphill. But I'll get what I can out the engines."

Warren looked apprehensive.

"So, you fancy doing some welding?" asked Gary.

"What do I do?"

"Cut round that and make sure the sparks don't hit your face," Gary replied, roughly marking a curve on the chassis with a pencil. "Before you do that though, there's something else needs doing, real urgent like."

Gary picked up an empty mug resting on a tyre. "I work better with tea. Three sugars mate!"

Warren sauntered off to the kitchen, before poking his head into the living room and gesturing to his sister.
"What's the matter? asked Nadia.
"I was hoping you could show me how to make tea?" replied Warren.
Nadia smiled and switched the kettle on.

Ralph sat in his rocking chair, looking out across the darkness of the school grounds, with the moon lighting the distant hills.
A couple of hours had passed since he last heard the screeching of welding from his workshop and watched two unlikely friends hard at work. Warren had taken to mechanical engineering like a duck to water.
What with all the noise, Ralph was pleased that his cottage was on the fringes of the school grounds, far away from rooms occupied by the boarders and house masters. But still, any member of staff out for a late-night walk was bound to have heard the banging coming from his workshop. It was a relief that nobody had complained.
While the three teenagers slept peacefully, Ralph's thoughts turned to the hoax kidnap and the likelihood of the Director being somehow involved.
His brother never trusted the Director. There was something about the way he moved his head, like a hawk scanning the horizon for prey. Bernie considered him morally bankrupt; a man driven by greed who had created a cold, loveless existence for Warren.

But what reason did he have for killing him and his sister? And what was his link to Fergus MacLean?
After contemplation in the dead of night, when the world was so quiet he could hear a mouse scurrying under the bookshelf, Ralph settled on a course of action. He believed that investigating the Director's background, as well as that of Fergus MacLean, might lead to answers.
For that, he needed the help of the only other person his brother had trusted at Farrington Towers.

Chapter 36

Ralph failed in his effort to stay awake all night.
He opened his eyes to see the sun's reflection piercing through a gap in the curtains.
Warren was asleep opposite him, on the sofa. Ralph crept upstairs, avoiding the creaky fifth step, and saw Nadia wrapped under a blanket on his bed.
There was a noise that didn't register for a moment. A faint murmur in the distance, in contrast to the sound of the morning birdsong. Ralph went to the back door and stepped out on to the lawn, damp with morning dew.
The noise seemed to be getting louder. He heard powerful bursts of acceleration followed by regular deceleration.
That was one of the good things about Beacons Grange; there was so little noise. A single country lane leading to it was seldom used by anything other than school traffic.
Whatever was approaching was not school traffic.
"What is it?" asked Warren, rubbing his eyes.
"Sounds like motorbikes," said Ralph, concerned. "Maybe five or six of them. Wake up the others. We need to move."
"Okay, but where's Gary?"
"What, he's not here?" questioned Ralph. "Great! Just great!"

Several minutes passed and the noise from the motorbikes had stopped somewhere close to the school.

Ralph, clutching a 3 Wood he kept in the closet, was keeping a lookout through a peephole in the second bedroom, which he used as a study. It wasn't designed to be a peephole. It was just a feature of an old cottage with shoddy brickwork, which in places was held together with flint and even hay. A drab picture of stones piled on a beach, a gift from a departing teacher, normally concealed the hole and kept out the cold.

It was quiet outside and Ralph was relieved that the motorcyclists hadn't immediately descended upon the cottage.

He saw Gary walk into view from the direction of the quadrant. Wearing his stolen school uniform and carrying a pile of books under his arm, he whistled as he made straight for the front door.

He slammed the lion's head down hard against the oak.

"Oi! Warren! You up yet?"

"So much for anonymity," uttered Ralph.

"Who is this moron?" said Nadia, as Ralph headed downstairs as quickly as his old knees could manage.

"What on Earth are you doing?" Ralph asked angrily, closing the door quietly as Nadia crept down the stairs.

"Keep your hair on old timer," replied Gary, spotting the golf club. "No big deal. I just popped out for a Coke."

"What's wrong with water?" asked Ralph, annoyed.

"Nah," said Gary. "Needed something with sugar. Shattered after putting those mowers together."

Dumping the books down on the table, Gary slumped on the sofa and fizzed open his can, swiftly gulping it before belching loudly.
"I needed that!" he said. "I was hoping to grab another Mars bar too, but after I smashed the glass last night, the kids here must have cleaned it out. Get this though, they all left money on top of the vending machine! Even though they could've just taken it all for free. Total mugs! Must be about £25 quid here," he said, shaking a pile of coins in his pocket.
"You took the money? asked Nadia in disbelief. "We're all in here trying to stay hidden and you're wandering about stealing money in a school uniform that doesn't even fit you!"
"Keep your bra on! I'm not stupid!" said Gary. "That's why I took the books with me. To blend in!"
"Oh, blending in, are you?" fired back Nadia. She was not happy with the bra remark.
She looked at the pile of books. "So, tell me; what lesson might you have been going to at 5:30am with Anna Karenina, sheet music for a Beethoven violin concerto, The Catcher in the Rye and a Sudoku puzzle book? That's quite a reading list for one lesson!"
"I don't know!" shouted Gary. "One of your pompous classes about Shakespeare's operas or something!"
"Oh, Shakespeare's operas eh?" mocked Nadia. "Which one would that be? I mean, Shakespeare wrote so many famous operas!"

"How about the one about the snotty rich cow who thinks she's better than everyone else!"
"I'm here on a scholarship, actually. Not that you'd know what that is!"
"Are you calling me thick?"
"Quiet!" interrupted Warren. "There could be snipers out there for all we know!"
"Snipers?" laughed Gary. "Don't think so mate. I've just walked straight across the lawn and I promise you, there's no bloody snipers out there!"
At that moment, a bullet pierced through the lounge window, shattering the glass of the Spitfire painting on the wall.
"Get down!" shouted Ralph, as a hail of bullets sprayed the cottage, leaving a trail of holes across the lounge wall. "Get to the workshop!"
As the teenagers squirmed across the floor, Ralph grabbed Warren's leg. "You remember the name of that cafe?" he asked. Warren nodded, then scrambled ahead. It was only when he reached the workshop that he wondered how Ralph was going to escape.
Nadia could barely believe her eyes. There were three sit-on lawnmowers and one of them had been painted pink.
"What the hell is that?"
"That's your one. Girls love pink, don't they?" replied Gary, looking pleased with himself.
"You actually don't have a brain, do you? I told you that we needed to be as inconspicuous as possible! Unless our entire

escape route is lined with pink azaleas, I'm going to stick out like a sore thumb!"
"Oh, I see what you mean now," said Gary. "I thought inconspicuous meant something else. Like, the total opposite of that."
Nadia looked at him with both pity and anger.
"You two need to stop arguing and we need to get out of here!" interrupted Warren, as he tightened the strap on a faded orange helmet.
"Where's Ralph?" asked Nadia.
"Don't worry about Ralph. We'll catch up with him later. Put your helmet on."
Nadia looked around. "I don't have a helmet!"
"Aye, you do!" said Gary, presenting her with a pair of goggles and a helmet he'd roughly cut from a large yellow tin of motor oil.
"I am not wearing that!" said Nadia, emphatically.
"Yes, you bloody well are!" said Gary, firmly. "And you'll be glad you did when you find out how fast your oh-so stupid pink lawnmower goes!"
"What are you wearing then?"
"Nothing! So be grateful for what you've got!"
With that, Nadia climbed aboard her mower.
Gary plonked the tin of oil over her head, before giving it two firm whacks on top to make sure it wouldn't fall off. A drop of oil leaked down the side and dripped over Nadia's cheek.
"There!" said Gary, placing the goggles over her face. "You never looked better!"

Gary stepped on to the middle mower and removed a gleaming new helmet from under a cloth on his seat. He looked at Nadia and winked.
"Seriously, if we get out of this alive, you're dead," she said.
"Okay, the workshop door rises up from the bottom," said Warren, interrupting the bickering pair. "As soon as there's enough space, we go. Aim for the school building. These guys probably won't follow us there and bail out. Nadia, you lead the way. And don't forget, there's no brakes."
"What?" shouted Nadia. "You never said that…"
"Engines on!" shouted Warren.

Three FPF guards, who had entered the house and were sweeping the downstairs area for occupants, heard lawnmowers at the far side of the cottage. They ran through several rooms and tried to open the door to the workshop. But it was locked.
The workshop's garage door rose steadily, as the sunlight blasted through.
"Five, four, three, two, one, go!" shouted Warren, and all three pressed down firmly on their accelerator.
The top of Nadia's tin helmet clipped the rising door as she passed under, just as the assassins shot their way through the side door to the workshop.

Chapter 37

The three lawnmowers sped along an undulating stretch of grass from the caretaker's cottage, around the side of the sports centre and towards the heart of the school.
Warren was stunned by how fast he was travelling. He needed to take his foot off the accelerator over some of the dips in the grass, otherwise he risked being thrown clean off his seat. Along the downhill section, he was going so fast that his face was vibrating, even though he had adopted a low, aerodynamically efficient position.
So, he was surprised to see his twin sister edge past him on her bright pink machine. She was crouched even lower and made no attempt to slow down for the dips, seemingly relishing the challenge they presented.
Gary was close behind. "Maybe that'll get her off my case!" he thought. He'd deliberately painted the mower with the best engine bright pink. Not that she'd thank him for it.
Warren pointed behind and Gary turned around to see three motorcycles in pursuit. The riders were dressed from head-to-toe in black, with black helmets and gloves too.
Then came a flash of light and a piercing noise, different to the buzzing shriek of the mowers.
"Holy shit! They've got guns attached to the frigging bikes!" shouted Gary.
The mowers sped across the school's car park, towards the security office.

Tony Burt, the Security Manager, ran out and waved his arms frantically, but the mowers blasted by. The pink mower was so close that Tony shrieked and cowered against the wall.
As Nadia roared by, she sarcastically uttered Tony's catchphrase under her breath.
"You can't go in without a pass and the only person who can pass you a pass is me!"
Nadia had heard Tony utter that line in the same smug tone a thousand times.
She then followed a path towards the school's historic clock tower, with her pink mower kicking up stones as she turned sharply left, briefly tilting on two wheels before heading straight along a gravel road that led to the quadrant.
The boys were right with her, but two motorbikes were closing in. A third had peeled away.
The quadrant is a large area of grass that students are not allowed to walk across. It's divided into four symmetrical squares by two paths running north to south and east to west, and decorated with award-winning flower beds. Even stepping one foot on the grass was enough to earn you a detention.
Nadia cut straight across it, leaving thick tyre marks and churning up the manicured turf. The head gardener, known to be almost as precious as the caretaker when it came to floral displays, began gesticulating wildly, but dived for cover as gunfire echoed around the grounds.
In the centre of the quadrant stood a statue of King George III, who ruled when Beacons Grange was founded some

250 years earlier. The eyes of the stature were disproportionate to the size of the head and gave the impression of following you around. The statue would spook pupils passing by it alone.
Nadia circled the statue, hoping that the motorbikes would struggle for grip on the recently watered turf. But the riders could easily turn on their multi-terrain bikes, kicking up huge sprays of mud and grass. Within seconds, the quadrant looked like a speedway track.
Surrounded the quadrant were cobbled stone passageways, decorated with ornate sculptures. Nadia tore along one of the passageways at full speed. She took her foot off the accelerator to take the top bend, but barely slowed down at all and couldn't avoid scraping the wall. She struggled to build momentum and one of the motorcyclists closed within shooting range.
Then, suddenly, Warren appeared from nowhere, slamming into the side of the bike, which smashed hard against the stone wall. The unconscious rider rolled across the cobbles like a rag doll, with the motorcycle spinning in a heap.
Managing to keep his mower facing the right way, Warren led the way towards a large building, where doors had been left open by cleaners who had fled the chaos.
The three mowers entered the dining hall, which was clean, ready for the breakfast rush, but mercifully empty.
Nadia found herself on two wheels again as she tried to turn on the polished wooden floor of the grand hall, where portraits of former Headmasters and Royal patrons lined the walls.

The spaces between the mahogany dining tables were just wide enough for a mower to pass.
The rapid gunfire of a semi-automatic weapon ricocheted off Nadia's engine hood, fired from the second assassin.
Gary breathed a sigh of relief too when he felt a bullet brush the side of his helmet.
He feared that Nadia's oil tin would not be as effective.
Other shots had been more erratic and bullets peppered the dining hall, causing an eight-foot canvas of Reverend Oliver Greenwood, Headmaster from 1870 – 1882, to plummet to the floor.
Spotting its thick gold frame, Gary leapt off his mower and grabbed it, hooking the side of the frame under the hood latch of his mower.
"Are you stealing that?" asked Nadia, dumbfounded.
"No! I'm using it as a shield. He won't be able to see me through it!"
"Yes, but you won't be able to see where you're going, you idiot!" replied a bewildered Nadia.
"Just get out of here!" said Gary. "I've got this one."
Nadia shrugged. He's got courage, she thought. If nothing else.
The motorcyclist skidded on the slick floor, turning his bike around on a sixpence to face the mower at the opposite end of the dining hall. He watched as the other two mowers exited, towards the canteen.
The assassin couldn't see who was on the mower opposite him, as they were obscured by a giant canvas. There was a chance that it was the Subject. He'd be in line for one hell

of a pay day if he could kill him. Take early retirement, buy a villa in Spain, get himself a younger wife.
The rider turned the throttle with his right hand and wrapped his left hand around the trigger of the machine gun. He promised himself he wouldn't stop firing at the painting until there was blood seeping through the bullet holes.
Across the hall, Gary poked a finger through the canvas, which was harder than he expected. It wasn't so much a hole as a strip that flapped down.
"What the bloody hell am I doing?" he said to himself. "All this to impress one stuck-up rich girl?"
He heard tyres screeching.
Gary closed his eyes and stuck his foot down.

Nadia led Warren through the canteen, where the smell of bacon drifted in the air. She caught a glimpse of a chef poking her head above a worktop, looking beyond Nadia and ducking back down. Nadia looked behind her to see a motorcycle fast approaching.
"Go!" she shouted to Warren, who put his foot down.
Nadia roared along the corridor, passing the Headmaster's office, where she noticed that the door was slightly ajar and a pair of eyes were peeking out.
Nadia flashed her lights.
"Get inside!" she shouted, as a hail of bullets were fired, showering a row of lockers outside the office.
Mr Richardson slammed the door shut, breathing heavily as he dropped to the floor, grateful to still be alive.

"Was that Nadia Fisher?" he thought, before pressing re-dial and demanding to know how much longer the police would be.
Nadia slammed into double swing doors, which flung back partially until Warren hit them again, smashing the lower hinges clean off and leaving the door dangling loose. This caused the biker to slow down, allowing the mowers to pull a few vital yards ahead as they made their way back outside along a path, before coming to a set of steps. Nadia was thrown from side-to-side as her mower bounced around wildly.
Having not expected steps, Warren barely had time to alter his speed and leapt past Nadia with all four wheels off the ground. He was relieved to reach the bottom in one piece. He tucked back in behind his sister as she smashed through a set of barriers, ignoring a 'Construction Personnel Only' sign.
The mowers made their way along the concrete ground floor of an empty library, which within two months was scheduled to be officially declared open by a minor Royal. Nadia drove towards a circular ramp, which was to offer wheelchair access to the upper floor.
She looked behind her to see the third motorcycle closing in. But where was Warren?
Nadia skidded out wide as she reached the upper level, losing momentum. Spotting a sheet of blue tarpaulin beyond the concrete pillars at the far end of the empty floor, she headed straight for it, weaving to ensure that her pursuer couldn't get a clean shot.

She knew from her school tours that the building was not yet completed and that beyond the tarpaulin was a sheer drop to a skip full of rubble.
Just as the mower was about to rip through the sheet, she jumped off and slid across the floor, showing incredible agility to grab on to the edge of the unfinished building.
She expected to see a black motorcycle follow her bright pink machine straight over the precipice. But sadly, the rider was quite aware of the possibilities presented by tarpaulin on a construction site.
He screeched to a halt, laughing as he stepped from his bike. He looked over the shoulder of the young girl clinging to the edge of the building, with oil dripping down her face under a makeshift helmet.
"If you thought that was going to work, then you watch too many movies!" he said.
He stood on Nadia's hand, softly at first, but then he applied more pressure, causing her to scream.
"Oh, I'm sorry!" teased the assassin. "I didn't see your hand there! Don't worry, it'll soon be over."
He raised his right foot in the air and Nadia saw his steel-toed boot above her head. She closed her eyes. Then she heard a strange firing noise, before the assassin roared in pain.
Two more shots followed and he staggered backwards, over the edge of the building and into the skip below.
Warren walked over and peered down.
The assassin was groaning. His left leg had bent back almost double, in a manner that made Warren physically recoil. It

didn't help that he had three six inch nails embedded in him either.
"Nail gun!" grinned Warren, holding it up. "I came across it downstairs."
"Wonderful!" replied Nadia, sarcastically. "Can you please just help me up?"
"Are you two okay?" came a voice behind them. It was Gary, who looked out of breath as he jogged towards them both as Nadia clambered to safety.
Warren was pleased to see him. So was Nadia, although she didn't show it.
"What happened to the other one?" asked Warren.
"Oh, don't worry, I dealt with him!" said Gary, brushing away the question like it was nothing.
"Great. Then we'd better move as…"
"Wait!" interrupted Gary. "Aren't you going to ask me how I did it?"
"Well, I wasn't going to," replied Warren, confused. "You implied that you didn't want to offer an explanation?"
"Yeah, well, I thought you'd ask for more details, to be honest," said Gary, crestfallen. "I mean, it was pretty cool."
"Okay, do continue," said Warren.
"Well, it was a bit like a bull fight," said Gary, tilting his head and looking to the sky. "He was at one end of the hall, I was at the other. Neither of us was going to back down. But something told me that only one of us would be walking out alive. It was like two gunslingers in the wild west, waiting to see who would draw first. Then, his back wheels started spinning. Smoke was rising in the air like…"

"Oh, please!" burst out Nadia. "Spare us the drama!"
"What is your problem?"
"My problem is that we're being hunted by assassins and we're stood here listening to you spout total nonsense!" said Nadia. "There could be other motorbikes with machine guns looking for us now and we need to get out of here. We don't have time for your made-up, wild west fantasies. Do you understand?"
"Okay," said Gary, embarrassed. "I'll tell you about it later then."

Chapter 38

When he heard the sirens in the distance, Ralph crawled out from under his bed.

He afforded himself a chuckle. He'd dragged down the duvet from the side of his bed so that it brushed the floor and concealed him. If he'd have been playing hide-and-seek with a three-year-old, he'd expect to be found within seconds. So, what were the chances of going undetected by three gunmen combing the cottage?

But he was lucky. He'd heard an intruder place one foot on the creaky step, then the noise of the mowers came from the workshop.

The assassins had never returned.

Ralph looked out of his bedroom window and saw a black motorcycle and a lawnmower side-by-side, heading across the fields to the north. Ralph couldn't make out the faces, but two people were on the bike and all three were wearing school uniform.

It looked as though the passenger was wearing his old tin of Pennzoil as a helmet. Strange, as he was sure it wasn't empty.

Ralph gathered up his most treasured belongings, including the Spitfire painting, which he found on the floor, and placed them inside a bag. He picked up his favourite flat cap from a hook by the back door, brushed his hand along the camellias one last time and left Beacons Grange forever.

He found his bicycle, complete with a wicker basket. He didn't look back as he pedalled away from the caretaker's cottage towards a cycle path that ran alongside the lane leading to the school.
The occupants of the passing police cars barely glanced at the old man making slow progress due to the slight gradient in the road.
Whilst still within a couple of miles of the school, Ralph had seen three ambulances heading towards Beacons Grange. He hoped that there were no students or teachers among the casualties.
Several miles later, a recovery vehicle passed by, heading back towards town, carrying the wrecked remains of two mowers and two motorcycles. One of the bikes was split in two.
After that, the roads had fallen quiet as the day descended into darkness.
Ralph felt as though his old legs couldn't pedal another inch, but there was still some way to go before he reached the home of Gerald and Yvonne Fisher. It was some relief that they'd moved closer to the Beacons so that they could see Nadia at weekends, even if they were normally taken up by tennis competitions.
His thoughts turned to a conversation he'd once had with them. Whilst Gerald and Yvonne felt that they had chosen Nadia after forming an immediate bond with her through an adoption agency, it was in fact they that had been carefully selected by Ralph and Bernard Page.

Gerald and Yvonne had come from working class backgrounds and had carved out moderately successful careers in their chosen field. The had both excelled at sport, Yvonne could speak French and Spanish fluently and German competently, whilst Gerald was well known in local jazz clubs as a multi-instrumentalist.
Yvonne studied Biology and later helped establish protected marine environments in Britain and its overseas territories. However, she sacrificed her career, as it involved too much travel and she wanted to spend more time with her adopted daughter.
Gerald developed a range of equipment for testing the force and strength of various materials. His machines were used by companies all over the world to do anything from measuring the bounce of a ping pong ball to ensuring the lids of medicinal bottles couldn't be opened by young children.
When a costly patent row went against Gerald, despite overwhelming evidence that a Chinese manufacturer had made exact replicas of his designs, Fisher Force Solutions Ltd had to take out loans to stay afloat.
Despite these struggles, Gerald and Yvonne never wavered in their love and support for Nadia. Without the money to support her rapid rise through the junior tennis ranks, Gerald packed up everything he thought possessed any value and drove to a car boot sale one Sunday morning.
It had been quite a productive first hour. Yvonne had sold some of Nadia's old sports equipment, including tennis racquets and hockey sticks she'd grown out of, whilst

Gerald was amazed at the interest in his modest collection of vinyl records, predominantly from the New Romantic era.
Then, an old man had leaned in and whispered, "Don't make a scene, but you need to get that painting off the floor."
Ten minutes later, the Fishers packed drove away in a rusting Vauxhall Meriva with a life-changing sum of money.

Ralph wondered if the Fishers would recognise him as the buyer of the painting when he knocked on their door. He also wondered how they would react to knowing the truth about Nadia's identity.
He was about to find out.
Whilst he was apprehensive about meeting them properly, Ralph was looking forward to sitting down somewhere warm, perhaps with a cup of tea. He'd been riding for six hours and his knees were wobbling.
He left his bicycle around the corner from the couple's modest semi-detached home and walked past once to ensure it wasn't under observation. He was on his way back along the road when the porch lights flashed on, illuminating the ornamental gnomes in the front garden. Ralph ducked down, just in case, but he couldn't see anyone, so he kept walking towards the driveway. It was then that a noise shattered the peaceful tranquillity of the night.
A sudden burst of gunfire. Then, five seconds later, another round was fired.

Ralph hobbled across the driveway and rolled under a row of fir trees lining one side of the front garden. He stayed there, petrified and motionless, as two men ran out, jumped on black motorbikes Ralph hadn't even seen, and sped away.

"I'm so sorry, Nadia!" he said to himself.

"I'm so, so sorry."

Chapter 39

Not for the first time during their long walk through the countryside, Gary looked embarrassed.
"Do you really expect us to believe that?" laughed Nadia.
"That's what happened!" argued Gary.
"You have to admit," grinned Warren. "It sounds unlikely."
"No word of a lie! That's what I said!"
"Let me get this right," said Nadia. "When you collided with the motorcyclist, you were thrown in the air. But you managed to miraculously cling on to the dining room chandelier. You then landed safely by adopting a leap and roll technique that Jackie Chan taught you when he gave a talk to The Wirral Young Farmers' Association, because that's exactly what he does during a break in filming, then, you strutted up to the rider and placed the giant portrait over his head. And your exact words were: 'You're no oil painting now!'"
"Yeah!" said Gary.
"Well, that all makes perfect sense, as you're clearly James Bond!" laughed Nadia.
"I'm telling you, that's what happened!"
"Oh, come on!" she said, looking up to the heavens. "There's no way you could have reached that chandelier!"
"Don't believe me then," said Gary, storming off, muttering under his breath.
"Oh, don't be a baby! I was only teasing. Those mowers were amazing. I mean, without you, I'd probably be dead!"

Gary turned around. "I gave you the fastest one. That were deliberate, you know? What with you being a girl."
"What's that supposed to mean? What? So, women can't drive now?"
"Oh, for Christ's sake!" said Gary, turning back up the pathway. "I can't win with you!"

Having decided to ditch the one surviving mower and the motorcycle for fear of being spotted by the FPF, the three teenagers walked along what used to be a railway line. Like many others, the line was closed by Dr Richard Beeching in the 1960s. There were remnants of railway line and sleepers along the path.
"So, Warrain eh?" said Nadia, giving her twin brother a nudge.
"What are you laughing at, Flower?" he joked back, as Gary trudged off ahead at pace. "Should we tell him to slow down?"
"Leave him," replied Nadia. "He'll keep going until he's about one hundred metres ahead, hoping we'll say sorry. And when that apology doesn't come, he'll stop and claim that it's the two of us who have been dawdling."
"How can you possibly know that?" asked Warren. "You barely know him."
"I don't need to. He's not overly complicated. So, is he a friend of yours?"
"I'm not sure."
"What do you mean, you're not sure?"

"I've only known him two days," said Warren. "And almost everything he's told me so far has been a lie. Still, they've been the best two days of my life. I know that I turned up with news that has impacted negatively on your situation, and I'm sorry for that. But for the first time, I feel, well, alive. Up until now, my life's been remarkably uneventful."
"Ralph told me about it last night," said Nadia. "Sounds like your father, well, our father, went to extreme lengths to keep you safe."
"You could say that," replied Warren. "Consider where we are now, on this old rail track. If the Director was managing this scenario, there would be a team of electricians ensuring that none of these lines were live. These sleepers would be deemed a trip hazard and would be covered in cushioned padding. There would be botanists scouring the path for any plant species that might trigger an allergy. Any thistles would be cordoned off and guards would be stood between me and the thorns. An entomologist would be surveying the insects to determine the risk of one biting me, even though I would be wearing a protective suit with a layer of netting strong enough to withhold a sustained attack from a swarm of African killer bees. A meteorologist would be monitoring the wind speeds with an anemometer and elite FPF guards would be combing any buildings ahead. There would even be a no-fly zone in the skies above us, to ensure I wasn't fatally wounded by a falling ice block from the toilet waste or something like that."
"That's ridiculous," said Nadia.
"That's been my whole life."

"Trust me, you have nothing to worry about here," she said, bending down. "I'll even touch the old live rail to show you."
Warren turned around as Nadia started shaking violently whilst screaming.
There wasn't a hint of a smile from Warren. Instead, he looked at her in pity.
"Factoring in the presence of tunnels, the rail line here couldn't have been powered by overhead cables, so the operator would have adopted a 750-volt DC third rail system, with the conductor rail supplied by direct current," explained Warren, matter-of-factly. "Clearly this section of broken track is not connected to a generating station, so your efforts at a prank were poorly conceived."
He leapt across the sleepers to another section of track with connecting conductors and held his hand over a separated section of old line.
"Now, whilst highly improbable, this section could theoretically still generate elect…"
And with that, Warren suddenly jolted and flew backwards in to the long grass that ran alongside the abandoned line.
"Warren!' screamed Nadia, running over to him in a state of panic.
Warren opened one eye. He couldn't hold back a grin.
"You swine!" she smiled, hitting him playfully.
"Got you!"
"So, you do have a sense of humour after all?"
At that moment, Gary called out from far ahead. "Oi, you two! Come on! I thought we were in a hurry!"

Chapter 40

It had been dark for a couple of hours by the time that the three companions found a hay barn on a dairy farm. It had been an exhausting day and one in which Gary had gone from hero to zero.

Whilst his engineering brilliance had contributed to their escape from a team of assassins on armour-plated, gun-wielding motorcycles, Gary had been humiliated as dusk fell.

He'd insisted that cow tipping was a real thing.

Warren had never read about such a phenomenon, but was intrigued by Gary's description.

Gary had sworn on his life that he'd once knocked over "pretty much a whole swarm" in one night.

Warren, who thought it pointless to tell him that the collective term for cattle is a herd, doubted his friend's account of cow tipping. He knew that cows, unlike horses, couldn't sleep while standing up because they are unable to lock their legs.

Nadia had quickly ascertained that Gary was prone to extraordinary levels of exaggeration and regularly resorted to plain lies. So, she merely rolled her eyes when he'd claimed to have been cow tipping "loads of times."

When they came across a mixed herd of red and black Angus cattle, Nadia gently questioned Gary's courage, knowing full well that he'd take the bait.

"Okay, I'll prove it!" he said.
Gary leapt over a gate and marched confidently towards a cow. Warren had to admit, it was standing and yet seemingly inactive. Maybe it was asleep.
Gary strutted up to the cow and pushed it with two hands. It didn't fall over.
"Just checking," he said, as though everything was going to plan. "This one's definitely asleep, so it'll work. Definitely. This is going to be legendary!"
Nadia raised her eyebrows. "I think you're right about that!"
Gary took a few steps back before sprinting towards the cow. He leapt and turned his body into the side of the animal, tucking his legs into a ball. To his surprise, the impact was much like running into a brick wall. He landed with a thud on the ground, while the poor cattle ambled away.
"Are you okay?" shouted a concerned Nadia, feeling guilty for her part in it. Gary was writhing around on the floor, gasping for breath.
"I'm fine," he wheezed. "Just winded."
"Didn't work then?" sniggered Nadia.
"Nah,' puffed Gary. "Must be a different breed. It worked on them black and white ones. What are they called?"
"Zebras?" joked Nadia.
"Oh, you're funny!" said Gary, sarcastically, starting to get his breath back. "You know what I mean."
"What's that down your leg?" asked Nadia. "It stinks!"
"Oh, Christ!" groaned Gary as he stretched out his left leg. His school trousers were covered in cow dung.

Warren couldn't help but laugh.
"It's not funny," moaned Gary. "I'm covered in shite!"
"It is sort of funny," said Nadia, unable to hide her laughter. "Come on, we'll find somewhere to settle down and get you cleaned up!"

By the time that they stumbled across the farm, it was almost midnight.
Warren was pleased to find that the barn was unlocked and the door didn't creak at all. There was no machinery inside, just piles of hay rolled into bales.
He slumped down on the hay and opened his bag. The food and water supply had been replenished at Ralph's cottage, although five of the six bottles were empty again. The major bonus had been a bag of *Murray Mints* that Ralph kept in the workshop. Gary had stuffed them in his pocket without asking, although he told the twins that the old timer said it was okay.
"He said we should savour them, as they were the last bag of *Murray Mints* ever made," lied Gary. "Ralph bought them literally as the factory was closing down. In Murray."
"I thought they were named after the creator, not the town?" asked Nadia.
"Nah," said Gary. "Murray's in Scotland. You know Murrayfield, where they play rugby? Well, that's where the factory was. All Scottish players suck mints at half time. They have too. Part of their contract."
Nadia and Warren didn't have the energy to question it.

As Warren laid out the evening's rations, Nadia told Gary to take off his trousers.
"You what?" said Gary.
"I'll clean them for you," said Nadia. "We passed a utility room and the door was open. There's hot water there."
"You'd do that for me?" asked Gary, surprised. The girl hadn't exactly been overly nice to him.
"Well, you can't wear them in that state, can you? And it's only right that the female does the washing, don't you think?"
An alarm went off in Gary's head, like the question was a test.
"I was being a moron," he said, humbly. "Honestly, what was I thinking, running into a bloody great cow? I should clean them myself."
Nadia smiled as Gary trudged past her.
"Gary?"
"Aye?" he replied, turning around.
"What you did with those mowers, fixing them up like that. That's the most amazing thing I've ever seen."
Gary beamed with pride, before walking across the courtyard in trousers covered in cow dung.

The trio's presence in the barn did not go undetected for long. When Gary turned on the hot tap, pipes started rattling as the old boiler in the 16th century farmhouse thundered into action. Whilst all seemed fine to Gary, the farmhouse was rocking.

After enjoying several glasses of cheap whisky, Brian Cooper had fallen asleep before *Countryfile* had even finished. It was the only TV show he ever watched, although most years he'd sit down for the Grand National too, if he remembered when it was on.

Brian hadn't replaced his television in three decades. It had a built-in VHS player, but he only had two video cassettes. *John Wilson's Dream Fishing* and *Four Weddings and a Funeral,* which he'd won in a tombola at a country fair in 1995. He'd not got around to watching it and wasn't the slightest bit interested in ever doing so.

As the pipes chugged into action, Brian woke. He switched off the TV, pulled on his jacket and slung a shotgun over his shoulder. He'd slept in his boots, so didn't need to worry about putting them on.

Brian pushed open the front door, which he hadn't locked in 30 years. He had nothing worth stealing.

Chapter 41

For three consecutive years, and for seven out of the last nine, one of Joy Hillier's bakes had been named best in show at the annual cake-making competition at Dolgellau Women's Institute.
When she first joined, the contest only allowed Victoria sponge cakes. An amendment to open-up the category to broaden the competition's appeal was only narrowly approved by the committee. Joy was among those who voted against change. It might also have had something to do with the fact that Joy was aware that hers was the best Victoria sponge, as she made jam from strawberries and raspberries grown on her own farm.
Last year, the cake competition had attracted thirteen entries, one more than the previous year, although seven less than the record amount recorded in the 1950s.
This time around, the committee decided to accept no more entries after the one hundredth application form was submitted.
The reason for the surge in interest owed much to the prize being offered by Farrington Enterprises Incorporated.
The Farrington family had supported the Dolgellau W.I cake competition for over forty years, with first Charles and then Douglas Farrington serving on the judging panel and presenting the trophies. It was a convenient community engagement for them, being only thirty miles from Farrington Towers.

The tradition had been continued by Dickie Page and the W.I was grateful for his donation of a £50 book voucher to the winning entry. In 2012, Dickie also funded a new set of shields and trophies.
However, when Joy wrote to Dickie early in the summer, asking if he'd once again agree to be a guest judge and sponsor, she mentioned without any assumption that it was the branch's fiftieth anniversary.
Joy had nearly fainted when she received a response. Not only would Dickie be delighted to take his usual place on the judging panel, but he would award £5,000 to the winner. When this was reported in the local newspaper, the W.I was flooded with membership applications. Initially, most were accepted, as they came from within the local community, as members had spread word of the prize before it made headlines. Within a week, the branch was receiving applications from people across Wales and beyond, all claiming to have an affiliation with Dolgellau.

Come the day of the competition, Joy, the branch President, was amazed by the standard of the entries. There was coffee cake, carrot cake, lemon cake, coconut cake, chocolate fudge cake, red velvet cake, chocolate mousse cake, strawberry cheesecake, Boston cream pie, black forest gateau and even pineapple upside down cake. And of course, Joy's own four-tiered, multi-jam Victoria sponge. Despite the fierce competition, Joy felt her cake was still the one to beat. However, she was not happy with Linda Thornbury. Linda had never shown any aptitude for baking

in six years as a W.I member and yet she'd produced a six-tiered layer cake with glazed icing and ornate, Indian-inspired decoration.
If Linda was declared the winner, Joy was prepared to call for an investigation into third party involvement.
It was approaching the time that the four-person judging panel would inspect the entries, which meant that Joy would have to find the unusual man who had declined to give his name. Instead, he insisted on being referred to as 'the Director'.
Like all the W.I members, she was saddened to hear that Dickie was unwell and couldn't attend. Joy was grateful that the Director had stepped in as a replacement at the eleventh hour, but he seemed disinterested.
Since he was introduced to Joy and other committee members, the Director had been tucked away inside a luxurious mobile command centre parked outside the village hall, where the W.I held the cake competition. Inside, the command centre, the Director was seething as he listened to the latest news bulletin on a major incident at Beacons Grange.
The Director was already regretting his decision to judge the cake competition.
He blamed Hisoka Saito.
The Director had ordered that a phone call be made to the Women's Institute to confirm that Dickie Page would, regretfully, be unable to attend and judge the cake competition. Of course, he'd opted not to tell them that

he'd murdered the old man and was planning on citing poor health for Dickie's absence.
However, Hisoka suggested that the Director step in to take Dickie's place on the judging panel, as the competition coincided with the Ashta squadron's attack at Beacons Grange.
"What better cover for the execution of two teenagers could you have?" he asked. "One hundred cake baking old ladies give you the perfect alibi!"
So, the Director agreed to attend, on the condition that he be kept informed of progress from the mobile command centre.

Mitchell Johnson had insisted that the assassins would carry out their duty with speed with stealth.
But things evidently hadn't gone to plan.
During its last transmission, the Ashta squad had identified Gary Morton heading towards the caretaker's cottage. Three of the motorcyclists had retreated to cover all conceivable exit points: The road leading to the school, a path that cut through woodland, and a small track across a field that linked to a disused railway line. With the approval of the Director, the other three motorcyclists had moved in on the cottage with the intention of executing all its occupants.
The Director was listening to events unfolding on the radio transmitter when Joy Hillier knocked on the door of the mobile centre.
"Cooey!" she said, seemingly oblivious to the presence of FPF guards as she stepped into the command centre.

"Just to let you know that entries are now being placed on the tables and tasting will begin shortly. Now, when it comes to judging, I tend to look for the cakes that are one hundred percent home-made. Some use off-the-shelf jam, which is fine of course. But I think it's good to reward those who make the extra effort, wouldn't you agree?"
"Jam, yes," replied the Director, who'd barely been listening and desperately wanted to return to his headset for the latest news.
"I have a couple of work issues to deal with and it must be done before the day's trading ends in Japan. Do you mind?" he said, leading Joy to the door.
"Not at all! Of course, they're a few hours ahead of us over there, aren't they? Funny place Japan, isn't it? They take a lot of photos, don't they, the Japanese? Not that I've ever been there."
"I'll be with you soon," said the Director, ignoring Joy as he closed the door firmly behind her.
She was startled by the door slamming and considered the Director rather rude.

Ten minutes later, the Director's mood had worsened. There had been no word from the three men sent in to carry out the assassinations. The three riders blocking exit roads had left the school undetected upon hearing sirens. They were unable to provide any update on the status of the Subject or Subject B.

The BBC's breaking news report had been vague. There were reports of gunfire and the first reporter on the scene had spoken to eye-witnesses in a frantic state of excitement.
Year 8 pupil Jenny Tewson said she looked out of her dormitory window to see three lawnmowers tearing across the school quadrant being chased by black motorbikes. One of them was pink and being driven by a girl with a tin on her head.
Sixth Former Stephen Amos said that the school's King George III statue had been blown to pieces.
Year 7 pupil Emily Offord had slept through it, but said that the night before, all the chocolate was stolen from the vending machine.
"What the hell is going on there, Johnson?" fumed the Director.
Mitchell had no answer. However, he had ordered the three members of Ashta that had returned to Farrington Towers to provide a full report. He had also sent out a reconnaissance unit to recover the three missing men and their equipment.
Joy knocked on the door for a second time.
"Cooey!" she said, smiling as she climbed the steps.
"Just to let you know that we're ready for judging. Now, there are so many entries that the committee thought it might be best if we pick the best one of each type of cake, as we know you're a busy man. Then you can just sample each one of the twelve finalists along with the other judges. Besides, they all start to taste the same after a while, especially cakes with glazed icing, which I must say doesn't

agree with me. It's so sweet and superficial, don't you think? But then, each to their own, as they say!"
"Yes, icing. Lovely!" said the Director.
He hadn't been listening.
"I'll be with you soon. Just a little hold up with the Japanese. It's like they're speaking another language!"
Joy laughed as the Director led her to the door.
"I do like those trees they make though," she waffled on. "The banzai trees. Oh, hang on, it's not banzai, is it? That's where they fly the planes into enemy ships, isn't it? Oh, my memory! What do they call them, those little trees?"
Joy was still talking as the door slammed shut.

An hour later, the news painted a confusing picture. Miraculously, no injuries had been reported among the pupils and staff at the school, although police had confirmed that there was evidence of sustained gunfire in several locations around the grounds.
The detective inspector suggested that there would surely have been fatalities had the incident occurred later in the day.
There was growing concern for two missing persons. Ralph Page, the caretaker, had not been seen since the incident and his cottage appeared to have been the initial focal point for the attack. Mr Page had worked at Beacons Grange for four years and was previously an award-winning landscape gardener.
Also missing was a fifteen-year-old pupil, Nadia Fisher, a promising tennis player.

Police could also confirm that two military-equipped motorcycles and two modified lawnmowers had been recovered from the scene. Three unidentified males had been transported to hospital with serious injuries under police guard.

While the Director had been glued to the news, Mitchell Johnson had been busy.
Just as vital information came in on a person of interest, he also received confirmation that FPF guards disguised as medical staff had recovered the three hospitalised members of Ashta. Maybe his luck was starting to turn.
"Good news, sir," he said to the Director. "We have retrieved all three guards before police could question them."
"None of this is good news!" replied the Director. "I believe the word you used was conspicuous! No, that's wrong. It was stealth. You said your men would operate with stealth. As in undetectable to radar. I'm certain that, if you look up stealth in the dictionary, Johnson, there will be little mention of firing machine guns whilst chasing lawnmowers along the corridors of the country's most famous boarding school!"
"Sir, things didn't go to plan. But we still…"
"Didn't go to plan?" interrupted the Director. "No, Johnson, things did not go to plan. I'm wondering how they could have gone any worse. I'm supposed to have at my disposal some of the finest ex-military personnel money can buy and your assassination squad is supposedly the crème

de la crème! Skilled in hand-to-hand combat, firearms, explosives, weapons, engineering and with advanced motorcycle riding tuition. But it appears they've been outfoxed by a girl riding a pink lawnmower, doesn't it?"

"Yes sir," said the humbled American. "But this isn't over yet."

The Director looked bemused.

"Well, of course it's not over! I'm hardly going to leave the matter at this far from satisfactory conclusion, am I?"

"No, sir."

"So, come on then," continued the Director. "You found Bin Laden in that raid that's so confidential that you've mentioned it to just about everyone you've ever met. Surely you have an idea as to where the Subject might be hiding now?"

"The most logical location would be the home of Subject B's foster parents," replied Mitchell.

"Excellent. Find them now and find out what they know."

"What if they know nothing?"

"I'm afraid they've caught me in a bad mood," said the Director. "No more mistakes. We clean up everything."

There was a knock on the door of the transportable command centre, before it flung open.

"Cooey!" said Joy, with less gusto.

She was becoming frustrated by the delays caused by their guest judge.

"Joy!" enthused the Director, as though he was pleased to see her. "I've dealt with the Japanese, so I'm ready for the tasting!"

"That's wonderful," replied Joy, relieved. "I know you're a man in great demand, but if we could do the judging now we'd all be grateful, as the photographer from the *Gazette* needs to go."
"Suits me fine," said the Director, as he marched purposefully into the village hall.
Joy struggled to keep up with him.
"All of the twelve finalists are on the far table," she said, scampering behind the Director. "The panel wasn't in agreement on all the entries. With some, it's a bit of a case of style over substance, if you know what I mean? But you'll see that the standard is very high. Of course, some of the sieved icing sugar on the sponge cakes has faded, owing to delays. Entrants weren't allowed to make any amendments to cakes once they'd been placed on the table, you see. However, if you did want to see a picture of the Victoria sponge when it looked its very best, I did ask the photographer to take a picture?"
The Director scanned the twelve cakes for five seconds.
"The winner is…that one!" he declared.
He hadn't even picked up a fork.
Linda Thornbury squealed with delight and hugged her friend, an Indian cake maker who'd been handing out business cards.
"But, we're supposed to discuss it!" pleaded Joy, trying to put on a brave face. "There are four judges on the panel and everyone's opinion is equal!"
"I don't have time for that," said the Director.

The Gazette photographer quickly placed Linda next to her winning cake, before calling in the Director to pose with a cheque for £5,000.

A few of the W.I members asked for Joy to be in the photo too, as she'd done so much to organise the event. But she'd disappeared. They didn't find her wiping away tears at the rear of the building.

The photographer snapped five quick shots and ran out of the door, as his editor rang his mobile for the fifth time to tell him to get his arse down to Beacons Grange or look for another job.

Chapter 42

Farmer Brian Cooper had no intention of firing his shotgun.
His gun was designed for shooting skeets, not people, as Brian was an accomplished clay pigeon shooter. Still, he'd happily wallop someone over the head with it if they'd broken into his property.
He made his way around the side of the farmhouse and towards the boiler room, where he saw the silhouette of a figure on their knees, scrubbing. He didn't notice the peculiar smell, as he lived on a farm and was used to such odours.
"What the hell are you doing, boy?"
Gary, petrified, looked up to see the barrel of a shotgun.
"Please, don't shoot me," he stammered for the second time that week. "I'm just cleaning my trousers. I'm so sorry. Please don't shoot!"
Brian lowered his gun.
"Have you soiled yourself?" he asked, disgusted.
"No! It's cow shit," answered Gary, apologetically. "I fell in it."
Brian groaned as he realised what the boy was using to clean the trousers.
"Bloody hell, that's a grooming brush. For horses! That's made of proper goat's hair. Cost me a small fortune!"
"I'm sorry," said Gary. "I'll pay you back!"

"Oh, don't worry," said Brian, lowering his gun. "What are you doing out here?"
Gary told Brian how he and his two friends had been walking for their Duke of Edinburgh Award. They'd pitched up a tent for the night, but then they heard noises outside. It was a lynx, which had escaped from the zoo. It urinated over the tent to mark its territory, so the three of them had to flee.
That was how they'd ended up at the farm.
"I see," said Brian. "Well, you'd best take me to your friends."
The two walked across the courtyard, with Gary holding his wet trousers over the front of his pants.
When Brian entered the barn, he saw Nadia and Warren breaking apart a bale of hay to make a soft bed.
"Right," said Brian, resting the gun by his side. "You two need to give me a better explanation for why you're here than the load of bloody nonsense I've just heard from this lad," said Brian, pointing at Gary. "Otherwise, I'm calling the police."
"I was just saying about the Duke of Edinburgh…" said Gary, shivering, before he was silenced by the farmer.
"Not another word from you! Escaped lynx, honestly! Now, I know something must have happened for three kids your age to be out here alone at night. So, tell me the truth and you never know, I might be able to help."
Warren stood up and looked the farmer in the eyes.
"My name is Warren Farrington. I escaped from my home at Farrington Towers two days ago. I've never been beyond

the perimeter wall before, but people seem to know about me and my family. I escaped as I was led to believe that my twin sister, Nadia, was in danger. Having found her, we now suspect it was a trick to place us both in the same location. We're being hunted by elite soldiers, probably working for the man employed to protect me. And here we are."

"And who's he?" asked Brian, nodding over to the boy who was turning blue from the cold.

"That's Gary Morton. He's a compulsive liar, as you've already discovered. He is travelling with us."

"We're mates!" butted in Gary, through chattering teeth.

"Well, we've not known each other long," shrugged Warren.

Brian Cooper looked at Warren.

"You look like your father, you know? In fact, you both do."

"You knew my father?"

"Yes, and I'll tell you all about that later," said Brian. "First, let's get you inside. I'll prepare the spare rooms and I'm going to run you a hot bath," he added, turning to Gary.

The old boiler couldn't produce enough hot water to fill the bath tub, so Brian filled up a kettle that had been in the family for fifty years, and put it on the stove.

Having twice emptied boiling water into the tub, he went back to the kitchen for a third time. One more refill should be enough, he thought.

As he awaited the kettle's whistle, Brian turned on the radio, just in time for a news bulletin.

A short time later, with Gary relaxing in the bath and his clean jeans drying on a cast iron radiator, Brian passed a cup of hot chocolate to a grateful Warren and Nadia. He talked about the days when he was a tenant farmer on Farrington land.
Brian was a fruit specialist and grew hundreds of varieties across the seasons. He'd sell raspberries, blackberries, strawberries, rhubarb, loganberries, elderberries, plums, pears, figs, honeyberries, you name it. People would come from far and wide to visit his farm shop.
Douglas Farrington charged him no rent. All that he asked for in return was a daily basket of fruit for the Towers.
Brian's sons had a great childhood, growing up in an old cottage with countryside to explore. But it all unravelled following Douglas' death. The farm was designated as poor agricultural ground and was closed.
Brian found work eventually, taking on a dairy farm in southern Wales. The hours were long, conditions were poor and the profit margins had been drastically reduced by the buying power of supermarkets.
His wife struggled to adapt and eventually packed her bags and left. There wasn't anyone else. She was just deeply unhappy. She got a good job in Liverpool and kept in contact. Brian still saw his children occasionally and was proud that his youngest son, Elliott, was keen to follow in his father's farming footsteps.
"I had a lot of time for your old man," said Brian, putting on a brave face while relaying painful memories. "He gave me and my family a good life for a long time."

"I'm so sorry for everything," said Warren. "I had no idea what was happening to the farms."
"I know that. It all came from that strange bloke. The Manager, or whatever he calls himself."
"The Director," answered Warren.
"That's him. Didn't even give me his proper name. Said the farm was unprofitable because it was unfertile, but that wasn't true. Far from it. It was good land. It still is. He did the same to a lot of farms across the estate. I think there's one or two left, run by tenant farmers who've spent their life savings taking the fight to court. But they'll be out soon too. Your dad though, he was a top bloke. If there's anything I can do for you in return, I'd be happy to help."
"Thank you," said Warren. "If this situation is ever resolved and I take over the estate, I will reinstate the farms."
Brian shook his head. "You're a good lad, but don't go saying things you don't mean."
"I mean it," said Warren, finishing the last drop of his first ever cup of hot chocolate. "That's a promise."
"Good, isn't it?" said Brian, noting Warren's enjoyment of the drink. "I added a touch of Irish cream as it just gives it a little kick! It'll help you sleep better too."
"Best drink I've ever had!"
"Before we head to bed, would you mind if I switch on the TV?" asked Nadia. "There must be something on the news about what happened earlier."
"I'm afraid I can't, my dear," replied Brian. "Doesn't work. Only plays VHS. Fancy a bit of fly fishing with John Wilson instead?"

"No thanks! Would you mind if I used your phone then?" asked Nadia. "My parents are going to be worried sick!"
Brian wasn't sure what to say. But he couldn't let Nadia pick up the phone.
Fortunately, Warren came to his rescue.
"I know they're going to be worried, Nadia, but we can't make that call," he said. "There's a chance that the Director or Fergus MacLean or whoever it is that's trying to kill us, will be monitoring calls made to your family. We might give away our location. We have to trust that Ralph will reach them."
Nadia reluctantly agreed, although she desperately wanted to let Gerald and Yvonne know she was safe and well.

Chapter 43

The following morning, after a good night's sleep, Warren found an unwrapped VHS cassette next to the TV.
He peeled away the transparent protective cover, made of regenerated cellulose, which he wouldn't have been allowed to go anywhere near at the Towers. A blank sticker slipped out.
He scribbled down 'Farrington Secret Files' on the sticker and put it over the label on the *John Wilson's Dream Fishing* video. He left it on the coffee table.
Warren hoped that, if the FPF were on his tail, they'd feel compelled to watch it.
After eating porridge for breakfast, sprinkled with enough sugar to have smashed Warren's daily calories limit, the four set off across the hills in Brian's Land Rover Series III, which his father had bought new in 1982. The Land Rover had never let Brian down. However, in no way could it be described as comfortable!
Gary complained incessantly as the vehicle bounced across the rough terrain. Nadia told him to stop whining and consequently had to pretend that her head didn't hurt after she knocked it against the roof as the vehicle leapt over a huge mound.
Brian was avoiding roads on Warren's advice. He couldn't recall ever having so much fun at the wheel and joked that, for once, a Land Rover was being used as it was built for;

crossing rivers and taking on rocks, rather than being used by suburban mums to pick their children up from school. After an hour, Gary could take no more and said he was going to be sick.

It was some relief to Nadia too. Pride prevented her from admitting it, but she was finding the journey every bit as awful.

"Bloody hell!" said Gary, as he jumped out the back. "My arse is killing me! Up and down, up and down. It was like being on a ship in one of them things with the massive waves. What are they called?"

"Tsunami?" suggested Warren.

"Toon Army?" laughed Gary. "Nice one! They're up and down all right! Up one year, relegated the next!"

Suddenly, Gary leaned over the stream.

"You're displaying all the symptoms of nausea inducing motion sickness." said Warren.

"I'll be okay. Just give us a minute."

After stretching her legs and having a drink, Nadia returned to the Land Rover, sitting in the front passenger seat. She looked at the radio. It was covered in dried mud, like the rest of the vehicle, but Nadia turned it on and fiddled with the frequency knob to see if she could pick up a transmission. As she raised the volume, Brian came running over.

"No, turn it off! The radio doesn't work!" he shouted.

"I think I can get it working," protested Nadia. "I was picking something up."

"You'll get nothing out here, I promise you that!"

"Honestly, I was getting a reception," argued Nadia. "Maybe it's clearing now we're out of the valley?"
"I'm telling you that the radio doesn't work!" insisted Brian, raising his voice and bringing about an uncomfortable silence.
But Nadia wasn't one for giving up easily.
"I don't want to come across as ungrateful, but what's going on, Mr Cooper? Last night, you wouldn't let us watch the news as you said the TV wasn't working, which looks suspicious when you have a current television licence stuck to your fridge with a promotional magnet from *Tractor Monthly* magazine."
"You didn't want Nadia to use the phone either, Mr Cooper," said Warren, backing up his sister. "I could sense your relief when I advised against making calls."
Brian Cooper twisted open the lid of his flask, sat down on a large rock and poured tea into the upturned lid.
Brian looked away from the twins. "When I was boiling the kettle last night, I had the radio on. I heard the news and I didn't want you to hear it. I've been trying to stop you hearing about what's happened."
"What's happened?" asked Nadia.
Brian wasn't sure if he could look Nadia in the eye, but he took a deep breath and faced her.
"Police said they were hunting for a girl missing from Beacons Grange. Said they were increasingly concerned for her welfare after they found…"
Brian's mouth suddenly felt too dry to speak.
"They found what?" said Nadia, her voice trembling.

"After they found the girl's parents..."
Brian Cooper's voiced tailed off.
"I'm so sorry."
Nadia's eyes filled with tears.
"Your parents were found dead at their home," said Brian, solemnly. "I don't know any more. I turned the radio off as I was worried you might walk in. I just didn't want you to hear about it like that. Didn't want you to hear it like this either."
Nadia walked a few yards to the edge of the stream and gazed out across the Brecon Beacons. She collapsed to the ground and her knees sank into the wet, moist grass.
Warren consoled her, but he didn't say anything. He just knelt too and allowed her to cry on his shoulder, even as the mud seeped through his trousers. For the first time in his life, he felt like somebody's brother.
Gary couldn't help but remember the time when he heard that his mother had died and quietly wiped away a tear too.
They might have stayed there in silence for hours, had it not been for a light buzzing noise. Nadia and Warren stood and listened as it grew louder. Then a drone appeared around the side of a hill, forty metres off the ground.
Warren was about to shout to the others to make for cover when he saw Brian pointing his gun into the air. Gary's natural inclination was to dive to the floor as the sound of a shotgun shattered the tranquillity of the countryside, before the drone crashed down on the rocks.
"Fair bit bigger than a clay pigeon," said Brian. "I'll pick those things out the sky blindfolded!"

"We'd best get moving," he added, as Warren and Gary piled into the back.
"Wait," said Nadia, drying her eyes. She walked up to the damaged drone and pulled off a fragment. "This is a tracking device. You wouldn't happen to have any strong tape in the Land Rover, would you?"
"Doesn't look like it," said Brian, having rummaged through the glove compartment.
Nadia put her hand through her hair. "Don't worry. I've got an idea."

Chapter 44

Ralph Page pedalled up to the 12ft high security gates obscuring a baroque-style mansion, typical of someone obsessed with all things German.

He pressed the button next to the gate and waited for a response. Anna's security guard checked the monitor, which displayed live images from each of the four cameras around the property. Through the darkness, he saw an elderly man slumped over the handlebars of his bicycle.

"I need to speak to Anna Kraus," said Ralph, talking into the speaker.

"What's the purpose of your visit?" came the response.

"To discuss the superiority of American oatmeal over healthier alternatives from Scotland," said Ralph.

He hoped Warren was right.

The gates slowly withdrew as Ralph pushed his bicycle up to the front door.

A suspicious Anna stayed hidden as her security guard, a gentle giant from southern Norway called Magnus, helped the exhausted cyclist into the lounge.

Ralph had been able to puff out enough information for Magnus to ascertain that he was Dickie Page's older brother and needed Anna's help to save the Farrington twins.

Convinced he was telling the truth, Anna walked into the lounge, having been listening close by.

"Thank you, Magnus, can you leave us for a moment?" she asked, politely.

"I'll put the kettle on, shall I?" suggested Magnus.
"Can you fetch a fresh bottle of mineral water too, please? I think that would be appreciated by our guest."
Magnus nodded before heading to the kitchen.
Ralph knew very little about Anna Kraus, although his brother had once written about her meticulous planning and remarked that she showed genuine affection for Warren's wellbeing. He hadn't mentioned how attractive she was, or that she spoke as quietly as a mouse.
Warren himself had spoken about her with warmth and felt that, aside from Dickie, she was the only person who disapproved of the extreme safety measures imposed upon him at Farrington Towers.
Anna waited patiently as Ralph took time to catch his breath. It had been three days since the extraordinary events at Farrington Towers, when Dickie had been killed for aiding Warren's escape. For his actions, Anna considered Dickie as nothing less than the greatest man she'd ever known. The following evening, the Director had terminated her employment at F.E.I with immediate effect.
Anna had no doubt that the morning's events at Beacons Grange, which she'd been following on the news, was linked to Warren's escape and that the young girl who was missing was also involved. Was she the second Farrington twin?
Magnus arrived with a tray.
"Anna insists on serving German coffee," he said. "It's quite a distinctive blend. Like most Berliners, Anna drinks it

black, but we have Kaffeesahne, if you prefer it white."
"Kaffeesahne?" queried Ralph.
"It's condensed milk from Germany. Anna is very loyal to her homeland. The food isn't as bad as people think, but the music is dreadful!"
"That's a sweeping generalisation!" smirked Anna, who was used to Magnus' teasing.
"And these?" asked Ralph, pointing to snake-shaped cookies half coated in chocolate.
"Spritzgebäck," replied Magnus. "A German cookie. A little dry for me, but Anna loves them."
"You clearly miss home," remarked Ralph, addressing Anna as he reluctantly took a bite of the cookie. Like most people, he had a negative perception of German cuisine.
"Perhaps she'll show you her secret room?" suggested Magnus. "It's a shrine to Anna's favourite personality from German history."
"Thank you, Magnus," interrupted Anna, clearly wishing to close that topic of conversation.
"If you need me, you know where I am," said Magnus, understanding the hint.

Over the course of the next hour, Anna listened intently as Ralph provided details of Nadia's life and the morning's events at Beacons Grange.
He took an immediate liking to Anna, although he suspected that there might be a darker side to her. Who was the subject of her shrine and why would she keep it hidden?

One thing was certain. His brother had trusted Anna Kraus. Warren trusted Anna Kraus. So, Ralph had to trust her as well. What were his options otherwise?

Early the next afternoon, an ambulance arrived at Anna's house. The blue lights were flashing, but the sirens were silent. The gates opened without the driver needing to press the buzzer.
Fifteen minutes later, two paramedics wheeled a stretcher back through the front door. On top was a body covered with a blue sheet.
Anna wiped away tears as the paramedics loaded the stretcher into the ambulance, before she climbed in too.
As the ambulance made its way through the gates and back on to the road, a man jogged up alongside it.
"Everything okay?" he asked. "I live a couple of doors away..."
"Nothing to worry about," replied the paramedic through the window. "An elderly gentleman suffered a heart attack. I'm afraid we were too late."
"That's terrible," said the jogger. "I'm sorry for holding you up."
After watching the ambulance disappear in the direction of the hospital, Stefano Gallo jogged to a car parked further down the road, just in view of Anna's house.
He radioed KR1.

Inside the ambulance, Ralph appeared from under the blue sheet. Anna thanked the paramedics for their assistance and

they expressed gratitude to Anna for her extremely generous contribution to the Ambulance Service.
Magnus suddenly appeared behind the ambulance in a dark black Range Rover with tinted windows. He looked in his mirror one more time and was satisfied that they weren't being followed. Having spent eight years with the Norwegian Intelligence Service, Magnus had been perfectly aware that Anna had been under surveillance since she'd been fired by the Director.
He flashed his lights and the ambulance pulled to the side of the road.
Anna hadn't doubted that Magnus' plan would succeed, but she was still relieved to be safely inside the Range Rover.
"Where are we heading then, Ralph?" asked Magnus.

Chapter 45

Brian Cooper gazed out of the window of The Cabin, a roadside café popular with truckers.
His young companions were each sat with a cup of hot chocolate, which came to a combined cost of £2.40.
Sheila, who had worked at the café for forty years, said she didn't know how some places got away with charging two pounds for a hot drink. "But folk flock to these places, don't they? All queuing up for chocolate sprinkles!" she said, shaking her head.
The children had eaten porridge, doused in sugar, at Brian's farmhouse, so weren't hungry. However, Brian had been tempted to order a full English breakfast as he'd seen one being served to a van driver, the only other customer.
"Your eggs look great!" remarked Brian, as Sheila placed the plate on the table.
"They ought to be!" piped up the van driver. "She's made a million of 'em!"
The van driver started chuckling as he loaded bacon, fried tomato and poached egg on to his fork, dunked it in a dollop of brown sauce and opened wide.
"Oi you! That's my line!" said Sheila, jokingly.
"Rick's in here all the time," she said to Brian. "Can't say we see many kids though."
"We're just passing through," said Brian, hesitantly.
Sheila called over her shoulder "No need to explain. I know who you are."

She squirted washing up liquid into a saucepan used for baked beans and ran it under the hot tap.
"Rick?" she called out, with her back to the seating area.
"Yes Sheila?"
'Would you mind just moving your truck further forward? That way, nobody can see the Land Rover from the main road."
"Why?" asked Rick.
"You heard about those kids they're after?" she said. "The ones missing after the shoot-out at the school?"
"Oh, that's you lot, is it?" smirked Rick, as he wrapped a rasher of bacon inside a piece of bread and butter and stuffed it in his mouth.
"Course I can!" he said, wiping his greasy fingers on his trousers while still chomping.
Rick rose from his seat, shuffled out as quickly as his nineteen-stone frame would allow and climbed into his van, which belonged to a garden ornaments company.
Sheila noticed the horrified look on Nadia's face as she watched Rick walk outside.
"He's actually lost a bit of weight, believe it or not!" said Sheila as she put some fresh oil in a frying pan and threw on three rashers of bacon. "That's why half his arse is hanging out of his trousers!"
Warren looked at Brian intently.
"We can't stay here," he said.
"Nonsense!" said Sheila, who overheard. "You can and you will! Ralph knows you're here and he's on his way. So, sit down and drink your hot chocolate! And you?" she said,

turning to face Gary. "I know you said you've had breakfast, but I've seen lettuce with more meat on it, so I'm cooking you up a bacon butty and I'll hear no quarrel about it!"
"You know Ralph?" asked Warren.
"You could say that," she replied, without explanation. "He told me to look after you until he arrives."
"Ralph is coming then?"
Warren was relieved. This was the spot where he'd agreed to meet the Ralph, but he didn't say exactly when.
"He won't be long," said Sheila, buttering a slice of bread. "Brown sauce or ketchup?"
"Ketchup would be great!" beamed Gary.
"Coming right up," she said, as Rick strutted back into The Cabin.
"Right," he said, pulling up his trousers again. "Put the kettle back on, Sheila! I'll wait until this old boy shows up before heading off. Quiet day anyway."
"Give me one minute," she said, in the manner of someone used to doing several things at once.
Rick settled down with *The Daily Sport,* pretending not to look at a photograph of a topless model.
"Sir," said Warren, approaching Rick.
Rick looked up from his tabloid, wondering if he'd ever been addressed as 'sir' in his entire life. He gazed at the nervous boy stood before him.
"If you've heard the news, you'll know that we're being chased?"

"Lunatics on motorbikes with machine guns, I heard," replied Rick.
"That's right. And when Ralph gets here, we need to keep where we're going and who we're with a secret, if you understand my meaning?"
"And you don't think I can keep my mouth shut?" replied Rick, offended.
"I don't think that," said Warren. "I was just asking…"
Rick scratched his chin and looked thoughtful.
"Three kids? Sure officer, they were in here early this morning," said Rick, talking to nobody in particular. "They sat over there, by the door. Don't see many kids in here. These kids asked me where I was going. They wanted to get out of the country and asked if anyone could help. I said I only do national routes. They offered me cash if I'd take them to Fishguard, but I wanted nothing to do with it. They ended up jumping in with a guy who'd done a drop near Swansea. Where was that bloke from, Sheila? Was he Belgian?"
"Dutch!" she replied, while wiping a table with a sponge. "His truck was orange!"
"Not all Dutch trucks are orange, Sheila!" said Rick, rolling his eyes.
"I thought they always did orange, the Dutch?" she said, like a confused old lady. "The football team plays in orange. Well, they did in the seventies, I know that much."
"I used to drive a TNT truck and that's orange and I'm not from bloody Holland!"

“Well, I thought he was Dutch!” said Sheila. “How do I know? I was busy! Anyway, they were definitely trying to get to port.”
Rick stopped the charade and looked up at Warren.
“That good enough for you?”
“Remarkable! You’ve done this before then?”
“Once or twice,” replied Rick nonchalantly, returning to his newspaper as Sheila brought out a bacon sandwich and placed it in front of Gary.
“That one’s on the house.”
An hour later, a dark black Range Rover with tinted windows pulled up alongside Brian Cooper’s Land Rover. The tall, blonde haired man behind the wheel didn’t move, but the back door opened and out stepped Ralph Page. Warren was amazed to see him walk in to The Cabin with Anna Kraus.
Warren didn’t know what was going on, but he started to feel a little better about his survival prospects.

Chapter 46

"Who the bloody hell is Nena?" asked Gary.
"A German singer," replied Anna. "One of the greatest pop stars of the 1980s."
"Listen lady, I don't mean to be rude, but have you got anything that isn't German?" asked Gary, as he heard a rock ballad playing through the speakers. "I mean, no offence, but this is shite."
Anna looked wide-eyed at her young guest.
"Exactly how am I not supposed to take offence to such a slur on an icon of my homeland?"
Anna had led her guests into a secret room, accessed via a hidden entrance in the hallway of her home. Having heard that Anna had a room dedicated to her favourite historical icon, Gary, much like Ralph, had been apprehensive about seeing it. It was a relief that it didn't contain anything sinister, aside from the saxophone solo blasting out from the room's four speakers.
"What is that?" groaned Gary, with his hands over his ears.
"That's the title track from *Question Mark*, or *Fragezeichen*, the second studio album by Nena," said Anna. "I love Nena. I went to see them perform their first single, *Nur Getraumt*, on *Musikladen*, which is very much like your *Top of the Pops*."
The room was full of Nena memorabilia, with outfits, records, posters, ticket stubs, musical instruments and even framed T-shirts hanging on the wall.

Anna walked towards a black leather jacket in a mahogany frame, stopped and stroked the glass.
"This is the very jacket that Nena wore in the original video for *99 Luftballons*. But this is my favourite item," she continued, gazing lovingly at a framed vinyl record.
"It's a limited edition first release of *Ecstasy* by The Stripes, the group Nena sang with before forming her own band. It's priceless to me. I believe I have the world's most extensive collection of Nena memorabilia, although there is a café in the guitarist's home town that has the roller boots featured in the video for *Irgendwie, Irgendwo, Irgendwann* in 1984 and the synth keyboard played by Uwe Fahrenkrog-Petersen when they recorded *Kino*."
"Why's there a gas mask?" asked Nadia.
"The promotional video for *99 Luftballons* was filmed at a Dutch military camp. There were some explosions but it all got a bit out of control and Nena wore this exact mask when the smoke became too thick."
"You're weird!" said Gary.
"This is all fascinating, Anna," said Ralph. "But we really need to be cracking on."
"Of course," said Anna. "I'll turn the music off, although anyone entering the house would not be able to hear it. The walls are sound-proofed and there is no way to see in here from the outside, so we are quite safe."

In the hallway, posters of famous Germans were framed and displayed. Anna had more than two hundred in her collection, although most were in storage, as there was only room for twenty on the wall.

She rotated some on an annual basis, ensuring an even split between men and women. Among the ten females were Anne Frank, Marlene Dietrich and Sophie Scholl, while the ten males included Michael Schumacher, Oskar Schindler and Johann Sebastian Bach.

In such company, Gabriele Susanne Kerner, better known as Nena, seemed out of place. But the pop star's poster was the only one never altered, as it concealed the entrance to the underground shrine.

After a history lesson on one of the biggest German pop groups of the mid-1980s, the six-strong group of Anna, Magnus, Ralph, Warren, Nadia and Gary spent the day engrossed in research. Anna had two old laptops, which she had given to Warren and Nadia to use, whilst she worked from an iMac as the Nena room was transformed in to a miniature control centre. Magnus was using his own laptop to aid in the complex research.

Some of the group sat around a glass top table which protected and displayed a selection of Nena records, on seats accessorised with red balloon-shaped cushions.

After five hours of scouring newspaper archives, family history websites, electoral rolls, maritime records and worldwide health data, the team had unearthed startling information.

"Okay everyone," said Ralph, as he briefly halted the research. "We've found several more fascinating accounts that strengthen our case. There's no doubt about it, the

MacLean family have been targeting the Farrington family for generations."
Ralph had set up a family tree on a large sheet of paper and taped it to the wall, in a spot where Anna had temporarily removed a guitar once played by Jürgen Dehmel, Nena's bassist.
The sheet of paper was in fact the back of a hand-signed poster of German tennis player Tommy Haas. His career hadn't quite panned out in a way that might earn him a position on the hall of fame, so the poster was sacrificed. However, Steffi Graf ensured tennis was represented in the hallway.
The aim of the group's research was to find out all they could about Fergus MacLean. Who is he? What is his background? Where is he now?
The obvious place to start had been Cameron MacLean, as it was the one documented link between the Farrington and MacLean families.
The death of Douglas Farrington had been widely reported in the media, both nationally and internationally. Ralph felt that Warren and Nadia should be tasked with a different aspect of the group's research, as he was aware that photos of Douglas being swarmed by bees while blood spurted out of his body were widely available on the internet. Instead, it was Anna who investigated the circumstances in detail.
She discovered that, whilst Cameron was only charged with causing death by dangerous driving, there was some evidence to suggest premeditation. At the inquest, the coroner remarked that it was unusual to transport estate

agency boards without securing them properly. MacLean's business partner, Ted Hawfinch, confirmed that on every other occasion, Mr MacLean had secured all boards during transportation.

One local newspaper published a picture of Cameron, taken several months before Douglas' death, when his estate agency was photographed after winning an inter-business bowling competition. Anna noticed a distinctive logo on Cameron's T-shirt. She was amazed to discover the logo was designed for the Canadian round of the 2002 World Motocross Championship.

So, he was also present when Tara Farrington was decapitated by a tree, supposedly felled by a beaver.

Scanning through documents relating to the criminal charges filed against him after Douglas' death, Anna came across a copy of Cameron's employment record. He had spent a year working in the sorting office at the Royal Mail from November 2002. That meant he could conceivably have been involved in planting the black widow spider inside Kala Farrington's didgeridoo.

Prior to that, he had worked for several small firms including a beachwear firm, which filed accounts with Companies House between 1997 – 2000. From the list of creditors named by the administrators when *Lenny's Beachwear* went into liquidation, it appeared the shop sold everything from flip-flops and beach towels to dinghies and inflatable orcas.

Cameron's name came up in a search on the British Newspaper Archive website. The *Isle of Wight County Press* of

21 May 1999 reported on a court appearance of Leonard Gillett, who had been fined by the local authority for contravening health and safety regulations. He had failed to properly secure several inflatable items for sale outside his shop, *Lenny's Beachwear,* which had led to the tragic death of Phoebe Farrington. Many other inflatables were seen blowing away, including a crocodile, dolphin and a Nemo clown fish.

After a short hearing, the charge was dropped as the Crown Prosecution Service agreed that Mr Gillett had given reasonable instructions to his assistant, Cameron MacLean. Mr MacLean had promptly disappeared after the fatality.

It was too much of a coincidence. The evidence pointed to Cameron being a serial killer.

But why was he hell-bent on wiping out the Farringtons?

Ralph gave Nadia and Warren the job of researching the history of his father, Hamish MacLean.

As Nadia had extensive experience with computers, whereas Warren's access had been strictly limited to heavily monitored use for educational purposes only, she took the lead.

Hamish's name cropped up in several science journals and periodicals. In an article published in *New Scientist* in 1987, Hamish MacLean was named as the lead scientist on a privately-funded expedition to the Antarctic. This was shortly after Charles Farrington announced plans for his own trip.

Six months later, Charles Farrington was dead. While the tabloids focused on the unfortunate manner of his demise,

scientific journals published the extraordinary results of his research.
Farrington's claims were universally approval. MacLean's own theories were considered as ill-conceived by his peers and his key research paper on climate change was ridiculed. Hamish's name didn't come up again in esteemed periodicals.
Nadia discovered that on the day Farrington was awarded a posthumous Nobel prize, Hamish died of an acute myocardial infarction, or heart attack, leaving heavy debts to Cameron, his only surviving son.
There was a second son, Hamilton, but he had disappeared on a school trip when he was twelve.
Gary, who was still nursing a sore bottom from the Land Rover experience, was asked to dig up any information on Hamilton MacLean, using Anna's smartphone. He made a half-hearted effort after checking to see how Liverpool had fared in their midweek game.
He found many newspaper articles, as there was a week-long manhunt for Hamilton involving hundreds of police officers and thousands of volunteers. All that was found were fragments of clothing and his favourite bear, near the bottom of a waterfall.
However, the disappearance and presumed death of Hamilton didn't appear to have any significance with regards to the emerging picture; that the Farrington family had unknowingly been the nemesis of the MacLean family for a very long time.

Genealogy websites led the group to Hamish's father, Gavin MacLean. In the months leading up to his death at the age of thirty-two, Gavin had been on the payroll of a logging company in the Brazilian state of Para. His place of death was recorded as a hospital in northern Brazil, where he perished from an infectious wound.

The fact that his death came only days after that of Ernest Farrington in a wood chipping machine in the rainforest nearby added to the compelling case against the MacLeans. Ralph was so convinced of a long-running saga that he was simultaneously investigating the circumstances behind the death of Ernest's father, George Farrington.

Ralph was a keen historian and like his brother, he knew the names of heroic RAF pilots, including George. Despite his personal interest, he'd never taken the time to find out the names of the three Luftwaffe pilots that had engaged George in a fierce battle on that fateful day in 1940.

Ralph visited the website of the British Forces Records, finding Farrington's name amongst the 1,300,000 archives. He then cross-referenced the incident with The Deutsche Dienststelle (WASt), a German government agency which maintains records of those who served in the Heer (army), the Kriegsmarine (navy) and the Luftwaffe (air force) during the Second World War.

It was no great shock to find the name Angus MacLean, a British Nazi sympathiser, listed among the three pilots. Indeed, it had been MacLean's plane that had been credited as firing the shot that downed Farrington's Spitfire and

would subsequently crash land on top of the ambulance transporting him to hospital.
Documents held by the WASt gave details of Angus' previous employment. They were thorough, as the Germans suspected some in the British Free Corps of being spies. The documents revealed that Angus had worked as a security guard at the British Museum, during the period that Stephanie Farrington died under a collapsing Tyrannosaurus Rex.

As the day progressed, as did the scale and longevity of the MacLean family's murderous campaign.
Tributes to Stanley Farrington hailed his expertise as a mountaineer, but there appeared to be no link to a MacLean until Magnus found a report in *Illustrated London News.* It published a photo of Farrington's support crew as they returned to port at Portsmouth. One of the men had the name 'MacLean' stitched into his rucksack, under the cross of St Andrew. Family ancestry records suggested that this man was Iain MacLean.
Magnus tried to unearth more details about Iain's life. The trail led to the St John's Authority Port off the tip of Newfoundland, Canada. The port recorded a missing vessel on the same night as the sinking of the Titanic in 1912, which was also the night Egbert Farrington had died.
Few details were known about the two-man crew, captained by Iain MacLean, who had identified himself to the harbour master during an authorised departure. Maritime documents reveal that he was transporting drilling equipment. No

distress signal had been received, but the vessel was never recorded again.
Ralph suspected that Iain had set off with the intention of sabotaging Egbert Farrington's efforts to lay deep sea communication cables. Could his actions possibly have also impacted the trans-Atlantic crossing of the Titanic?
The group struggled to find information going back any further, although there was one advertisement of interest in a newspaper reporting the death of Gertrude Farrington in 1826.
Gertrude had been to South East Asia, visiting Malacca, Penang and Singapore to sign key trade deals. Shortly after her return, she was found dead with a weathervane lodged in her skull. The police didn't suspect foul play, but Nadia believed she knew who was responsible. An ironmonger with a shop close to Gertrude's house had placed an advert in the same edition of the newspaper. He sold everything from door handles to blacksmith nails and had a fine selection of weathervanes.
The name of the ironmonger? Calum MacLean.
Nadia then found a record of the death of Gregor MacLean in a South African prison in 1899. Gregor had been jailed for his role in a mining accident which had resulted in the death of Richard Farrington.
With everyone else in the team occupied, aside from Gary, who was reading football transfer gossip, Ralph had investigated the story of John Farrington, who had been pierced through the heart by a statue on a pirate ship's bowsprit.

Ralph focused his research on the British sailors of the merchant navy who had been captured by the pirate, Ching Shih. He was particularly interested in the sailor who had turned traitor.
The National Archives at Kew Gardens holds records going back to the 17th century of naval personnel who received the death sentence for mutiny, as well as those who were court marshalled.
In 1810, after a long journey back from the far east, seven sailors previously held captive were present at a posthumous hearing into the actions of boatswain Lachlan MacLean.

"*Word had reached Britain of the death of the traitorous Mr MacLean,*" said Ralph, reading the sworn testimony of one of the sailors.
"*We believe that Ching Shih killed him with her own sword, before hanging him in full visibility of passing ships. This was not intended as a warning to the East India Company, but as a demonstration of power to those serving in the Red Fleet, her army of thieves which dominates the seas off China.*
It was - and I hope shall forever remain - the only occasion when the demise of a fellow sailor filled me not with sadness, but satisfaction. For Lachlan MacLean was a most loathsome individual. He was a man who had forsaken friendship, loyalty and his King for personal wealth.
MacLean boasted about the riches lavished upon him as we were tied up and forced to sleep on a stone floor without food or water, while

Madame Ching's ships plundered from British merchant vessels, thanks to secretive trade information he had provided.
Moments before we were rescued by the heroic John Farrington, MacLean had been preparing dumplings coated in gu, a Chinese poison made from the toxins of five deadly animals. He had intended to force us to eat them.
It wasn't until we had returned to England that news reached us of Farrington's tragic death. If the reports are accurate, Farrington was statuesque as Madame Ching attacked his launch. Consequently, he was speared through the heart by a sea goddess statue on the pirate ship's bowsprit.
I hear on the streets, people talking about evil spirits. No doubt, the false claims of a curse made by our murderous captor Lachlan MacLean have been twisted and mistaken for a truth. Perhaps it makes for a more interesting story for the drunkards to spread in the taverns, for the ears of those who perceive China as a mystical land of magic and wonder.
MacLean did indeed claim that the jade dragon retrieved by Farrington was inflicted with a curse, but he did not speak the truth. All seven of us surviving captive sailors witnessed MacLean being handed the ornament by Ching Shih herself. She only said it was an artefact of great historical importance and made no reference to mystical powers.
It is my opinion that our rescuer, John Farrington, was in fact poisoned. Poisoned by a dumpling hidden in his pocket by the wickedly cunning Lachlan MacLean."

Chapter 47

"So, you're not cursed then?" asked Gary.
"The evidence suggests otherwise, don't you think?" sighed Warren.
"Told you!"
They had taken a break from researching, partly to allow Warren and Nadia an opportunity to absorb some of what they'd learned.
"Good news though, eh?" Gary continued. "About the curse, I mean?"
"Not sure about good news," replied Warren. "It's certainly a positive that it's not necessarily my destiny to suffer a grisly death because of a cursed Chinese ornament. On the other hand, it's depressing to discover that generations of your family, including your own mother and father, have been murdered by people they never knew existed. Also, from an entirely selfish perspective, it's frustrating to find that I myself have lived an unnecessary life of solitude. So, from that point of view, not necessarily good news."
"Well, no," said Gary. "Not when you put it like that."
Nadia struggled to form an emotional connection with the Farrington men and women she had read about.
She could sense Warren's growing bitterness at the realisation that his entire life had been a pointless charade. However, her own thoughts were on the people she considered to be her true mother and father; Gerald and Yvonne Fisher.

Not one to be cooped up all day in front of a computer, Magnus had embarked on his regular afternoon run.
Upon his return, he reported that there was no sign of an FPF surveillance unit. So, they were all okay to come out of the Nena room for a break, so long as they kept the blinds closed and stayed in the kitchen, out of sight of the two cameras Magnus had spotted in the trees surrounding the house.
Nadia was perched on a long, oak worktop in the kitchen. She felt tired, although she wondered how she could possibly sleep after all that had happened?
Ralph, Anna, Magnus and Warren made their way back down to the Nena room with a tray of drinks and snacks. Gary found himself alone in the kitchen with Nadia.
He was pretending to enjoy a snack that Anna had served. It was speculaas, a type of shortbread that looked delicious, not least because the biscuits were shaped like elephants. But they were too spicy for Gary's palate. He was desperately looking for a place to spit it out without Nadia seeing.
As far as Gary was concerned, his efforts in churning out the soggy mush into a tissue whilst pretending to blow his nose had worked brilliantly, but Nadia knew exactly what he'd done.
Not that she cared.
Gary was nervous. He knew he hadn't said the right thing to Nadia on a single occasion in the short time that he'd

known her. He also understood he was probably incapable of finding the right words in the current situation.
Still, he felt he should at least try.
He saw a few bottles on the side, most of which had German labels on. There was Bärenjäger honey liqueur and Kuemmerling, as well as a bottle of Bailey's Irish cream.
This gave Gary an idea. He started going through Anna's cupboards and pulled out a tub of milkshake powder. Then he went looking for the fridge freezer, which was concealed within units matching the rest of the kitchen, something he'd never seen before, except on TV.
He grabbed the milk from the fridge and in the freezer found a tub of vanilla ice cream. He scooped out two lumps and dropped them into a blender, along with several teaspoons of milkshake powder, milk and a generous splash of Bailey's.
"What are you doing?" said Nadia, covering her ears.
"Just making milkshake!" he replied loudly, compensating for the noise. After twenty seconds, he switched the blender off and poured the milkshake into two glasses.
"This is one of my specialities."
"Let me guess," mocked Nadia. "You won the bartender of the year competition? No wait, you invented milkshake?"
"My mum showed me how to do it," said Gary.
"Sorry," said Nadia. "Didn't mean to be nasty. Bad day, that's all."
"Try it," he said, passing a glass to Nadia. "Mum would make this for me as a special treat. She wouldn't put as

much Bailey's in as I have though, especially when I was really little."
"I doubt that your mum added any whisky at all when you were little!" said Nadia.
"Not whiskey! It was Irish cream, like this."
Nadia laughed. "This is whiskey, Gary! I think your mum made this for you when you needed a good night's sleep. Or when she needed a good night's sleep!"
Gary read the label.
"Frigging hell! Well, like they say, you learn something new every year! So, what do you think?"
Nadia took a sip and wiped away a frothy moustache. She had to admit, it tasted divine.
Gary was beaming with pride. "Don't mean to sound rude or nothing, but my mum once told me this would help me pick up girls!"
Nadia wasn't offended. "Do you miss her?"
"Like crazy," replied Gary. "She'd be dead chuffed you like the milkshake."
"Dead chuffed?" said Nadia, raising one eyebrow.
Gary frowned. "Never were too good with words."
Nadia laughed, before realising he hadn't made the grammatical mistake deliberately.
"What were they like?" asked Gary. "Your folks, I mean."
Nadia shrugged. "I don't know. Just normal, you know?"
"When I think about my mum, one time always pops in my head," said Gary. "When I were little, I got hold of some red paint. Nicked it from school. One night, I painted the Liverpool badge on a wall near my house. I know it sounds

daft, but I thought it looked great! Anyway, turned out this wall was the side of some bloke's house and he comes banging on my door. Says he knows it were me and that he was calling the police because it was paramount to vandalism."

"Tantamount," corrected Nadia.

"Right!" said Gary. "Anyway, turned out he was a bloody Everton fan and he thought I was taking the piss. But I never meant that. My mum though, she tells him to his face that it can't have been me, as I'd been out shopping with her all day. I reckon she's where I get my lying gene from. So, I think I got away with it right? But later, she dragged me outside with a couple of sponges and made me scrub the whole thing off the wall. Learnt my lesson, you know? Makes me feel better thinking about it. If only for a bit."

Nadia smiled as she recalled a moment she hadn't thought about for a long time.

"At the end of the school year, Beacons Grange hosts a big awards gala. All the nominees and the parents dress up in ball gowns and tuxedos, all wanting to look their best. When I was in Year 7, I was nominated in a few categories, so I was invited. Mum looked so beautiful that night. When we walked into the dining hall, people were wearing pearl necklaces and designer dresses. But it was my mum who turned everyone's head. Dad, on the other hand, didn't even own a suit. He didn't want to spend money he didn't have just for one night. So, he bought this suit from a charity shop which was way too tight and had ridiculously big shoulder pads. Mum thought it was hilarious."

Nadia took another sip of her milkshake.
"We found ourselves chatting in a group which included Lyndon Anderson. His son, Archie, was the boys' sports captain and the worst kind of privileged bully. Anyway, straight away, Lyndon pokes my dad's shoulder pads. *'Tell me who fitted that suit Gerald, and I'll call my lawyer!'* he said. Some of the other dads fell about laughing as Lyndon Anderson is loaded, so they think they should. My dad would never have done anything to embarrass me, so he just smiled. But my mum wasn't having it. She had this mischievous look.
'That's one of the problems Gerald has, I'm afraid,' she said. *'He's always in his workshop, hammering and welding for hours. The result of all that manual labour is this incredible, muscular frame.'*
"She grabbed Lyndon's hands. *'Most suits are made for people with soft hands who work in offices all day counting money. What do you do, Lyndon?'* she said. *'I'm a senior partner at Anderson & Wilkinson Financial Management Solutions,"* he said, like he royalty. My mum looked like she felt sorry for him. *'Well, I suppose one good thing about that is you can easily find suits to fit your tender frame,'* she said. *'But that's not so easy with my Gerald with these biceps! And the thing is, Lyndon, in my experience, all that hard work tends to pay off in other departments, if you know what I mean?'*
"Then she went in for the kill. *'I like a real man and you'll find most women would say the same. I would ask your wife, but she's over there chatting up the waiter. She does know that he's only a Sixth Former, doesn't she?'* And with that, she took my dad's hand."
Nadia was embarrassed when she realised she had tears in her eyes, but she was smiling too.

"It gets easier you know?" said Gary. "As time goes by."
"Yeah?" sniffed Nadia.
"The day my mum died, I was at the hospital. I remember the nurse coming out to see me. And I knew what she was going to say, just by the way she tilted her head and smiled in that weird way nurses do, like they've got bad news but let's pretend it's all going to be okay. When she said it, it felt like my heart was screaming. It wasn't making a noise, but it felt like it was and I thought that the whole world could hear it. That probably doesn't make any sense. Anyway, it's not so bad now. It still hurts. But not so much."
"Do you think she's watching over you?" asked Nadia.
"I don't know. Sometimes I lie in my bed and I ask her to send me a sign, just to let me know she's there, watching me. Then nothing happens and I think she's gone forever and I'm on my own. Then other times, like just now, it's like she's talking to me, telling me when I've poured enough milk in the blender. And I don't feel like I need a sign at all. Anyway, I just wanted to check you were okay. Not that anything I say will help."
"Strangely, I think it has," said Nadia.
She touched his hand, briefly but tenderly. "Thank you."

Chapter 48

It had been a humbling few days for Stefano Gallo and Frank Stone.

They'd been humiliated by a teenager who had first escaped the world's most guarded property from right under their nose and later deprived them of their weapons and uniform, leaving them stranded in the middle of a lake.

It was a relief for both men to discover, during a meeting of security personnel that every member of the FPF was ordered to attend, that they were not the only ones who'd been made to look foolish. Mitchell Johnson's ego had also been bruised by successive embarrassments.

Even the excitement caused by the shooting down of a drone had only led to more frustration.

As Mitchell explained during the meeting, an FPF drone had picked up a Land Rover travelling across wild terrain. In its last transmission, the drone recorded footage of the Subject with Gary Morton, as well as an adult male who took aim with a shotgun just before the camera feed was lost. However, the tracking device was still operating and moving slowly through a nearby field.

Mitchell hoped that either the drone was still in operation, or was now in the possession of the Subject.

When an FPF unit reached the location an hour later, guards found that the tracking device had been attached to the tail of a cow. It was held in place by a girl's hairband.

Unfortunately for the Head of Security, the day was to get even worse.

Three FPF units arrived at Brian Cooper's dairy. It hadn't taken long to find an address for the registered owner of the Land Rover after the drone had recorded the number plate. The guards found evidence that several people had eaten and slept at the farm and tyre tracks were found heading into the hills.

There was no clue as to where they could be heading. However, there was a VHS cassette that the guards thought could shed light on the Subject's next move.

They scribbled down many notes in case the video contained cryptic information. Their optimism started to waver during episode two, in which fisherman John Wilson visited the Scottish Highlands to catch three types of common skate in the saltwater lochs. Two guards spent three hours watching six episodes before Mitchell Johnson finally accepted that it had been a time-wasting trick conjured by a cunning young opponent he had seriously underestimated.

The primary person of interest became Brian Cooper. The registration plate of his vehicle was circulated amongst the FPF and technical specialists had gained access to highway cameras in a bid to trace him.

Stefano and Frank were given a different assignment. It was low on the list of priorities, leaving them in no doubt as to how the Head of Security felt about their professional conduct over recent days.

Their job was to take over surveillance of Anna Kraus.

It was considered unlikely that the Subject would attempt to contact the recently fired Head of Lifestyle and Education. However, FPF unit F2, which had been staking out Anna's home for two days before being re-assigned, did report one interesting development.

On their last night of surveillance, F2b had seen an old man matching Ralph Page's description arrive by bicycle at the property. Anna Kraus' security guard had helped the cyclist inside.

Frank and Stefano arrived in Anna's neighbourhood.

As several hours had passed since F2 had ended surveillance, Stefano thought it wise to jog around the block, to gain an insight into the layout of Anna's property and its exit points.

Frank stayed in the surveillance car, an unremarkable Ford Mondeo, happy to let his more physically fit partner do the leg work.

Within minutes of parking up, Frank was surprised to see an ambulance approaching in his mirrors. It passed Stefano while he was on his second jog around the block. On his third circuit, he saw the ambulance exiting Anna's driveway. Timing his movements to perfection, he jogged on the spot before running up alongside the emergency vehicle. The paramedic wound down his window and Stefano asked what had happened.

An old man had passed away from a heart attack.

Stefano jogged to the Mondeo and immediately informed KR1 of Ralph Page's possible demise, before sitting patiently for several hours.
But Stefano couldn't shake the feeling that something wasn't right. Wasn't it odd that the paramedic would reveal details of someone's condition to a passing jogger? And where was Anna Kraus' Range Rover? Had the security guard taken it out while the house wasn't under surveillance?
Frank initially thought Stefano was worrying about nothing. Indeed, everything seemed to be in order when Anna Kraus and her security guard arrived back home in the Range Rover, presumably from the hospital.
But Frank was just as suspicious as his partner when a delivery arrived at the property a few minutes later.
A white van pulled up with what appeared to be four garden statues loaded in the back. They were heavily protected by bubble wrap and cellophane. The two FPF guards couldn't quite make them out through the live feed from a camera hidden in a tree overlooking Anna's property. But three appeared to be life size figurines and the other depicted an animal, as it was standing on four legs.
The Scandinavian-looking security guard picked up the figurines one at a time and took them inside the house. He was helped by the delivery driver, who must have been almost twenty stone and kept having to pull his trousers up.
Frank took his spaniel, Bandit, out for a walk and tried to cross in front of the garden ornaments delivery truck as it exited Anna's property, hoping to initiate a chat in the same

way Stefano had done with the paramedic. But the driver ignored him and carried on up the road.
"We need to go to the hospital," said Stefano, as Frank and Bandit returned to the Mondeo.
"Why?" replied Frank.
"To find out about that body. We need to confirm it's Ralph Page. Otherwise, we're working on assumption."
"Okay," agreed Frank. "You go to the hospital; I'll take Bandit round the block again and maintain surveillance."
Frank leant back and shook Bandit lovingly.
"I'm sorry, old boy! But we've got to go out again."
Bandit rolled over and snuggled into a blanket that had been put down to prevent the Mondeo getting covered in dog hair.
"Oh boy, I know you're tired!" Frank said, soppily. "Last time, I promise!"
He put on a tweed jacket and flat cap and set off with an exhausted Bandit. He walked twice around the block and was having to pull on the lead as Bandit became increasingly reluctant to move.
Just as Frank was starting to wonder what was taking his partner so long, his mobile rang.
"We've got a real problem," said F8b.

There was no dead body.
Stefano had found that out himself. The paramedic he'd spoken to that morning had spilled the beans, before Stefano had left him unconscious on a stretcher in the back of his own ambulance.

Frank shook his head. Once again, they'd been tricked, this time by an old gardener.
"How are we going to explain this to the Director? He already thinks we're incompetent."
But Stefano wasn't ready to make the call to KR1. He wanted to investigate further. He called the garden ornaments company, having taken down the number from the side of the van. He pretended to be an angry customer, complaining that one of the statues delivered to Anna Kraus' address was broken.
He wasn't surprised to be informed by the helpful secretary that she had no record of a delivery to that address. She suggested that Rick, the driver, was probably doing a favour for one of his mates down at *The Cabin.*
So, that was where they headed.
Frank and Stefano made for convincing truck drivers as they sat down for a bacon butty and a cup of tea. They even bought a Kit-Kat for the road and made a big deal out of putting a pound in Sheila's tip jar, for which she thanked them.
Frank had twice tried to engage the café owner in a conversation about the missing schoolgirl, but if she knew anything, Sheila wasn't forthcoming with information. He might have pressed further, but his attention turned to the van pulling up outside.
Rick Merchant walked into *The Cabin.*
"Any cake left, Sheila love?" he called out as he headed straight for the café's only toilet.
"I'm out of lemon drizzle," she replied. "Carrot cake okay?"

"Lovely!" said Rick. "Cup of tea too!" he added, just before the door to the toilet closed.
Stefano snuck outside. "Give me a shout when the sarnie's ready. Just popping out for a fag."
"I don't blame you!" replied Sheila, as she turned the bacon over. "Rick tends to clear the place pretty quickly!"
Stefano walked away with his back to the café. He stopped for a few seconds as though he was lighting a cigarette, then disappeared round the front of Rick's van. He peered through the window and smiled as he spotted the dashboard camera.
The door was unlocked.
Frank and Stefano watched the startling footage together in the Mondeo, having left *The Cabin* without waiting for the bacon to fry. The camera clearly showed the old man and the two Farrington children being covered in bubble wrap and loaded into the back of the truck, before being delivered to Anna Kraus' house.
Despite much protestation, Gary Morton had been wrapped up whilst in a crawling position, to give the impression of a four-legged animal statue.
"Why do I have to be the animal?" he complained.
"Because I've only just thought of it and I'm nearly wrapped up already!" replied a female out of shot, presumably Nadia Fisher.
Frank called KR1 and explained that they had irrefutable evidence that all three people of interest were hiding out with Anna Kraus, along with Ralph Page, who was very much alive and kicking.

Mitchell Johnson had congratulated them on their outstanding initiative.

The two friends relaxed, with Bandit slouched across the back seat. There was a sense of relief and redemption. They were expecting a further instruction from KR1 to await back-up, before moving in to apprehend the Subject and Subject B. When the radio transceiver lit up once again, Frank picked it up and was surprised to hear the voice of the Director himself.

His orders left F8a in shock.

"What's the matter?" asked Stefano.

"That was the Director. He's sending in the Ashta squadron again."

"I thought they were three men down?" said Stefano.

"I guess a few guards have been promoted," shrugged Frank. "If this had happened this time last week, they'd have probably promoted us!"

"Could you do that?" asked Stefano. "Kill unarmed kids?"

Frank thought for a moment. "No. Not without a bloody good reason. Why does he want them dead? There's something going on here that we don't know about."

"What do you think of him?" asked Stefano. "The Subject, I mean."

Frank smiled. "He used to call me the giraffe."

"The giraffe?" replied Stefano, before chuckling as he looked at his friend. "I see what he means. It's the ears!"

Frank took his friend's remark in good jest.

"When he was little, he drew me a picture of a giraffe. He did it for a few of the staff."
"Yeah, I know," said Stefano. "I was a tapir."
Frank burst out laughing.
"I liked the kid back then," continued Frank, sensing his partner was adequately embarrassed. "Before the Director came up with that stupid rule about us not being allowed to talk to him and not saying his name. Can you remember?"
Stefano nodded. He liked the boy too.
"On each one of his pictures, he wrote a fact about the animal you looked like," said Frank. "And do you know what he wrote on mine?"
"Something about the long neck?" guessed Stefano.
"He wrote that giraffes have the biggest heart of any walking animal. When he gave me the drawing, he said that was why he knew I was a good person."
Stefano looked at his partner, who hadn't expressed any affection for the Subject in years.
"He was a lovely boy," said Frank. "But we betrayed him. Stood there, ignoring him, when all he wanted to do was talk. Just for the sake of obeying orders."
"It was our job, buddy."
"And what's our job now, Stefano? To sit here and watch while they all get massacred?"
Frank looked down to see that he was twisting a ring around his finger.
"I nearly lost this," he said. "When I was out in the middle of that lake, I wasn't worried about hyperthermia or even the rollicking we were going to get off Johnson. I was

worried about this ring. It was my dad's. He was wearing it when he was killed in the Gulf and they brought it back with his body. Thought I was going to lose it when the Subject took it from me. He could have just thrown it in the water, couldn't he? If he was that sort of lad. But he didn't. He left it on the rock and gave me a nod."

"So, what are we going to do?"

"Something stupid," replied Frank, with a tone of resignation. Stefano smiled as Frank jumped out of the car. He turned to face his friend. "Whatever happens, Stefano, it's been a pleasure to…"

"Don't you dare!" smirked Stefano. "None of that shit!"

Chapter 49

When the buzzer sounded, everyone in the Nena room froze.

Anna nodded to Magnus to respond on the intercom. He could see on the monitor exactly who it was. It was one of the two men in the new surveillance unit spying on the property.

"Who is it?" asked Magnus, with none of his usual warmth.

"My name is Frank Stone of the Farrington Protection Force."

"What do you want?"

"You have to get out, now," said Frank. "An assassination squadron is on its way. They know that the Farrington children are with you."

"There is nobody here but myself and Anna Kraus," said Magnus, trying to maintain a degree of calm in his voice.

"We have no time," said Frank, urgently. "We've been to *The Cabin*. We found a dash-cam in the delivery van. We know those were not garden ornaments. You must get out of there."

"Does the Director know the children are here?" asked Anna, speaking over Magnus' shoulder.

"Yes. We reported it to Farrington Towers," replied Frank. "Me and my colleague, Stefano Gallo. I'm sorry. We didn't expect him to send assassins. Please, let us help you."

"Why would you do that?" asked Magnus.

"Because," said Frank, hesitating. "I'm the giraffe. Tell the boy, I'm the giraffe."

The line went quiet for a moment, before the gates jolted into life. Frank squeezed through the gap and Stefano drove through as soon as it was wide enough for the Mondeo.

He left the engine running, jumped out and was almost alongside his partner by the time Magnus opened the front door.

"We have to separate the twins," said Frank, forsaking pleasantries. "It's their best chance."

"Why?" asked Anna, appearing behind Magnus.

"The Director has given instructions that the FPF is not to fire on the Subject or Subject B, unless they are together. If they're both here, they're going to kill them. If they split up, they have a chance."

"What do you suggest?" said Anna, as a helicopter approached in the distance.

"One of them must leave," said Stefano. "Frank will take them somewhere safe. I'll stay here and help you fend off the FPF."

"I'll go," said Warren, stepping forward. "Hopefully, some of them will follow me."

He shook hands with Stefano.

"The tapir," he smiled. "Take care of my sister."

"I will. Now go!"

Frank Stone patted Stefano on the back before jumping in the car. Warren leapt into the back seat.

"Keep your head down!" said Frank, as he drove out through the gates.

"What's the dog's name?" asked Warren, as he rested his head against a spaniel who looked nonplussed by the ensuing drama.
"Bandit."
"He doesn't look a particularly lawless dog," noted Warren.
"He's not," replied Frank. "But he loves Burt Reynolds."

Frank was turning right on to the road when he looked in his mirror and saw someone running behind him.
"Oi! Wait for me!" shouted Gary, whilst running in a peculiar manner, clinging on to his jumper. He ignored calls from the others to return to the house.
"Wait!" shouted Warren, looking out of the rear window to see Gary chasing him along the road.
"Christ! Just what we need!" said Frank, as he screeched to a halt.
Gary looked knackered as he ran out of stamina in the final few metres to the car. He reached the Mondeo, opened the rear door and leaned against it.
"Where you off to?" he panted. "I thought we were mates!"
"Well, not sure about mates," replied Warren.
"Just hurry up and get in!" shouted Frank.
But it was too late. Gary heard something click behind him and as he turned around, a bright flash appeared from the bushes. The bullet hit him straight in the chest.
Gary slumped to the pavement.

Frank had no choice. He put the car in first gear and accelerated away as Warren shouted Gary's name.

He looked back through the tyre smoke to see the boy in the Liverpool shirt lying by the side of the road.
Nadia screamed from the door of the house and was about to run to Gary's aid, but as more bullets were fired, Magnus stopped her and dragged her inside.
"What weapons do you have?" he shouted to Magnus.
"A bass guitar, a synth keyboard and lots of vinyl records," replied Magnus, as he led Stefano along the corridor. He could hear windows being smashed somewhere in the property as Magnus pulled back a picture of a female singer Stefano didn't recognise, before stepping into a hidden passageway.

Chapter 50

"Keep your head down!" shouted Frank Stone, looking in the mirror as three motorcycles closed in. "I'm sorry, but we can't help him now. Just stay down!"

Frank flew along the country roads at a ridiculous speed, passing fields of grazing sheep. But he couldn't shake his pursuers.

The high speed and uneven road surface meant the assassins had to resort to hopeful shots and only a few bullets pierced the Ford's bodywork.

After ten miles of driving along country lanes, Frank nearly had a heart attack when he came around a corner to see a flock of sheep blocking the road.

"Shit!" he yelled.

Frank veered off the road, smashing through a wooden gate as the closest pursuer slid off his bike and into the flock.

"Kerry hill sheep," noted Warren, looking out of the window. "They're quite distinctive with the black patches over their eyes."

"You're checking out the sheep?" shouted Frank. "How about you just keep down. We've still got two on our tail!"

Frank drove across the field before smashing through another fence and into a courtyard covered in giant clumps of mud that had peeled away from tractor wheels. He kept his foot down as chickens clucked as they ran about aimlessly.

"Orpington chickens," said Warren. "Good egg layers and popular for their meat quality."
"What are you, Doctor Doolittle?"
"Just been reading up about farming lately," replied Warren.
Frank headed towards a gravel driveway before turning sharply, bringing the Mondeo to opposite lock as he pointed the car straight along the centre of a huge dairy barn. On each side, cows poked their head through railings to eat a mix of hay, grain and nutrients.
"Holstein-Friesian," remarked Warren. "Ideal for dairy production. May or may not be perceptible to cow tipping."
"That's not helping!" said Frank, as another hail of bullets struck the Ford. "Just stay down!"
"There!" shouted Warren, ignoring Frank's request. "A slurry pit. I figured they'd have to be one here somewhere!"
"A slurry pit?" repeated Frank.
"It's full of animal waste," said Warren. "A death trap for anyone or anything that gets stuck in it. I've got an idea."
Frank maintained a high speed, trying to avoid the potholes on the driveway around the farm's perimeter.
He could see that the motorcycles didn't like the bumpy terrain, as both fell further behind. Then, at Warren's direction, Frank turned hard left, driving straight between the open doors of a large timber barn. Inside, hay was rolled into bales and piled up thirty feet high on both sides.
Frank accelerated through the gears before smashing through the far end of the barn. Timber was thrown everywhere as the Mondeo slammed into the side of a shocked motorcyclist, who had lost sight of the car.

Frank hit the brakes and was mightily relieved to see the Mondeo's front wheels teetering on the edge of the slurry pit. The motorcyclist frantically tried to climb up on to his bike to avoid drowning in the foul-smelling concoction.
As Frank reversed and sped off, the last remaining rider pulled up.
"Help me!" shouted the panicking assassin as his bike sank slowly under eight foot of slurry.
The last rider shut his visor, twisted the throttle and skidded off in pursuit of the Subject.
Frank was heading up a bumpy track beyond the dairy when Warren told him to turn into a maize field.
"Why the hell do you want to go in here?" shouted Frank.
"It's sweetcorn! It's over ten foot tall. We're lucky that this maize hasn't been harvested yet."
"Lucky?" groaned Frank.
"Just keep your foot down!"
Warren crawled between the two front seats and opened the electric sunroof. Grabbing Bandit's blanket, he wrapped it around his hands and held it over his face to try and protect himself from being lacerated by the crops.
"What are you doing?" yelled Frank. "You'll be sliced to shreds!"
"Just drive!" shouted Warren, with his knees balanced on the head rests of the front seats. "Keep it straight, between the rows if you can."
It was difficult to see as the green leaves and tall storks of the maize crop whipped his face, but as he raised his head, Warren saw what he was looking for.

"Turn left, now!" he shouted.
Frank obliged, although the motorcyclist in pursuit wasn't going to be shaken so easily.
"Just keep it straight!" said Warren. "And put your foot down! We need more speed!"
Frank did as he was told, but he was petrified as to what was happening, as he couldn't see anything but maize. If a gate, road, wall, fence or something worse suddenly appeared in front of him, there wouldn't be a damn thing he could do about it.
"Faster!" shouted Warren, as he looked behind to see the motorcyclist edging closer.
He was ten metres behind and had fired off more rounds, although it was difficult to hit a target with the rough terrain. "Give it everything she's got, Frank!"
"I am!" yelled back F8a, just as an almighty noise descended upon them. A flash of red metal appeared through the corn and passed by in an instant. Then, a second later, came a horrible sound, like metal going through a grinder.
Warren dropped back down and slumped in the back seat next to Bandit, his face bleeding from several lacerations.
"What the hell was that?" asked Frank, his heart pumping faster than it had done in years. "Did you just play a game of chicken with a bloody combine harvester?"
"Yes," said Warren, puffing out his cheeks. "Yes, I did. Sorry it was so close. It's tricky to accurately gauge speed at such a distance, but I figured that if it was harvesting at 7mph and we were travelling at 42mph on a sustained trajectory of ninety degrees, we'd just make it. But I'll hold

my hands up and admit that my calculation was slightly off. The harvester must have been going closer to 8mph."
"Misjudged?" said Frank, angrily. "I'll say this once and once only. You ever put Bandit in danger like that again and you're on your own, you hear me?"
Warren was surprised by F8a's anger.
"Understood."
"Good!" said Frank.
Frank was relieved to see an end to the maize, as he turned out of the field and drove back along the driveway.
He grabbed his mobile, but had no signal. He stopped the car, spotting a trailer behind a wall, with hay rolled into bales and stacked four high.
The trailer had been left at the top of a long, recently harvested field with a steep gradient.
"What are you doing?" asked Warren.
"Trying to get a signal. I need to find out what's happening with Stefano."
Frank climbed on to the trailer and leapt athletically to the top of the bales. The beautiful view as the sun set over the hills barely registered as he checked his phone. He was relieved to see he had a faint signal.
"Warren, stay out of sight for a few minutes. That first rider must still be out there."
Frank dialled and was waiting for his partner to answer when a bullet hit him in the shoulder. He fell to his knees and saw his mobile fall between the bales as one of the motorcyclists, dressed all in black, emerged from behind the wall.

He took his helmet off and Frank saw the man who had been introduced to all members of the FPF just a day earlier. Fergus MacLean.
"I can't tell you how good a shot that was," said Fergus. "This is a Walther P38. It was my great-great grandfather's during the Second World War. It's a pretty useful gun, certainly compared to the Luger P08, which it replaced. But still, from that range, it isn't easy to hit a target in an elevated position, especially with the cross winds. Not to mention the injury to my right arm following my fall back there. Still, I should be grateful that they were sheep and not cows, I suppose!"
Fergus smiled as he walked towards Frank.
"You were trying to call your partner, am I right?" said Fergus. "Seeing as I interrupted you, I shall fill you in on what I've heard on my radio. Anna Kraus' home has been blown to pieces by a rather uninspiring combination of machine guns, hand grenades and rocket launchers. As for your friend and the others, well, they've blockaded themselves in a safe room. So, we've hit them with incapacitating agents. Sleeping gas, if you prefer. They won't survive for long with all the smoke seeping in, I'm afraid."
"You're a murderer!" shouted Frank.
"Just doing my job. You, on the other hand, you should be ashamed of yourself. Disobeying an order from the Director."
"I am a guard of the Farrington Protective Force," said Frank, on his knees. "I protect the Farringtons, you prick."

"Oh, resorting to insults?" chuckled Fergus, pointing the gun at Frank once again.
"Where is the Subject?"
"What Subject?"
Fergus fired and Frank roared out in pain as the bullet struck his left shoulder. He was knocked back off the hay bales, landing with a thud on the ground next to the trailer.
"I would very much prefer not to use too many bullets. They're very difficult to obtain in this country," said Fergus, walking round the bales to see Frank clambering back up to his feet.
"This gun is sort of a relic, you see?" he added. "There were millions of them once, but now, not so many. So, I'll ask one more time. Where is the Subject?"
"He's in the car," replied Frank, before a third bullet struck him in his left kneecap.
"No, he isn't!" said Fergus, frustrated. "I checked and all I saw was your bone-idle dog, which couldn't even be bothered to bark!"
Fergus held the German firearm against Frank's head.
"I know you're here, boy," he shouted. "In among the hay bales. Come out and I spare this man's life. If not, I will kill him, I promise you that."
There was no response.
"Five seconds! Or I kill him and burn the hay anyway!"
Still no response.
"Goodbye F8a," said Fergus MacLean.
But he didn't count on Bandit.

He jumped over the wall, raced under the trailer and leaped up at Fergus, who was momentarily knocked off his feet. He grabbed the spaniel as it tore at his black jacket and tossed Bandit to the floor, kicking the dog violently.
Bandit yelped in pain.
Fergus turned around to see Frank desperately trying to drag himself under the trailer. Fergus would have hunted him down and killed him, but suddenly, a hay bale fell from the top of the trailer, crashed to the floor and started rolling down the long, steep slope across the field.
A bemused Fergus saw the Subject's head just visible at one end in the centre of the bale, his eyes closed as he thundered down the hill.
Fergus left his helmet behind and ran to a nearby tree. He re-emerged on his motorcycle, sporting dents and scratches along the paintwork, and set off in pursuit of the rolling bale.
Frank used his one good leg to drag himself to the rock wall. He mustered the strength to pull himself up.
In the distance, he saw Warren being caught and forcefully removed from the bale by MacLean, who was holding the gun to his head. Frank looked up to see a black helicopter approaching in the distance.
Frank felt the car keys in his pocket and looked over to the Mondeo. It was thirty metres away.
He had to make it.

Chapter 51

"I'm pretty sure that's Kim Wilde," said F9b, one of six Ashta assassins in the home of Anna Kraus.

"Kim Wilde's not German!" said F9a, who after ten minutes of searching had found a concealed entrance behind a framed poster in the hallway.

"What's being German got to do with it?" asked F9b.

"Look around!" said F9b, who'd long been frustrated by his colleague's lack of intelligence. "Beckenbauer, Schumacher, Beethoven! What do they all have in common?"

"Oh, I see!"

Another guard, F15a, had been setting an explosive charge on the titanium door.

"Get back!" he yelled, before a monumental blast not only blew the door from the wall but obliterated the entire hallway.

Once the smoke had cleared, the guards stepped into a dark passageway behind the titanium door.

"They've tripped the switch," said F15b, flicking an unresponsive light switch.

"Revert to night vision," ordered F9a, as the squadron moved tentatively forward.

They were stopped in their tracks as music started blasting out of the speakers.

"What is that?" asked F9b.

"That's *99 Red Balloons*," replied F9a. "That wasn't Kim Wilde. It was Nena."

"Why's it so loud?" asked F9b.
"They're toying with us," replied F9a, his gun poised. "Stay alert."
With his next step, F9a fell forward, tripping over bass guitar strings utilised to garrotte his ankles.
Suddenly, the lights came on, momentarily disorientating the assassins, who were still wearing optoelectronic devices.
Stefano appeared in front of F15a, smashing an electric guitar over his head. Magnus jumped out too, knocking F15b unconscious with an Oberheim OB-X synth keyboard.
"Man down!" shouted F9b. "Fire at will!"
He shot aimlessly around the room until he was struck in the side of the head by a bowling ball used in the video to Nena's 1983 German top ten hit, *Leuchtturm.*
He hadn't seen Nadia launch it from across the room.
Guard F9a desperately cut himself free of the makeshift snare that had sent him tumbling over. As his vision adjusted to the light, he surveyed the unfolding chaos.
Stefano Gallo was smashing a drum kit over the head of F17a, who'd been disarmed. A blonde-haired giant of a man had floored F17b with a saxophone.
Then, F9a felt a searing pain as a circular object sliced his cheek. Feeling blood trickling down his face, he turned to see Nadia Fisher removing a vinyl from its sleeve and launching it towards him.
He ducked as a 7" single of *Haus der drei Sonnon* flew by. He grabbed his gun, looked up and saw his attacker preparing to launch another record.

"Subject B!" he said, taking aim.
Magnus was the first to spot the danger. He ran across the room, jumped over the sofa, knocking two red balloon shaped pillows on to the floor as he dived in front of Nadia as F9a fired.
Anna screamed as Magnus crashed to the floor, protecting Nadia below him.
Nadia clambered out, her hands covered in blood.
"Oh God, Nadia!" shouted Anna.
"It's not mine. It's not my blood. It's Magnus!"
"No!" cried Anna, shaking her friend and security guard. But there was no response.
She looked across the room at F9a, who reloaded his assault rifle and took aim at the former Head of Lifestyle and Education.
But he didn't see his panicking partner behind him.
Disillusioned and smarting from a broken jaw, F9b staggered back to the spot where F15a, the only member of the squadron trained to operate the M9 Bazooka rocket launcher, lay unconscious.
F9a picked up the weapon.
"Fire in the hole!" he shouted.
Anna remembered F9a being blown to pieces before everything turned to black.
When she regained consciousness, the Nena room was full of smoke. She wafted her hand helplessly, trying not to breathe in.
Just as she thought all was lost, Anna remembered the gas mask.

Chapter 52

Frank Stone had experienced extreme pain before.
There was the time when he crashed his wooden go-kart and broke his leg when he was nine-years-old. Then there was the time he threw a wounded soldier over his shoulder and ran one hundred yards across a battlefield, despite the shrapnel that had ripped a hole in his backside.
But the pain of driving with three gunshot wounds was something else entirely.
The wound on the left arm was serious. Frank couldn't raise it at all and certainly not enough to grip the steering wheel, so his left hand rested on the gear stick.
The first bullet had hit his right shoulder, but Frank found that by carefully moving his elbow outwards and turning his hand anti clockwise, he could grip the centre of the wheel just sufficiently for driving.
The worst part was changing gear. With his shattered kneecap, the pain of pressing the clutch was beyond anything that Frank had ever known. The veins in his face contorted and he screamed as he accelerated.
"Why didn't they give me an automatic, eh boy?" he said, laughing through tears as he glanced back at Bandit, who'd escaped his own encounter with Fergus MacLean without serious injury.

Frank kept his speed steady, hoping that nothing would cause him to come out of fourth gear as he made his way back to Anna's house.
He saw the smoke rising above the horizon long before he arrived. Sirens were flashing everywhere and three fire crews ensured that no burning ember burst back into life. You could barely see anything through the thick smoke emanating from the burning carcass of Anna's house.
Frank opened the car door, wincing in pain, before turning to Bandit. "I need you again, boy! Go find Stefano!"
Bandit leapt into the front seats, pouncing on Frank's lap, which caused him to cry out again. He watched as his dog disappeared in the smoke.
He could hear emergency services personnel trying to work out what had happened.
"Neighbours are saying they heard machine guns and bombs going off like it was World War Three!" said one firefighter. "If there was anybody in there, there's no way they're coming out alive."
Bandit started sniffing around the rear of the property, treading carefully around the scorched wood. Then, he started barking. Like he'd never barked before.
Frank heard him, howling through the smoke.
"Check the dog!" he yelled, with all the strength he could muster. "The dog! He's found something!"

The firefighters didn't know who was shouting, but several of them ran towards Bandit, who was barking over one spot. Through all the commotion, a firefighter could make out the faint sound of music under the rubble.

"Is that *99 Red Balloons*?"

A firefighter kicked aside a burning wooden kitchen cupboard full of burnt German food and the sound became louder. Then, chunks of brickwork and a framed poster of Albert Einstein were tossed out of the way.

And there it was. A latch to an underground bunker.

Two firefighters worked together to lift it and a huge plume of smoke blasted outwards, forcing them back.

When they turned around to check inside, Nadia was already climbing out, coughing and spluttering and with her face dripping with sweat from the searing heat. She was swiftly followed by Anna and Ralph, still clutching the gas mask once worn by a German pop singer he'd never heard of. It had saved their lives. The fire crews and paramedics rushed in to place fresh oxygen masks over their faces.

Stefano was the last to appear, carrying Magnus over his shoulder. Firefighters helped pull the unconscious man through the hole. "We need a paramedic here now!" yelled one.

"Is there anyone else down there?" asked another firefighter, as Stefano clambered out.

"That's all of us," said F8b. "Two bodies. Both intruders. There's nothing you can do for them. The others escaped and barricaded us in."

Medics appeared with a stretcher. Stefano put his hand on the shoulder of the female doctor. "He has a serious gunshot wound on his back below the right shoulder and

shrapnel wounds in his lower right leg. It's in a bad way," he said. "Please take care of him. We all owe him our life."
"Well, him and this dog!" replied the doctor.
"Bandit?" said Stefano, surprised to see the spaniel. "Where is Frank? Come on boy, where's Frank?"

It took some time for his partner to be extracted from the Mondeo.
"You really shouldn't be driving in such a condition," joked one of the paramedics, noting the three bullet wounds.
Frank initially laughed, but winced when it caused him pain.
"No more jokes please, Doctor!" he said.
"Oh, I'm not a doctor," replied the paramedic, as he cut into Frank's left leg under a local anaesthetic. "I'm just a janitor. But, you know, there's been a lot of cutbacks in the NHS."
Frank laughed and winced in pain once again.
"Sorry about that!" said the Doctor in a light-hearted tone, hoping he could save the leg.
"Listen, lifting you out of here is going to cause you a huge amount of pain," continued the Doctor. But don't worry, when you finally get to the hospital, you're going to be surrounded by friends!"

Chapter 53

Anna held Magnus' hand as he was placed into the ambulance.
She watched as it weaved around other emergency vehicles on its way to A&E.
She cried, knowing that had it not been for Magnus and Stefano, who had fought side-by-side armed with a variety of musical instruments against a team of assassins, they'd all be dead.
But they'd succeeded. And Subject B was still alive.
Nadia? Where was Nadia?
Anna looked around and saw her crouched over the body of Gary Morton. Amid the chaos, nobody had seen him lying face down on the pavement further up the road.
Anna put her hand on the crying girl's shoulder. "I'm so sorry."
"None of this was his fault," sobbed Nadia.
She turned to face Anna. "He saved my life. I know he came across as a fool, but he had something about him. Something I quite liked."
Nadia kissed him tenderly on the forehead.
"I'll never forget you."
Then came a strange sound. A groan. Nadia sat up.
"Gary?" she said, before leaning back down and putting her ear to his mouth. She could hear breathing.
Then, Gary opened his eyes, blinked a few times and sat bolt upright. He looked around at the scene of devastation.

"Christ, that hurt!"
"Gary! How are you alive?" asked Nadia. "You were shot at point black range. I saw it!"
"Oh right, yeah!"
Gary felt his chest and could feel glass everywhere. He lifted his jumper and a smashed frame of a Nena record fell to the ground. The vinyl was badly dented, although otherwise remarkably unscathed, considering a bullet had struck it.
"That's *Ecstasy* by The Stripes!" said Anna. "Were you stealing this?"
"Sorry," said Gary. "It's just you said it was priceless."
"Priceless? To me, yes! But worthless to anyone else!"
Nadia was apoplectic with rage.
"You mean to tell me that while we were trapped in there, with assassins blowing up the house with a rocket launcher and leaving us to choke to death under a pile of rubble, you were taking a nap after stealing a pop record?"
"Oh, you've changed your tune!" said Gary. "Just now you were kissing me and saying you'd never forget me!"
"That was before I realised what a selfish, ungrateful thief you actually are! I can't believe this! I mean, do you realise that if it wasn't for a dog coming to our rescue, we'd be dead? Dead, Gary! While you were sleeping on the pavement!"
"Oh, shut up! I was hardly sleeping! I was shot in the chest, you know?"
"More's the pity that it didn't go through the vinyl and do the job it was supposed to!" shouted Nadia, her voice breaking.

"Nadia, I'm sorry."
"You don't get it, do you?" raged Nadia. "Warren is gone. They have him and now they want me. The last thing we need is you screwing everything up. Just get out of my sight."
Gary trudged off. After a few yards, he looked back at Nadia, but she didn't turn around to face him.
"Nadia?" he pleaded, apologetically.
"Just go! I don't want to see you again."
"He just makes me so angry," said Nadia, as Anna consoled her. "Every time he does something good, he messes it all up by doing something stupid."
"You could look at it the other way," said Anna. "Every time he does something stupid, he tends to make up for it."

Chapter 54

When Hamilton MacLean reflected on his childhood, he couldn't recall what it was about Aunt Rosie that made him want to see her so often.

She lived an isolated existence in the Highlands. From the age of eleven, Hamilton would visit her most weekends, as his father and brother were glad to be rid of him.

And yet, when he was there, the two rarely talked. Sometimes, Aunt Rosie would ask about what happened to her sister, Hamilton's mother. She was seeking clues as to what *really* occurred, although Hamilton didn't know, as he was only nine when she fell down the stairs one night and didn't wake up.

Growing up had been difficult. His father drank heavily and was consumed by his hatred of a man Hamilton had never met. His brother, Cameron, was two years older and turning out just like his father.

Hamilton took after his mother, who he had loved dearly. Then suddenly, she was gone. The night father had taken off his clothes and thrown them on a fire behind the house.

Hamilton would perform all sorts of jobs for Aunt Rosie at weekends. She would wash the dishes, clean the floors, do the laundry and polish the furniture, while Hamilton repaired the fencing around the cottage and tended to the garden.

After heavy rainfall, sections of the stone wall along the road would occasionally collapse and he'd rebuild it.

When there wasn't much to do, Hamilton would drag a little rowing boat from the stony beach into the loch nearby and go fishing. He had only ever caught two fish, which was four less than he had seen being caught by osprey on the same loch. Yet Hamilton would sit in the boat for hours, enjoying the peace and serenity.

He was never paid for the work he did at Aunt Rosie's. He didn't expect to be. The cock-a-leekie soup was ample reward for his efforts. He would eat at the table with Aunt Rosie and usually they wouldn't say a word to eat other. They were like a married couple, although she was over forty.

After dinner, they would read at opposite ends of the sofa. Sometimes, their feet would touch in the middle, and they would smile and carry on reading.

Aunt Rosie had many novels and regularly attended book fairs, where she would seek out anything to do with the natural world or Greek mythology, both subjects which fascinated her nephew.

Hamilton would sleep in the spare room, which was far more comfortable than his bed at home. Aunt Rosie would keep the landing light on until he was asleep, as it was an old cottage with lots of creeks that could frighten a child with a wild imagination.

Every Sunday roast, Hamish would arrive, beep the horn and wait for his son in the car.

He had never knocked on the door and hadn't spoken to Aunt Rosie since Hamilton's mother had died. Hamish never waved at Aunt Rosie and neither would Cameron.

Cameron's loyalty was to his father and they both knew how Aunt Rosie interpreted the night Maisie MacLean had fallen down the stairs.
Hamilton missed Aunt Rosie during the week. He would have liked to have lived with her all the time. It would be inaccurate to say that he disliked his father. The two simply didn't have much of a relationship, as Hamish was so distant.
Hamilton didn't know much about his work, although important people and even reporters had visited all the time in the weeks before his expedition to Antarctica.
After the expedition, everything changed. There was no money. Journalists stopped coming to the house for interviews. He was shunned by his former colleagues. The blame, as far as Hamish was concerned, lay with one person: Charles Farrington.
He was driven by his hatred of the man.
Whenever Maisie dared to confront him about it, Hamish resorted to violence. Hamilton would defend his mother, even wrapping himself around his father's leg on one occasion, until he was kicked out of the way.
Cameron would defend his father and couldn't understand why his mother and brother failed to see that Farrington was to blame for everything that had gone wrong.
Maisie was worried about the effect that her husband's obsession was having on the children, particularly Cameron. That's probably why she said what she did.
Hamilton couldn't remember exactly what she'd shouted on the night she fell down the stairs. It might have been "You

can't let a dead man get the better of you." It might have been "He's dead and he's still a better man than you." Either way, that was the last thing she ever said.

After a while, Hamilton decided that he wanted to stay with Aunt Rosie permanently.
He imagined ways to make it happen. Then, when Hamilton was twelve-years-old, his school organised a residential trip to the Lake District.
He wanted to go. His father had been drinking heavily since reading that his rival could be in line for a posthumous Nobel prize. So, a week without being kicked around the house held a certain appeal for Hamilton, although school life was only marginally less miserable.
His entire year group travelled in two coaches. During the only scheduled stop, Mr Tilley, the PE teacher, ordered the boys at the back of the first coach to hand over the pornographic magazines that they'd been holding up to passing motorists, including a *Help the Aged* minibus. This only brought more grief for Mr Tilley, as the pupils responsible speculated what he planned to do with the magazines.
In the evening, the pupils were told who they would be sharing a tent with. Hamilton heard his name and waited for his three camping partners to be announced. When the name of Luke Burchill was called out, Hamilton groaned. Luke had made Hamilton's school life a misery. He taunted him for having a hint of a moustache, for getting rubbed down in the shower by Mr Tilley, even though it never

happened, and spread all sorts of rumours about his mother. He would regularly mock Hamilton for wearing trousers too small, as his father couldn't afford a new pair.
"Miss, Academical is wearing shorts again!"
That's another thing he did. Luke Burchill would call him Academical, because Hamilton Academical was the name of a Scottish football team.
The first day of the residential hadn't been so bad. In the morning, Hamilton had managed to get dressed inside his sleeping bag without Burchill seeing his willy and telling the entire campsite how tiny it was, or how hairy it was, or that he didn't have a willy at all.
Hamilton's group activity had been mountain biking, and he'd ridden with a boy called Ashley Tilley. Ashley told him all about the graphics of the new Sinclair computer. If Hamilton ever bought one, Ashley had loads of demo cassettes that he could borrow. Hamilton didn't really know what Ashley was talking about, but he was friendly and made it a pleasant day.
In the evening, Luke Burchill found a hair in his jacket potato, but Hamilton was spared this time. Instead, Burchill proclaimed that it was a pubic hair belonging to Rowan Griffin, who was widely acknowledged as having the hairiest willy.

On the second day, Hamilton and his group went rock climbing. This held little fear for him, as he'd often climb near Aunt Rosie's cottage. He'd walk over the red coloured marsh that ran alongside the river, before climbing the peak with no name. Then, he'd see how fast he could make it back down to the river by riding on the black slates. Not that anybody at school knew about this.

So, when Hamilton froze while perched on a rock overlooking a gulley, nobody was surprised.

"Don't shit your pants, Academical!" shouted Burchill, who was climbing up behind him.

There was indeed a smell emanating from the shaking, pale-faced boy who the instructors were trying to coax down from the mountain.

Eventually, the instructor carefully guided Hamilton down. Everyone could see his legs shaking and heard his whimpering cries. His harness was removed and Hamilton had to face the jeers of all those who had been denied a chance to scale the mountain because he'd 'bottled it'.

On the walk back, the group stopped for a break, during which time Hamilton crept up to an ancient stone wall just off the pathway. He leapt over it, slipped his shoes off and flicked off his tracksuit bottoms as quickly as he could. He then pulled down his soiled pants before trying to put his trousers back on.

It was then that he heard a shout.

"Oi, Academical! What you up to?"

It was Luke Burchill. Having seen Hamilton's flailing arms, he took it upon himself to investigate. As he scaled the wall, Hamilton was kicking leaves on the floor.

"My God!" said Burchill. "You haven't?"

He grabbed a stick and poked it through the leaves, before raising Hamilton's blue pants in the air.

"Academical's shit his pants!" he yelled down to the group. He ran down the hill laughing, telling everyone that he was right, he did smell shit up the mountain!
Luke Burchill revelled in the glory of humiliating Hamilton MacLean.

For the rest of the walk home, Hamilton walked alone at the back of the group with his pants in a plastic bag. The supervising teacher had insisted that leaving them in the undergrowth was akin to littering.
For many years after, that supervisor and every boy sleeping at the campsite that night would consider their behaviour. Were they partly responsible?
Certainly, nobody offered any defence for Hamilton. Not a single adult or child.
It started at dinner time, when one boy, and Hamilton really couldn't recall who, sabotaged his entire meal by putting wet mud over it, solely for a cheap laugh.
"Academical's crapped on my fish fingers, sir!"
This opened the floodgates to ever more preposterous taunts. First, Hamilton had shit all over the shower block, then on the driver's seat of the school coach, then on the porch to the cabin where the female members of staff were sleeping. The taunts lasted until midnight and came from every corner of the campsite. The three boys in his own tent joined in, led by Luke Burchill, even as they heard Hamilton sobbing in his sleeping bag.

The next morning, Burchill was terrified. He was telling the teachers that it wasn't just him, it was everyone. But he felt guilty as hell.
Hamilton MacLean was missing.
Tracks were found on a mountain path alongside a river and fragments of Hamilton's clothing were pulled from barbed wire several miles away. Days later, his ripped trousers and Teddy bear were found on rocks at the bottom of Ritson's Force, one of the largest waterfalls in the Lake District. Eventually, rescuers lost hope. Hamilton was never seen again.
Which is exactly how he planned it.
He'd had some help from Aunt Rosie. She had discarded Hamilton's clothing in convenient locations. They'd shopped together and bought two of everything in preparation for the vanishing act. But it was Hamilton who had formulated the most important elements of the plan. If he'd just run away, people wouldn't have stopped looking. If he had run away after being humiliated in a way that might lead a troubled young boy still mourning the loss of his mother to do something stupid, well, that was different. Not only would the search soon end, he'd also be able to gain revenge on those who had made school life so hard.

Aunt Rosie attended a memorial service held for Hamilton a month after his disappearance.

She wept for her nephew, who she'd left happily reading a book about ungulates of the Serengeti by a roaring fire at her isolated cottage.
For over a year, Aunt Rosie and Hamilton were on high alert. He wasn't to go near the windows and even when he ventured out for a walk, he would usually go out heavily wrapped up and at quiet times of the day. There were surprisingly few occasions when they feared being discovered.
Hamish died just months after Hamilton's disappearance, although that had more to do with the success of his dead rival than mourning his missing son. Hamilton's big brother Cameron never once visited Aunt Rosie, even when he was old enough to drive.
Aunt Rosie devoted her life to supporting Hamilton. They would read during the day, and while she never strictly followed the national curriculum, Hamilton excelled at science and mathematics. All sorts of educational books could be found at the fairs she attended.
Naturally, there were days when the two argued, and Hamilton would blame Aunt Rosie for his isolated existence in the Highlands. But ultimately, he was happy.
Then, one day, when Hamilton was sixteen-years-old, he was reading at the opposite end of the sofa to Aunt Rosie when their feet touched, as they often did. But on this day, Hamilton chose to lean over and try to kiss his aunt on the lips.

Aunt Rosie was desperately sad as she watched Hamilton leave the cottage a few days later. But it was for the best and on that point, they both agreed.
With the money she had given him, Hamilton travelled south and rented a room in London, where he set about making a name for himself. Albeit a different name, of course.
He was mesmerised by the pace of city life and by the diversity of the people, yet astonished by the lack of focus exhibited by those around him. Their lives seemed to be dominated by distractions and he took full advantage to rise rapidly through the ranks.
By the age of twenty-two, he was an Investment Manager at a FTSE 100 company. Having later launched a hedge fund, he was catapulted to fame when a string of investments in internet start-ups reaped enormous profits. Despite his growing reputation, he rejected all requests for media interviews, opting to stay out of the spotlight. He had his reasons for not wanting exposure. There were people out there who might recognise his distinctive, angular features.
Then one morning, as he walked passed a newspaper stand near Canada Water Station on the Jubilee Line, his heart stopped. A billboard reported the suicide of Cameron MacLean.
He picked up *The Times* and read it in his office, arriving as he did long before anyone else. As far as the press was concerned, all his brother had ever achieved was killing the celebrated naturalist Douglas Farrington with an estate agency 'Sold' board and a swarm of bees.

However, the article also mentioned that he'd left a young son behind. A nephew Hamilton never knew he had.
He shed a tear as he looked across at the high-rise buildings of Canary Wharf. He had hoped that, one day, he might be reunited with his big brother. Now, that could never happen.
He was there, at Cameron's funeral. He didn't enter the church, as it wasn't an occasion where he might blend in anonymously. There were only a handful of people present, including Cameron's estranged wife and Ted Hawfinch, his former business partner. Hamilton saw them touch tenderly outside the church and suspected that they'd been in a relationship for some time. He could also see how little his brother's wife, who he knew was called Morag from the newspaper reports, seemed to care for her son.
Morag didn't even notice the boy wander out of the church and find a spot under a giant oak tree, in a corner of the graveyard where the headstones were illegible and slanted at unusual angles. He crossed his legs and opened a book.
"Hello," said Hamilton. "You must be Fergus."
"How did you know that?" asked the boy, wondering if the man had magical powers.
Hamilton was surprised by the boy's appearance. His clothes were creased, his hair was long and greasy and the sole of his right shoe had almost fallen off entirely.
"I'm a relative of yours," said Hamilton. "I've just been away for a while."
"Are you going to look after me then?" smiled the boy, revealing teeth that belonged to the Middle Ages.

"Doesn't your mum look after you?" asked Hamilton, taken aback by the boy's question.
The boy shrugged. "She'd rather somebody else did, even though she does love me lots and it's the hardest decision she's ever had to make. I'll be all right on my own though. I'm nine soon!"
"I see," said Hamilton. "So, what's this book you're reading?"
The boy handed it to him. "My dad left it for me. I don't know why, as it doesn't have any animals in it. He knows I only like books about animals."
Hamilton opened the book.
'The Story of the MacLean family.'
"Maybe I can read it instead?" said Hamilton. "Then, if I think you'll like it, we can sit down and read it together? I'll buy you another book in the meantime. One all about animals!"
"You'd do that for me?"
"Yes, of course. I've got to go now, Fergus, but I promise I'll see you soon. I'll bring you a book and a new pair of shoes too. How does that sound?"
"Sounds great!" yelped Fergus.
Hamilton slipped out of sight. He placed the book inside his coat pocket, and as he did so, came across a folded newspaper article. It had been there for several weeks and something had stopped Hamilton throwing it away.
"The Most Difficult Job in the World?" ran the headline. The article was all about Farrington Enterprises Incorporated, which three months on from the death of

Douglas Farrington had yet to find the right man to head up the demanding role of Director.
It was time for Michael Manalton to remember who he really was.

Chapter 55

It had been two days since Gary had suddenly re-appeared in the multi-storey car park opposite the Birkenhead YMCA.

A lot had happened in the week since he'd run away, but not at the car park where those staying at the YMCA would hang out at night. Some would smoke, some would drink, but most just sat about chatting.

Occasionally, a couple from a local church would show up and try to pretend that Baptists are cool. When they didn't bang on about Jesus, they were all right.

Gary was briefly treated like a celebrity, as he'd been in the local newspaper, what with having gone missing.

"Morton! Where have you been?" sneered Dylan Maguire, who was the first to see him emerge from the darkness. Dylan had a naturally menacing look that made him seem permanently confrontational. "Trials for Barcelona?"

This earned a laugh from the handful of others hanging about.

Gary said nothing, which was unlike him.

He'd spent most of the day wallowing in self-pity. Initially, he was embarrassed at being exposed as a thief by Nadia. He spent two hours wandering around, thinking of all the things he wished he'd said to her on the pavement outside Anna's house.

Like reminding her that he'd given her the fastest mower.

Like reminding her that he'd made her an amazing

milkshake. Like reminding her how he'd risked his life, even though this thing with the Scottish family had nothing to do with him. Like reminding her how he'd be better off without her anyway.

All of which made him angry and upset. Gary couldn't decide whether he really liked or really hated Nadia Fisher. She was driving him insane, even when she wasn't around.

He'd jumped on a bus and asked the driver if he was going to Birkenhead. The driver had laughed, but told him he could take him one way to the train station at Machhynlleth for £4.70, where he could get a train into Swansea, and from there he could probably get to Birkenhead.

Having been dropped off outside an old stone building, Gary could barely believe it when he was told a ticket would cost him £53.30. He didn't have that kind of money on him. He'd left the two wads of cash Warren had paid to him in the pocket of the combat trousers. They were still hidden in a locker at Beacons Grange swimming pool!

Using the money taken from the vending machine, he bought a ticket to the next station, Caersws, for £8.60. Then he hid in the toilet for four hours until he finally arrived at Birkenhead North.

During the trip, Gary thought about the boy who vanished in the Lake District.

Something about it niggled at him. It didn't make any sense. How had his body never been found?

Long after the sun had set, Gary walked from the train station to the YMCA, without really wanting to reach it.

He saw the building in the distance, but he could see cigarette smoke rising above the walls of the third floor of the car park. So, he headed that way.

The idea of hiding a missing person appealed to several of the residents, although none had given Gary the time of day before he'd run away. In the end, he crashed out in Dylan's room.
He barely slept at all. Gary's stomach was grumbling and the tissues stuffed down the side of Dylan's bed gave off an unpleasant aroma.
The following morning, Dylan said he'd bring Gary a slice of toast after his breakfast, but he forgot. Then, they'd wasted the best part of two days in town with Clinton Botting, another resident. They'd been looking for a video game in charity shops.
The release of FIFA '19 meant that people would be flogging their older versions to second-hand shops or even donating them to charity shops. The boys found FIFA '18 in the second-hand game shop, but weren't happy paying £15 for it. So, they settled on FIFA '17 instead, which cost £3 from the hospice shop.
They'd been playing for four hours, rotating on a winner-stays-on basis. This rule had been initiated by Clinton, as he knew he was the best player. He'd been hogging one of the two controllers throughout the afternoon.
Clinton's winning streak meant that he'd ignored his dinner, provided by the YMCA, so Gary gratefully tucked into a bowl of spaghetti Bolognaise and two slices of garlic bread.

Clinton was leading 4-1 against Gary, who was of course playing as Liverpool. Bored of losing, Gary's mind was on other matters.

"So, did I make the front page then?" he said, keeping his eyes on the screen.

"Don't know!" replied Dylan, eating *Frazzles* on the bed. "I only saw it online."

"Did it have my picture?"

"Yeah, like, way down at the bottom," replied Dylan. "It was mainly all about your step-mum."

"Irene?" scoffed Gary. "What's it got to do with her?"

"She reckons you ran off just to make her feel bad," said Dylan. "They had a picture of her crying and holding a photo of you. She told them all about your dad's court case and your permanent bullshit disease."

"Compulsory Lying Disorder," corrected Gary, not caring as Clinton slammed in a fifth goal.

"To be honest, she came across as a bit of a bitch," said Dylan. "Woman Hitler!" added Clinton.

"You what?" said Gary.

"It's an anagram. Where you mix up the words to make something else. Woman Hitler makes stepmother."

"You sure?"

"Yeah!" said Clinton, before moaning as a long-range effort slammed back off the post. "You were lucky. Should have been six!"

"You got a pen and paper?" asked Gary, putting his controller down.

"Christ's sake mate! Can't it wait until the game's over?" whined Clinton.
Gary found a purple felt tip and a leaflet about debt advice on Clinton's desk. He scribbled down the words 'Woman Hitler' and quickly realised they couldn't be re-arranged to spell stepmother.
"What are you talking about! Half the frigging letters are wrong!"
"Oh, hang on!" said Clinton, who hadn't paused the game and was dribbling the ball through a motionless Liverpool defence. "It's mother-in-law! Oi, look at this, your guys aren't moving! Pretty realistic for Liverpool's back four!"
"Of course!" said Gary, scribbling on the leaflet again. "It's a frigging anagram!"
"Told you!" said Clinton.
"I'm talking about Michael Manalton!"
"What are you going on about?" asked Dylan.
But Gary didn't answer. He stood and ran out of the room. On the staircase, he leapt passed a startled manager who'd been under intense pressure since Gary disappeared from his care a week before. As he barged through the front door, he tried to work out the fastest way to the Kirby family farm. He hoped he could remember the way, as he'd only been there twice before.
Clinton and Dylan looked out the window to see Gary sprinting up the road.
Dylan picked up the leaflet and looked confused by Gary's jumbled letters.
"Who the hell is Hamilton MacLean?"

Chapter 56

The monthly meeting of The Wirral Young Farmers' Association (WYFA) was nearing its conclusion, which was a relief for those present. It had been an interesting but tiring evening in the barn at Chas Kirby prosperous arable farm.

WYFA meetings had been held inside his barn on the last Sunday of the month for the past three years. Not just because his three children were on the committee, but also because it was the only heated barn with space to accommodate the twenty-four members.

The WYFA President, Elliott Cooper, who was studying agriculture at college, started the meeting with a news briefing.

He outlined the main points of an information pack distributed by the regional power network operator, offering advice to farmers working near overhead electrical cables following eleven serious incidents over a twelve-month period.

In other news, applications were open for the Cumberland Agricultural Show. Member Sally Jennings was hoping to become the youngest supreme champion with her Limousin-sired Heifer, Prince of Darkness.

Later in the evening came a much-anticipated talk by Phil Cropper, a potato forum representative for the National

Farmers' Union. Mr Cropper spoke about the growing demand from overseas for high quality British potatoes.
As was customary, the WYFA presented Mr Cropper with a hamper of products, donated by local farms. Roy was particularly looking forward to sampling the award-winning cider made at the Tomlin family's orchard.
As the meeting came to an end, Elliott Cooper announced that anyone interested in registering for a committee role should speak to the membership secretary, as a formal vote was scheduled for the Annual General Meeting in two months' time.
Elliott expected to continue unchallenged in the role of President, although he needed a new Vice President. Gary Morton had only attended two meetings all year.
So, Elliott was as surprised as anyone when the elusive Vice President burst in.
"I need your help!" he shouted before bending over, trying to catch his breath. He'd run six miles in forty minutes.
Gary had been thinking about what he'd say and had it all planned perfectly. But stood before the group, everything came out wrong. He said something about three lawnmowers and assassins on motorbikes and being shot by a sniper while a house was blown up by a rocket launcher. But he was talking so fast that none of it made sense to anyone.
Gary hadn't noticed that most of the other young farmers were laughing.
Tanya Kirby was the first to have a dig.

"Why did you run here? Couldn't you just have driven your Lamborghini?"
"You shouldn't be here anyway!" chipped in Daniel Woodcock, a three-time winner of the young sheep shearer of the year competition. "Aren't you supposed to be playing for Liverpool tonight?"
"He doesn't play for them now, he signed for Real Madrid, remember?" shouted Wilf Tomlin, who worked at his father's lucrative cider and apple juice business.
"I'm not lying!" pleaded Gary.
"Like you weren't lying about the tomb of the Egyptian pharaoh you found under the septic tank on your farm?" piped in Rodney Morris as laughter filled the room.
Gary was humiliated. A tear rolled down his face.
It was Elliott who noticed that his Vice President was fighting back tears.
"We didn't mean to upset you. It's just you've always let us down. Too many lies, Gary. And what you're saying now is preposterous. Even for you."
"I'm sorry," said Gary, not looking at anyone directly. "I've been a fool. I've hardly said a word of truth to anyone in this room and I don't deserve help. But I need it. I know you think what I'm saying is bullshit, but it's not. I swear on my dad's life."
The room fell quiet.
"You all know my dad. You all know the last thing he said, before the guards took him down to the cells. Said he never wanted to see me again. That was why I ran away. Without dad, there was nothing left for me here. Which if you think

about it, is a pretty shit situation to be in. Then I came across another lad who was running away. Warren Farrington."

Gary saw a few people shaking their heads, but they were at least listening, so he carried on.

"We started chatting and somehow, we got on. Helped each other out. He was trying to find his sister, the girl from Beacons Grange. I fixed the bloody mowers they've been talking about on the news. And I like her too, even though she can be right hard work. But then I let them down. Like I let everyone down. But this time, I'm going to make it up, because they're my friends and I haven't had one of them in a long time. I know that's not your fault. But still, I'm here and I'm asking for help. Because I need it. I really, really need it and so do my friends. They're going to die otherwise. They're going to be murdered by the Director of Farrington Enterprises Incorporated, who's really a man called Hamilton MacLean and his family have been killing people for two hundred years. That's unless I stop him. So, who's with me?"

Gary turned to face the members of The Wirral Young Farmers' Association.

There was silence.

"I'm with you," said a gruff voice from the back of the room.

Gary smiled before embracing the farmer whose grooming brush he had ruined.

"Dad?" said Elliott Cooper. "How do you two know each other?"

Chapter 57

The Director was excited.
His masterplan was finally coming to a successful conclusion.
He smiled as he sat, his hands clasped together, gazing but not really looking at a 15th century painting by Sandro Botticelli that hung on the walls of KR4.
Like the rest of the world, he'd heard the rumour that Kala had given birth to two children as she was dying on the steps of Farrington Towers in 2003.
It was one of those things that conspiracy theorists always talked about. Did the Americans really land on the moon in 1969? Did Adolf Hitler really die in a Berlin bunker? Is Warren really the last Farrington?
The Director had to find out for certain. For many years, his search yielded nothing. Then, he had a lucky break, as a Doctor sent a greetings card on Dickie's 80th birthday. The postal mark led him to Graham Draper, who was living with a new identity in an overseas territory in the Indian Ocean.
It was Fergus who made the long journey and spent three weeks hunting down the retired doctor. Eventually, he found his man and extracted the truth. Violently.
The good doctor only said the baby girl was named Nerida.
If he knew anything else, he took it to his grave.
The hunt could begin.

The Director was excited yet nervous, even sitting where he was most comfortable, at the head of the Louis XIV table. He felt like he was meeting the Subject for the first time, whereas of course, he'd seen him practically every day for over ten years.
"Should I address him as the Subject or call him Warren, now that the situation has changed," he thought.
Mitchell Johnson radioed to confirm that he was heading to KR4 with the Subject, who had been restrained by the FPF since the helicopter had captured him at a maize farm.
As he waited, the Director thought about eating one of the truffles on the table. But he wanted everything to look perfect, so he resisted. There were still six truffles, which seemed ridiculous given that two of the Executive Committee were dead and another had been fired.
Professionalism amongst staff had undoubtedly dipped since the dismissal of Anna Kraus. Fifteen members of staff had also resigned, including two long-serving observers in the Control Room. So, a little disorganisation was to be expected.
Finally, the Subject entered, along with Mitchell Johnson, Hisoka Saito, Fergus MacLean and six guards.
"Please, Warren, have a truffle," said the Director.
"You called me Warren? I don't recall you ever referring to me by my name."
"Well, things have changed. I never envisaged putting you on a helicopter either!"

"I see you're working in partnership with a murderer now?" said Warren, nodding towards Fergus MacLean. "You planned the kidnapping hoax together, did you?"
"I'll explain everything," said the Director. "You deserve to know. But please, have a truffle."
"I'm not hungry."
"I have them specially made in Belgium by the world's leading chocolatier," said the Director in a persuasive tone.
"I don't want a truffle."
"Please, have a truffle and I will not ask you again!" repeated the Director, his voice becoming gradually louder until he shouted the last word, slamming his fist down on the table.
Of everyone in the room, Warren appeared the least startled.
He picked up a truffle and placed it in his mouth. It tasted divine, but he screwed his nose up and winced.
"Oh, that's disgusting! Where's the bin? I need to spit it out!"
The Director smiled as Warren took a crystal glass from the centre of the table and dribbled the chocolate down its sparkling sides.
"I am such a fool," he said. "I continue to underestimate you, Warren. Even after today's events, when I lost four of my assassination squad. I consider myself fortunate that dear Fergus should return in one piece. The first time you met him, he had a bird costume on, of course. It seems so long ago, doesn't it?"
Warren remained silent.

"I must say, your performance today was quite marvellous," continued the Director. "A combine harvester! I mean, that blew me away! I'm told the FPF are having quite a job scraping up all the body parts."
The Director laughed.
Warren noticed that Hisoka Saito smiled nervously, as you'd expect of a man living in constant fear.
"I was a little disappointed that it wasn't you who had died in such a messy fashion," said the Director. "It would have been a fitting way for a Farrington to bow out. It would certainly have upheld the legend of the curse."
"There is no curse," replied Warren. "I know everything. Behind every death of a Farrington, there has been a MacLean driven by a pathetic, illogical sense of vengeance. You're working alongside the last MacLean, Fergus. He must have suckered you in to a deal. Let me guess, he gets his revenge on my family and you get full control of Farrington Enterprises Incorporated?"
"Oh, don't look so pleased with yourself!" said the Director. "I receive alerts when internet pages containing certain information about my past are accessed. It happens once or twice a year. It's usually a journalist getting too close to the truth and I need to 'manage' the situation. When fifty alerts came up in one day, I knew that you were finally fitting the pieces of the jigsaw together. You and your sister, Anna Kraus, the old caretaker Ralph Page and the brainless Gary Morton. So, I trust you know who I really am?"
Warren looked surprised.
"You?"

"You still don't know, do you?" laughed the Director. "I must say, I'm disappointed, Warren. I assumed you knew! Someone in your wonderful little rebellion accessed the necessary news reports. Did you not read about the missing boy in the Lake District?"
Warren sighed as it all fell into place.
"Hamilton MacLean?"
"At your service!" smiled the Director.
"So, you must be…"
"Fergus' uncle," interrupted the Director.
"Michael Manalton!" said Warren. "I can't believe I didn't work it out. I even said to Ralph that it was an unusual name."
"I don't know why I chose an anagram," said the Director. "Well, let's be honest, it was arrogance. I loved the idea of infiltrating your family business and destroying it, whilst even giving you a clue as to who I really was."
"You can't claim you were rubbing our noses in it. I cannot recall a single occasion when you have been referred to by that name. You've always been the Director."
"Of course," replied the Director. "I was naïve. The anagram increased the chances of being found out. That is why I eventually insisted on being referred to only as the Director. I know people found that a little, what's the word?"
"Dictatorial?"
"I wouldn't go quite that far," replied the Director. "But yes, there is a degree of assumed superiority about the title."

"So, where does this leave us, Hamilton?" asked Warren. "Do you mind if I call you that?"
"Not at all. I would like that."
Hamilton finally picked up one of the truffles.
"Delicious!" he said, licking his lips. "If it's acceptable to you, I would love to relay the story of how I did it."
"Did what, exactly?" asked Warren. "How you murdered a harmless old man who loved bow-ties? How you assassinated Gerald and Yvonne Fisher?"
The Director looked as though he was about to strike the table in anger again.
"Careful, don't want to put a dent in the table!" remarked Warren. "It's a Louis XV original, if I'm not mistaken?"
"Louis XIV!" bragged the Director.
Warren laughed. "I don't think so."
"Why do you say that?"
"The backs of the seats are rigid and upright and the legs are straight with a rectangular seat," said Warren, lying with a conviction he'd never have possessed prior to meeting Gary. "17th century, it is not. Somebody has taken you for a ride."
The Director smiled.
"Bravo, Warren! You almost fooled me. I must say, I like this new, street-smart style of yours. All that playing outside has done you good. It feels like you are finally a worthy adversary and adds a degree of gravitas to our final confrontation. To think, just last week you were petulantly throwing books across KR2."
Warren stared at him.

"A lot has happened since then. This life you made for me, it's over. You're finished here."
The Director snorted.
"No, Warren. Honestly, how do you think this will end? Your sister, Ralph, Anna, your ridiculous friend who pretends to play for Liverpool. They're all dead."
"I don't think so."
"What makes you think that?" asked the Director.
"The way your eyes keep pointing towards the exit. The way you're manipulating your jaw to moisten a dry throat. The slight leaning back of the head and the fact that you stopped tapping your feet during that last sentence. That all tells me you're lying. My sister is not dead. If she was, I would be too."
"Maybe you're right," shrugged the Director. "The truth is, I don't know. I wish I did, but having blown up Anna's house, my men had to leave the scene before we could confirm who was dead and who wasn't."
The Director looked to Mitchell Johnson. "Any news?"
"Nothing confirmed, sir. We know that several ambulances have left the scene with injured patients. Also, there's no sign of the Ford Mondeo at the maize farm."
"There's no way F8a could have driven away," interrupted Fergus, surprised at the news. "I shot him in both arms and the leg at point black range."
"Don't worry, Fergus," said the Director. "You've not let anyone down. You have returned Warren to us, so even if others have survived, we still hold the trump card. That's

more than the collective efforts of Johnson's personnel. All they've done is lose the Subject and take out our own men!" Mitchell Johnson was red-faced, as he had been all week.
The Director rose to his feet.
"Come Warren, let's go outside."
"Why, so you can kill me?"
The Director looked offended.
"Warren, I've been preparing for this day for over a decade. My family has been waiting for centuries. I am not going to ruin the moment by doing something rash and unworthy of our glorious shared history. I give you my word, you will return to the Towers alive."

Hamilton MacLean
(1976 -)

Chapter 58

Moments later, the Subject and the Director were walking side by side around the south lawn.
It was the first time, at least that he could remember, that Warren had walked outside without being accompanied by the FPF.
"When I was at school, my history teacher set me an assignment," said the Director, breaking the silence. "He asked me to answer this question: Was Hitler evil? Initially, I thought the answer was simple. But the more I thought about it, the more I questioned what evil really is. A human is not born evil; they become evil. And it's usually love that causes it. For Hitler, that was the love he had for his country. A country he fought for in the First World War and which was humiliated at Versailles. Hitler's actions are now described as evil, but they were actions driven by love."
Warren gave a look that suggested he disagreed with the Director's opinion.
"I don't ask you to agree with me. I'm merely stating that people are not inherently evil. I am not inherently evil, Warren. Like Hitler, I am driven by a sense of injustice. In my case, it's not a love for my country, but for my family. Not just the father I lost, but for my brother and the nephew he left behind. Young Fergus. This love doesn't come without conflict. Now, today could be the culmination of two hundred years of vengeance by my

family upon yours. The day when the tables are finally turned. But do I feel happy about it? I'm not sure. Does a great general look across the battlefield at his depleted but victorious army and rejoice? Or does he contemplate the sacrifice of those who have fallen?"
"We are not at war," replied Warren.
"Oh, but we are," said the Director. "And we have been for a long time. And now we're at the end and I don't know how to feel about it. I want you to know that, Warren. You have given my life purpose. When I ran away at the age of twelve, I did so to leave behind my father and brother, as they were obsessed with revenge. And yet in time, I came to understand their anguish. Soon, you and your sister will be dead and I will run Farrington Enterprises Incorporated with my nephew at my side. Then, we will be compensated for two centuries of humiliation. As soon as we find your sister's charred corpse, we can end this. But still, there is great conflict in my heart, as I am not inherently evil. I will miss you, Warren. I really will."
Warren laughed.
"Are you mocking me?" asked the Director.
"I'm merely fascinated by your philosophy," said Warren. "Science would suggest that you are inherently evil. I'm certain that analysis of your brain's functioning would reveal minimal activity levels in the prefrontal cortex. That's why you lack the empathy of more principled people, who tend to have an enlarged amygdala, a part of the brain that formulates an emotional response."
"That's fascinating!" said the Director.

"There you go again. A perfect example of psychopathic behaviour," said Warren. "You feign empathy, but your natural abnormalities mean that you care little for what I've said. Most of our brain's activity can be attributed to hereditary genetics. A balanced, nurturing childhood might have gradually made you more considerate of others, but you were denied this. Which is unfortunate."

"So, I am inherently evil after all?"

"Yes," replied Warren. "You most certainly are."

Chapter 59

Jonathan Hawkins had been given several nicknames in his life.
He'd been John, Johnny, Little John and there was also a day when a friend had come up with J-Hawk, although it never caught on.
But never was Jonathan known as Jonty.
However, when Jonathan's passion for reptiles and amphibians progressed to such a degree that he decided to establish a business selling them, he needed a company name.
He didn't normally have pythons in his shop, as his primary area of expertise was lizards and frogs, but he couldn't resist calling his business *Jonty Pythons.*
It wasn't long before the regulars at his small shop referred to Jonathan as Jonty.
It had been another quiet day. A woman had come in to buy some crickets for her daughter's leopard gecko. A man had asked about an ideal first pet for his son and was surprised by Jonty's view that corn snakes aren't as child-friendly as some proclaim. A regular customer had popped in and as usual repeated fake news stories that he'd read online. Today, it concerned an anaconda found dead with a three-metre bull shark in its stomach.
He hadn't sold much. He rarely did. If it wasn't for its secretive work at Farrington Towers, *Jonty Pythons* would have gone under long ago.

Jonty had been secretly breeding the golden poison frog of Colombia in his flat above the shop for almost a decade. He only had one customer for this unauthorised breeding and that was all he needed to make a good living. He didn't know what they did with the tiny amphibians, although he knew that each frog carried enough toxin to kill ten people, so Jonty suspected that the buyer had sinister motives.
He never asked questions though and an American at Farrington Towers had once made it clear that he was to never divulge details of his arrangement.
He certainly didn't advertise the breeding side of the business, as he didn't want to attract the attention of authorities. The only time he'd had any cause for concern was in the early days, when he traded solely through the internet. Fortunately, they'd never traced the black widow spider that caused a fatal injury back to him.
Every month, Jonty would travel to Farrington Towers to deliver a batch of freshly-bred poisonous frogs to replace the old ones. Because of the income they generated, Jonty had great affection for the amphibians, so he would name them, usually after characters in his favourite comic books. Jonty was in the process of naming the new batch when the shop bell rang. The man entering was short and wore a black exercise top that revealed his bulging muscles. Jonty Hawkins vaguely recognised him from somewhere, although he didn't look like the sort of person who kept lizards as pets. He looked a little Italian, thought Jonty, shortly before a punch was thrown and everything went black.

The following day, Stefano Gallo arrived at the outer security post of Farrington Towers, driving Jonty's Volvo estate.
There wasn't any cause for alarm as far as the FPF was concerned. Jonty's arrival was scheduled for 5:30am and because of the dangerous cargo, four additional guards were on hand to ensure safe passage of the amphibians to the Farrington laboratories. It was a job Stefano himself had been occasionally assigned to in the past.
"Hey man," said Stefano, to the guard who approached his window. "How's it going?"
Stefano was wearing a bright orange chemical suit given to him by Jonty Hawkins. Well, Jonty really didn't have much say in the matter. He was now 'resting' in his flat with his legs and arms tied together, and wasn't likely to wake up for a while.
"We were expecting someone else," said the guard.
Stefano was relieved he hadn't been immediately recognised by F6a. Despite Anna's insistence that the disguise would fool his own mother, Stefano was not so confident. He knew his nose was distinctive, even if comparing it to a tapir's snout was a little exaggerative.
"You're expecting Jonty, right?" said Stefano, in a laid-back monotone drawl. That was his general perception of people who like comic books and breed poisonous frogs.
"Jonty's been hurt, so he sent us instead. Says he's like, sorry, and hopes it's not a big deal for you guys."
"What's happened to him?" asked F6a with authority.

"Royal python," said Stefano, maintaining a mellow attitude. "Ten-footer. Bit his arm during feeding. He had his glove on, but she got him just above the wrist."
"Is he okay?" asked F6a, without any genuine concern.
"Yeah man!" laughed Stefano, like it was a stupid question. "It's a python, they don't have any poison. Nasty bite though. She just gave Jonty something to remind him to drop the chicken a bit quicker next time!"
"I'm pleased to hear it," said the guard, peering in the back seat. "Is this the cargo?"
"We didn't come all this way for nothing!" smiled Stefano, before breaking into a yawn.
"You okay?" asked F6a.
"Yeah, it's just the time, man! I don't know how you guys get up and do this every day. I mean, I don't mind, as Jonty's paying me, but I wouldn't normally get up until way later. Especially as I was up playing Dead Rising 'til I don't know what time last night."
"Dead Rising?" questioned F6a.
"Serious?" frowned Stefano. "It's a zombie apocalypse game dude, you should try it."
"So, have these got names?" asked F6a, looking at the frogs hopping around in the clear container secured in the back. He knew from the fact file on Jonty Hawkins that the frogs were always given names. The last ones had been named after the *Holy Order of the Jedi Knights.*
F6a didn't know what that was and didn't care.
"Yeah, man. All these guys get names!" replied Stefano. "Jonty's been reading *Saga*, so we got Alana, Hazel, Klara,

Marko and Gwendolyn. That one's a little bit sexy so she's Sophie and the evil looking one is Prince Robot IV."
"Did you describe one of the frogs as sexy?" asked F6a, with a look that let Stefano know he held him in the utmost contempt.
"Well, yeah!" said Stefano, embarrassed.
"Sexy for a frog. I mean, I wouldn't personally have sex with it. Not literally."
"You are so lame!" remarked Nadia, in a tired drone that made it seem as if uttering the words was as much energy as she could exert.
The attitude matched her appearance of short, jet black hair, layered pale foundation with flashes of blue mascara and a nose ring, in stark contrast to her orange suit, which was designed to protect people working with industrial chemicals, but worked just as well when handling poisonous frogs.
"Ignore her," said Stefano, looking at F6a. "She's new. She wanted to come along as she thinks she's going to meet the recluse. Hoped he'd be into girls who believe in vampires."
"No I don't!" bit back Nadia. "Shut up!"
F6a didn't explain the countless reasons why she wouldn't be allowed anywhere near the Subject.
"You'll need to remove that nose ring, ma'am. Before the security post at the delivery entrance. Or they'll remove it for you and that wouldn't be pretty."
Nadia rolled her eyes. She looked vacant, but was anything but.

"*Saga,* right?" asked F6a, smirking as he turned back to face the unusual man behind the wheel.
"Yeah," replied Stefano. "It's like a space opera. You got these two parents from different races escaping from this like, intergalactic war. And they got this baby and sometimes…"
"It's okay, I get it," interrupted F6a.
He turned around and walked up to his colleague, F6b, who was smirking. "Did that guy say the frog was sexy?"
"Yeah," replied F6a. "These two are weirder than the usual guy."
"That's saying something!" said F6b, dialling a number seconds before he heard a mobile ringing in the Volvo.
"Jonty's phone?" said Stefano, answering the call.
But there was nobody there. F6b had already hung up.
"Hello? Hello?" continued Stefano, only too aware of what was happening.
"So, should we let them through?" whispered F6b.
"Yes," replied F6a. "They obviously work for Jonty. They creep me out, just like he does. Besides, the lab's running low on poison. Place an extra unit with them, just to be on the safe side."
And with that, Stefano and Nadia were on their way. Not with a container of the deadliest amphibian in the South American rainforest, but with the harmless and remarkably similar Hispaniolan yellow tree frog.
With newfound confidence in his acting ability, Stefano started to believe that Anna's plan might work.
Nadia had never doubted it.

Chapter 60

Ralph intuitively thought about sprinklers as the clock ticked over to 8:15am. Normally, he would be watering the quadrant lawn at Beacons Grange.

Instead, he was wearing blue overalls and a matching cap bearing the logo of an oatmeal company. The same logo was proudly displayed on both sides of the white van he was driving.

He had driven up to the first security post on the Farrington Estate, but there was a hold-up. There wasn't supposed to be a delivery from *McCall and Oats* until the following day.

"You can ring the office, but there won't be anyone there. It's my farm, you see," said Ralph, hoping the information Anna had provided was correct. Anna had told Ralph that the owner of *McCall and Oats* didn't answer his phone before 9am.

The FPF guard made a call and it went through to voicemail.

"This is your first visit here?" asked F6a, already sensing it was going to be a long day and a bad one to pull a double shift.

"We're a new supplier," replied Ralph, with a Scottish accent. "We received a visit from Anna Kraus last week and we signed a temporary contract to provide oatmeal. Just one delivery a month for six months."

Ralph handed over the contract and the guard inspected it.
"First delivery is due today," added Ralph, confidently.
"8:15am, so I'm right on the money. Not a minute too late or too soon, like she said."
"Well, I'm afraid there's a discrepancy. We have it down for tomorrow," replied F6a. "You'll have to come back."
"I damn well won't! I've got two bags of grain. Barely worth the diesel money from Dumfries! It's today or nothing. If it's nothing, I don't mind, but you can explain it to that German lass, as to be honest with you, she terrifies me."
The guard looked at Ralph and a trace of a smile crept across his face. That had been most people's perception of Anna Kraus.
"Okay," said the guard, who didn't want to cause more problems for a kitchen team in disarray following Anna's departure.
"Park your vehicle between the two purple marks."
Ralph did as he was told and a huge scanning machine moved slowly over and around the vehicle, like a car wash. A smaller device built into a transparent section of road provided the FPF with an X-ray view of the underside of the van.
Ralph was asked to remove several objects from the vehicle. These included items that Anna had positioned there to add authenticity, including an old music cassette of country classics, the remnants of a service station breakfast, yesterday's newspaper, loose change and a Great Britain road map stuffed under the seat.

Other items, including the jack and a spider wrench for changing a tyre, were also removed before Ralph was told to step out of the vehicle and stand still for two minutes on a marked spot in a quarantine zone.
Having passed the first security check, Ralph drove the van alongside the western side of the Towers, with fields and trees on one side and the perimeter wall on the other.
He couldn't believe that they'd contemplated climbing over it, considering the amount of guards and the heavy artillery positioned along it. Then again, as rescue plans go, the one they'd eventually come up with seemed equally as unlikely to succeed.
Ralph was flanked by four black motorcycles, ensuring he maintained a speed of 10mph as he headed towards the second security post at the trade entrance of Farrington Towers.
There, he was forced to stop.
"I'm afraid Anna Kraus isn't here today," said guard F14a. The FPF had been instructed not to offer an explanation why. "You'll be meeting a sub-team manager before we carry out compliancy tests on the oatmeal."
Ralph nodded and F14a proceeded to place a metal band around his right wrist.
"You're lucky!" said the guard. "The wristbands have only just arrived. Should have been ready half an hour ago."
"What's it for?" asked Ralph, knowing exactly what it contained. One had killed his brother, after all.
"It's just so we can monitor your whereabouts," said F14a.

Ralph could tell by his demeanour that he considered an old man no threat.
"You'll have restricted access to Zone 6. There's a canteen and they serve a good breakfast. You can go there during the compliancy testing, if you wish. You will not be able to access other areas. If a door doesn't open, it's because it hasn't recognised your wristband sensor and you're not authorised to enter. Do not try and force your way beyond your authorised access zone. Is that understood?"
"Perfectly," replied Ralph. "What happens otherwise, just out of curiosity? Does the wristband explode or something?"
The guard smiled nervously. "Of course not! But we monitor all visitors through a tracking device in the wristband. If you were to enter a zone where you're not authorised, you may be forcibly removed."
"Couldn't I just take the wristband off?"
"Not without this," said the guard, holding up an electronic key that locked the two ends of the band around the wrist. "There's nothing to worry about. I'm just telling you this, as I'm obligated to. It's like safety instructions on a plane. They have to go through the drills, but nobody ever tries to open the door mid-flight!"
"It's all a bit extreme, isn't it?"
"Well, he is the last Farrington," replied F14a.
"He is indeed!" said Ralph, praying that the other Farrington had successfully delivered the non-poisonous frogs and that his wristband wouldn't be causing his death within the hour.

Meanwhile, at the main entrance, reserved only for staff and visitors deemed important, a loud, obnoxious redhead called Ellen Hadley-Smith from the Department for the Environment, Food and Rural Affairs (DEFRA) was proving a nuisance.
"Are you serious?" she complained as X-ray scanners offered her no privacy to the eyes of the FPF guards monitoring the screens. "This is an infringement on my human rights!"
"That's why, if you look over there, you'll see we have an all-female monitoring unit," said F2a.
"This is beyond comprehension!" fussed Miss Hadley-Smith. "This is worse than when I met the President of the United States. I'd expect such an invasion of privacy from the Americans, but I thought we operated with more decorum!"
"Would you rather I put the gloves on and checked you the old-fashioned way?" asked F2a.
He immediately regretted it.
"Was that a threat? What's your name? Do you have a badge number? I'll be making an official complaint to your superiors!"
F2a braced himself for another barrage of abuse as he asked the woman to remove her stilettos, which matched her designer white suit.
"Are you joking?" she said. "I was told that I wouldn't be going anywhere near Master Farrington. Besides, what do you think I'm going to do, stab him with my shoe?"

The guard raised his eyebrows. "Strange as it sounds, that's exactly the type of risk we have to consider."

In KR1, the behaviour of the stubborn representative from DEFRA had attracted the attention of the Director. An irate, opinionated junior environment minister was the last thing that he needed, but the Director had little choice but to comply with the government's request for access.

Two days ago, information was leaked to the press about the number of birds killed by lasers at Farrington Towers. A petition to have the lasers removed had attracted over a million signatures in just 24 hours.

The Director wasn't happy about granting DEFRA access to inspect the lasers, especially as the woman they'd sent evidently had pre-conceived opinions. He had no idea that the woman at the main entrance was the same woman who had leaked the details to the press in the first place.

The same woman he had fired six days earlier.

After an extensive makeover, Anna was enjoying the opportunity to act, something she'd enjoyed at university. She felt she'd played the role of an obnoxious minister to perfection.

The Director immediately disliked the DEFRA representative. Growing frustrated by her incessant bird-loving monologues, the Director reminded Miss Hadley-Smith that whilst one million people had signed the petition, most of the population had chosen not to, despite extensive media coverage.

"So, you believe that the overwhelming majority of Britain's hard-working population agree with the practice, do you?"

she said, infuriated, whilst waving a copy of the leaked list of birds obliterated by the lasers. "Need I remind you that my party outlined, in its election manifesto, numerous pledges to the environment stating, and I quote…"

"Settle down," gesticulated the Director. "This isn't a political broadcast."

"Very well," said Anna, relieved that she'd been interrupted, as she wasn't sure what the Conservative party's pledges on the environment had been and certainly couldn't quote them!

"Mr Director, you killed a hen harrier," she said, calming down. "They're on the red list, critically endangered, with just a handful of breeding pairs remaining in this country. The whole world now knows what you're doing to birds and I can't leave without major concessions. I'm sure you understand my predicament?"

"The lasers are necessary," replied the Director, wearily. "We must protect the Subject from all possible eventualities, including birds of prey. Did you know that Stanley Farrington was killed by a golden eagle?"

"Whilst climbing Mount Everest, if my history is correct," responded Anna. "I hardly think the last Farrington is going to be picked up by a hen harrier and dropped from the top of Farrington Towers!"

The Director smirked.

"Need I remind you, the last person who fell to their death here did so having been bitten by a black widow spider?"

"That is not an acceptable argument," replied Anna, removing a document from her bag.

"This petition has caused the government huge embarrassment. Columnists are having a field day. *The Daily Mail* has claimed on its front page that the government is giving preferential treatment to people of power and privilege. If we allow you to continue killing birds, we can wave goodbye to the next election. You know it, I know it. I have with me an official request from the Secretary of State ordering the immediate removal of the lasers."
"Absolutely not!" replied the Director.
"It is the opinion of the Prime Minister that you would strongly regret non-compliance with this request," smirked Miss Hadley-Smith.
"What do you mean by that?"
"Well, it would be a shame to have to pursue allegations of bribery and corruption with regards to South American infrastructure contracts won by F.E.I," she grinned. "We've obtained evidence that casts suspicion upon Hisoka Saito and, by association, you too. We also have documents from the Sea Shepherd regarding your links to shark-finning operations in Japanese waters. The government can either brush these matters under the carpet, or place them at the top of its political agenda."
The Director smiled as he faced a woman who had laid her cards on the table and revealed a strong hand.
"Excuse me for a moment, will you?" he said politely, before consulting Mitchell Johnson.
"We lose our artillery if we shut down the lasers, am I right?"

"That's correct sir," replied the Head of Security. "They operate from the same power source. We'll lose the defences around the perimeter wall, so that's the anti-tank and air-to-air missiles."
"Can we do anything about that?"
"Do we really need to?" replied Mitchell. "Is all the safety necessary now? Three days ago, we flew in the Subject by helicopter for Christ's sake!"
"It's not about protecting him anymore!" whispered the Director impatiently. "It's to keep the others out! You think his sister, Anna Kraus, unit F8 and the rest of them aren't going to come here and attempt a rescue?"
"Okay," said Mitchell. "It'll take a while to re-route the power via the back-up generators though."
"Do it. I'll speak to the lawyers later and see what we can do about these veiled threats from the government. This woman doesn't know who she's dealing with."
The Director turned around, gave a broad smile and walked towards his guest. "You win! We're turning off the lasers."
"And the nets?" pushed Miss Hadley-Smith.
"We'll take them down immediately."
And with that, Mitchell Johnson walked over to the control panel in KR1 and shut down the lasers and artillery protecting the perimeter of Farrington Towers.

Chapter 61

Ralph Page sat in a corner of the canteen.
He ate croissants and a selection of jams and marmalades, although he regretted not having opted for a bacon and egg bap, seeing as it could conceivably be his last meal.
He chewed slowly, as he didn't want any of the guards to question why he was sticking around long after the compliancy tests on his oatmeal had been successfully completed.
Tucked away in Zone 6, the canteen was in a part of Farrington Towers that had never been accessed by the Subject. Warren was theoretically permitted to enter Zone 6, but there would need to be considerable preparation for such an event, as it presented numerous dangers.
As well as housing the employee canteen, which was also used by trades people, Zone 6 incorporated the medical facility. Directly adjacent to that was a warehouse accommodating the Farrington family's collection of vintage and veteran motor vehicles, some of which were purchased by Howard Farrington, who in 1904 became the first man to surpass 100mph.
The engine and wheels of his Farrington Flyer were kept in the warehouse. The hole in the tyre caused by the arrow of a native was still visible.
Warren though, had never seen this warehouse.
At the most westerly point of Zone 6 were the science laboratories. This was where food, drinks, clothing and all

materials that the Subject could conceivably encounter, was tested in an incalculable number of ways.
It was in one of these rooms that Nadia and Stefano had spent two hours meticulously extracting the non-lethal bodily fluid produced by three dozen harmless tree frogs, before passing the fluids to an engineering team.
Like Jonty, the two amphibian experts were not told that the fluid was to be placed into the inner chamber of every electronic wristband in time for a shift change at 8am. The frogs needed to be replaced every month to keep the toxins at a level high enough to trigger immediate paralysis. Having carried out their work, Nadia and Stefano were required to change their wristband from the ones they'd initially been fitted with.

Because Zone 6 was an area where deadly toxins were extracted from the golden poison frog of Colombia, not to mention the area where the FPF carried out testing on weaponry, it was located as far away from the Subject as possible.
There were three rooms and two guarded check points between the laboratories and KR5, the library. This was the closest point to Zone 6 that could feasibly be visited by Warren. Therefore, Zone 6 wasn't an ideal launch pad for any attempt to rescue him.
That's why the FPF guards on duty there were surprised when the two *Jonty Pythons* employees emerged from the laboratories with bright orange chemical protection suit

hoods covering their faces and charged through the first check point.
At about the time when one of the guards was picking himself up off the floor, wondering how on Earth the laid-back frog expert had managed to break several of his ribs and immobilise his partner, Stefano and Nadia were wreaking havoc in the canteen. Ralph's croissants were among the items to be knocked from tables, before Stefano grabbed a woman in a white suit, seemingly at random, and put her in a choke hold.
In KR1, the Director didn't need to be told by one of the wounded guards that there was a code red situation.
He was watching the carnage unravel on screen.

The man in the orange suit looked up at the camera overlooking the canteen exit.
He was holding a needle to the neck of a petrified woman, who moments earlier had been enjoying a bowl of exotic salad.
"Let us through that door now, or she dies!" Stefano shouted, almost spitting out the words.
Anna thought he might tone it down a touch, and perhaps loosen his grip ever so slightly.
"Sir, what do I do?" shouted Julius, the Chief Observer, as the Director looked at the monitors. But he didn't respond.
"Sir, that's the DEFRA minister. What if he kills her?" said Julius, nervously.
"Open the door," said the Director, finally.

"Alert KR5 and get a second unit on the check point there. There's no way they're getting near the Subject."
A thick, titanium door slid open and canteen employees who had worked at Farrington Towers for years saw a room full of old cars that they'd heard were there but had never actually seen.
In KR1, three red dots started flashing incessantly on screen as, for the first time that anyone could remember, visitors had entered a room without authorisation. They represented the two supposed employees from *Jonty Pythons* and the unfortunate DEFRA minister Ellen Hadley-Smith, who looked to be in tears as she was dragged through the vehicle storage warehouse.
The Director, meanwhile, ordered Julius to bring up facial close-ups of the two culprits. He studied them intently as the images appeared alongside one another on the central monitor.
"It's her!"
"Who?" asked Mitchell, now joined by Fergus and Hisoka. It was mandatory for the Executive Committee to head to KR1 in a code red situation.
"Subject B! That's the Farrington girl. And there's only one person I've ever seen with a nose like that!" added the Director, pointing to the male suspect.
"Stefano?" said Mitchell, not entirely convinced that the gothic-looking man with the jet-black hair was one of his finest men.
"It would certainly explain how a frog expert was able to smash through one of your check points and floor two

guards, wouldn't it?" said the Director to his Head of Security. "Shame he was never so efficient when he worked for you!"

The Director continued to gaze transfixed at the monitors, as a unit of the FPF unsuccessfully tried to convince the man in the chemical suit to put down the needle and let his hostage go.
He could see the three dots still flashing on the screen, showing that visitors with identification codes LABV1, LABV2 and GOVV1 were beyond their authorised zones.
"You are to initiate the poison sequence of LABV1's wristband with immediate effect," the Director shouted to Julius.
The Chief Observer turned around. "Sir, the guards, they might be able to convince him…"
"That's an order!" shouted the Director.
Julius tapped the code into the computer and closed his eyes. He didn't look up at the screens to see Miss Hadley-Smith wriggle free of her captor as he suddenly weakened. Stefano took two faltering steps across the corridor and fell forward, the side of his face hitting the wall before his body scraped pitifully down to the floor.
KR1 fell quiet as everyone watched the monitors.
Nadia grabbed the needle from Stefano's motionless hand. One guard tried to prevent her from doing so, but was surprised by the teenager's agility. Nadia weaved around him, before charging towards the remaining FPF guard with the needle raised in the air like a dagger.

"Initiate the poison sequence of LABV2's wristband," the Director yelled.
Julius shook his head.
"Now! I'm ordering you!"
"No!" replied the CO, stubbornly.
He'd been considering his future at Farrington Enterprises Incorporated for some time. At that moment, he knew his stint there was over. He was okay with that, if the alternative meant executing a fifteen-year-old girl.
It was Fergus MacLean who intervened and aggressively pushed Julius away from the control panel. He activated the wristband while the Director kept his eyes on the screen. He saw Nadia dodge another guard as she leapt beyond the second check point, before running at speed along the central aisle of the library. She was fast.
As she passed the history section, she started stuttering. As she reached the geography and travel books, she fell to her knees.
KR1 fell silent as Subject B slumped face down on the library floor.
"Fergus," said the Director, quietly, still looking up at the screens as if he was expecting the Farrington girl to have miraculously survived the poison. "Take over here. The Chief Observer is relieved of duty. Johnson, have the two bodies moved to the medical centre and meet me there in ten minutes. You'd best make sure the woman from DEFRA is okay too."
"Where are you going?" asked Fergus.

"To speak to the Subject. He deserves to know that his sister is dead."

Chapter 62

Fergus MacLean couldn't help but feel that the death of Nadia Fisher had been an anti-climax.

She'd done superbly well. She'd managed to fool the FPF to gain entry to the Towers and progress beyond Zone 6 into KR5, which could conceivably have been occupied by the Subject.

Admittedly, the lack of a plausible escape plan dampened his admiration for the teen, but nonetheless, she'd orchestrated the single most successful attempt to infiltrate Farrington Towers and therefore warranted a degree of respect.

Yet, the sight of Subject B lying on the library floor, having suffered the fatal effects of amphibian poison, wasn't the ending Fergus had envisaged.

Having ordered that the cowardly Julius Reed be escorted from the building, Fergus looked up at the monitors and could see that the bodies of F8b Stefano Gallo and Subject B Nadia Fisher, or Nerida Farrington, were being transported to the medical room by Mitchell Johnson and three guards.

They carried out the duty with dignity, covering the bodies with blankets, as you would expect from men who had lost comrades on the battlefield.

The Director, meanwhile, was on his way to the medical facility with the Subject, who had been under heavy guard in the padded cell of KR8 since his recapture three days previously.

Trevor King was sat in his usual spot in KR1, hoping for a promotion now that the CO had been dismissed.
Two other assistant observers had resigned in recent days, leaving only two people manning KR1. Therefore, Trevor was keen to impress the newly-appointed member of the Executive Committee.
"What should we do about Ellen Hadley-Smith?" he asked Fergus MacLean.
"Who?"
"The junior minister from DEFRA."
Fergus shrugged. "Where is she now?"
"She's being looked after by the FPF in a private room in Zone 6, sir," said Trevor. "Monitor 39."
Fergus looked up. The minister didn't seem so feisty now she'd been dragged around with a poisonous needle against her neck.
"Leave her. She got what she came for. We shut down the lasers, didn't we? She can finish her coffee, then go."
Trevor felt compelled to argue. After such an ordeal, surely it wasn't right to just dump her at the exit gate. But he didn't want to come across as non-compliant, so he dutifully relayed instructions to the FPF.
Fergus was gripped to monitor 42, which he'd enlarged so that it dominated the third unit of sixteen monitors. He saw the Subject walk into the medical unit. Normally, this would require countless safety implementations. But a great deal

had changed since Warren's escape from the Towers. Still, several yards behind him stood two FPF guards, and the Director was at his side.

Fergus turned up the volume on the control panel and the transmission from the medical unit echoed around KR1.

"I'm sorry," he heard the Director say. "We had no choice but to kill her."

The comment did not illicit a response from Warren, who was leaning over one of two stainless steel autopsy tables. His hand was trembling as he held the blanket that he'd pulled down, revealing his sister. Her eyes were closed.

"You're going to pay for this."

"Seriously?" laughed the Director. "You're going to pay? Is that the best you can do?"

Warren clenched his fist.

"I thought you might come up with something more imaginative," mocked the Director. "Call me a bastard, or even just a son of a bitch!"

Warren's anger was visibly growing.

"I know, I'm upset too!" grimaced the Director. "Believe me, it's not at all how I planned it. I had something far more elaborate in mind. For me, this lacks the style of a traditional Farrington death."

"Style?" fumed Warren.

"Maybe that's the wrong word," pondered the Director. "You know what I mean. Kooky, unorthodox, random. That's better. Random. It's not as random as I'd have liked. Fergus wanted to fulfil his circus stunt idea with African elephants, lions and a human cannonball. But he just

couldn't source the animals. If it was just a few years ago, it wouldn't have been a problem. Did you know, we had a touring circus with tigers and lions as recently as 2012? Can you believe it? In this country!"
Warren didn't respond.
"I couldn't believe it either!" continued the Director. "But it's true. His plan had something to do with an inadvertently opened lion cage. You know, typical Farrington stuff. He put a lot of time into it, but it's not possible now. He's almost inconsolable. We need to have a good think and come up with something extra special for you now!"
With that, Warren swung his right fist.
But the punch never landed. The FPF guards had anticipated the move and pulled him back, forcefully holding Warren's arms behind him as he wriggled around on the floor.
"That's better!" said the Director, crouching over Warren. "I'm so pleased that you are still trying to win. I feared that you might be so depressed about your sister's death that you would give up and wail mournfully through your final days. That would have been awful, for me and for Fergus. We'd have taken very little satisfaction from killing you in such a sorry state."

Fergus spun around on his chair in KR1 and laughed at his uncle's quip, but Trevor King looked concerned. He'd been monitoring the movement of others inside Farrington Towers.

"Sir, I have detected a presence in the vehicle storage warehouse in Zone 6."

"Is it unauthorised?" responded Fergus.

"Not as such, sir. It's a visitor with authorisation across Zone 6, but normally the warehouse is closed off. It is currently open and unguarded from the canteen, as the FPF at the closest check point are aiding the minister from DEFRA. My guess is that the visitor has taken a wrong turn."

"Who is it?"

"This chap," said Trevor, as an image of an elderly gentleman with blue overalls and matching cap appeared on the monitor.

"Cyril McCall of an agricultural supplies company called *McCall and Oats*. First visit. He's delivering oatmeal, sir."

"Then why's he climbing into the driver's seat of a Rolls Royce?" asked Fergus.

Chapter 63

Ralph had slipped unnoticed through the open door to the warehouse, taking advantage of the confusion following a doomed rescue bid by two amphibian experts.
And there it was. His Rolls Royce Silver Ghost.
What a sight she was. The most beautiful machine ever built as far as Ralph was concerned.
She'd been well looked after, that he could see. Ralph only hoped she would start first time.
Driving a Silver Ghost required a small amount of skill and a good deal more experience. Bernie, could never get it right, but Ralph had the knack. It was a balancing act. You had to carefully judge when to press the ignition switch at the top of the steering column, and it was best to use the starter handle if the car wasn't used much. Then you had to accelerate with steady speed control and use the governor lever to prevent stalling.
Ralph smiled as the old girl fired up first time.
"Why did I ever doubt you?" he said, patting the steering wheel with affection.
It was at this point that Fergus decided to transmit directly to the medical room.
"We have a problem with one of our visitors," he said, as the Director listened to his nephew on the ICS. "He has fired up a Rolls Royce in the warehouse."
"Who?" replied the Director, looking towards a camera in the corner of the medical facility.

"An elderly man delivering oatmeal," said Fergus.
"Can't you deal with him?" asked the Director.
"I thought I should tell you, as that's the next room to you," said Fergus.
He then looked at the screen in amazement. The Rolls Royce was on the move.
Fergus didn't even have time to issue a warning before the car smashed through the wall of the medical facility. The guards leaped out of the way and the Director cowered in the corner as Ralph emerged through the flying debris, just about stopping the Rolls Royce before it slammed into the autopsy tables.
The Director couldn't believe what he was seeing through the dust of smashed plasterboard. Stefano Gallo had risen from the dead and grabbed the Subject, while Subject B jumped down from her own autopsy table and leapt in the front passenger seat.
"Go!" she shouted, as Ralph rolled the car into reverse.
One of the FPF guards clambered up on to the side steps of the Rolls Royce, originally made so that passengers could board with dignity. But Stefano threw a punch and the guard fell back on to the rubble as Ralph drove through the warehouse.
He roared with joy as his old beauty steadily picked up speed while bearing down on the wooden garage door.
"What's going on?" screamed Warren, leaning over the back of his sister's seat. "You were dead!"
"I'm hardly going to explain it now, am I? Just get down!"

The Director ran through the hole in the wall and watched as the Silver Ghost sped across the warehouse, smashed through the garage doors and bounced across the south lawn.
"Initiate the poison!" he screamed. "For Christ's sake, initiate the old man's poison! And fire the artillery!"
Fergus had already tried on both counts. But the artillery was out of commission, having been shut down with the lasers.
Ralph winced and took his right hand off the wheel as eight tiny needles pierced his skin. It was painful, but the fluids from the back of a Hispaniolan yellow tree frog didn't have the same effect as the golden poison frog of Colombia had had on his brother.
He looked in his wing mirror and saw the guards and the Director disappearing in the distance as the mighty six-cylinder engine roared towards 50mph.
Most employees on the lawn seemed bewildered by another startling development at Farrington Towers. They didn't take much notice of the woman running along the pathway.
"There she is!" shouted Nadia, pointing towards Anna.
Ralph gently released the accelerator, as the temperamental motor didn't like sudden changes of speed. Anna flung herself head first into the back seats, her feet kicking Warren in the face.
'We're going to make it!' thought Nadia, as Ralph steered towards the gap in the perimeter wall that hadn't yet been repaired following his brother's day of destruction in the F-22.

Warren looked up to an artillery point on the perimeter wall and noticed that the guns were not manned and that the lasers had disappeared. He couldn't comprehend how they'd orchestrated a rescue. He'd spent three days stuck to a Velcro wall in a padded room with nothing to do other than contemplate escape, but with the trapdoor having been welded shut, he hadn't come close to a solution. Yet somehow, his friends had found a way.

Then, once again, his world was turned upside down.

Quite literally.

After briefly tilting on to two wheels, the Rolls Royce went over, with the sparkling front windscreen smashing as it scraped along the concrete just beyond the perimeter wall. Warren scrambled out of the wreckage to see the Director casually running towards him, accompanied by a strong contingent of FPF guards.

The Director slowed to walking pace and clapped, as his guards roughly dragged the other occupants out from under the car.

"Well, this must be my lucky day!" said the Director. "We only installed these pop-up bollards two days ago. A temporary measure, just while we're repairing the wall. I've seen how effective they are on cars using city bus lanes and I thought they'd be perfect! I don't suppose you'll have known about that, would you, Anna?"

"Took you long enough to work it out," she shot back. "Let the kids go!"

"Let them go? I can't do that!" said the Director, smiling. "But I'm obviously going to have to finish you all off

quicker than I intended. I mean, you lot are wearing me out!"
"Sir!" came a shout from a guard upon the perimeter wall, who was frantically pointing across the hills. "We've got trouble! There's a tractor approaching."
"One tractor?" shouted back the Director.
The guard looked out through a pair of military scopes.
"Yes, sir!" replied the guard. "There's someone hanging off the side of it, waving a banner."
"A banner?" repeated the Director.
"Wait, there's three tractors!" shouted the guard. "Make that five! No, seven! They're fanning out, sir. The tractors are fanning out! There's an army of them!"
"That banner, what does it say?" yelled the Director.
"The Wirral something," replied the guard. "The Wirral Young Farmers' Association."

Chapter 64

Warren stared in amazement at the astonishing array of agricultural machinery tearing up the green fields of the estate.
He hoped that the guards would loosen their grip, as they seemed equally as dumbfounded by the tractors, diggers, combine harvesters, muck spreaders and even a round baler travelling towards the perimeter wall. But the guards kept a firm hold.
"There must be twenty of them!" marvelled F2b.
"More like thirty!" replied his partner, fearfully.
The noise was sensational.
"It's Gary!' shouted Nadia.
Warren looked again. The tractors were too far away to make out faces, but the lanky frame of the boy hanging from the side of the lead tractor was unmistakable.
Gary cheered jubilantly as Brian Cooper sliced in front of the row of tractors, churning up the field in his Land Rover as he signalled for the front loaders to lead the assault, like a general commanding an army.
Seven loaders lowered their buckets.
"Charge!" shouted Gary, who had hitched a ride on Elliott Cooper's machine.

Across the field and the car park, close to the main entrance of Farrington Towers, the Director made a frantic call to

KR1, demanding that power be restored to the perimeter artillery immediately.
"But what about the woman from DEFRA?" argued Fergus.
"There is no bloody woman from DEFRA!" shouted the Director. "She's in on it! Get me power now!"
"Two minutes!" responded Fergus.
"They'll be on top of us in two minutes!" shouted the Director. He looked around and saw FPF guards milling around.
"What are you doing?" he screamed. "You, man the artillery posts!" he shouted to a guard on the perimeter wall. "And you, find the motorbikes and get out there!"
Hamilton MacLean then turned to his Head of Finance.
"Don't just stand there, Saito, do something for once!"
"Like what, sir?"
"The jet! Find Major Reynolds and use the bloody jet!"
Hisoka nodded and ran off in the direction of the F-22.

The front loaders were only two hundred metres away from the main entrance when power was restored to the perimeter defences. Within seconds, the first armour-piercing shell was fired by the anti-tank guns.
"Holy shit!" shouted Brian Cooper as the shell exploded near his Land Rover, leaving a crater in the ground and filling his cabin with smoke.
Another shell landed under the front wheel of Jimmy Kirby's green tractor. Jimmy was unable to avoid the blast and the front end of his machine dug into the ground.

Tanya Kirby screamed as her brother's tractor somersaulted violently over.
Tanya was about to jump down from her front loader and run to help, when she saw Gary Morton leap from Elliott's tractor and sprint across the field, even as shells exploded around him.
One landed close enough to send him flying in the air. But with his face covered in mud, Gary picked himself up and reached Jimmy's tractor, dragging him out of the cabin, shaken but unhurt.
Gary lifted him over his shoulder, staggered across the battlefield and lowered Jimmy into the front loader of Tanya's tractor, telling her to retreat to the top of the hill, out of range of the shells.
Elliott drove back over to Gary.
"Jump on!"
As he clambered aboard, a hail of bullets struck the metal chassis and the two boys ducked down.
"Crap! Not them again!" said Gary, as he emerged to see four black motorcycles skidding in the dirt.
Gary surveyed the carnage. Smoke was drifting across the field and a few machines were on fire. Patrick Kemp's combine harvester took a direct hit, but he scrambled out and climbed aboard Daniel Woodcock's tractor, until his McCormick was hit too, sending it toppling over. They were both limping back up the hill.
Elliott and Gary kept their head down as more bullets flew into the side of their tractor. Gary poked his head up and

saw the motorcyclist skidding around, kicking up a rooster tail of mud before heading back towards them.
The assassin was about to start firing again when he was knocked violently from his bike by a bale of hay.
Gary looked across the field to see Chas Kirby sending bales rolling down the hill like agricultural wrecking balls, wiping out two more of the motorcyclists.
Sally Jennings, famed for her prize-winning cattle, was gleefully crushing the bikes in her New Holland T7 as the riders fled.
Another motorcyclist made the mistake of driving alongside Ted Miller's manure spreader and was buried beneath several tonnes of the most unspeakable stench.
But still, the anti-tank shells kept coming.
"We have to do something about those guns or someone's going to get killed out here!" yelled Gary.

Hisoka Saito was sweating profusely in his Saville Row suit as he keeled over next to a bemused Australian pilot.
"Major Reynolds!" panted Hisoka. "I want you…"
He couldn't talk. He had a sudden urge to vomit. The sprint across the lawn was the most physical exercise he'd attempted in years.
"You want me?" smirked Jack. "Crikey mate, I didn't know you felt that way. Don't get me wrong, you're a good-looking fella and I love what you've done with your hair. But I'm not that way inclined."
"No, you idiot!" wheezed Hisoka. "I want you to use the jet and destroy those tractors!"

"No can do, mate!"
"That's an order! You hear me? Get in the jet now!"
"Can't do it!" said Jack, nonplussed. "I'm suspended from active duty, remember? After the whole Dickie incident."
"I gave you an order!" shouted the Head of Finance. "You obey me or find yourself another job. Hurry up, before they ruin everything!"
Jack smirked, evidently not bothered by the threat.
"All right mate. You're the boss!"
Jack punched in his five-digit code and Hisoka entered the second part of the code, known only to members of the Executive Committee.
The canopy rose upwards.
"Now, hop on in and strap yourself in!" said Jack.
"Hop on in?" queried the Japanese.
"Well, I'll need a co-pilot, won't I mate? It takes one man to control the jet and a second to fire the missiles. We'd best get on with it too as those tractors are closing in."
The Head of Finance reluctantly climbed into the co-pilot's seat and raised his arms as Jack tightened his harness. He picked up a helmet and placed it over Hisoka's head.
"Fits like a glove, mate! Must be your lucky day!"
Jack wriggled into the pilot's seat of the F-22, lowered the canopy and initiated the thrusters. As the jet propelled forward, Hisoka's heart was racing. He was terrified and something about his being there didn't feel right.
Jack edged the jet towards the perimeter wall.
"This is Major Jack Reynolds calling KR1. Requesting access to the outer grounds."

"What are you doing?" came the reply from Fergus MacLean.

"I'm under orders to engage the hostiles, sir," replied Major Reynolds.

"Then permission is granted," said Fergus.

A section of the south lawns lowered, leading to a sloped road that led under the perimeter wall. It rose again towards a runway about fifty metres beyond the wall, where Jack could see that the tractor army was sustaining heavy damage.

"KR1, do me a favour?" said Major Reynolds. "Tell the guys on the artillery posts to keep those shells well away from me!"

"Affirmative!" came the reply, before Major Reynolds switched channels and conversed with his co-pilot.

"Okay mate, you can start firing missiles at these kids now."

"How do I do that?" shouted the Japanese.

"You should see a yellow lever to the left of your seat and another to the right."

"Yes, yes! I see them!"

"Terrific mate. Now on three, just pull them up together. You've got to put some welly into it though or it won't work. Ready?"

"Just hurry up!" shouted the Head of Finance.

"Right you are, mate! Three, two, one, now!" yelled Major Jack Reynolds.

The rocket boosters under the co-pilot's chair were fired up and a split-second later, the corrupt Japanese millionaire

was propelled into the air with a force fourteen times greater than gravity.
Hisoka Saito would have screamed if he'd been able to. He must have been two hundred metres above the ground when he realised that he'd initiated his own ejector seat. There was a moment of relief as his chair fell away and the parachute automatically opened, allowing Hisoka to float down to the ground. Unfortunately for the Head of Finance, he was inadvertently struck by a shell fired from an artillery posts on the perimeter wall.
Major Jack Reynolds watched as his body landed with a thud.
"Crikey! It wasn't his lucky day after all!" he said, before shutting down the engines.

Chapter 65

Mitchell Johnson hated doubt.

He felt that his greatest strength was his ability to focus on a singular objective. To segregate and eliminate inner conflict to execute his job with ruthless efficiency.

But he was struggling to justify his recent actions for Farrington Enterprises Incorporated.

He'd killed men before and it had never bothered him. Like the great US Army commander George S. Patton, it was Mitchell's opinion that soldiers who suffered post-traumatic stress or required counselling after conflict were weak.

It was something he'd never suffered with. Because deep down, Mitchell Johnson knew that the men he'd killed stood on the wrong side of justice.

But not Samuel Tau.

Samuel was a good man. When he had been asked to conspire in a plot to murder children, Samuel hadn't buckled.

"Go to hell!" he had told the Director. And he had died for it. Right in his arms.

And the memory of it was tearing Mitchell apart.

He'd gone along with the Director's request to mobilise the Ashta and issued the order to kill three innocent teenagers. He stood by, once again, as the same unit was sent to kill Nadia Fisher's foster parents. Then, he'd kept his mouth shut as the Director tried to kill the twins at Anna Kraus' home.

Two of his best men, Gallo and Stone, had defied orders and put their lives on the line for what was right.
But not you, Mitchell Johnson. Not you. You just stood there and watched it happen.
And now, stood in KR1, he watched Fergus MacLean jump around with glee as anti-tank shells rained down on an invading army of agricultural machines driven by young farmers. Mitchell was still doing nothing.
What sort of a man was he?
Fergus threw his hands triumphantly in the air as a shell slammed into another tractor, sending all four wheels off the ground before it crashed heavily into the turf, which resembled a battlefield of scrap metal.
Mitchell couldn't believe what he was about to do, but if he was the man he thought he was, he had no choice.
He strode across KR1 towards Fergus, who turned around just in time to see the American's fist slam into his face. He dropped to the floor like a stone.
Despite all his combat experience, Mitchell hadn't thrown a punch since a team brawl at a baseball game when he was thirteen.
"Get out of here," Mitchell said to Trevor King, the only other conscious man in the Control Room.
Trevor did as he was told.
"This is the Head of Security, Mitchell Johnson," came an announcement that rang out from the ICS across Farrington Towers. "I order the Farrington Protective Force to stand down. I repeat, all FPF guards are to stand down. Vacate the artillery posts immediately."

Chapter 66

Gary was relieved to see that the guns had stopped firing and FPF guards were deserting their posts along the perimeter wall.
He urged Elliott to drive on.
The guards on entrance duty dived out of the way as Elliott's tractor smashed through the huge glass windows of the quarantine zone. Others in the Wirral Young Farmers' Association followed, demolishing the front gates, sending fragments of wood, brick and glass flying.
Dozens of Farrington Towers employees fled the carnage and ran towards the car park.
The Director, who had ordered the guards in F2 next to him to ignore Mitchell Johnson's directive and keep hold of the Subject, dived to the floor, closed his eyes and put his arms above his head to protect himself from the flying debris.
He clambered to his feet to see Gary leading his agricultural army across the manicured lawns of Farrington Towers.
FPF guards headed for cover as tractors, combine harvesters, a Land Rover and even a manure spreader rolled over the crumbled entrance gate.
The Director was amazed to find that Richard Farrington's walking cane, which had hung proudly over the main gate for generations, had landed right next to him. The carved jade dragon was miraculously intact.

As far as he was concerned, the battle wasn't lost yet.
His attention briefly diverted by an overturned Rolls Royce, Gary clung to the side of Elliott's tractor, scanning the grounds of Farrington Towers.
He saw a man in orange overalls engaged in a fight with an FPF guard in black, while a woman in a white suit was helping an old man in blue overalls hobble to safety.
Gary didn't realise who they were.
Further up the lawn, he saw Warren and a girl in another pair of orange overalls being dragged away by the Director and two guards.
"Nadia!"
Gary pointed to the twins, who were nearing the front entrance of Farrington Towers. "Head over there!"
"Whatever you say!" replied Elliott.
"Can't you go any faster?"
"This is all she's got!"
"Just my luck to jump aboard the slowest bloody tractor out the lot!" moaned Gary.
"This is a classic! 1981 International 3688, top of the range. They don't make them like this anymore!"
"Top of the range?" mocked Gary. "I've seen prams with bigger front wheels. It's like two Penny Farthings with an engine in the middle!"
Elliott laughed. He was starting to like his Vice President.
Although it didn't have the speed of the modern tractors, the International 3688 closed in on the Director, the guards and the twins. Gary was perched on a panel above the giant rear wheel, clinging to the roof for balance.

Suddenly, he launched himself off the side.
Elliott couldn't believe what he was seeing as Gary landed directly on F2b, who had been pulling Nadia along by her hair.
The WYFA President ploughed ahead, steering straight at the Director and F2a, who had no choice but to let go of Warren as they dived clear of Elliott's rampaging tractor.
As Gary landed on F2b, Nadia was thrown forward and escaped the guard's grip.
Gary quickly clambered to his feet and slammed his fist into the ribs of the muscular guard with all the strength he could summon, but it barely seemed to register. The guard laughed and grabbed the lanky teen's head, before effortlessly pushing him down to the floor. He shook his head pathetically at his young opponent, before taking two steps forward and leaning over Gary with his fist clenched.
"Nighty, night, hero!"
Then came the knockout blow. But not for Gary.
The guard slumped to the floor, as Nadia stood behind him with a silver ornament in her hand. It was the Spirit of Ecstasy, the female figure cast in silver, which had fallen off the bonnet of the Rolls Royce when it crashed.
"You took your time, didn't you!" said Nadia, as Gary lay on the floor. "What have you been doing for three days?"
"You what? I've just saved your bloody life! Again! Thought I'd at least get a thank you!"
Nadia's appearance softened.
"You're my hero," she said, before kissing him on the cheek.

Gary blushed, with a strange grin on his muddied face.
"Whatever that look is, stop it now," said Nadia. "You look weird."

Chapter 67

Hamilton MacLean was clutching Richard Farrington's walking cane as he chased Warren across the front of Farrington Towers.

Even though he could hear the Director's deranged threats, Warren could easily outrun him.

That being so, he regretted his decision to head up the stairs of the perimeter wall.

Although he'd never been allowed up there, he knew there were 204 steps to the summit, eleven more than the spiral staircase at Covent Garden Station, which was apparently a challenge for City commuters.

There was a competition among some of the fitter guards in the FPF on who could reach the top in the quickest time. Stefano Gallo had once achieved the feat in one minute and fifteen seconds, almost a minute faster than his partner, Frank Stone, who had collapsed with exhaustion at the top and vowed to take the elevator in future.

Whether it was adrenaline, or a natural fitness that owed much to Anna's balanced diet and exercise routine, Warren couldn't be sure. Either way, he leapt up the stairs two at a time and barely slowed his pace, even as he neared the top. Nobody had a stop watch running, so nobody knew that when Warren bounded to the summit, he'd knocked two seconds off Stefano's record.

Warren ran along the perimeter wall. Looking down, he could see the lasers were back on, forming horizontal red

beams that stretched across to the wall on the opposite side of the lawn.
He reached an artillery check point and looked behind him to see the Director stumble breathlessly to the top of the stairs.
He had a murderous look in his eyes.
Hamilton raised the walking cane above his head and made slow strides towards Warren, who was stood behind the anti-tank gun.
"You're a coward!" said the Director, dripping with sweat. "Like every Farrington before you."
"And you have failed. Like every MacLean before you."
Hamilton laughed menacingly. "We'll see."
"Come any closer and I'll fire!" said Warren. "This is an M5 3-inch anti-tank gun. At this range, they won't scrape up a piece of you any bigger than a penny."
"You're not going to kill me!" smirked the Director. "You don't have the guts."
Then suddenly, he charged.
He was right. Warren wasn't a killer.
The Director leapt around the side of the gun shaft, swinging the cane viciously as Warren ducked behind the artillery's steel cover. He dodged another blow, but slipped over as he did so.
Warren instinctively held up his legs to block his face as the Director lashed out again and felt the jade smash against his leg, breaking his fibula.

He yelled out in pain and tried to stagger away. But in his panic, Warren made a fateful mistake. He went the wrong way.
He dragged himself to the end of the perimeter wall and looked down at the crumbled debris from where it had been blown up by Dickie in the F-22.
Hamilton MacLean paced slowly towards Warren Farrington.
"I could barely have planned this any better! Richard Farrington's old cane landing at my feet like that. It's fate! It's the perfect ending for the last Farrington. At least, the last Farrington the world will ever know about."
The Director screwed up his face with two centuries worth of bitterness as he held the cane aloft, ready to deliver the fatal blow.
Warren looked down. There was no way he would survive the fall, let alone the laser beams.
He closed his eyes and lifted his arm in a vain effort to try and prolong his life, if only for a few seconds.
As he did so, Warren heard a strange sound. A sound he had never heard before. Then came a solid thud and Warren opened his eyes to see Hamilton stumbling back. A hand-carved, wooden boomerang dropped to the floor.
The Director roared in pain and rubbed his head as he turned to see Nadia at the top of the stairs.
"How the hell did you find your mother's boomerang?" he yelled, before staggering back to the artillery post.
He pushed around the gun shaft and aimed at the turret above the staircase.

"Run Nadia!" shouted Warren, as the Director fired. Nadia dived down the steps as the shell exploded, demolishing the turret. The Director smiled as he reloaded. Warren was driven by a need to protect his sister. He shuffled back towards the artillery post and was relieved that, while indulged in shooting, the Director hadn't turned around. He'd assumed Warren incapable of movement, what with his fibula broken in half.

Warren reached out and carefully, quietly, grabbed the walking cane from under the Director's legs whilst he was moving the shaft back around so that it was once again pointing at the turret.

"You still alive, girl? How about one more, just to be sure!"

Warren dragged himself around the side of the gun and wedged the walking cane into the shaft, with the jade dragon becoming lodged tightly at the end.

He moved his hand away just as the Director fired.

The blockage caused a deafening explosion as the shell imploded inside the gun. It ricocheted back down the shaft, with shrapnel blasting back in the face of the Director.

Warren couldn't hear anything aside from a deafening piercing whistle, but as he looked back up, he could see Hamilton MacLean clutching his scorched face. He stumbled backwards and over the edge of the perimeter wall.

Warren lunged forward and caught his outstretched hand, but the Director's feet hit the lasers two metres below the wall and were instantaneously scorched.

He screamed while desperately clinging to Warren as the putrid smell of burning human flesh drifted upwards.
"Hold on!" screamed Warren, clenching the Director's hand with all his strength. But he didn't have the strength to pull him to safety.
Hamilton MacLean looked up.
"Warren, I'm sorry."
For a moment, Warren was prepared to forgive him.
"Sorry I never killed you when I had the chance!"
Hamilton reached up with his left hand and grabbed Warren by his bullet-proof vest in a bid to drag him over the edge. He was pulling down while swinging precariously in the air, impervious to the horrific injuries to his lower legs.
"We die together! That's how it was meant to be."
Sweat was dripping down Warren's face as he reached across his shoulder and tore off the Velcro fastener on one side of the vest.
He teetered over the edge as it slipped partly off.
The Director's tormented screams echoed around the estate as he dropped another few inches, with the lasers burning through his shins.
Warren gripped the second and final Velcro strip.
"Goodbye Hamilton MacLean," he said, as he tore it away and watched the bullet-proof vest slip off his body.
Warren was momentarily blinded by a huge surge of electricity, generated as the Director struck the lasers.
He peered back over the wall as his eyes re-focused. Far below, the charcoaled body of Hamilton MacLean was

slumped face up on the underside of the Rolls Royce far below.

Warren heard someone approach behind him. It was Nadia. She dragged her twin brother away from the edge, before picking up a fragment of jade.

"You know what? Maybe the dragon is cursed after all."

She smiled, before tossing it over the wall.

Chapter 68

Anna and Stefano claimed to be representing the Crown Prosecution Service when they visited Irene Morton and Dean Mack, a labourer at the Morton farm.
They sat down with a cup of tea and had an informal chat about Irene's stepson, Gary Morton.
Gary, they said, had been questioned by the police about his involvement in a major incident at Farrington Towers, where two people had been killed.
Irene had heard about it on the news. A man had reportedly died after falling from the perimeter wall and another perished due to a malfunctioning ejector seat.
She looked pleased to hear Gary might be involved and couldn't wait for the lawyers to leave, so she could post something about it on Facebook.
The two prosecutors explained that they couldn't ascertain how much of what Gary Morton had told them was truth and how much was fiction.
"You know when he's telling lies!" interrupted Irene. "His mouth moves!"
She laughed at her own remark.
"I know," said Anna, laughing with her. "We need more time to question him. That's where you come in."
"How can we help?" asked Dean Mack, while holding Irene's hand.
It hadn't needed that for Anna to conclude that there was far more than a professional relationship between the two.

"We know that this boy is troubled, Irene," said Anna, feigning a look of concern. "The police believe that he is responsible for both deaths at Farrington Towers. We're talking about murder, Irene. He could be behind bars for a long time. But everything he says is a lie."
"He's been like it for as long as I've known him," said Irene. "During his dad's court case, a medical specialist said he had Compulsory Lying Disorder."
"Yes, we know about that from the records," said Anna, as Stefano took notes. "Is there anything else he's done? If we can charge him with a small offence, we can hold him for questioning for another day or two."
"Like what?" asked Irene.
"Has he threatened you in any way?" replied Anna. "Or been violent towards you?"
"No, he's all mouth!" chipped in the labourer.
"Dean!" said Irene, giving him a look that suggested he should keep quiet.
"He came back here one time," said Irene, facing the prosecutors. "He told me he was going to finish the job his dad had started. Now, to me that sounds like attempted murder!"
"Is it true?" smiled Anna.
"He didn't use those exact words," shrugged Irene. "But I'd stand up in court and swear on it, if it helps?"
"Thanks Irene," said Anna. "Yes, we could hold him on suspicion of causing someone to fear immediate unlawful violence. Why did he threaten you anyway? Did he feel harshly treated?" asked Anna.

"I guess so," replied Irene. "He was so angry about what happened the day Neville attacked poor Dean. He said we'd pay for our lies."
"He was telling the truth about the two of you, wasn't he?" asked Anna, tenderly. "He did see you together on the day that your husband assaulted Dean, didn't he?"
"Yes," sniffed Irene. "Not that he deserves any sympathy. That was the only time he ever told the truth in all the years I've known him. All that Liverpool Football Club rubbish and pop stars coming here for Sunday roast. Honestly!"
"It's okay," said Anna. "I understand why you did it. It must have been hard, having to lie in court about that."
"It was, but we had no choice," said Dean. "Irene would have lost the farm otherwise and Gary would've got it instead. Besides, truth or not, doesn't justify what Neville did. The guy tried to kill me!"
"It's fine, Mr Mack," said Anna, calmly. "I'm not here to interrogate the two of you. I'm on your side. I wouldn't ever condone perjury, but I understand why you did it. You could have lost everything if Gary's testimony was believed by the jury. You your job, and Irene the farm."
"Exactly," said Dean. "That's why Irene had Neville change his will afterwards. Cut his son out entirely. The lad's a loser."
"You turned a father against his only son through your lies and deceit," said Stefano. "You're the loser."
"You what?" said Dean, surprised by the sudden change of tone.
"Thank you both for your time," said Anna, standing up.

Stefano pulled a recording device out from under the table. "You two better get yourself a good lawyer," he said, as he turned and followed Anna out of the door.

Chapter 69

The re-elected Vice President of the Wirral Young Farmers' Association looked good.
He'd been suit shopping with Warren, a treat for them both after a month of hard work at Farrington Towers and to celebrate the cast being removed from Warren's leg.
They had all been very busy.
Nadia and Warren had focused their efforts on Farrington Enterprises Incorporated, shutting down nearly all its subsidiaries and integrating the few remaining noble business practices into the company founded by Dickie Page, *Batwing Limited.* Ralph had been appointed Chairman of the board.
Because of his close links to the farming community, Gary was tasked with re-establishing tenancy agreements with farmers on agricultural land around the Farrington Estate. Brian Cooper was among those who expressed a wish to return to his old farm, while Gary had marked out his own patch of land too.
The perimeter wall had come down. Stefano had organised its destruction, in between visiting his partner in hospital. Frank had become good friends with the Norwegian security guard in the next bed, until he'd been discharged. Magnus was making an incredible recovery and was already getting used to walking with a prosthetic foot. He didn't have the stomach to look at his back in the mirror, but

Anna promised him that the surgeons had done an incredible job of the skin graft.
Frank's arms were recovering, but it was going to take a while to build up strength in his left leg, as his knee had been entirely rebuilt.
He was fortunate not to lose it.
Bandit had been staying with Stefano at Farrington Towers, although it was often Gary who took him out for a walk into the woods beyond the old wall, sometimes joined by Nadia. On one occasion, Gary had pointed out the giant cedar tree where his adventure with Warren had begun.

Then came the day Gary had been looking forward to with trepidation and excitement.
His lawyer stood outside Her Majesty's Prison in Liverpool for the second time in as many days. Well, she wasn't a lawyer, professionally speaking, but Anna Kraus was becoming used to deception.
Her previous visit had gone pretty much as expected.
Neville Morton had gone through the whole spectrum of emotions when presented with the truth. He'd cried when Anna relayed the story of Gary's heroic actions at Farrington Towers.
Anna smiled as her young friends approached.
She tucked an exposed part of Gary's tie under the collar of his smart, ironed shirt. "You want to look your very best for your father."
"Thanks."

"You're welcome," said Anna. "You're quite handsome when you're not wearing a Liverpool shirt! Ready?"
"Just a minute."
Gary took Nadia's hand.
"Good luck," she said, hugging him tenderly.
Warren stepped forward and shook his hand.
"Thanks," said Gary. "I owe you one for this."
Warren laughed. "You don't owe me anything. It's me who owes you, mate."
A smile swept across Gary's face.
"What?" said Warren. "Why are you smiling like that?"
"You called me mate."

AUTHOR'S NOTE

Now that you've finished *The Last Farrington*, I would be hugely grateful if you could leave feedback about the book on Amazon. I've only printed 100 copies to gauge reader reaction before making a concerted effort to seek agency interest. So, opinions are appreciated!
Alternatively, email me at: benmorrisaah@gmail.com

This is my first attempt at fiction. Since 2011, I've been the editor of AAH (All About Horsham) Magazine and it's been nice to move away from reporting and let my imagination wander.
I found that elaborate ways of killing off the Farrington family would only come to me while I was walking on the South Downs with my spaniel, Otis. So, if nothing else comes of it, writing the book has at least got me out of the house.
I must thank Sonia Morris for her wonderful illustrations, my mum Boo for her encouragement, and my sons Max and Nicholas for their excellent suggestions.

This first edition published by AA Publishing Ltd, 2018

ISBN: 978-1-9164360-0-8

To contact the author, please email:
benmorrisaah@gmail.com